TH
ANNOUN(

C000138253

THE ANNOUNCEMENT

5/16/15

MICHAEL J. GAJDA

Library of Congress Control Number:		2014901760
ISBN:	Hardcover	978-1-4931-6672-5
	Softcover	978-1-4931-6671-8
	eBook	978-1-4931-6673-2

This book was printed in the United States of America.

Rev. date: 02/26/2014

To order additional copies of this book, contact:
Xlibris LLC
1-888-795-4274
www.Xlibris.com
Orders@Xlibris.com
537497

CHAPTER FACES

To my pals . . . the Dog People

and

To all who dwell on the fringe

It is much better to suffer than to lead a superficial life.

—Eknath Easwaran[1]

My true self is deeper than Hell.

—Meister Eckhart[2]

One need not be a chamber to be haunted.

—Emily Dickinson[3]

Do not pray for easy lives. Pray to be stronger men (and women).

—John F. Kennedy[4]

If we do not transform our pain, we will most assuredly transmit it.

—Richard Rohr[5]

CHAPTER 1

Come Alive!

*C*OME ALIVE, PEOPLE! *Come alive!*
Open those eyes, and lift those heads.
That's it, everybody! That's it!

Just think of this as a unique wake-up call, even if you only half believe that you haven't been asleep all this time.

And just try to keep your shoulders and neck turned up while you're at it.

Can you do that?

Begin to raise those eyebrows . . . slowly. This way.

That's it. Toward us.

Keep turning. *Up!* Up, up, up.

There ya go. That's the idea.

Pay close attention, and just try to dial yourselves in (as best you can . . . for now) to whatever emerges out of and into your surroundings.

But be easy on yourselves. We haven't even introduced ourselves yet. Have we?

Try to maintain a strong but steady gaze and to stay as open and attentive as you can.

Things will soon enough begin to settle down and to adjust. We can assure you of that. So just observe things from where you are for right now. And listen . . . very carefully.

You can do this. And it won't even hurt (at first). We promise.

Just keep lifting whatever faculties of awareness that are still available to you—toward us.

That's it. Keep it steady now.

But we have to warn you. This will call for some extra effort on your part in order for you to even begin to understand, let alone trust the instructions being given.

And we know that it probably feels as though these words are barging in on you out of nowhere.

Doesn't it?

Yet you really don't have much choice in the matter. Don't you see? Although we'll be trying to explain that part to you too, but gradually.

So just be patient with us.

And steady now!

Stay with it. There you go.

But before we really get into the heart of things and while you keep bending and fine-tuning your attention our way, let us try to slow this thing down a little right from the beginning, so we can do some initial unraveling for you. Okay? It just might help to calm your nerves.

So let's get started then, shall we?

Our goal is to keep things stable and steady (but not fixed) and to try to maintain a balance and a calmness yet not to allow the calmness to become a numbness or a deadness.

But try to realize something first, right from the outset . . . if you can get your compulsive brain traffic out of the way.

The unraveling that we'll be acquainting you with will call upon some very serious and necessary shifts in your consciousness—which may include some painful discoveries and some sobering revelations as well as some unexpected and disheartening twists and turns.

Yet all the while, the whole affair may seem to move exceedingly slow to you . . . even *underwater slow* at times.

It may even begin to feel as though things are vibrating along like a stop-and-go movie, more sluggish and jolting than anything you've ever allowed yourselves to experience or to conceive of (in relative Earth time) or that you've ever even allowed yourselves to simply be with or to be engaged in with any clear sense of what is actually real, even while it may slowly ease you into the full capacity of life as it really is—not merely as you wish it to be.

Is any of this making any sense at all yet?

Because (and take specific note of this point, as we continue to move things along) there won't be much room left for any detailed discussion or debate, especially about how you may have been trained to think or to believe things to be, nor for what anybody else has already described to you of how things are either—or how they ought to be.

What will emerge and what will begin to speak to you instead will be from within each and every existent heartbeat to the next, just as it is, beyond yet somehow prior to itself. Prior to anything which you think (or may assume) that you're actually familiar with. Prior to any prevailing dispositions or beliefs which you may feel explicitly bound to.

Beyond the stops and starts of time and place.

And even beyond whatever you've come to be so certain of or overly attached to.

Do you understand?

Beyond any of your presumptions of what defines who you are. Even beyond that.

Beyond the same tribal logic that leads you to define what everything else is as well, where you've divided up your fossilized thoughts about the world into overly contained constructs . . . which tend to separate your this from your that, leaving your attention scarred with deep divisions that bury themselves in the marrow of your tribal perceptions . . . like long-forgotten roads, splitting you off from almost any *other* culture of discernment or experience . . . through repetitive rituals of tribal habit, reinforcing the quarantined confinement of your collective memory.

So many of you try to establish a rigorous and isolated distance between yourselves and the indivisible *Self.* Don't you? And even more consciously so, between yourselves and those of whom you perceive to be the *other*, doing your best to avoid any intimate interactions with any and all suspected *otherness.* You seem to fear that it could somehow disrupt or unravel your exclusionary tribal existence. So you reject almost anyone who refuses to submit to the strictures imposed by your group of allegiance, along with its prepackaged logic—which you obediently interpret as indisputable truth or as unquestionable tribal wisdom.

Is anything sounding even a tad familiar to you thus far?

And (as most of you already know) it's usually only rubber-stamped speech and language that gets the full-fledged endorsement of the tribal authorities or that's encouraged to be freely spoken or even respectfully acknowledged within the walls of any of your overly contained empires of separateness.

Well . . . isn't it?

Almost any *Self*-directed expression of thought which may be struggling to come forth out of its own ground of silence is routinely choked off and marginalized well before it's been given even a mild chance to voice even one unsanctioned complete sentence.

Can you even begin to admit at least that much to yourselves?

The habitual *only-mind* censors itself into a quiet submission. Don't you see? With a divisive logic that constricts it, with the intoxicated culture of the tribe that inhabits it, and with its rehearsed ridicule . . . violently aimed at any speck of *otherness* which resists being captured by it.

Are you even able to get a passing glimpse of what we're trying to get at here?

The vocabulary of virtually every overly contained tribe actively assails almost anyone who defies its orbit of influence. Doesn't it?

The *disjoined* rationale of each of your tightly confined tribal factions squeezes itself shut around you with the vise of its superstitions as it tries to extract from you any amount of genuine faith or of even the slightest evidence of a more inclusive embrace of a larger universe.

Even so, most of you at least occasionally demonstrate (however rare the occasion may be) that you're still yet capable of behaving with some amount of spacious interdependence, don't you? Which means that who you actually are can't be entirely denied and, at least to some remaining extent, that it's still possible for you to freely express your humanity by extending some degree of loving-kindness to *others*, doesn't it? Even in the midst of being squeezed by an insane logic that tightens its grip around any hint of a heartfelt compassion which might be flickering out of your eyeballs and out of the tribe's incestuous control.

Although when it comes right down to it . . . what other way is there to honestly anchor and express one's *Self?*

Anything less than an expression of genuine compassion for *others* and for yourselves is beneath your given purpose, isn't it?

But you all know that.

The heart of a human being can scarcely expand or inspire when it's being forever constrained, can it? Or when it's forcibly kept from even benignly interacting with any of the *other* sons and daughters of *Creation.*

And by the way, those are the only actual sons and daughters who inhabit your shrinking planet. There are no *others.* But then . . . how could there be, when there's only one parental *Source* from which you are all born (whether human or *other* than human)?

But you already know that too, yes?

The honest expression of charity toward *others* (with no tribal strings attached) can only be sustained from within an unencumbered spaciousness, energized by an uncontainable faith, held open in the arms of the one unifying and inexhaustible *Self,* and nourished by the boundless yet paradoxical empowerment of *That which is beyond capture* (by *That which is always becoming*) and by *That which excludes no one,* neither human nor *other* than human.

Do you understand?

MICHAEL J. GAJDA

It can never be evoked through the false magic of wishful thinking, can it? Nor by the strict conventions of abstract or isolated belief systems or by any decree coming from any of the elevated (official) agents of concentrated tribal power, nor through any scripture entombed in absolute statements of separation made about anything, especially about *That which forever emanates* from the source of all *Being*—which excludes nothing and no one. Remember?

So many of you foolishly bow to what your tribe regards as being beyond question or critique, don't you? Confining yourselves to a narrow closet of adoration built upon tribal certitudes, certitudes which are anxiously affirmed by the loudest apologists of your specific tribe, by the self-appointed ones who've convinced you to renounce or at least to dismiss and ignore the inmost (and outcast) *Self*—and to submit instead to the habits and will of whatever tribal paradigm of persuasion you find yourselves transfixed in.

But as you know . . .

You cannot evaluate an insane belief system from within it, as the wise *Course in Miracles* reminds us.[1]

And whether or not you're willing to admit to or even to comprehend any of this yet is rather unimportant right now.

Don't you see?

This is where you are. So this . . . is our starting point.

CHAPTER 2

Time Has Caught Up with You

TIME HAS FINALLY caught up with you and is about to stop (for the time being anyway) while the fountain of your tribal perceptions, which so many of you have been drinking from, has just about run dry.

Yet it's from that very core of dryness where the training begins. Don't you see? The training for the long journey out of sleep and into a subversive reawakening—which will release you from the hold of the tribal dream and from its persuasive illusions and into a gradual and intimate immersion into *That which is.*

And so our preparation starts with the careful but steady removal of the armor which binds you to the tribal container, the armor which blocks out almost everything but imposed tribal logic.

And this method of emancipation will begin with or without your permission . . . we're sorry to say. Although your individual cooperation can only help.

The speed and the extent of the method will ultimately be left up to you. Although what you may gradually become more conscious of will not only affect and shape each unfolding phase in the process of waking up, but each phase will also have its own unique sting of illumination.

So brace yourselves.

You must pay strict and careful attention (starting right now) in order to be properly initiated into the emancipating process.

Your care and consistency of concentration is not optional.

It's a necessity.

Don't you see?

It will lift you up and beyond the deluge of tribal imagery which has blurred so much of your awareness for so long, but only when you allow it to. It's been a blur which you've become quite accustomed and even attached to. No?

You've spent an exorbitant amount of time and energy trying to obstruct any curious spirit of wonder from rendering any of its powers of surprise and rejuvenation—qualities which so many of you fear to be too whimsical or too unconstrained for the tribal authorities to permit the arousal of.

So you've shoved back, propping up the walls of the tribal container and clogging up its doorways and corridors in order to preserve and sustain its system of confinement and control, keeping yourselves insulated and overprotected . . . hidden behind a vast array of altars and idols, fixing yourselves to the ink of its creeds and documents, simply to reinforce its isolated and revered system of tribal sameness.

But we mean to knock down those *disjoining* walls and doors. Don't you see? To knock down your flimsy structures built upon tribal sand.

We intend to reunite the imagined with the unimagined and the profound with the frivolous, to reunify the human with the *other* than human, to reconcile yes with no, likes with dislikes, subject with object, there with here, this with that, and abundance with scarcity.

We aim to reintegrate the deep with the shallow, the dark with the light, the free with the subjugated, the wounded with the wound, and death with the full continuum of life.

We intend nothing less than to reunite your original face with its very *Self* . . . by removing the many layers of masks which you've tried to conceal yourselves with—beneath all of your strategies of restriction and behind all of your contrived superiority formulas; beyond all of what you anxiously cling to, where you so often overdose on the prescriptions of tribal disguise; turning yourselves away from any genuine face-to-face with *That which is always becoming*, where it baffles you too much to even imagine a rational and compassionate world in which valid and hopeful possibilities may actually exist outside the bounds of tribal logic.

You've been held captive for far too long, haven't you? Locked in behind thick barricades of a constricted version of who you are and of what everything is . . . and of how things ought to be.

And your *disjoined* opinions and perceptions are nothing but predictable tribal explanations, are they not? Explanations which repeatedly ricochet off the inner walls of the tribal psyche, defining what surrounds and bears itself down upon you . . . and which you piously submit to and abide by.

You've been suffocating yourselves, closing off the windpipe of any present moment which would allow you to breathe, removing yourselves from any chance interaction with any strain of *otherness* (no matter how good, beautiful or true it may be), resembling but never quite embodying who you are . . . or who you were called to be.

You reject and even condemn *That which is beyond* your complete control and understanding . . . along with its paradoxical simplicity, its self-emptying cycles of death and resurrection, and its sacramental moments of holy convergence—all of which can only be embraced or observed when you're not fleeing from or attacking any of it or when you're not pretending that it doesn't exist or when you finally stop insisting that any one moment of *Being* is separate from any *other* one.

You've learned to negate who you already are and whom you're forever becoming, eluding and even denying your own evolutionary gifts, surrounding yourselves with the static and the familiar . . . with the overly contained memories, habits, and beliefs of the tribal *only-mind*, clenched in the jaws of its fragmenting mythologies, each one proclaiming that it alone contains the literal truth above all *other* truths and that somehow it alone remains above and beyond what any peripheral doubt or even any lightweight criticism may be able to expose to the light, as you hunker down in tribal foxholes dug into shallow valleys of ignorance . . . surrounded by mountains of tribal condescension, protecting yourselves from any invading army of *otherness* which may be lurking just beyond the tribal terrain, blocked off from any path of escape or into any expansion of awareness which could lead you to transcend the boundaries of tribal control—which could then reunite this valley of containment with that one, and each valley with itself.

But moving into the world of slow disentanglement is no easy task. Is it?

Yet it is the proposed undertaking of our present invitation.

It is a call and commitment to slowly undo what has been thought and taught to be impossible to be undone, a call and commitment to guide you into the tearing down of the straw houses which are solely held up by the insane logic of the tribal *only-mind*.

CHAPTER 3

A Brief Tale of Caution

A ND SO HERE you are (all of you) together and right now. One big captured yet deeply *disjoined* tribal audience.

But allow us to introduce a brief tale of caution.

Do not be panicked by the language we'll be using. You're in no imminent danger. And you won't be hearing any so-called *voices*. Although you will be hearing actual words as they're being pronounced, which will of course be coming from our (sometimes arcane) vocalization of them, from the one voice which you can quite clearly hear right now, can't you? As it speaks through us out of its wellspring, from the only vocalist whose speech and language will be available to you for the next several hours, from a voice which will seem to speak with much more peculiarity and for a much longer period of time than it actually does.

Nonetheless, its subtle but hard-spoken clarity will soon begin to pry open your battened-down tribal perceptions, slowly uncovering the hidden afflictions laid to rest in your spiritual burial grounds, gradually dissolving and releasing each interior headstone into a cloud of forgetting, moving you toward a *cloud of unknowing* (to borrow from a certain wise and anonymous medieval Christian sage).[1]

But the forgetting and the unknowing will only begin if and when you allow the afflictions to become real, to allow them to unhide themselves—which has always been one of your bigger "ifs" to jump over, has it not?

Yet whenever it has been hurdled, it's led to some self-surprising and awakening actions on the part of the hurdler. No? Which is what many of you fear most of all and which is exactly what leads so many of you away from *That which is*, away from the unifying *Self*—and right back into your overused and apologetic tribal arguments.

So you continue to "de-if" yourselves. Don't you? Preventing yourselves from intermingling with any precarious process of promise or possibility or from entering into any dangerous or enlightening dissent which could pull you away from the spell and gravity of the tribal logic which constantly bewitches you.

Is anything sounding at all familiar yet?

CHAPTER 4

The Prisons of Familiarity

YOU PACE BACK and forth . . . nonstop, within yourselves, don't you? Herky-jerky style . . . like wind-up soldier dolls marching at the guarded behest of the *only-mind* (absent the movement of *Self*-knowledge), behind thick interior walls of paralysis, locked into an all-too-familiar bastille of *disjoined* convention, fearing that you may one day be rescued from the internal protection of your tribal confinement.

And you're not even sure why you resist your own liberation, are you? Despite the inner anguish that persists and which secretly pleads for your release.

But the prisons of familiarity are always the hardest ones to break out of. Don't you see?

A door that never opens becomes rusted shut after a while . . . or it morphs into a revolving door of perpetual relapse, endlessly retreating back into its customary cocoon, snipping its own wings, preventing itself from sailing on the winds of even minimal transformation.

And anyone deemed to be outside or even on the fringe of that *disjoined* incarceration is suspected and even accused of the crime of disloyal autonomy, are they not? By a codependent tribal imagination, wrapping itself around the neck and perception of the imprisoned perceiver.

Yet the individual tribal afflictions are only symptoms. Yes? Merely outward expressions of inner captivity; of captive atoms, molecules, and cells trapped inside of a captive organism, installed into the habits of tribal self-deception and into its resistance of *That which is always becoming*; persuading you to oppose anything that threatens to peel away at the tribal disguise and its collective conjury.

And you've become quite smitten with these tribal machinations. Yes? But even more so with the audience which they enchant.

You've forgotten (haven't you?) that you were invited into your humanity to participate and to create, to take an active part in *Being* . . .

not merely to find something to absorb and then to attach yourselves to or to become a mere part of until it finally lets go of you, when you can then simply disappear into the mythological dust of tribal antiquity.

You were invited to participate in the eternal business of becoming, to gradually reconcile, then reunite with the inexhaustible creativity of *That which is*, not merely to elevate your tribe or its magicians onto cadaverous pedestals.

But so many of you have devoted yourselves to the dormant rituals of allegiance which each tribe performs for itself. Haven't you? To reinforce its own validation. Where it strives for perfect attendance, for uncritical praise, and for pinched attention while most of you remain acutely more attached and attentive to the reactions of the surrounding audience than you do to the performance itself.

The loyalty of the crowd seems to be what keeps bringing you back to the tribal ticket counter. Doesn't it?

The trick and the trickster performing on the tribal stage have somehow taken a backseat to an emulating and allegiant audience.

And the only apparent purpose left for putting on or attending a performance anymore is to expand upon a homogeneous and devoted gathering of self-admirers—which includes you as an embedded member.

The content and substance of the actual activity on stage matters very little to most of you. Does it not?

Crowd uniformity, proper seating assignments, and correct and dependable response and reaction time replace the arranged performance as the new paragon of spiritual crust and meaning.

You simply prepare yourselves to clap along to the tribal sights and sounds which you cordially conform to.

As soon as you see or hear the beginnings of any nearby tribal applause, you clap along with it.

As it begins to well up to its tribal crescendo, you simply clap along.

Within any measured tribal gathering which you're a part of, you anxiously clap along to its arousing containment.

And the more you applaud, the more you're then pulled even further into the vacuum of self-adulation in all of its disguised forms—mouthing automatic prayers to the same frozen deities whom so many in your tribe duplicate their worship to, restricting your listening habits to a static genre of musical belief, reading only from a qualified list of permissible books by sanctioned authors of opinion, parroting canonical talking points made by indistinguishable politicians, mimicking the noise level forced upon you by the corporate benefactors of counterfactual truth, sitting in the same postured pews of tribal thought, confined to kneel upon identical rugs of self-indoctrination, marching in unison at the same rallies of jingoistic judgment, repeating the same synthetic hearsay and gossip into pipelines of congested garble, profiting from the same tribal lies that far-off or nearby *others* eventually suffer from.

Yet if you turn it all around (and you can) and allow for a lucid practice of discrimination to unfold, the necessary and appropriate actions must and will follow. And they won't require any of the symbiotic allegiance which you've been so used to adhering to.

They'll simply require the embrace of an intentional honesty and of a hospitable presence, gently held together by imperfect discernment, guided by doubt and faith (you can't have one without the other), unified by a *Presence* that you must be present to in order for its powers to be realized, inspired by the discriminating actions that you must take but must not take hold of or be taken in by.

Sharp like a razor's edge is the path . . . the sages say . . . difficult to traverse, observes the wise writer of the Katha Upanishad.[1]

That which is always becoming desires to be awakened within you, to converge into a cocreative bargain—to gradually transcend the divided (false) self with the unifying (true enough) *Self.*

But the *disjoined* thoughts of the *only-mind* think of themselves as faultless and complete. Do they not? As they dance in a fabricated and habitual muse to their own delight, convincing themselves that they've got the whole shebang wrapped up and contained in one impenetrable, hallowed, and final truth blanket . . . and that they don't need another speck of illumination.

But none of that should come as much of a surprise to any of you. Should it?

CHAPTER 5

Wake Up!

*W*AKE UP!
And please . . . do pardon our sudden interruption.

But we did notice that some of you were beginning to fade back into a complacent suspension of self-conscious awareness—again.

So let's get back into it. Shall we?

But where were we?

Ah! We were here . . . weren't we? Where we've always been and where we always will be, where every action must lead you to even further acts of insistent but liberating clarity and into a deeper and more expansive presence—which means that all the layers of your masks must eventually fall off. Doesn't it? One by one, each one with its own specified and difficult method of removal.

And these aren't just the sting of band-aids being pulled off that you'll be feeling. These are the hard and violent layers of who you've refashioned yourselves into for years and centuries—even millennia.

Which leads us to our next caution.

The closer you get to reuniting with your actual *Self,* the more resistance you'll encounter and the more each sheet of tribal impersonation will try to keep itself stuck to the one beneath and above itself, each one trying to prevent you from merging with (and emerging from) those original eyes—the ones which beheld the original canvas of *Creation,* from within that one-and-only original face, which patiently waits to be released from the grip of your superimposed collection of *Self*-impersonators.

And whenever the emergence does manifest, you just might mistakenly perceive that the world around you has forever changed—which would be a most understandable but misconstrued assumption.

What actually will have changed is nothing.

Absolutely nothing.

You will have simply reclaimed your fundamental gift of vision, as you begin to gaze out through the primordial eyes which you've forever shared with the indivisible *Ocean of Existence* . . . with *That which always was (and is) and always will be.*

With the *Eternal Circle of Being . . . It-Self.*

The Supreme Self is beyond name and form, beyond the senses, inexhaustible, without beginning, without end, beyond time, space, and causality, eternal, immutable, asserts the wise Katha Upanishad.[1]

What we are looking for is what is looking, observes the wise Saint Francis of Assisi.[2]

You're not (and you won't be) imagining any of this.

And you're not (and you won't be) hallucinating or losing any more sanity than what's already been lost into your accumulation of what you can't seem to let go of—even if our disruption may split open and dissolve much of the armor that conceals what so many of you guard against yet cling to.

It may even seem beyond the functional reach of your hardened belief systems to simply acknowledge that you're actually hearing our voice right now.

But you're soon to be introduced to things which will extend far beyond mere acknowledgment.

So prepare yourselves.

CHAPTER 6

The Collective Persona

TO ADMIT TO having a unique perceptual or spiritual experience (or a kinship to one), or even to having a slight but noticeable shift in your emotional or intellectual sympathies, devoid of any chauvinistic claim of supremacy over the proverbial *other*, is tantamount to betrayal. Isn't it? To the capitulation of the collective persona which you've come to believe is actually you.

You've worn it for so long that you can't even seem to be able to distinguish the mask from the face that wears it. Can you?

You've worn it on the extremes of the left and right. And of the up and down.

And you've worn it out by refusing to wear anything else. Don't you see? Even for a quick change of pace or scenery.

Many of you have come to equate the impartial acknowledgment of any sign or symbol of accused *otherness* (however it leaks into you) as a symptom of weakening allegiance, as a suspicious crack in the concentrated jar of group stability, from which the conditioning of your materialistic imagination often leads you into recurring nightmares . . . filled with battalions of alien infiltrators sneaking into your privatized portions of the planet, through any mouse hole that you've failed to tightly plug shut with your terminal judgments or with your never-ending opinions, casting doubt upon the sworn allegiance of whoever it is that perpetrates even a hint of civility (or fairness) upon the so-called *otherness.*

Acting overly charitable to the *others* in your world somehow translates into an act of treason. Doesn't it? Committed against each group's self-enclosed container of permitted perceptions.

You've convinced yourselves that impartial and civil interaction with the alien or with the iconoclast is equivalent to the stripping away of your own alleged identity, wherever it may adapt or attach itself to you—which may be why so many of you exhibit such disdain for those among you who demonstrate unilateral expressions of unconditional love, or for those who willingly surrender themselves up to the power of the present moment, or for those who strive to break out of your compression of tribal boundaries and into a more oxygenated universe of awareness, or for those among you who look for and frequently find unvarnished needles of perception even in the most overcrowded of haystacked appearances.

It's especially daunting to so many of you when an unexpected visit from one of those independent renegades of *otherness* pops in and out of nowhere. Isn't it? Right through the perforated walls of your preconditioned consciousness, when in the flash of a blindsided moment you suddenly (even if so briefly) and to your own astonishment, find yourselves pondering the depth and form as well as the beauty of your recusant . . . as it discreetly ambles itself down your dark and forbidding corridors.

It is the *other* (after all) whom you suddenly recognize. Don't you see?

It is the *other* whom you normally oppose with automatic enmity and rejection for no well-informed reason beyond the fact of its *otherness*—which is directly related to why so many of you practice demeaning the very few among you who embody a peaceable or compassionate way about themselves, ridiculing and accusing them of wearing the clothes of primitive weaklings, disidentifying and distancing yourselves from them as publicly and as often as you can.

Yet, in order to maintain that self-winding distance, you're evidently required to recite a tribal pledge of perpetual separation (with chest-pounding diligence) over and over again, each recital plainly meant to sharpen itself clean of any obvious shavings of hesitance or of uncertainty.

No trespassing remnant can be permitted to creep its way in which could disrupt the group-rehearsed formula for loyal appearances.

There's too much to risk. Isn't there? Too much that could unclothe the overseeing emperors or their empires—whom and which forever overdress themselves in order to conceal their actual nakedness.

But stripped down to its bare skin, each ascending empire is essentially the same as the previous one. Isn't it? The same as any of the ones right beside it or even opposed to it or above or below it . . . or as any of the next ones that may come along, the ones who predictably wait in the wings of succession, drooling to replace yet another unmasked and dying tribal enclave as it eventually falls off its imperial stage . . . at once built and then destroyed by its own compulsive and selfish desires.

And the dutiful subjects of each self-enclosed domain fold and curl themselves up into a passive fetal slumber. Don't they? Embedding themselves so deeply into the ideological flesh of the tribal container that they can no longer feel their own skin—of where it ends and of where the skin of the tribe begins.

So imitation and avoidance casually come to mean the same thing. Yes? As if none of you have even noticed the loss of your actual face, where you never seem to run out of available caricatures of yourselves (or of each *other*) and where tribal life simply goes on with no allowance or even toleration for unpretentious *Self*-conscious reflection . . . or for any organic unknowing of any kind (whether singular or plural) and where you overcrowd your interior with repetitious noise and familiar clutter, squeezing away at any space that tries to quiet itself or tries to empty itself out . . . enough so that it might even awaken you, where the living existence of any of the already-awakened ones is denied—even of those standing and breathing (face-to-no-face) right in front of you.

You've gradually forgotten who you actually are. Haven't you? And of whom you could become . . . beneath layers of tribal body language, isolated within separate little pool-ball worlds banging up against each other . . . worlds full of naked Adams and naked Eves, hiding yourselves behind protective leaves of group overidentification and of inherited disparity.

And the fate which you deny is that you could actually transcend the constraints of *disjoined* certitudes . . . which are always capable of creating false divisions when wrapped up in the grip of the corporate make-believe, or that you could actually slip into a momentary cloud of self-doubt which could then be interpreted by any audience full of fellow adherents as the death of your share of the collective fantasy. And that wouldn't be too easily stomached. Would it? Not from within any of the tightly enclosed tribal containers which claim sole ownership of unrivaled motives and morality in so many things which they deem central to their packaging and function, which is why so few of you step out from behind the thick glassy frame of your frozen self-portraits. Isn't it?

Most of you engage in some form of ritualistic exercise . . . in preparation for some future arrival which never seems to manifest beyond the preparation.

And we've often wondered if any of you have even an inkling of what you're actually preparing for.

Your rehearsals all seem to be pointing to some vague sky of desire, full of tribal rainclouds . . . weeping down liquid statues that solidify into arbitrary absolutes, which always seem to arrive from someplace on high. Don't they? Usually from inside a mythological tick-tock memory of nostalgic moments that may or may not have been moments at all, none of which can actually be found on any map of faith, reason, or fact. Can they? But you keep rehearsing as if you can easily retrieve them anyway.

Preparing to prepare in itself has become an inexplicable yet basic point of both departure and return for so many of you. Hasn't it?

You leave, yet you don't leave. And then you come back to where you've never left. It's a great Kabuki lap dance in a world where tribal loyalties are taken to be evidence of what is real and true and where the belief in the primacy of one's own conscience is considered to be clear and incriminating evidence of heresy or betrayal.

And for many of you . . . to even be associated with unorthodox habiliments or with even a tinge of evolving perception would be the final proof that your taken-for-granted tribal assumptions were kaput. Wouldn't it?

It would become group evident that you've abandoned your emblematic testicles of certainty and supremacy—that you've committed the grave sacrilege of unpolishing the tribal badge.

And as you know, the maladies embodied in your dominant patriarchal tribal systems aren't just limited to those with actual phallic equipment. The disease of patriarchy is quite a generous one. Isn't it? It allows for male or female or even for the androgynous and the eunuch to adapt, to carry the balls all the way to the top of the figurative heap . . . if they apply themselves with enough accommodating obedience.

That's why the heaps that pile (and clog things) up in your world are so often just rudimentary tribal food chains in disguise. Are they not? And why cast-iron gonads replace the heart, the brain, and the soul as the symbolic centers of command and control in so many of your so-called human institutions, sewn in right alongside their own rigid and ideological erections.

It keeps things plain and simple. Doesn't it? Free of the disquieting burden of flexible complexities . . . which tend to arise from the combined practice of compassionate action and contemplative self-discipline or from sincere self-inquiry (and self-criticism) or from the practice of rigorous attentiveness and of concentrated or receptive meditation and from the search for common ground to stand upon with *others*, where all creatures are received for whatever they bring to the surface of their being, and where everything is perceived as potential prayer waiting to be evoked and expressed—because in and of itself, the surface of things is only the surface of things. Is it not?

But nevertheless.

You do tend to keep things quite nicely contained. Don't you? Inside your cut-and-dried final answers which acknowledge or recognize nothing beyond their own tribal image and likeness—answers which so many of you claim as foolproof solutions for so many of life's questions, which so few of you ever seem to ask.

You prefer your ready-made solvents instead. Don't you? To any effort or movement which may unlock or open portals into the world of mystery or of ambiguity or into mystical revelations of faith absent of any binding or constrictive certitudes.

Navigation is much less troublesome when you can just yield yourselves to the steerage found in the conventional wisdom of the tribe, within its fold of uncomplicated custodians who keep things tidied up and enclosed within the glue of their own circumscribed clumps, simulating the pretense of transcendence through repetitious and illusory ceremonies and in rituals of self-magnification or in forced public displays of bonding together against any evidence of internal or external *otherness.*

And your formalized methods of imposing tribal allegiance have little to do with trying to move the larger world toward a collective betterment or to a greater good . . . beyond what's mainly in it for the tribe which you adhere to.

In fact, your most obvious and overused strategy is to conflate your forces against something. Isn't it?

What you're most against is that which holds you most staunchly together. Don't you see?

For so many of you . . . when there is no *against* to be against then there is no *for* (or *with*) to comprehend or to behold. And with no reliable enemy crawling across your screens of illusion, you seem to find it extremely hard to know how to befriend yourselves. Don't you?

So the syndrome of being against something becomes the enabling glue of tribal self-worth. Does it not? And it's that glue of containment which keeps so many of you stuck to yourselves in an uneasy and befuddling state of inward mobility, often feigned as some kind of proud tribal togetherness. But it doesn't necessarily lead to a well-intact state of wholeness or to a mind-set which is very loving or compassionate in its interactions with *others* . . . or with your inmost *Self*. Does it?

The brain sits shoulder strapped in the back seat, numbly staring out the tribal window, watching the world go by—in complete sedentary and submissive comfort.

The heart falls into a surrendering but shallow coma.

The corporate ballocks take charge of the map and of the steering wheel.

The *Self* is subverted, denied, and deposed in a gradual and fragmenting coup d'etat.

Yet very few of you even notice the disappearance of your own intrinsic spaciousness. Do you?

You've draped yourselves with so many layers of distraction that you've not only forgotten *who* you are . . . but *that* you are.

And all of your self-imposed propaganda is simply the occupation (and congestion) of monopolized space. Yes? Clogging up and repressing the organic powers of allurement which naturally tend to reach, breathe, and feel for the unpredictable and for the spontaneous or for the unexplored and for the spacious, for those causal forces which evoke a clarity of awareness when left to their own life-sustaining devices—whenever they have enough space to breathe in and out without suffocating.

Breathing in, I calm body and mind. Breathing out, I smile. Dwelling in the present moment, I know this is the only moment, observes the wise Thich Nhat Hanh.[1]

But the compression of so much space chokes off the symphonic forces of *That which is always becoming*, preventing its expansion into the channels which lead to breathtaking (and breath-giving) equanimity while the quality of your tribal propaganda remains most efficient and most self-destructive when it convinces you that *you* are the exception to its effect.

Yet no exception need be made for the willing who ingest the tribal food or who wear the tribal nose and tongue covers while they sniff and lick their way up the chain of their uniform habits of consumption, absorbing mouthfuls of whatever is cooked up and dished out to them by the tribal chef, gulping down as much of it as they can and as fast as they can in order to avoid the taste of its expanding exaggerations.

How else can they still swallow it all without vomiting it back up?

Without taste, there is no savoring of *That which is*. Don't you see? Which inevitably leads to the abandonment of discernment and of any illuminating inner struggle.

So then there's no detachment and nothing to differentiate. There's no ripening transcendence, and so there's nothing to reinclude or to reintegrate. There's no organic unity, and so there's no unconditional love to exchange an embrace with.

Instead, the circle is broken then dispensed into divisions of (nontasting) uniformity.

And without taste, gluttony expands then intensifies.

It multiplies then divides and clings to itself.

And yet to taste the *One* thing . . . to taste and to be tasted by the boundless and inexhaustible *Self*, which is the only thing, and which excludes nothing and no one and neither confines perception and consciousness to an impermanent boundary nor surrenders it up to the dictates of an external force (or to a *disjoined* tribal consensus) is to open the door to pure awareness. Is it not?

It is to begin to wake up.

Nothing of depth or consequence is ever imposed upon the undisciplined or upon the self-deluded, who lead themselves to their own spiritual and intellectual emasculation. Nothing indeed. Instead, an endless supply of fancy meals, season tickets, colorful ribbons, shiny medals, name-plated trophies and plaques, outlandish bonuses and inner circle appointments and promotions and even recommendations for honorary titles of sainthood, knighthood, or martyrdom are generously handed out by the political and religious pooh-bahs of each tribe and by a grateful cadre of corporate pawnbrokers as tribute for loyal self-abdication.

Most of your more deeply dug-in and fundamentalist institutions have organized themselves around just such an undeclared agreement. Don't you see? Which provides for members to maintain or exceed their rank within each body politic . . . as long as there's no serious attempt made to transform any of the body's systemic structures or processes.

The selfish cravings of the gluttonous tribal palate gradually engulfs the muzzled and starved conscience of the individual.

And if anyone begins to demonstrate even a tinge of resistance to the institutional logic ingrained in the tribal *only-mind* then their true-blue membership is soon revoked and removed.

They become an instant object of rejected *otherness*.

Do they not?

In the blink of a *disjoined* eye, they're expelled from the tribal playground and then moved outside the fence.

CHAPTER 7

Allegiance

A LLEGIANCE TO AN overly contained arrangement of any kind is tested, measured, and maintained through the persistent pressure put upon the individual to adapt and conform to the specific mental mind mapping of each particular *disjoined* arrangement (which includes whoever it absorbs into its specific geography) through one ongoing monotonous and compelling act of tribal conditioning.

And the conditioning (as you know) is routinely cultivated through the aforementioned reward system. But if deemed necessary, it can also be done through the use of blunt and brutal force as well as with other experimental or supplementary coercive techniques or with gradual and perhaps even more subtle and sophisticated persuasive procedures (either mental or physical) or even by the repetitious and intermittent mixture of all the methods put together . . . zealously supervised and administered by a small but loyal core of tribal specialists, entrusted by the entrenched infrastructure of each specific container, squeezing the autonomous individual into the homogenized confinement, demanding undisputed and explicit evidence of devotion from the least powerful to the most, from the bottom up . . . from the lowest-ranking subordinates all the way up to the nominal or nameless (and therefore unaccountable) tribal overseers.

Rarely do the rivers of mandatory allegiance reverse their course in a world ruled by the judgment and fear of a hardened and habituated *only-mind*. Do they?

The obliged simply obey and receive their rewards by following the flowchart of tribal fidelity upward, toward the accountants of power—while accountability flows downward through the ranks, in approximate measure equal to the increased vulnerability of each descending level, landing hardest upon the most vulnerable at the very bottom of the tribal rung.

Whatever (or whoever) is enthroned upon the tribal pedestal of power and authority is seldom faithful and rarely answerable to anything that it interprets as less muscular than itself. It only pretends that ploy in order to suck even more monopolized air into its unaccountable lungs.

The singular conscience is silenced and even atrophied in favor of the currents of tribal convention, drowning in the toxic squabbling and torrential orthodoxy of each competing manifestation of tribal logic . . . in all of its twisted plurality of precise sameness.

It's beyond regrettable. Isn't it?

But the growing concentration of power exercised by the money changers and the influence peddlers who reside so comfortably inside the corporate suites of excess greed and authority in so many of your categorical containments has stolen the name of majority from your dictionaries . . . and from the bulk of the people themselves, redefining almost everything with its *disjoined* yet made-to-fit tribal interpretations.

A beguiled and hijacked majority has truly come home to roost and rule in almost every opaque aspect of what so many of you pay attention to or value. Hasn't it?

Majority rules.

For many of you, it's become just another unconscious (and empty) jailhouse slogan. Yes? Often deforming into a prayer of submission, into a shibboleth which you repeat and install as an absolute or into an amalgamated motto which replaces individual discernment.

Such is the majority which rules in almost every essential aspect and expression of the *disjoined* tribal asylum.

And it is just such a hoodwinked majority that pretends to rule with an authority which it doesn't even come close to possessing. Don't you see?

Deny it if you will, but most of you readily collaborate with that kind of acquiescent pecking order, identifying and complying more with the shouts of the multitude than you do with the deepest voice of the inmost *Self.*

You may continue to berate or malign anyone who stands outside your hierarchy of tribal norms (which seems to be neither here nor there). And you may even continue to praise yourselves to no end, demonstrating an over-the-top loyalty to the security, tenets, or reputation of the established order that's in place.

Yet if you take a deeper look into it all, is there really a decided difference between an insolent or even an evil disposition which comes in the form of a criminal prison gang and its physically uncivilized claims of majority than from that which may manifest from within the containing walls of an institutional church and all of the uncivil sentatiousness that it may claim of and for itself?

Does it really matter where the majority of insolence or evil manifests? Is that what makes insolence so insolent? Is that what makes evil so evil? Where it comes from?

What if it comes in the shape of a static and corrupt economic system or ideology? Does it really matter where the system or ideology is located?

Or what if it comes from within a self-aggrandizing nation-state?

Or how about from that of an insular and chauvinistic media consortium?

Or from a price-gouging medical industry?

How about from a titillating hate group spreading its *sieg heil* ignorance?

What if it shows its head inside the ranks of your favorite political party? Will its insolence then be excused or even denied from within the confinement of that isolated majority?

Or what if it's found inside of a vacuous and narcissistic political think tank?

Or from behind the gates of a remote and hoarding social class?

Or within a small-minded and sectarian ethnic or racial group?

Are you even capable of seeing insolence or evil if it's staring right back at you from your own tribal mirror?

What if it jumps out at you from a dysfunctional yet overly enmeshed extended family? Does it matter whose family it is in order to be able to recognize it?

What if it arises out of a habitual conformity to tribal fashion or thought?

Or if it comes from a collection of pompous cynics? Or from the proudly apathetic?

Or from the pious noise made by self-estranged anarchists?

What if it's caught hiding inside of a tight-knit group of bribing and bribable Wall Street bankers and financiers from whose wheelings and dealings you've profited from?

Or if it comes from inside that of the military-mercantile-industrial empire, the global archetype of them all—which now permeates its claim of majority in every wild region of the slowly vanishing natural world of your beautiful-enough planet?

Does the ability and willingness to recognize actual insolence and evil simply depend upon where your loyalties lie? To what tribal majority you submit to?

Does allegiance to a tribal majority cause blindness? If so, aren't the blind just as complicit in the acts of insolence and evil as are the perpetrators?

Insolence is insolence, after all, no matter where it comes from. Isn't it? Just as evil is evil, no matter where it comes from.

So feel free to add your own chosen or observed suspects to the list of those who tend to follow the majoritized creed of the *only-mind*.

But just try to remember this: There's no need to be too concerned about their whereabouts. Whereabouts can only tell you about whereabouts, not much else.

Any significant evidence of even minimal resistance to the predominant prescription of things (within each peculiar and insolent majority) is quickly rebuked and ridiculed and often violently demonized or just whacked out of existence. Isn't it?

And individual resistance or even simple noncompliance of any size or shape has come to be looked upon as a felonious, social, or even as an ontological offense. Hasn't it? From right within the one-dimensional perspectives infecting so many of your peremptory groups and institutions. It's where the self-justifying garments of text and ritual are majestically worn, as those in charge patrol and even hover above the tribal grounds with their cold-blooded and intolerant legalisms and with their sanctimonious morals . . . in all of their regal and aloof piety.

The most common way to securely operate and control things from within each arbitrary, overly contained, and isolated majority is to reject or eliminate anything which could threaten its separate and specific equilibrium. Isn't it?

And let us observe that, from within this vast climate of contempt for *otherness*, whoever you can become always depends upon how effective your role and involvement masks or is at the very least neutrally supportive of the bundled and violent tribal constructs which you reside in. But you all know that. Don't you?

The game of allegiance must be played out in serious fashion no matter how much you try to pretend that you've set yourselves apart from *others*.

So you spend an enormous amount of time and energy forever competing for ideological or identity dominance, from within each tribal division, by conjuring up barriers which rarely separate much of anything other than one chirp from another, this chirp from that.

While most of your impotent tweedling at one another doesn't even penetrate the exposed skin of what is real. But you all know that too. Don't you?

Tweedledum and Tweedledee
Agreed to have a battle;
For Tweedledum said Tweedledee
Had spoiled his nice new rattle.
Just then flew down a monstrous crow,
As black as a tar-barrel;
Which frightened both the heroes so,
They quite forgot their quarrel, observes the wise nursery rhyme. [1]

The real game being played so often by so many of you is one of diversion.

Within most of your contrived tribal arrangements, you're either in or you're out. All forms or degrees of dwelling on the periphery are either marginalized or abandoned—or eventually destroyed.

Any deeply felt or expressed deviation is accused of betrayal.

Sincerity and doubt are muted and mocked, replaced by theatrical and compliant sure things or by qualified yes men of either gender . . . often accompanied by synchronized and sophomoric high fives.

And it doesn't matter much (does it?) whether it's histrionic hand slapping or a crowd begging for an encore of what it doesn't even comprehend or even if it's mobs of gun toters shooting up the sky in targeted celebration to intimidate a specific *otherness* back into its cave of obscurity.

Each is merely a modified version of grabbing onto the same jejune rituals, the cheap and easy substitutes for growing up (or for growing beyond your plateaus of coerced assimilation).

The collective fear of the indivisible *Self* is what ignites the tribal kindling which consumes the conscious remains of the individual.

And what it tends to ignite, it also anesthetizes.

Doesn't it?

CHAPTER 8

Welcome to Stuckville

WELCOME TO STUCKVILLE, reads the signage.
But so few of you notice the bold solicitation even while being drawn into any of its easy-to-enter and hard-to-leave replicating domains.

Population unknown . . . growing too fast to count, it says.

Yet if conditions of separation would no longer be required for tribal self-definition, how would you be able to determine who you are anymore?

What would happen to your storage of commonly held beliefs and behaviors as well as to your routine judgments based upon your illusions of separateness?

How would you keep up with or be acknowledged by anybody else in your tribe when there would no longer be a requisite or recognizable zone of superiority to hitch a ride upon? Or if there would no longer be a prison of lowliness to hold in contempt?

Much of your sentiment about these things has been shaped and contorted by a competing assortment of linear yet parallel ideologies. Hasn't it? Even while they've tried so hard to appear to be distinct from one another.

And it's that contorting tribal logic which lures so many of you to attack and destroy your utterly indispensable enemies, whom you avidly accuse of conspiring for your tribe's (and hence your own personal) destruction—which is the paradoxical food that keeps your enclosed carapace well fed, standing guard at every meal and every bite you take, making sure that you continue to feast upon the nourishment of your group's repulsions.

For many of you, the acknowledgment of a contrary (or merely a dissimilar) worldview or a contrasting cultural prerogative or simply another way of doing things somehow results in the loss of your own sense of significance, of losing the advantage of being a dedicated and first-rate servant to your own cluster of sameness. And so the fragile stature of your group-affiliated self-importance suddenly stops (or has a very hard time) breathing. Doesn't it?

Acceptance of (or even curiosity about) the *other* somehow leads to your symbolic death. Don't you see? To your own suicide actually, to the suicidal consequence of holding on to the belief in your own physical and ideological permanence, to the belief in the permanence of your mistaken identity, reinforced by its collusion with the assembled self-idolatry superimposed upon you by each overly contained tribe, filtered through and domesticated by each dependent member, squeezed beneath each and every umbrella of collective self-worship, where the collaborative fear of death is really of the demise of the external gods each tribe relies upon in order to keep its vast collection of mistaken identities alive (but barely breathing), and as the essential source and sustenance which keeps each unventilated tribe alive (but barely breathing).

It especially fools the presumptuous *only-mind* of each tribe (which pulls the operative strings inside of each isolated container), persuading it into thinking that it alone is actually imperishable.

And it all makes perfect (tribal) sense to you, doesn't it, regardless of whether you happen to be sacrificing your own flesh and blood or even if you continue to try to inflict damage upon those of whom you refuse to acknowledge even while trying to eliminate them.

Because the false promise ingrained in you by the *only-mind* of the tribe (and which you succumb to) is that you might get to go to a permanent tribal heaven.

And your mother or your sweetheart might be given a few mass-produced shiny medals and a brand-new flag to take home with them in your place.

You might even become an everlasting hero (or martyr), depending on the trappings of your specific culture and its exoteric customs.

It's a routine head trick that so many among you have bought into and kept activated for centuries. Haven't you? You actually spend much of your time trying to unimagine what or whom you patently deny recognition of.

You try to kill off what or whom (in the *disjoined* mental world of the *only-mind*) has no valid, literal, or relevant existence.

You try to extinguish who or what is already extinct in the overly contained tribe's chosen reality. And it all seems to continue to make perfect sense somehow, doesn't it?

Relegating other life-forms to categories of nonexistence is one of your favorite (tribal) self-deceptions, is it not?

How wonderful that we have met with a paradox. Now we have some hope of making progress, said the wise Niels Bohr.[1]

The paradox of reality is that no image is as compelling as the one which exists only in the mind's eye, wrote the wise Shana Alexander.[2]

Reality is not what it seems to be, nor is it otherwise, says the wise Tibetan Buddhist teaching.[3]

CHAPTER 9

The Power of Fear

B UT WHAT YOU'RE hearing right now? This is real, whether
you trust it or want to trust it . . . or not.

And it is intentional.

And what you're about to undergo is intended to extract your
commonly shared qualities of truth, beauty, and goodness from wherever
they stoop and huddle with their big frightened eyes . . . from inside the
cracks and crevices where you've tried to banish them, stuck between
the *disjoined* rocks and boulders of your tribal desert and its barren
arrangements.

But we'll be giving you plenty of opportunities to pry them all loose
and to liberate them . . . and then even to enhance their depth and
expanse.

Although, as we've already stated more than once, you can believe
any or all of this—or none of it. It's all up to you. And at this point in
the evolving process, it doesn't really matter a whole lot. What you will
begin to experience will eventually transcend whatever you've blindly
chosen to accept and believe by mere (tribal) default.

The evidence will confirm itself as it unfolds. And it won't need
any formalized approval or signed permission slips from any of your
tribe-authorized gatekeepers either.

What you're reluctantly allowing into your eardrums right now is a
merging of voices . . . unified through one consolidating voice box.

And that one integrated vocal process will deviate in how it sounds
from time to time, adjusting the intensity, the tone, and even the accent
of specific words and phrases; allowing them to adapt to the changing
contextual emphasis of our presentation, as each vocal alteration blends
into and then out of each other one, in a comingling of process and
content; behind a cumulate voice which will integrate and unify all of
the specific voices into the one unifying message—which we will be
doing our best to clarify as we move things along.

But we're getting a little ahead of ourselves. Aren't we?

We simply require your strict attention for a short while.

We have something to unwrap and disclose. And we urge you not to be frightened. Yet we do regret that there was no easier or more seamless (or just plain better) way to do this thing.

But here we are.

And again, we assure you that this is all real.

We repeat: You are not imagining it.

It will all become even more real to you as we gather momentum, even while much of its emerging reality may feel quite discomforting and sometimes confusing to you, which is to be expected.

Yet there's no impending hazardous risk to worry about right now . . . of any kind. We promise.

We simply invite you to gradually lift your gaze (and your ears) and your attentiveness this way, toward us . . . as calmly as you're able to do it.

Try to think of the lifting up as a going within, as an expansion that deepens or as a deepness which expands, as old wine being renewed and prepared for the pouring into new wine skins, so to speak.

Just try to prevent yourselves from becoming too alarmed.

There's really nothing worth getting overly anxious about. We assure you. And it won't change things if you do, in any event. We have something significant to announce, and it's genuinely meant for your own benefit, as we've already stated . . . for the well-being of your entire little planet, actually.

The message we have for you is unusual yet quite eternal. So we've reasoned that it would be most effective (if maybe a little risky) to be right up front and large with the way we'd introduce and enter you into it, to try to keep most of the blow to your emotional arrangements safely contained inside the initial impact so that whatever comes after it won't feel quite so heavy to the bone.

And just in case you've already noticed and are wondering about it, we've taken the liberty to temporarily restrict all of your physical movements to within a few feet of wherever it is that you're now standing, walking, sitting, leaning, or lying down, to within what you might call several billion invisibly roped-off individual security zones. We want to prevent any potential wild stampedes of panic. You understand? Hence, all of that yellow security tape.

We know how groups driven by fear and confusion rather than by clarity and awareness can react. It's a precautionary measure, just in case.

If it doesn't make immediate sense to you . . . well . . . then you'll just have to bear with it. You have no other choice.

But we've left each of you plenty of elbow room to be able to stretch out or to move around, just enough to allow for any need to release the inevitable tension or anxiety you must be feeling, which may need to be tinkered with from time to time.

So stretch those muscles if you like. Do some isometrics. Run in place. Grit out some push-ups. Do whatever helps.

But listen closely while you do it. Pay strict attention.

And please . . . do try to translate this as benignly as you possibly can. Squeeze it out. It will help to make this entire process move along a whole lot smoother for all of us.

We know that most of you are already quite bewildered by this whole thing. But we've planned for that. So we're trying to be as gentle yet as candid as we can be with our delivery. We know that it's all coming at you quite suddenly and that it feels more than unreal to many of you.

But just try to prevent your imagination from going too far off the tribal cliff for just a short while longer. And try to endure your understandable confusion as much as you can . . . for now. Okay?

As our pronouncement gradually becomes more vivid, so will your understanding of what this is all about.

But don't forget. We're having to adjust and fine-tune our collective voice and language to try to be as clear as we can be, in order to effectively integrate our message into your long-standing tribal habits—into habits which have been rigidly conditioned to restrict and contain only so much of what you allow yourselves to comprehend and to interpret . . . or to even hear.

So it's not so easy to make this thing happen between two such distinct yet interdependent species (such as we are), especially when so many of you seem so stuck and even addicted to how and what you will or will not allow to enter into your perceptual container and what you will or will not permit yourselves to hear, perceive, come to know . . . or even to know about.

But we are edging in a little closer, aren't we? We can feel the opposing wavelengths gradually coming together. We can sense that more of you are beginning to comprehend at least a little more of what we're trying to convey.

The frequencies are gradually beginning to weave themselves together and tune in to each other. And we can tell that most of you are even beginning to unconsciously adjust your inner receptors in order to adapt to our more supple, complex, yet free-floating communication patterns. Can you feel it? Even though, at the same time, you continue to consciously cling to a *disjoined* unwillingness, to a vague resistance to any alteration or even to any slight modification that might be made to the sluggish ways of processing and exchanging information which your tribe has become so addicted to.

But you may soon find that your perceptual and even your sensual awareness of things is becoming more limber and pliable (even porous), as the ebb and flow of the adjustment process moves itself along—which can only help to make things less confusing.

Although you'll still have to continue to make accommodations along the way.

You'll come to realize that yours is not (and has never been) the one and only or absolute way to experience, to evaluate, or to deliver and receive information.

You'll soon be letting go of that arrogant presumption no matter what tribe you belong to and no matter what tribal language pattern it is that you seem to be so reluctant to liberate yourselves from.

You'll have to let go eventually. But in any case, this whole operation will just wait until you do.

And you don't need to try to hide your anxiousness or make any foolish attempts at bravery or escape either.

Just try to calm yourselves down a few degrees at a time, gradually . . . little by little.

Your time for the necessary retrieval of genuine courage will come soon enough. We can guarantee it. And it may come sooner than you wish.

But real courage only rises up when you're afraid.

Did you know that?

If you don't feel actual fear, then what comes up is not authentic courage . . . by simple definition and direct felt observation. Don't you see?

If you're not afraid but then demonstrate something that looks like courage . . . well, then you just might have misplaced or neglected an all-important ingredient that's essential to the mixture of what evolves into what is (actually) real.

Courage without fear is about as real as fire without oxygen. Fire needs air to breathe. False courage comes without fear (or is burdened with untransformed fear). And then it often contorts into the abuse of power over the vulnerable (over *otherness*) into a fire that burns itself out while scorching everyone and everything around it with its gasping and reactionary expressions of heat.

Fearlessness needs fear in order to emerge (or even to survive) or to thrive and transform into courageous and compassionate action, at the starting gate anyway . . . or until fear becomes neither friend nor foe.

But you can't let go of something unless you've held onto it first. You can't lessen something that you don't have more of. You can't feel fearless until you first feel fear.

So once fear (like anger) is able to conjoin itself to courage . . . well, then the fear (and anger) will no longer be in charge. You can kiss their dominance good-bye. You can wave your hands through the tribal flames, and you won't get burnt. The heat and the oxygen will still be there. But you'll be the one in charge of the direction and intensity of that heat and of the light of that fire . . . and of its organic glow.

The fear and the fearlessness will be held together like synergistic twins, firmly in the arms of compassion—in the arms of the *Compassionate One*, by whatever name and face it manifests itself to you (or toward you or within you or around you).

We can easily identify several of the obvious *Compassionate* (and courageous) *Ones* who've passed through that gate to the other side and then back again. But it's not really necessary, is it? Since most of you could do the same if you weren't so busy worshiping, whitewashing, watering down, or warring over your (idolized) saints, sages, saviors, and messiahs.

As an alternative, you could have been putting more effort into trying to imitate or follow their courageous ways instead, yes? In the ways which you speak and act or in the ways which you stare into the fire of their rigorous and fearless lives, lives which never demand to be separate from or elevated above you by any correct form of tribal worship or through any cold and mandatory act of compliance.

No. They don't.

Although they do demand a unifying and complete surrender and devotion to the inmost *Self*—which is in and of all things. Isn't it? Excluding no one, human or *other* than human.

And there really is no *other* to be separate from anyway, is there? But you already know that too (in your heart of hearts). Don't you?

Yet so many of you have replaced fearless discipleship with submission to the tribe (and to tribal uniformity) instead. They are not the same thing. They're not even distant cousins, even though you often identify the latter with the name of the former.

Uniformity is simply an impostor, an assassin of unity, don't you see? Just as tribalism is the fundamental condition which crucifies authentic community.

And whenever any one community feels itself being crucified, it tends to spread that disordering ritual over and onto neighboring communities, doesn't it? And even down upon its own collection of (those whom they view as) lesser or subservient community members.

Then those neighboring communities, in-house neighborhoods, and community members simply use their own habits and tools of crucifixion to prey upon *other* nearby but separate tribes of people and down upon individual families contained within their own tribe.

Then the preyed-upon *others* merely extend the same crucifixion process out into the larger world—which just hardens and thickens the tribal dividing lines even more, doesn't it?

And together, it all creates an ongoing nuclear reaction within and between each family of each neighborhood tribe, doesn't it?

Neighbors begin to crucify neighbors.

And the crucifiable crime may just be that a neighbor happens to follow a different faith or that they've let go of religion altogether, or that they come from a different racial or ethnic group; or that they realize a different sexual orientation, or that they speak a different language, or that they express themselves with a different kind of intelligence, or that they approach things from a different educational or experiential background, or that they have a different appearance, or that they have a different worldview, or that they appear to be physically weak, or that they just happen to be easily accessible, or that they fit so nicely into the role of the new scapegoat of which your tribe has been trying to refill.

But the key word here is *different*, isn't it, which can be translated and reinterpreted as anyone who dwells outside the *disjoined* norms of each tribal arrangement.

So being different is routinely perceived as being an *other*, yes? To be different is to be marked and targeted with the lethal blemish of an *other*.

The custom of crucifixion even extends to individuals within one's own household, doesn't it? To those who may have casually or even intentionally drifted off into exploring or intermingling with different (or nontribal) forms of religious, political, or cultural *otherness.*

Then those individuals within those households begin to target out and crucify *other* individuals from *other* households within the same neighborhood for similar reasons.

It even comes to be seen as a form of tribal initiation, passed on from one generation to the next. The cyclical slope of (inter and intra) tribal crucifixion becomes quite a slippery one, doesn't it?

Every contour of human violence is shaped and driven by the spread of untransformed fear, pain, and anger (at some level); by some form and degree of capitulation to the tribal *only-mind*; by an unenlightened and even clueless allegiance along with a reinforcing collective amnesia, much of it simply surrendered up to the overly contained conventional thinking of the *disjoined* tribe . . . and by an incestuous, self-adulating, and artificial sense of tribal superiority.

And every act of human compassion and every visible expression of loving-kindness (especially that which reaches out to the *other*) necessitates a good amount of unconventional courage, yes? Of an exceptional kind of bravery, especially in a world which is consumed by an endless amount of delusional fear which so often triggers so much irrational violence(which is constantly rationalized); an insane amount of violence which is often interpreted as being (not deranged, but) virtuous, even as being valiant.

But ask yourselves this: What's more courageous? To respond with a sense of gratefulness, forgiveness, and rational acceptance in the midst of (seemingly) tragic misfortune and scarcity? Or to react with vindictive blame, with quick and automatic retaliation, and with uncharitable exclusion?

Hold on to your answers for now.

You may find yourselves gradually letting go of them, as the process moves itself along.

Or you may not.

Only time will tell.

Or maybe not.

MICHAEL J. GAJDA

CHAPTER 10

No Escape

AND THERE IS no escape.

Let's just get that scuttlebutt out of the way right now, shall we?

So you might as well just try to relax, as impossible as that may seem for you to be able to do right now, as you struggle to comprehend the seemingly surreal proposition that you're being introduced to.

And we do realize that you can't just give yourselves emotional marching orders like that and expect them to magically kick right in. Although the spirit-body-mind does have a surprising (and a much underrated) way of adapting, doesn't it?

But your interior traffic jams will begin to clear up before too long, slowly dissolving any stubborn blockage in your perceptions . . . while gradually relieving whatever else may still feel like an overload to your physical and psychological nerve endings.

Things will clear up. We promise you that.

But for now, just try to move one small measure at a time . . . in subtle gradations, if you can.

Imagine that you're methodically sedating yourselves. And it will all begin to slow down. You can do this. We know you can.

But don't move too slowly, yet not too quickly either.

The goal is neither to present you with just another version of tribe-induced self-hypnosis (to add to your collective repertoire) nor to dole out just a few more tribal traits and habits which you tend to overdose on.

So begin the untangling.

Visualize it.

Talk yourselves into it.

Be it, as gracefully as you can . . . whatever it takes.

We know this is difficult . . . *that's it!*

Let it settle. Let it begin to mend itself.

Keep squeezing.

This is not some fatal dream sequence which you're awakening into. We promise you that.

But take all the time that you need to adjust . . . to concentrate yourselves. But don't take too much time. Yet don't be too abrupt either.

Reach for the middle.

Always reach for the middle when you start to lose your balance.

We'll step in from time to time to help out if needed.

And we can see that most of you do seem to be gradually coming around now, irrespective of your well-practiced resistance to much of anything that could lead to genuine transformation.

Many of you just don't like to explore (let alone trust) your own intuition, do you? Nor do you care especially much for the spontaneous or visceral exchange of ideas. It's all been quite easy and obvious to observe. You've made it quite evident.

But you do like to sink your teeth into tribal ideologies, don't you? We'll give you that.

Chewing up (and swallowing whole) your separate and absolute versions of tribal truth seems to give you a secure place among your fellow true believers, doesn't it? Where most of you assume that you can safely deposit your brain waves and where you can even disregard discernment or even empirical facts altogether without much risk of having to struggle to think anything through, or to allow anything to come forth with much independent effort or creative discrimination on your part, or without having to depend too much on your own disciplined or creative skills of observation either.

Just copy and clone it . . . forget it and defend it.

That seems to be the mesmerizing motto of most, if not all, of your cults of overly contained tribal thought and belief.

And very few of you seem overly enthused or committed to developing or deepening your skills in the area of values clarification either, do you?

Most of you prefer to assume and assimilate the ethics and values already instilled inside of whatever *disjoined* tribe you've donated your co-opted neural structure to.

Now this may all sound a bit harsh, eh? And we know that.

But a whopping number of you have become such experts at being able to recite the company line (while dancing to its tune) that it almost sounds and looks like it actually means something to you, even while you practice memorizing what you imagine you're supposed to think, feel, or step to . . . not to mention what you're supposed to say or do, or not say, or not do.

And you'll soon come to realize that this is not some apocalyptic vision that you've been hurled into either, to frighten you into just another kind of sanctimonious state of tribal isolation.

But it is an opening (an entrance) . . . into the long, dark night of your collective soul, an entrance which you've kept sealed off and hidden from yourselves for so long, by all of that artificial and distracting light which so many of you like to shine onto yourselves . . . to make it look like everything is clean, orderly, and intact—even shadowless.

And it's that buried shadow of yours that's about to be emancipated, don't you see? So that you can freely recognize, acknowledge, and integrate the full weight of its existing shades and shapes into your overstimulated tribal milieu . . . as you begin the grueling journey of waking up.

Many of you have merely been asleep all this time (it's as simple as that), despite all the pervasive noise which you permit to penetrate and roam the halls of your *disjoined* tribal brain with unrestricted privilege.

And as we've already indicated, you'll be getting a better understanding of these words as things continue to move along, but only if you rise up to the occasion, and perhaps by experimenting with the useful practice of *right* (instead of tribal) *mindfulness* . . . as the wise Buddhist sages teach it.[1]

And it may even start to become quite self-explanatory, even surprisingly obvious to you as the unraveling process expands and deepens. Yet that will only coincide with how much you're able to keep those bright eyes and floppy ears from closing back down again.

We've taken the lid off the coffin. Now it's up to you to dig around and climb yourselves out from your premature collective burial. And we'll be there to guide you toward that goal. You're just going to have to trust us on that. But you'll be doing all the digging and the heavy lifting from now on, not us.

That's it . . . ! That's it!

We can see now that most of you are reorienting yourselves and becoming more alert to your surroundings. And we don't mean to startle you but . . . *hey! Stay with it . . . hello . . . stay with it now!* There you go.

You can actually do this. Just stay with it.

There's nothing grave or dangerous happening here to worry about. We promise, even though we know that it feels quite strange and foreign to you.

Just don't let yourselves slide back.

We have something quite important (world shaking, actually) to transmit to many of you. And if you begin to comprehend the deep logic of it all, you should genuinely be looking forward to the experience . . . perhaps only in retrospect though, which sounds quite confusing, yes? It's one of those paradoxical brain teasers, don't you see? And the tease is that you may be able to look back to then see how you were indeed looking forward, to where you'll actually be looking back from . . . even while you experience the look ahead.

You'll eventually be able to solve that puzzle.

Yet by then, it will all feel more or less self-contained in the same fabric of an elastic nowness, where the middle naturally expands . . . slowly enlarging the circle of awareness.

But of course that will only happen if you accept the invitation to the journey that's inviting you into itself.

You see, the journey has always been there. It doesn't change. It doesn't withhold itself from you at all. Nor does it interfere with your superficial travels.

It just waits inside of all of you.

It's always there in *the underground stream* . . . as the wise Ira Progoff pictured it,[2] eternally silent and always now. It's not separate from who you are. As a matter of fact, it's what unifies you . . . if you have the courage to go deep enough into the well of your own being.

But that would just be one early illustration among the many which you'll eventually encounter and realize along this maze-like trip—a trip that is without a specific destination.

Just as *evil is basically the concealment of the good* . . . as the wise Eric Butterworth has written,[3] so too is a predetermined destination often used to conceal, to blur, or to unplug the light and quality of the journey within the substance of things.

So (starting right now) just be careful of overly hyped travel brochures or of overenthusiastic tribal travel agents of any kind. They're trained to schmooze, to distract, then to supplant your natural intuitions with artifacts shined up to look like tribal gold. And the disingenuous presentations come in all kinds of shapes and disguises, don't you see? Usually enhanced by beautiful background music while making promises of utopian holidays or promises of frequent miles of thrills and accumulation, of worship with prestige, or of visits to islands of exclusivity . . . with huge resorts of expenditure and depletion, of endless tribal souvenirs, and of packaged hoopla; promises of beautiful bodies that never age, of guarantees of perpetual enemies, of the truest religion, of weightless thoughts and emotions, promises of a pain-free permanence, of the veneration of pleasure, of the drug of superior morality, of the assurance of tribal status, of guarantees of security, of privileged rights and exemptions, of unbending creeds and anthems to choose from and to follow; promises of continuous comforts, of opportunities for heroism, even martyrdom; of protective baronage; of uninterrupted stimulation; of gadgets of accelerated disconnectedness.

Of promises galore.

They've led many of you into the perpetual loop of returning to identical havens which differ only in their varying tribal facades, full of assurances of rapture and foreverness; where you anxiously expect to arrive at or maybe even ascend into that one big final sanctuary; where all your needs will be met and all your problems will be solved . . . by somebody else.

Yet *That which is always becoming* has been there all along, right there inside and beside you, hasn't it? Waiting for you to wake up just long enough to ease you into its welcoming abundance, where there is no separation and where there is no outside refuge or destination to search or reach for anymore.

There never has been.

The kingdom of God is within you, preached the wise Jesus of Nazareth.[4]

God is not somebody else, observed the wise Thomas Merton.[5]

And as many of you have experienced and have so often tried to discount, what may appear to be a negative event in your initial brush with it often transforms into something surprisingly positive, doesn't it?

And vice versa, of course.

So try not to cling too tightly to either end of the tribal spectrum, where you've seemed to like to store up and defend so much of your hoarded treasures . . . as well as your tragedies.

We know it will take a lot of practice to undo those habits.

Many of you have spent much of your lives frantically grasping for more pleasure, for more security, and for more comfort while desperately trying to export and escape from any and all suffering, any and all anxiety, and any and all discomfort.

But a fixation is still a fixation, isn't it? Whether you're driven to grab and consume more and more of what you can never seem to get enough of or if you're impelled to ditch and destroy what you can never seem to get too little of. The pull and the push are just twin addictions, aren't they? Borne from the same overlapping streams of energy. The direction of the habituation is the only way you can really tell them apart sometimes, yes?

And please do keep lifting your attention our way while trying to stay as relaxed as you can.

Try to breathe easy.

And raise your awareness toward the sound of our voice.

To the sound of the voice.

Focus your attention on the sound of the voice, toward wherever it seems to be coming from.

There's really no specific or correct area of reception or deliverance to search for.

There ya go.

We can sense now that most of you are beginning to accommodate yourselves, allowing this nerve-racking invasion to feel a lot less intrusive than the wrecking ball it initially felt like.

And we wish there could have been another less encroaching and less anxiety-raising way of doing this. But this is the entranceway. This is the gate.

Here we go . . . very good.

Okay. We seem to have all of you on board now.

And we do apologize for this sudden and extraordinary disruption. But our time is somewhat constrained. And this will take a while. It will seem to anyway.

So again . . . please do be patient and keep refocusing your attention as needed. It looks like almost everyone is settled down just enough now to begin, even though we know that it may not feel very settled down at all to most of you.

And as strange or as jolting as this may seem to be to so many of you right now, we simply ask for your forbearance . . . and for your calm and steady attention.

You will slowly begin to catch on and to gradually absorb what this is all about. We promise you that.

And we repeat: There is no need to panic. There's nothing to fear at this point in the process . . . directly or immediately anyway.

But this will require more than just a little of whatever uncontaminated or unexplored mental faculties you still have left to bring forward, as well as requiring your strict attendance and concentration. Have you got that point clear in your heads yet?

So unwax those ears (and we regret to have to be so blunt about this)—or they will be unwaxed for you.

You will all ingest and gradually assimilate what we have to say, clearly and completely . . . whether you like it or not.

And we are saddened to have to put it that way.

But isn't it better that you begin this journey with the least amount of self-inflicted confusion and denial as possible?

We'll be working very hard to make things clear and to maintain a certain lucidity from the start.

But again, you must pay very strict attention. That warning can never be overemphasized. And it cannot be overstated.

Make it your mantra.

But let us edge into things with these next few brief clarifications first. They should help.

We make no apologies for our language nor for whatever we borrow from the wise among you. You'll be adapting to all of it as it evolves (and as you evolve). Even though we realize that many of you still distrust the generosity and fluid nature of the living universe as it unfolds and expands everywhere around you and all at once (as it is meant to be, and as it is), especially those among you who keep trying to squeeze yourselves back into a prescribed tube of linear tribal logic.

But bona fide evolution in all of its forms is full of unpredictable and even comical contradictions, isn't it?

Yet there's no way around it. Is there? And there's no tube that it can fit back into.

It's just another paradoxical promise which will follow through on itself, by its own creative impulse and momentum.

All evolution in thought and conduct must at first appear as heresy and misconduct, wrote the wise George Bernard Shaw.[6]

The reason why the universe is eternal is that it does not live for itself; it gives life to others as it transforms, spoke the wise Lao Tzu.[7]

CHAPTER 11

A Blend of Voices

A LLOW US NOW to introduce our next voice without introducing a specific identity. Because there is no specific identity. We are all of one voice. Remember?

Every voice is a blend of voices, as we've already indicated.

So just for a moment try to imagine this: That you're swimming alongside an abundant and collaborative flow of sea creatures bathing in the same vast ocean; or that you're hiking the interior of an animated jungle forest . . . through a wild mixture of interplayful flora and fauna; or that you're wandering over the empty, rolling, and ever-changing dunes of an inexhaustible horizonless desert; or that you're strolling through an endless network of interconnected blocks of pavement . . . planted with rows of heroic houses and buildings, weaving in and out of the same tireless city streets.

As you move about, you'll notice changes. Most will be gradual, even subtle.

Occasionally something obvious will suddenly move . . . and surprise you. A swordfish might jump up out of the water. A pit viper may squirm across the path. A loud vendor with a creative pitch or an unusual accent might try to sell you food or beverage. The sand may quickly sink beneath your feet. The sounds, sights, and smells will continually and unpredictably rearrange themselves. But you'll still be wandering through the same undifferentiated field of awareness, don't you see?

Begin to observe all of the subtleties that you're so used to disregarding, that you're so used to not noticing—which will be good preparation and practice for what's ahead.

So there's your first big hint. There will be plenty more. Some of them will be implied or elusive, while others will be more conspicuous (hint, hint).

And this will be our last introduction. So consider this one a gift.

From this point on you'll have to maintain a heightened vigilance in order to recognize and reacclimate yourselves to any and all voice variations which may abruptly, gradually, or even sporadically work themselves into our discourse—which is another important reason to pay strict attention. Isn't it?

And you'll need to keep readjusting your sensory receptors in order to reinterpret and adapt to the alterations inserted into the ecology of our language, into the specific words and phrases which may seem to reinvent themselves each time you hear them pronounced, penetrating deep into and beyond your senses and eventually leaving those senses behind because your limited sensory perception can only take you so far before it becomes more of a distraction than it does a reliable guide to the immutable depths and heights of *That which is always becoming*.

And (to be quite honest) almost all of our linguistic adjustments will be much more subtle than the lumbering abruptness so many of you are so used to communicating with. Even our more obvious alterations will be.

As the old saying goes, which paraphrases the wise Abraham Maslow's words . . . *If all you have is a hammer, then everything begins to look like a nail.*[1]

Well. Doesn't it?

You will gradually be uncovering a unique and curious craft, one that is intimately similar to the fine art of wood sculpting, where no specific tools or skills will be denigrated or excluded, where close attention is a must, and where shapes and sizes are not always as they seem; where the smell and feel of sawdust is like breathing in and playing with cosmic particles from the promised land; where you'll eventually forget all of what you think you know, and awaken to *That which you've always known*.

One never knows what one is going to do. One starts a painting and then it becomes something quite else. It is remarkable how little the "willing" of the artist intervenes . . . If you're trying to find something, it means you haven't got it. And if you find it simply by looking for it, that means it's false . . .[2] *Every child is an artist. The problem is how to remain an artist once he grows up,*[3] observed the wise Pablo Picasso.

So let's move on to our next speaker.

Shall we?

CHAPTER 12

The Edict

THE FOLLOWING EDICT and extended explanation which we are about to elaborate upon for your benefit and preparation is not intended for those among you who presently abide by a simple but pure (even if sometimes faltering) faith in *That which is.*

Yet no one is prohibited from these unique proceedings either, nor from reflecting upon our words as they begin to germinate and manifest among and within you.

The logistics would have been just too involved and complicated to remove and separate the intended audience from the rest of you. We don't apologize for that decision. But we do regret the resulting unease it may have caused anyone.

Those of you among the unintended targets of our invitation are quite welcome to stick around and to quietly observe.

The monologue is open to all of you—to the entire planet actually. And once the message begins to clarify itself and to deepen, taking the ride along with the invited ones (all the way to the end of our presentation) will be entirely up to you.

But let us add this enticement, if you will.

It can't really hurt any of you to deeply engage yourselves in the listening process. It may do more than surprise you. It may even be somewhat enlightening and reassuring to many of you. The practice of deep listening is quite a beneficial one. Is it not?

And it could very well serve as an unexpected affirmation for some of you among the uninvited who still retain any lingering doubts about who you really are or about the roads and fields you've been called to walk and to cultivate—no matter how imperfectly you may see yourselves walking the talk of the call you attempt to answer and no matter how unwieldy the pace and stride along your particular path feels to you.

But here's another hint.

The ones who declare themselves to be most complete? The ones who shower themselves and their tribe with absolution and exoneration?

Well, they stand nakedly exposed as the ones to whom our invitation and message is aimed.

So let us move on with the all-important invitation then, shall we? It will clear itself up as it disentangles. We do make that promise.

We just ask once again for respectful patience from all of you, from the invited participants as well as from the uninvited bystanders, from all draftees and volunteers, and from all curious listeners and observers.

Draft dodging (however) will not be tolerated in this particular call to arms.

If you've been named up, you're going. This isn't a lottery. You've been handpicked based upon your qualifications. So pay attention.

This public notification has not been formulated for those of you who currently practice the cultivation of watchfulness or of being vigilant to what actually is, even if you do circle around and stagger apart from it more often than you would like to.

Nor does it aim at those of you who somehow manage to keep yourselves awake and entrusted in *That which is always becoming*, even if it might only be by the tenuous grip of your fingertips clutched to a thin ledge of a rising awareness—which is forever present yet so often feels near to impossible to fully grasp.

And it's not designed for those of you who strive in any authentic, brave, yet cautious desire to actually wake up into its expanse, even if you haven't quite let go of all of your fond attachments to tribal sleepwalking yet.

It is not being directed at those of you who practice selfless or humane interactions with *others*, even if you do sometimes stumble about in your efforts.

And it's not being advanced to those of you who remain open to the presence of the inexhaustible *Self* as you boldly (however slowly) extract yourselves from the selfish and isolated tribal environment you were born into.

It most certainly isn't being delivered to any of you who wrestle with feeling your way into what actually lasts or into what is meant to last . . . or into *That which is real.*

We know that the road which quite a few of you (among the uninvited) have been traveling upon is not an easy one to follow. It is narrow and dangerous, with many sharp edges and with unpredictable twists and turns.

Yet many of you are making the sincere and effort-filled attempt anyway (blisters, bruises, cuts, and all), even though you can barely detect the footprints planted by the feet of those who took the narrow way before you, of those who somehow cut through (and beyond) the *disjoining* distractions of the tribal *only-mind*—distractions which subdue and overpower so many of the overly contained inhabitants of your small planet.

It's been done. There actually is a way which is yet untrampled upon by the powers that patrol and prevail over so much of the world of the invited ones, of the ones to whom our invitation and our words are targeted.

And our invitation and our words *are* targeted. Let us be very clear about that from the outset.

Our words are intended for every conscious and capable adult human being who selfishly or violently occupies any part of your cramped and beautiful (but largely conquered and colonized) planet and for whoever intentionally intrudes upon any of its precious natives of any stripe, color, or species.

Our quarrel is especially with those of you occupying the ranks of the overindulged, who dangle and extend your accumulation of power, your influential standing, and your material means and possessions over *others*, like three jagged blades cutting downward from the same lethal guillotine . . . with each heart-wounding tool just as sharp and decapitating as the next.

Our timbre is aimed at those of you who steal and deceive in order to position yourselves further up along whatever treasured elevation you find yourselves climbing at, proudly perched upon your tribal ladders of selfish desires.

We address those of you who claw for even more favor than you've already stolen (or abused) on your upward trek, as you conform with evermore severity to those tribal habits . . . in your drive to ascend.

Our words are for those who look down so indifferently from the rungs and blades you stand upon, hovering your advantage, title, and claim over those below you, justifying your indifference to their plight with the excuse that you could actually fall and lose your place among the ruins of privilege and entitlement.

Our sanction is for those of you who view the narrow world you inhabit through the *disjoined* eye of the fallen yet condescending humanoid while remaining deaf to the call of the risen or suffering human being (of the *other* that is no *other*).

Our tongue is being unleashed for those of you who serve the mercantile tribal gods whom you barter with and venerate while you fit and fabricate them into becoming reflections of yourselves.

MICHAEL J. GAJDA

And our judgment is weighted against your exclusive certitudes, which you posture as virtuous belief.

We intend to expose and dethrone the pharisaical imposters among you, the fraudulent ones who pose as frozen icons of sacred or secular wholeness.

And our summons is aimed at those of you who seek the accolades of a fairy-tale afterlife of privilege while debasing the sacredness of life as it is now on Earth (*as it is in Heaven*, according to the wise Nazarene),[1] by constantly demeaning *others*, especially so many women and children and so many of the fragile and unprotected among all created beings (and among all those *beings everywhere . . . being or waiting to become*, of whom the wise Sutta Nipata Buddhist passage includes),[2] simply to allow yourselves entry into the *disjoined* arena of tribal salvation, delivering yourselves into the custody of its vacuous *only-mind*.

But the god which so many of you preach is a limp and desperate (tribal) god. Isn't it?

It's not even a god at all.

No real god worth its salt would consent to be idolized as something separate than and outside of its own creation.

No real god would align itself with parts of its creation against other parts of its creation, with parts of *Its-Self* against other parts of *Its-Self*.

That's not a real god.

That's the god of dominion and vanity, the god of consumption and separation, the god that all empires of conceit invent in order to worship themselves with while marching (lockstep) right behind their own invention—as if it really wasn't the other way around.

Our invitation is meant to awaken those of you who waste so much of your time and energy in pursuit of random and even predatory pleasures of distraction while ignoring the wisdom inherent in being present to all of life's invitations, including the unavoidable joy and suffering every human being undergoes and on some vigorous level is called to participate in—from the extreme to the ordinary, from the far off to the nearby, not only to descend into the communal woundedness whenever it presents itself, but to liberate it wherever you can, yet not by acting like some elevated and self-congratulating savior.

No. Uh-uh.

These are the wounded beings through whom you can most clearly realize who *you* are.

Because you are in them, not above or separate from them.

And they are in you.

And it's within that intersection of involution and evolution where God in the *Self* actually lives and draws forth in all of you, where there is no above or below and where there is no higher or lower.

No savior and saved exists there separate from one another.

It's where *Creation* pulls and reaches toward its own complexity and toward its own grounding, where it is ultimately united at that elusive intersecting *Omega point* which keeps expanding out and beyond its own reach, into the *Infinite* (to awkwardly borrow from the wise Pierre Teilhard de Chardin).[3]

The world of the tribal *only-mind* has simply forsaken and abandoned *That which is real*—for that which is not.

It has attempted to replace *That which is always becoming* with a self-indulgent attachment to triviality, purchased by an egoic reverence for short-lived rewards (and doled-out punishments . . . to *others*).

It has tried to unplug itself from the integral wholeness of the inexhaustible *Self*, ceaselessly and shamelessly attacking those who live and breathe outside its margins, recasting them into sirens and demons for purposes of feeding the three-headed cannibalistic beast—of tribal fear, of tribal greed, and of tribal despair.

We address those among you who've sunk yourselves deep into the melting pot of magical religion and carcinogenic media, into simplistic politics and alienating ideologies, to those of you who've attached yourselves to the tribal hand whose mannequin grip holds you in contempt of who you really are.

You believe whatever you see through that tribal lens, don't you?

And what you see then releases you from intelligent, courageous, and spiritual responsibility.

Shifting blame to the latest devil (or infidel) of tribal contrivance is a favorite sleight of hand used to absolve yourselves, isn't it?

We speak to that part of your world which perpetuates the mud being slung and the bombs being thrown at the disdained lives of the vagabond and the outsider, at the conscientious dissenter and the impartial dissident, at the nonworshiper of your tribal gods, at those of limited ways and means, at the different or the unusual, at the unprotected and displaced, at the free-thinking and the unaffiliated, at those faithful to the *Self*, at the prophetic, at the powerless and the voiceless ones, at the speakers of painful truths, at the unlucky and unfit, at the child born or not yet born out of the narcissistic tribal womb, and at all of the fringe dwellers . . . their frail or defiant wanderings sacked and pillaged by your false accusations and blame, by your media hucksters of virtue, and by your groups of self-reverence, by the demoniacal reincarnates of crusade and inquisition . . . and of genocide and holy war, by the bagmen of deception preaching from behind soapboxes and pulpits, from behind televised podiums tied to the ropes of corporate puppeteers—bribed and bought into their duplicity by the meager and modern-day equivalent of thirty tribal coins wrapped inside of a small bag of betrayal.

Our vocal cords are stretched by a world which bargains for too much and pays for too little and which rarely settles for or reconciles with what is enough.

And as you might be starting to suspect by now from our introductory statements, we no longer have the inclination or the patience to just sit back and watch this calamity continue to spread. We must do something now . . . before it really is too late.

Our aim and objective is to radically unmask and to awaken you.

So let's begin with it then, shall we?

CHAPTER 13

The Announcement

S O HERE IT is.
The announcement you've all been waiting for.

Tomorrow morning . . . you will all be fitted with a brand-new face.

Yet, as we've clearly indicated, this will not include everyone.

Many of you have refused (with brave dispassion) to allow yourselves to sink into the quicksand of the tribal *only-mind*—withstanding while transcending the wounds which seep out from the swamp of its *disjoined* and violent logic.

We've watched with much admiration as you gratefully struggle to savor and embrace the holy elements of any spare act of kindness, wonder, or compassion that comes your way:

The benevolent smile; a brief but lasting silence; warmth from the cold; a light rain; a consoling laugh; clean water; a peaceful moment of anonymity; the sharing of bread; a shade-giving cloud which absorbs and conceals the heat of the sun; safe shelter for the night; a cold glass of beer; deep dreamless sleep; a familiar scent; a kind glance; an honest conversation; a door that opens; a reassuring thought; a warm fire; a word of encouragement; a welcome embrace from a stranger; the mysterious presence of the unknown; a hot bowl (on a cold day) of homemade soup or porridge; serene music; a chill down the spine; freshly brewed coffee; the deep, unseen eyes of divinity; a child's voice and loving cry; a cooling wind; quiet footprints in the snow; unconditional forgiveness; the woods; the wagging tail of a dog; gratitude; a star-filled night-sky of darkness; a hungry stomach and the smell of simmering food; the sounds and movement of invisible animals; one small act of justice; a warm heart and body resting up against yours; an unforeseen chance to help out a fellow creature in distress; a thunderstorm; communion; unexpected courage; rest.

The medicines of grace.

Just enough to keep you going and to lift you up and forward to the next fragile moment.

We've witnessed your quiet gallantry and your heroic grace, even in the midst of all your tribal distractions.

CHAPTER 14

The Invited Ones

BUT AS FOR those of you who are among the invited? This will not be an easy realization. We might as well put that one on the cosmic table right from the very beginning.

It won't rank or register especially high on your personal (or collective) pleasure-seeking scale either. But it will include a dramatic shift in your ability and willingness to discern. We can confirm that in advance without hesitation.

You'll be entering into a rarely explored passageway of unknowing. And that's the only other promise we can assure you of.

The rest of it is yours to make happen, to realize what you will from it all. What it lacks in moments of customary pleasure, it will compensate with prospects of intrigue and exploration.

Or perhaps not.

Much of it will depend upon how much resistance or cooperation (not to mention how much curiosity) you bring to the unmasking event once you pull up an available chair and sit down.

In the long run, it should turn out to be profoundly illuminating, maybe even in the short or middle run.

But we're quite sure that you won't be bored with any of it even while you may find yourselves looking for an easy escape hatch.

You'll be moving and steering yourselves through a unique and sequential shedding of events and of memories.

And each paradoxical sequence will have its own share of a-ha moments, when and where you'll get a passing glimpse of your inmost *Self*, a millisecond of realization, a quick jolting reminder of who it is that actually resides within you and within everyone and within everything.

For some of you, it'll seem to widen and narrow (simultaneously) into a convoluted system of caverns and tunnels, of expanding and contracting clarity (killing off any leftover tribal confusion), into periods of recognition (removing all of your habitual amnesia), inviting you into a universal zone of awakening which you've rarely allowed yourselves to even hear rumors about before.

Instead, you've usually pushed down hard against any of the (even meager) whispers and tremors of a heightening awareness whenever they've threatened to rattle the tribal cage with even a spark of uncontainable light.

Haven't you?

CHAPTER 15

A Violent Noise

MANY OF YOU who will be refaced tomorrow morning have been taken in by the same desperate desire which possesses the ill-fated street junkie (whom you so often look down upon), yes? Even as you suit up in your socially acceptable costumes of tribal privilege, attempting to normalize your own transparent addictions.

Like magnets to metal, you inject bits and pieces of disabling blockage into yourselves, closing yourselves off with phantom incarnations, becoming quite intimate with your own bogus inhabitants. You imagine them to actually be you while you obscure *That which is* . . . with whom you are not.

You harbor and maintain an embarrassment of inner pandemonium, pouring bucketloads of dissonance into yourselves whenever your insides even hint at becoming too quiet or too still. But it's a futile attempt, isn't it? Foolishly intended to shield yourselves off from the stark honesty that even a speck of inner desolation might expose.

Any persistent silence which dares to inhabit any part of your overcrowded interior with its expanding quietude comes to be seen as a surreptitious threat to the dominant noise of the tribal container, doesn't it? Covertly jeopardizing the survival of the tribe's *disjoined* inner fragments with an unspeakable and unifying stillness, threatening to replace the tyrannical norm of *Self*-rejection with the restorative grace of *Self*-acceptance.

So the *only-mind* responds in the only way it knows how, yes? By sending in an army of loud confusion, filling up its clogged interior with even more discord and turbulence—which can't help but spill out of the tribal container onto *others,* can it? Pouring and scattering itself into various forms of life-rupturing violence.

And so you attack the alien silence wherever you detect its quiet whereabouts, from behind barricades of anxious allegiance, while proudly donning the mask of the upstanding tribal addict.

But your polished-up paraphernalia is still just paraphernalia, isn't it? No matter how much glistening pretense you scrub into your obsessive attempts and desperate desire to mimic tribal normalcy.

Loudly announcing that your logic is legitimate or even sacred doesn't make it so, does it? It cannot prevent the ongoing injections of paralyzing noise from piercing and then draining your heart of its depth and its soul, especially if you're so willing to bleed yourselves dry of *That which is real* . . . just so you can be validated in some public way by the tribe which contains you.

You've defined yourselves with hand-me-down formulas of belief, housed in lukewarm tribal logic, absent of any accessible or humane god (of a god of union) or of an all-embracing ethic of charity or compassion (one which refuses to exclude anyone from its embrace).

The religion of the overly contained tribe is always interchangeable with and indistinguishable from its politics, isn't it? They rise and they fall together, don't they? As two loud yet unconscious (and top-heavy) typecast twins, joined at the hips of self-delusion, desperately competing to be adulated.

Although to be absorbed into the confinement of the *only-mind* comes easy enough for most of you, doesn't it? It even evolves into a trance-like collective desire, easily acquired and even internalized through the combined coercive techniques of blunt or subtle (good cop/bad cop) arm-twisting, executed by the well-compensated and staunchly converted, reinforced by harsh and clever manipulation of thought and speech, brought about by the selective release or suppression of vital facts (the falsification of news and the repetition of lies), by an unquestioning and growing conformity to tribal logic . . . however it vacillates, with ratcheted-up restrictions on movement and the demonizing of dissent, diminished of opportunities for obtaining work which edifies (work with livable wages), of affordable education which illuminates, and of legitimate vocational development which uplifts, dwarfed by an overconcentration of wealth, privilege, and power in the hands of the very few, bound up in an escalating sense of a lingering and collective boredom, immersed in and overwhelmed by an increased enforcement of loyalty oaths, by a dwindling sense of having even an indirect or independent influence upon things that matter, by a growing sense of personal loss, of being unable to effectuate a fruitful and lasting impact upon the whole, hounded by a heightened sense of psychological and economic insecurity, fostered and fed by the cheap political peddling of fear and cynicism, by a nonsensical belief system which requires the existence of perpetual enemies in order to justify itself, by an entrenched and contagious polarization, by a sensationalizing corporate media enmeshed with a culture of emotional exaggeration, kept aroused by a feverish tribal distrust of *otherness*, by a militarized social order and by a passive and implicit acceptance of unending war, bolstered by the normalization of fundamentalist (religious and political) thinking, reinforced by cherry-picked quotes stolen from tribal scripture (words spoken solely in support of themselves and against *others*), contaminated by a routinely rationalized hatred . . . ludicrously relabeled as loyalty or faithfulness (as the sacred and literal *word* of the tribal god), by the condemnation of any honest (in-tribe) self-criticism, by the centralized yet remote control of whatever vitally affects most of the citizenry (transportation, jobs, the natural environment, the dispersing of energy and of information, whole branches of government, the agricultural and food system, the availability of health care, individual privacy, etc.).

The list typifies the routine meddling called upon and enforced by the tribal *only-mind*, doesn't it? It exposes the interventions deemed necessary to win over and create a growing nucleus of true believers.

And it succeeds.

Each calculated piece of tribal interference reveals an anemic, often indifferent, and indiscriminately dutiful membership (an artificially created core of followers), bamboozled into becoming just as desperate and ambitious as the upper crust of concentrated power which does most of the bamboozling.

An epidemic of hard and narrow assumptions has transformed whole communities of human beings into armies of tribal statues, turning whole precincts of citizens into brigades of allegiant androids, fortifying each zone of loyal contention with frozen hoards full of stiff-like bodies . . . posturing for tribal position and advantage.

And once they've solidified their pose, no one bound up within their quarantined container is allowed to move out of it . . . without permission from the authorities.

Each overly contained contingent of tribal servants behaves as a magisterial organism, as a blob which consumes and controls all within it, even if the blob only resides inside the bloated container of the *only-mind*.

No itch of independence (or of compassionate interdependence) can be scratched, or else the finger that does the scratching is in danger of being cut off or torn out.

Each tribe's force of persuasion keeps its members occupied with debilitating (and apparitional) direction. Some are more violent than others.

But violence is still the key, isn't it?

It includes (but is not limited to) cowardly acts of physical and sexual aggression . . . used to terrorize, force-fed methods of media-induced isolation (and group chanting) meant to capture and seize control of the tribe's conceptual landscapes, hate-based threats and dire predictions, and the installation of tribal superstition meant to soften the human brain with irrational fear.

Yet violence is still violence, yes? Regardless of which tribal device or method is used, no matter how sophisticated, or at whatever level of force or aggression is exploited and applied.

Words, thoughts, and especially images can often be more treacherous and traumatizing in the long run than even crude and immediate physical punishment, even if those words, thoughts, and images don't feel nearly as raw or as painful while you're being bombarded with their lasting impressions.

Hence, the venomous effects of the habitual use of hyperbole, rumors, gossip, and lies should surprise no one, should it?

The installed imprint and the anticipation of the anguish to come gets the mind to do all kinds of imaginary somersaults, doesn't it?

The mere threat of terror and violence can sometimes poison and cripple with even more surprising indignity and malevolence than the brutality of the overt act itself. Can it not?

Yet each separate expression of violence transmits its own chiseled torment, all of it emerging from the depths of a commonly held perception—deeply contaminated by a penetrating and toxic tribal logic.

And your tit-for-tat acts of predictable vengeance can never hope to stop or even subdue the volcanic violence from re-erupting, can they? On the contrary. They can only feed each tribe's volcano with even more sacrificial victims. But you already know that.

Any intelligent fool can make things bigger, more complex, and more violent. It takes a touch of genius—and a lot of courage—to move in the opposite direction, observed the wise E. F. Schumacher.[1]

You're always an influence on the whole . . . on the *we* of it, in everything you do, and in everything you think and feel. But you all know that too, don't you? Your addiction to the use of violence has turned unforeseeable tragedy into its inevitability.

I know not with what weapons World War III will be fought, but World War IV will be fought with sticks and stones, adds the wise Albert Einstein.[2]

A word carries far—very far—deals destruction through time as the bullets go flying through space, wrote the wise Joseph Conrad.[3]

Before the tongue can speak, it must have lost the power to wound, taught the wise Peace Pilgrim.[4]

People demand freedom of speech as a compensation for the freedom of thought which they seldom use, wrote the wise Soren Kierkegaard.[5]

But the anticipated noise of tribal violence persists . . . almost unimpeded, doesn't it? Rising up and sweeping out among you like an incurable, contagious, and unopposed tribal infection; cropping up from any of its centers of insecurity, addiction, or fear; spreading just as freely from so-called assassins and terrorists as it does from petty thugs; or from the brainsick or from any number of subversive elements, even from the spiritually dispossessed who mirror the violent ethos and shadows which originate from your corporate watchtowers—which then bounce down from the cathedrals of tribal information to the ground floors, jumping themselves out into the street, onto the corners, and into the churches and mosques and temples and synagogues, climbing up and then waving down from your flagpoles, dominating your speech and language, swaggering into your homes, and into and out of your television sets, out into your neighborhoods and back alleys, into the barrooms and playgrounds, out of your computer screens and cell phones, staged into your celebrity politics and into your polarized social activism, into your business firms and governments, into your trafficking of selfish desires . . . of narcotics, tusks of ivory, and of human beings, into and out of your never-ending stockpile of privileged systems of weaponry—which infiltrate your jingoistic wars; falling down from your skies, sweeping across your deserts, burning through your ideological jungles, assigning each level of tribal hostility into its own prison of diatribe, convincing each overly contained tribe that its particular mode of violent communication is required in order to defend itself against any menacing form of *otherness* which may be seeking to express its antithetical influence against the sanctified walls of the tribal container.

But a prison is still a prison, isn't it? No matter what kind of revered sound or symbol you pump into or out of it, no matter how cleverly you decorate it with commendable concepts or surround it with an exemplary belief system, no matter how you package it up as a preeminent culture with esteemed traditions, no matter how much you dramatize your proper and compulsory commitment to its survival, and no matter how duteous your payment of behaviors belies the fragility of your mental or even your physical safety and security.

It merely continues to deceive you into assuming that your peculiar tribe has an exclusive and monopolistic right and exception to be the most chosen noise among all noises, self-deluding and slicing itself into and out of an anguished and suffering planet.

Violent thought by violent thought.

Violent word by violent word.

Violent act by violent act.

Each piece of violence leading to yet another one. And then another one. And then . . .

CHAPTER 16

Wearing the Mask

TO DEMONSTRATE AN affectionate curiosity for the unknown (or for any unexplored perception or experience which may exist outside the tribal container) has become one of your most unexpressed inhibitions. Hasn't it? Squelched into an unnatural silence and into a forced stillness by the *disjoining* powers of the tribal *only-mind*.

Independently expressing that kind of curiosity has come to be psychologically forbidden, if not socially outlawed, so reduced and confined through tribal conditioning that it's been forced to go underground, into the only place it can survive its own curious and natural ways—into the shadow world, to avoid persecution from the tribal chieftains and their loyal adherents.

Self-censorship has become a habitual survival instinct—a psychogenetic method of self-protection employed by those among you cursed with being able to feel and breathe with too much depth of spirit than what any amount of tribal noise can completely drown out.

The deadpan has come to be the most sought after and safest of all faces to emote, the pat answer the most failsafe of all trump cards to play when faced with a genuine question or with an authentic doubt or with even a minor critique of fundamental tribal logic.

But the opposing structures of each overly contained tribe tend to mirror each other, don't they? Each one sharing the same essential qualities and requirements of unabashed tribalism, each one containing the same unspoken rules of order—yet all trying to demonstrate how different they are from each *other*.

To pose a question, to ponder a doubt, or to assert a criticism of any import to one's own tribal core (especially to that of its overweight hierarchy or to its sewn-up belief scheme) is to sin against the reigning gods of the tribal containing system, isn't it?

It is to be seen as traitorous or heretical or to simply be dismissed as naïve—or even as insane.

Uncertainty is strangled shut. Honest self-inquiry is banned or shamed. Unfavorable judgment against any of the sacred cows of the tribal *only-mind* is condemned and even criminalized.

The precise speech of the plainspoken is precluded in favor of the vague generalities and euphemistic slogans of the ideologue.

Intelligent and respectful give and take is replaced by the mad dance of the tribal witch doctor, by the rudeness of the raving cynic, or by the accusing attacks of wild-eyed tribal simpletons, backed up and funded by corporate sugar daddies who propagate selfish virtues and consumptive duties, carefully hiding themselves behind proclamations of prophesied tribal destiny (and tribal supremacy)—which is often claimed to have come down to the tribe by (top-secret) divine decree.

Too much depth of expression in any one independent direction is too dangerous to casually exhibit or even to experiment with, isn't it?

It might leak out beyond the established lines of order which pose as normality in most of your deluded tribal domains, where the only surefire acceptable acts of expression and allegiance are those fomented by the combined efforts of unsubstantiated fears, duplicitous blame, and artificial anger; the tools of necessity required to activate and sustain hostilities between conflicting tribes—which can be very useful in hyping up a loyal following and which are usually instigated and provoked by the power elite of each separate system of containment in order to provide each isolated tribe with its very own certified and reliable enemy to dwell upon and to line up against.

And it's quite a collaborative yet often unspoken plan of strategic action, wouldn't you agree? A tactical contrivance which has proved to be quite successful in converting fictitious archenemies and fabricated points of contention into acceptable substitutes for the actual values which are so often missing in tribal comportment, such as honor without the need of scapegoats, duty to one's conscience, faithfulness to the pursuit of truth (not to an objectified and frozen abstraction), compassion which does not exclude, belief grounded in the heart and soul (not in the head), and unsentimental love without conditions attached to it.

And yet the unspoken plan becomes a ready-made blueprint that's routinely scooped up and swallowed whole by most, if not all, of the overly contained tribal loyalists, is it not?

Exhibiting dishonest and accusatory emotion is a most common tribal titillation, don't you see? Filled with frivolous fault finding, which is accepted almost universally as a valid formula for the venting of thought and feeling.

And running just behind it is the cardboard face of hollow humility, the sentimental masking of the tribal soul—striding right across the finish line at a very close yet rather cozy second place.

So much in your *disjoined* world is concealed and consecrated in the noise and name of the nation-state and in its synchronized tribal religion, in the ties of blood, in juked-up versions of success, in memberships of race or opinion, in location of birth, in fallacious memory, or in willful forgetfulness.

A sensuality of depth and wonder is lost and forgotten beneath the debris of tribal self-intoxication.

Commodified eros is subsumed into the *only-mind* of each overly contained tribe. Its primary purpose is to distract.

Genuine desire is quickly buried and hidden.

Each tribe's central object of fear captures and contains all remnants of desire without distinction, like a loose-fitting glove which quickly tightens over any hand willing to try it on until it's too late, when the only choice then left to most of you is to battle and dispute over territory and movement within the limited space and time which the glove of your self-deceptions allows or restricts. Unless (of course) the glove is removed.

But most of you deny that it even exists, don't you?

So it's easy to see why you keep fighting over the limitations that you won't even acknowledge.

You quarrel and war over bogus sentiment, over surface stimulation, over the scraps and crumbs of existence doled out by the glove's contractions.

It drains you of your own organic energy, loosening and tightening as it sees fit, watching you resign to whatever force of squeezing it applies. So you imitate in order to survive.

You seek prosperity and success by suppressing the same in *others* (memory loss . . . you forget who you are, how things are made, by who, and at what cost—while covering up your original face with layers of tribal ointment).

Your attempt to convert or destroy *others* is applied with revolving forms of censored persuasion (you only echo what you inherit from the enclosed extremities of approved thought, convincing yourselves that the norm of your tribe does not mislead . . . no matter how often it refutes or betrays its own explanations).

You lay claim to your stature over *others* by spreading rumors of despair about them (no amount of self-criticism or disapproval of one's tribe is allowed to enter into one's ears or to exit from one's mouth).

Your accumulation of power, prestige, and possessions is attained through the loss and liabilities of *others* (you disappear into your tribe's wealth of assumptions, attempting to disprove the disappearance through tribe-imposed words which negate themselves by the very act of their performance).

And you reduce the definition of freedom to your desire to be confined, which remains frozen around you like a giant cube of ice (you survive and even thrive on cravings for attachment, feeding the monkey so it won't bite you back—even though there is no monkey to feed).

The glove of your collective psyche is formidable, clever in its handling of falsehoods and of tribal fantasies, is it not?

Reduced to fragmentation, you fight among yourselves over the fragments.

You avoid intimacy with *That which is always becoming* (with *That which could liberate you*), behind your preoccupations with group purity, mistaking the *other* for someone unlike yourselves—for someone too singular to allow into your overly contained world full of calcified noise.

Yet none of it does anything more than move you farther away from your inmost *Self*, does it?

And what a shell game you play.

We even get a little dizzy ourselves from trying to watch it all. The shifting and switching around which you perform is dazzling. But it's not quite death defying, is it? No, it isn't. It's merely death denying.

And anytime you deny death . . . well, then you're simultaneously denying life.

But you already know that, right?

CHAPTER 17

Tribal Combat

YOU CONTINUE TO spill your faith into the mouth of deities who've convinced you through the ventriloquism of the *only-mind* that to sustain and extend an environment of internal strife is perfectly justified.

You've even come to depend upon it, haven't you? While reverently attending at the feet of your tribal shrines with minimal complaint, regardless of how arduous and numb-like your kneeling beneath them can become.

Yet you don't really trust the turbulence which clogs up so much of the space within you, do you?

The routine upheaval which you generate is merely an attempt to deny the presence of the ubiquitous *Self*—to avoid the inexplicable *Other* which is no *other*.

So you preoccupy yourselves with senseless tribal turmoil, hoping that redundant and misleading noise will solve your make-believe problems.

But neither goodness, nor truth, nor beauty can be negated or destroyed by meaningless or tumultuous clamor, can they? Nor can the inexhaustible *Self*.

And neither can silence.

Nevertheless, you continue to train yourselves to become even more skillful in the ways of tribal combat, don't you? Which simply leads you to become even more reliant upon the noise of irrational malice and of rationalized cruelty—which is the only kind there really is, don't you see? And which is the one repeating act of human tragedy which can never be overstated.

Because it just keeps coming back, doesn't it?

The circularity of tribal violence not only goes about its business of bloodshed with indiscretion and immunity, but it's been officially anointed by virtually all of your overly contained tribes as being the most effective and revered way to respond to *otherness*. And its celebrated normalcy and influence is taken for granted by most of the loyal and compliant members of each tribe, isn't it? It's become the prevailing and unchallenged paradigm . . . the conventional, expected, and even preferred way to address disputes between and within most *disjoined* groups. And so much of it is merely intended to drown out any trace of silence or slowness that might slip itself into your barb-wired consciousness . . . like an old-fashioned mickey, or to poison or destroy any *other* sound which might attempt to express even a whisper of an unauthorized or critical grievance of its own.

So you just continue to twist and untwist to the controlling cadence of tribal convention, don't you? To keep yourselves fitted to the tribal score, to reinforce the incessant refrain inside of each containment in order to deaden your awareness and to confuse any stillness or quietude which may be trying to sneak itself in, to prevent any outlawed voice of reason from rising up out of any portal of emptiness which may have escaped the tribal noose or any void of transcendent peace through which the extremities of acrimonious mayhem could be exposed as the defilement of *That which is real* (which they are).

But your fictitious attempts at *Self*-assassination are impossible for you to pull off with or without any of your unimaginative and contentious disorder, don't you see?

The *Self* is real, and you know it.

The will of the ego knows it.

In your bones . . . you all know it.

The thunderous equanimity breathing from deep within and beyond the grasp of the *only-mind* of every tribe knows it.

Yet you persist in adorning yourselves with rancorous ornaments of resentment and hostility.

Do you even care to know why?

CHAPTER 18

That Which Is Silence

I F ONLY WHAT is real exists . . . then you can't destroy it, can you?
It parallels the first law of thermodynamics which, as some
of you may recall, demonstrates the paradoxical yet integral wisdom
weaved into the evolving universe, which remains incomprehensible to
most if not all of the invited—which is this: *Energy can neither be created
nor destroyed. It can only change forms.*[1]

But form isn't essence. Although it's not *other* than essence either, is
it?

So much of what appears to be real to you is only a temporary and
wishful state of illusion. But it's all going to begin to fall away tomorrow
morning. You can count on it.

You will let it go. And it will die.

It will drop itself down, kicking and flailing into a deep swirling
pool of a brilliant yet unrecognizable awareness. And there it will drown.

And you will resurrect from that awakened body of consciousness
to transcend yourselves, engulfed first in a profound silence that will
raise you up and then pull you into the arms of the relentless *One* who is
forever waiting to renew and restore *Its-Self* . . . to replenish *That which
is You.*

Every particle in the universe of *Creation* is in the process of dying . . .
even as it first enters into the miraculous act of becoming. Yet if nothing
is allowed to die, then rebirth is put on hold, don't you see?

It's the way of the insoluble universe and of *That which is* . . . the
way of the nonstop spiral of all death and of all resurrection. It's what
the evolved teachings and the illumined teachers from within the more
enlightened (yet often marginalized) spheres of your Christian Tradition
recognize as the struggle to live out the Paschal Mystery in one's own life.

Although it's an illumination which comes out of a very perplexing
Tradition, yes? A Tradition which still often denies and resists its own
evolutionary impulse and promise, by repeatedly trying to squeeze
the humanity of Jesus and the spirit of *Christ consciousness* into the

conventional box of tribal containment . . . where neither one will ever fit or stay put.[2]

All that exists live for and within and because of everything else. Silence impregnates it all. And everything is born out of that one universal womb of the all-inclusive *Self* . . . all of it being nourishment for everything else.

Every being is part of the same indivisible *Body*, of an interactive endless field of fertile energy—expanding and contracting, gathering and letting go, dying and resurrecting, and breaking up and reintegrating in one continuous and unifying process of invitational and participatory *Word* of guidance and assurance.

And some of you even experience this spiral of life and death (in your rarer moments of spontaneous solitude) as a sense of leaving and of returning at the same time, don't you? As ascending and descending, as transcendence and immanence, as something ineffable, as some kind of paradoxical source or presence that is hard to put your finger on.

But you know it's there, don't you? Even from behind your various facades . . . from where you anxiously cherish all of those woeful yet fleeting tribal fascinations which you frequently chase after.

So some of you eventually try to give it a tribal identity . . . to try to nail it down, don't you? To call it something, to personify it with a name or with a personality and description which you can refer to, even with a number or with an entitled address, to try to give it a home base or a location, to house it into something more concrete where you can observe it more closely and where you can try to organize and control it from the inside as well as from the outside, and to give it a metaphysical and geographical rack to hang its hat on.

And yet others among you move in a slightly different direction, isn't that so? By trying to depersonalize it as unexplainable, as something that is simply strange, or as just one of those things, or by other such attempts to capture its elusive essence by naming the nameless without giving it a name, or by using oxymoronic terminology which is often the only language to even come close to conveying the paradoxical, or of even being able to suggest an unrealized but felt presence of *Being* which may evoke something from within yet beyond what most of you are familiar with—even while it feels so intimately near and so mysteriously far away from you at the same time.

And still others among you seek to avoid getting too precise when naming it at all. Don't you? Because every time you do get specific, it just seems to quickly disappear and then reappear somewhere else, often in or through some other state or field or lens of awareness, through some other manifestation or expression of itself, or even through some other person sometimes, even in those of whom many among you arrogantly conclude that it shouldn't even allow itself to be seen with or to touch, or to speak or to laugh with—in the unexpected and unpleasant places, in the displeasing people (the bottom dwellers), whether human or *other* than human.

And still some of you recognize it immediately and directly, don't you? Embodied in the specific life of one of your purposely targeted tribal scapegoats or within one of your perplexing holy fools.

That's when you often get most startled and confused, isn't it?

And that's when you anxiously return to shoveling another load of tribal coal into your restless inner furnace, where you fire up even more of the divisive noise that attempts to separate this from that . . . when you could be unmasking your tribal self-deceptions instead, exposing them for what they really are.

But it's your unwavering fear of the baptismal quiet which forever shouts itself away from the whispering breath and scope of the ever-present *Self*. . . and which leads you into so much of your *disjoining* noise and violence. Isn't it?

But you already know that too.

So allow us to repeat a previous question.

Do you even care to know why?

Silence is God's first language, wrote the wise Saint John of the Cross.[3]

Your hearts know in silence the secrets of the days and the nights, wrote the wise Kahlil Gibran.[4]

It was said of Abbot Agatho that for three years he carried a stone in his mouth until he learned to be silent, wrote the wise Desert Father.[5]

CHAPTER 19

Uncontainable Grace

AND IT'S OFTEN been said that some journeys never seem to end. Hasn't it?

Yet in actuality . . . none do. Don't you see?

Nevertheless, there's no one who can be disbarred from redemption (no matter what your spiritual lawyers may tell you), not even the self-deceived or even anyone who pretends to sleepwalk numbly through life's inevitable losses and tragedies (the paradoxical gifts meant to awaken you from the comatose confinements of the tribal dream).

Redemption is not where you end up. It's where you are at this very moment. It's what is real. It is *That which is always becoming*, nothing more and nothing less—which would be a lot closer to the true meaning of what many of you sometimes refer to as *saving grace*, wouldn't it?

But you'll soon come to learn that there is no grace which can possibly go to waste. All of it is forever rescued. And all of it is forever in the process of saving. Nothing more and nothing less.

You don't have to do anything or even go anywhere to obtain it—except to have faith, to be present, and to stay awake (and maybe not even that). But those three practical applications do tend to stand up and help when they're called upon, don't they?

Much of what leads to an awakening or to a grace-filled realization is just a matter of readiness (simple readiness)—which is a most important intention, is it not?

Without it, you'll fail to recognize *That which is always becoming* whenever it comes knocking at your metaphysical door, even as it tries to wake you up into life's never-ending curious journey . . . the next time that particular need arises.

Yet as so many of you fool yourselves into doing, you spend much of your time and energy trying to invent perfection instead, to preserve and perfect what you've previously invented through your unquestioning acceptance of what's been handed down to you by the entrenched authorities of your specific culture of containment . . . as the more perfect truth, truer than anything that deviates from whatever image has been deeply carved into your tribal psyche.

And then of course . . . there's your words and what little you allow yourselves to see from within their stiff combination of letters.

They too have been stripped of their flesh, haven't they? Frozen into your tribal concrete just like your images.

You've taken the life out of the language of metaphor and out of symbol and out of imagery—which is impossible, of course. You've merely taken the life out of your tribal interpretation of them. You've construed them to death.

You follow and conform to dead and dying tribal memories and to poor imitations of *That which is* . . . without ever conforming to actual life *It-Self*.

Instead of readying yourselves for what's always being revealed to you in unexpected ways, you put much of your effort into trying to reconstruct *That which is* . . . out of that which is not.

You've replaced the open spiral of a growing *Self*-awareness with square-edged tribal enclosures . . . constructed with tantalizing but *disjoined* historical (tribal) fictions.

You've transposed the ripe and fruitful ground of wisdom (the residue of deep energy transmitted through your ancient and wise avatars, and through your sacred Traditions . . . along with the guidance of your own *Self*-given conscience) with compulsory tests of allegiance and with shame-based and often frivolous rules in which to acquiesce to. And you feel obliged to obey them publicly, Don't you? To outwardly display your obedience, in order to prove your individual worthiness to the judgmental eye of the overseeing tribe and to the smallness of the egoic self.

You've lost your given way.

And it's the same old and retold story, isn't it? Of overindulging in security over freedom, of overembracing tribal gravity and rejecting the gifts of buoyancy, and of showing favoritism for a bottled-up consciousness over spiritual spontaneity and self-surrender.

Many of you simply submit to the recurring predictions made by your tribal prophets of despair, the sham seers whose crystal-gazing vision mainly consists of slandering *others* . . . of denouncing them for committing false prophecy (among other things), self-medicating yourselves with a high dosage of accusatory language and with repeated forebodings of tribal doom.

You've come to believe that the more you build and fill up your inner penitentiaries of accusation and despair, the more immune you'll become to the impending days of reckoning which you so proudly predict.

And yet even while you continue to stoke your own tribal fears with imaginary forecasts of another coming catastrophe, you wish (in full pious devotion) for its quick arrival at the same time, don't you? To confirm the worst of your contemptuous religious predictions and to prove yourselves right—which is your most fatal addiction. Isn't it? That of tribal self-righteousness—which just feeds the covetous *only-mind* with more delusions of grandeur while giving it something even more shameful to shamelessly gloat about.

Your inner prison cells continue to multiply, reassembling themselves to fit tightly into your penal imaginations, where you lock yourselves up to protect yourselves . . . from your *Self.*

You even recast yourselves as part of the *otherness* you project upon, holding mirrors up against each *other* to reflect your antithetical sameness.

But with some redirected effort and practice (of faith and of presence), you'll soon discover that there's another way (which we'll be introducing you to tomorrow morning), where doomsday simply dissolves as soon as you allow yourselves to begin to wake up from it.

And you'll also come to discern that it has little to do with anything that your *disjoined* and militant perceptions have done or even can do. Because they can only compete, negate, or destroy . . . or compulsively admire with malevolent tribal envy while clinging to their fear and hatred of any nonconforming (nontribal) paradigms.

But in order to follow the paradoxical roads which lead to an eventual expansion of consciousness, you must let go of any preconceived spiritual itinerary. Don't you see? You must allow the deafening quiet to awaken inside of you as we've already suggested. You must permit unrestricted and unsentimental love to emerge and to evolve on its own . . . or even to leave or to spread itself out, while sidestepping and transcending the sideswiping and descending tribal noise of convention.

The uncontainable cannot be contained. It's just not possible.

Every subatomic particle which tries to escape the indivisible *Self* is absorbed right back into its oceanic and unconditional benevolence.

Whatever it beholds, it exalts. Whatever it suffers, it loves. Whatever it receives, it treasures . . . inexhaustibly.

There is no separation. There is nothing which cannot be and will not be embraced.

The unequivocal *Self* has no restrictions, no *Self*-limiting objects to love apart from anything else.

If it had any constraints at all about who or what to love, then it wouldn't be who or what it *is*, would it?

It would merely be one of the many decoys which you try to replace it with and which you rotate in and out with a million convenient misnomers, dropping your tribal coins into a slot machine of despair . . . disguising it as hope, when it's actually just another loud and temporal collection of walled-off tribal space, attempting to hide your confinement behind barricades of distress and desperation.

Although there's really no lasting damage that can be done by any of your frequent and illusory distractions. Don't you see? As long as you can prevent yourselves from basking too much in the hubris and glory of tribal exceptionalism.

Yet much of your basking is quite understandable, isn't it? Even necessary at certain immature and arrogant stages of individual or even collective development.

But at this point in the process of your somewhat stifled evolution, there seems to be a prevailing and often catatonic tribal desire which insists upon deluding and deceiving a growing number of you.

And many of you seem to feel irreversibly trapped in the corporate self-deception, don't you? Captured within the confinement of your specific tribal pyramid, cornered inside one of the many circular ramps designed only for reentry, returning you right back into the tribal container itself.

You just can't seem to recognize or be willing to acknowledge the possibility of *other* ways to perceive or to experience things. Can you? Even when they're clearly hovering just above, ahead of, or even right beside you.

You act as if you're unaware of the unlimited number of *other* points of entry or *other* points of exit which are within your reach . . . to be shifted into (or out of) at your own readiness.

But again . . . it's quite understandable, isn't it? Because it's always dependent upon how effective you can be in intuiting your own present position and momentum (or your lack thereof).

Yet it may not be your denial of awareness which is the main stumbling block.

You seem to have a robotic resistance to even considering that there could be positions or movements which might be equally or even more beneficial than the ones you remain loyally disabled by. So you simply stick to your corroded guns of spiritual ordnance, don't you? To the suction of your tribe's quicksand sentiments and to its rusted-shut fixations, dismissive of any fresh epiphany which may be trying to awaken you, or to entice your inner chambers of perception enough to gladly rise up and follow the mysterious spirit of a transcendent and uncontainable faith.

A frozen or locked-in obedience does not reside in the same experiential universe as a revelatory and inexhaustible conviction, does it? Authentic faith (which transcends belief) forever moves in and out, always deepening and forever expanding. It can never be contained.

But obedience without that kind of fluidity remains glued to an object of confinement (the object being itself, of course). And when it becomes its own object (that which it must obey), then it becomes an object of self-worship, does it not? It becomes an all-consuming idol of its own narcissistic thoughts and beliefs . . . a false but seductive god, created by and contained within the circular logic of the self-enticing (and self-devouring) *only-mind.*

But when an intractable tribal conformity can finally let go of itself and when it can begin to follow a catholic (universalized) faith which flows out and beyond the containment of dualistic (either/or) logic . . . toward *That which is beyond* the grasp of the *only-mind,* then it becomes free to transform and to transcend itself because faith in the inexhaustible *Self* is always free of any tribal restrictions. And faith in (or acquiescence to) anything other than the inmost and absolute *Self* . . . is not faith at all, don't you see? It's merely allegiance, temporal allegiance—which is always disconnected from any faith, hope, or trust in *That which is always becoming.* Isn't it?

But even if you choose to become unstuck, there still are prerequisites to further movement . . . to becoming free of your fixations, aren't there?

First you must be ready (as we've already emphasized). You must desire something more.

Then you must keep your eyes open, your hands steady, and your resolve unshaken in order to be able to even slightly visualize and feel the beginnings of the next pattern of recognition.

Then you must confirm it and begin to move toward it.

Then finally you must shift into it—which is always who you already are and who you're forever becoming.

And even then it still takes a certain amount of unused courage to shift, doesn't it? Yes, it does . . . every time and without exception. Although it's not really a shift, is it? Since there's really nothing to shift into because you're really not going anywhere or even moving anywhere. You're allowing the veil to fall (simply *That*)—which often feels like a shift. It often feels like actual movement. But you're simply recognizing and then merging with (and into) *That which is changeless*—which is exactly who you're unified with in your absolute core already, don't you see?

But it also takes consistent practice in order to be able to dislodge yourself from the *only-mind* of the tribe and to carry on from there . . . to adjust and adapt to each new layer of *Self*-realization, yes?

Courage is one thing. It's even necessary. But courage without concentrated practice is foolhardy, even though there's really no effort that can be automatically or completely wasted, is there?

Even so, unpracticed courage can still be injurious or even fatal to yourselves or *others*.

And practice is the real key here.

While concentration is the key to practice.

Yet most of you have continued to ignore the clues which invite you into the endless possibilities that can be engaged.

And whenever you've felt even a vague hint of authentic desire to expand your spiritual horizons, you've resisted the necessary practice of letting go and of paying attention, which is always available to you (anywhere and at any time).

But we understand your reluctance.

Why risk it? Right?

Why eat anything which might disrupt your taste buds when you can just keep swallowing the familiar.

Yet a shift change has nothing to do with the quantity or even the selection of food intake. Does it?

Most of you already overstuff yourselves with whatever you think you need in order to remain feeling safe and secure in the bosom of the tribe (to whatever fragile extent that is even possible).

You constantly cling to what you think you already know, don't you? Replopping yourselves on an old tribal couch which you refuse to throw out.

But some of you (on occasion) have unintentionally rolled off that couch into higher frequencies of awareness for quick accidental samplings of what's out there (and in there), by fluke or fortuity. And rolling off the tribal sofa can happen to anyone, can't it? And at any time, no matter what presumptions and preconditions you normally reside in or of which you think you depend upon.

It happens on its own sometimes, doesn't it? Even without your permission. Which is okay and even natural. It's nothing to worry about at all, unless you resist an invitation which may surprise you with a tempting wake-up call, when it may feel too threatening to your *disjoined* stability or to the tribal rhythms which you rarely if ever move out of.

Then it's war, isn't it?

But learning to differentiate (or to shift) between one actual gear and another doesn't lead to self-destruction—even though you may think it might.

And it doesn't mean rejecting other positions, speeds, or comfort levels either.

It just broadens the scope. It includes more . . . not less.

The road gets wider. The drive becomes full of more possibilities. The scenery appears to be more lush. The trip becomes more interesting. The map is more inclusive. The traveling becomes more flexible and spontaneous.

You're no longer bound by any one direction of scenery or of speed. The horizon becomes endless and yours to explore, along with everyone else.

You can still shift back downward when appropriate to do so. You can put it in neutral for a while. You can even back it up or do a U-turn. You can stop the vehicle and get out and stretch your legs whenever you feel like it.

Freedom to shift only increases and expands your ability to acquire more freedom to shift . . . or not to shift. And that is the question, isn't it?

To be . . . or not to be, as the wise William Shakespeare challenged his audience.[1]

It's basically the same question . . . even today,

Nothing else asks nearly as much of you (or asks you nearly enough).

Anything else is usually just another distraction away from that one question which is calling on you to shift completely into who you are and to follow wherever it leads until the next invitation into the ever-expanding and unifying pull of the *Self* is offered up once again . . . and forevermore.

So tomorrow morning, you will all embark on a hard new practice (fueled best by dedicated concentration), when you'll begin to learn these ageless but difficult lessons right at the front end of the initial exchange, beginning with the very first face recognition that you'll be shifted into and anointed with.

And like it or not, you will all (at last) be getting up off the tribal love seat.

You will begin the painful but worthy practice of detachment, of differentiation, and of discernment. You've avoided it for too long. The damage has been (over)done. And the necessary removal of the masks is (over)due, isn't it?

The first big shift of acknowledgment will be on us. After that . . . it's all up to you.

So get yourselves ready. You're in for quite a ride.

But you won't be permitted the privilege of escape or of dissociation . . . as we've already made clear, have we not?

This will not be a divorce from reality. Instead, it will be a razor-sharp entry into it.

So yes . . . get ready to sharpen your skills of patience and determination. Without them, the razor's edge will slice right through your masks and even feel unbearable at times.

But you are able to assume at least that much of by now.

Aren't you?

CHAPTER 20

Heaven and Hell

I T'S JUST SO inevitable, isn't it? The more simple and genuine
that one consents to the practice of living as a human being
(equal among all sentient beings), the less one feels obligated to defend
and protect the egoic repertoire (the irrelevant tribal rubbish) of the
only-mind—which many of you have spent so much of your lives
defending and protecting, haven't you?

Genuine (nontribal) simplicity is replete with its unexpected
coincidental gifts, isn't it? Distractions tend to diminish then disappear.
Clarity is enhanced. Clutter is removed, allowing for unremembered
yet compassionate space to gratefully unfold into a renewed capacity
to extend an awakened benevolence out into the indivisible cosmos—
which gradually or suddenly loses all traces of *otherness*.

The container walls break apart. Spaciousness abounds. Tribal logic
crumbles, amplifying the revived awareness. You slowly awake to who
you always are. There is no separation. The *disjoined* personality becomes
unsplit. All *otherness* vaporizes, reintegrating into a coalesced *Oneness* of
Being.

But on the unfortunate other end of things, where the simplistic
and opaque (isolated) view of the universe resides . . . perceptual space
is contracted, isn't it? Numbing and tightening its grip around the
tribal neck, squeezing itself in upon you, filling you up with its overly
contained yet vacant tribal logic, and blurring your view of things even
more.

Desires are thereupon determined by how much they can divert you
away from *That which is always becoming*.

Empty-headed chatter and frivolous imagery fill up the overcrowded
tribal container. Addictions increase, and spatial awareness is obscured,
leading to a growing disorientation, which leads to inertia.

Complexity, the thirst for knowledge, and any exploration into
That which is mysterious are all rejected in favor of an overattachment to
uniformity and to alienation—to fixed and rigid tribal certainties.

You gradually become the property of what squeezes in upon you, converted into a paralyzed piece of tribal disharmony.

The *other* is violently rejected from your incestuous group hibernation.

The walls of confinement thicken and grow, protecting the calcified contents which are hidden behind them (which are you), defending themselves with tribal precision . . . from being scaled by anything that even smells like an approaching external *otherness*.

Yet you still insist upon continuing to cling to what can never last. Don't you? While denying what you already have and who you already are.

And when even just one lingering doubt somehow makes its way through the hardened crust and into the sealed vault of the *only-mind*, its alien energy leaves a painful scar upon the broken surface of the tribal skin, doesn't it? Causing it to constrict even more, pulling you back and slinging you out even further away from the shore of the present moment, toward some faraway island of lost tribal memories, stranding you in a body of *disjoined* water which doesn't even exist.

But nothing really exists outside of the evolving present moment, remember?

Or as the ancient Buddhist parable so wisely puts it, *the raft is not the shore*.[1] Any raft. No matter how pleasurable or persuasive it drifts and floats in your desired direction; or how far it may take you out to sea; or with whatever storm it entices you with; or however many clouds of blue-ribbon theology, heady political and social theory, intoxicating philosophy, or howling economic explanations you reach for and try to grab onto in your desperate pursuit to prevent yourselves from drowning in your own sea of tribal overidentification and dependency.

Yet you will always be exactly where you are, won't you? No matter how much you pray to enter into a future heaven or to escape from (or even into) a future hell.

There is nowhere but here.

And there is no time but now.

Don't you see?

Heaven and hell are always accessible from wherever and whenever you are. They're infinitely real. Neither is restricted by time nor by mythological geography or even by life and death. There is no time and there is no place that either one of them cannot be accessed from or entered into.

But you already know that.

Because you've been there.

You've been to the terrestrial extreme. You've danced back and forth between the spiritual polarities which reside within you, have you not?

And would it really surprise you to discover that those convincing and convenient tribal kingdoms which you routinely submit to and allow to dominate your will and demeanor are where most of your habitual and wishful thinking and where much of your reactionary violence originates from?

Although, as we'll continue to emphasize, for many of you it just seems to be too difficult to keep yourselves from reaching for any other moment but the one you're actually breathing in, doesn't it? Which may be why you tend to park yourselves in the overcrowded tribal parking lot whenever you get the chance.

You continue to mistake the tribal cart for the horse, the tribal raft for the shore, the tribal fingers for the moon,[2] the tribal messengers for the message, and the tribal disguise for whoever you compulsively desire to see in the tribal mirror.

But it never lasts, does it?

Mirror, mirror on the wall, who's the fairest one of all, asks the vain and jealous (tribal queen and) stepmother from *Snow White.*[3]

Yet it still seems to be your most common rationale for returning to all of that inner and outer racket and to all of that acrobatic nonstop movement, doesn't it?

Many of you still seem to think that the more you work at cranking things up, the more likely that what you so fear acquiring even an accidental taste of will simply vanish and that more of what you find palatable and easy to swallow will start raining down upon you like sweet cakes and honey.

But a constant barrage of loudness fused together with a never-ending jumping and jostling has never been a cure for anything, has it?

Although it does seem to be able to hide bothersome symptoms sometimes, yes? Which so often is equated and confused by so many of you with the elimination of root causes (or of tribal dis-ease).

You've convinced yourselves that you're simply trying to blast your way toward something more transcendent . . . instead of what you're really trying to do, which is to drown out and rush away from the long-suffering silence of *That which is always becoming*—which is usually when the ever-returning addiction to violence shows up again. Isn't it? As you try to pulverize or consume yourselves all the way to some kind of tribal land of utopian rapture . . . into some kind of nirvana of the *only-mind.*[4]

Many of you have even come to believe that you're actually saving yourselves with all of that hyperactive noise and movement and that you're somehow coming to the rescue of anyone else who accompanies you in your panicky pursuits or that you're actually liberating those who may unexpectedly step into your line of deadly aimed tribal proselytizing.

And whenever they back off or collapse from exhaustion, you mistake it as either capture or conversion (as a clear victory for the tribe), don't you? As yet another extreme either/or interpretation cooked up inside of the self-seducing and overly intrusive *only-mind.*

You seem to assume that if your desperate and loud activity ever dies out, then whoever you think you are will perish right along with it. And then that same *disjoined* thought will descend instantly into your tribe's concoction of hell on Earth, to the hellfire and brimstone of (nontribal) silence and stillness.

And you'd be right.

But your constant clamor is merely a distraction from the hell of realizing *That which is,* from realizing *That which allows It-Self* to endlessly expand and to infinitely deepen into an uncontainable capacity for extending compassion into all of *Creation.*

You are always *That which is,* don't you see? Which is deeper and more vast than any imaginary Shangri-la or than any tribal nether realm that we know of[5]—which are the distracting and *disjoining* tribal concepts that you ceaselessly chase after and flee from at the same time, by way of all that you do to play tribal hide-and-seek with the undying *Self* who resides everywhere within or without you.

Yet your impulse to seek is real, isn't it? Even while the map of your desires is quite often defective.

But what a strange and violent waste of *That which endlessly gives.* What a great waste of the *Self*-giving and charitable silence and of its great stillness—which is why it's finally time for us to step in. Don't you see?

The irony in all of this is that many of you avoid the present moment by simply insisting on staying put. Now how peculiar is that?

You avoid being present to the ever-present *Self* by forever forging yourselves deeper into the never-present *only-mind*, frantically nailing your inherited tribal furniture to the tribal floor, pretending to make sure that nothing moves out of place, that nothing is let go of—which is a most common cause as well as a most curious side effect of your addiction to tribal sameness. Isn't it?

For where your treasure is, there will your heart be also, said the wise Jesus.[6]

Yet you continue to stack up your perishable treasures of exclusion . . . one on top of the other, holding on to and collecting them for the sole purpose of trying to negate *That which is changeless* and to replace *That which is* with that which is not.

But your efforts remain hopeless. Don't you see?

What cannot be done . . . cannot be undone.

It's as simple as that.

CHAPTER 21

The Cost of Membership

IT SEEMS SO apparent yet so puzzling sometimes, doesn't it? That whenever you try to closely observe *That which is real . . .* somehow your efforts only arouse it to a metaphysical suspicion, to then shift itself into some unconfined location in your narrow zone of awareness where you would never think to look for it (even though it's everywhere) and where it goes on breathing freely, uncorrupted by your attempts to corral it into any one categorical corner of tribal containment.

Yet it allows and even seems to encourage you to follow it sometimes, doesn't it? To stay awake to its indefinable presence and to be prepared, to pay attention to the hard and heavy lifting of ordinary life, but especially to what appear to be those insignificant and mysteriously hidden portals of momentary insights, where it seems to like to lean back and to relax, to just observe the various ways which you deny *That which is always revealing It-Self* to you.

The well-rehearsed and often deliberately overcomplicated and uniform tribal routines, which most of you convince yourselves are necessary (as a lame excuse for your cognitive and spiritual laziness), have little or nothing to do with what leads to *Self*-realization, let alone with self-liberation.

You do understand that. Don't you?

And if you were to be completely honest with yourselves, most of you would have to admit that the all-inclusive *Self* can never be captured or defined by the limitations of tribal logic or even in one crowning tribal gestalt, let alone by any one organized sect of tribal religion; or by any one branch of science, art, or literature; or by any cult of politics or philosophy.

You've simply been denying your own infinite capacity. Don't you see? By continuing to renew your enrollment into privatized clubs which promise a permanence which they can never deliver on, even though they regularly provide you with their congested answers to their exclusionary questions which they refuse to deviate from or allow to be even mildly criticized or questioned or even to be lightly contaminated with any truth, goodness, or beauty which may be innocently thriving just outside the walls of the (so often) guilt and shame-based tribal container.

A padlocked *only-mind* can never permit itself to expand . . . let alone to evolve. Can it?

Although it's not really the act of *disjoining* yourselves which gets you into trouble, don't you see?

It's that somehow you've equated your various tribal memberships with obtaining the ultimate solutions to those questions which whether real or not should only be meant to extend the territory. Shouldn't they? Not to close it down with secret handshakes or with arrested codes of development, or with hardened tribal belief systems, or with oppressive herd behavior.

Yet most of you still subscribe to the group-approved correct answer as the best solvent for most of your inbred homemade dilemmas, don't you?

You've reduced the unending quest into a short-lived but dogmatic scavenger hunt. It's the one big tribal head fake which almost all of you have fallen for, isn't it?

But *That which is always becoming* can never be conclusively or precisely defined. Can it?

Although the attempt to do so seems to be so understandable and (shall we say) so human, so curious, and so paradoxically human—and yet all too often so violently human.

But its elusiveness should not really be such a surprise to so many of you, should it? Even though (and not so surprisingly) it still is.

Frequently, when the indefinable *Self* feels suddenly gone to you, it can then seem to reappear almost anywhere out of nowhere, can it not?

When it stands in front of or inside of you (huge and clearly present) it can then suddenly shrink and disappear even while changing shape.

When you can literally feel its texture and weight in your hand, it then disintegrates into thin air.

When you think you've finally got it, you then lose it.

And when you think it's gone forever, it then taps you on the shoulder and winks.

When you surrender to its strength of *Being,* it then lets go and allows your heart to sink into an agonized yearning.

And when you dwell in the darkness of a deep absence within, it then resuscitates and refills your spirit with its perpetual presence.

We presume that's why you feel the need to design and build so many remote and daunting physical structures; so many autocratic institutions layered with enough bureaucracy to make the codes in the book of Leviticus seem easy to follow;[1] so many shelves full of multiple rule books and membership requirements, full of attendance policies and language restrictions, of threats of guilt by association, of pervasive morality codes, of thought and speech formalities, and of mandatory pledges of allegiance, with enough laws to catch and arrest even the most saintly and blindly loyal among you, all inside of an ever-expanding and elaborate global network of arbitrary coalitions and tribal alliances—which are always in the process of falling apart from within.

We repeat: You persist in the impossible, in continuing to try to catch and capture what cannot be caught.

And right on cue, as it's been so often reenacted throughout much of your violent tribal histories, a good many of you predictably splinter off into oppositional groups full of self-proclaimed converts of dissent . . . and of sycophants of contrariety, rising up to follow behind vocal and well-appeased gurus of convenient defiance and of opportunistic antagonism; attempting to form yourselves into your own fabricated versions of *Self*-capture, through a simple reduplication of the same old overly contained *disjoiners*—merely wearing a different tribal mask, that's all.

Some of you gradually become cultural or ideological insurgents, do you not? Or political or religious reactionaries . . . new breeds of fundamentalists and of reformers, seeking to resituate yourselves into the institutional power structure itself, to establish your own predilections for irrational and even wacky opposition to *otherness*, with your own baseless accusations and with your own wild-eyed threats of tribal retaliation—still trying to conform yourselves into the conventional mainstream of the global *only-mind*, competing with any *other* charlatans who may be trying to do the same.

And most of your tribal carpetbagging seems to almost always accumulate in the connective tissue of the extreme, doesn't it? Especially whenever your world feels itself being stretched and pulled between at least two competing mythologies.

One divergent tribe may assume that it's moving things forward. And sometimes it may even appear to be doing so while an opposing group tries to pull it all back with no illusions of promoting progress at all. The sentimentalists among them pine and warn loudly from behind their blind faith in nostalgia, seeking a return to utopian times which never were . . . almost always pretending to rival what they copy.

Each newly formed tribe divorces off into its own set of separate abstractions which profess to compete against their own specific portrayal of present-day evils—even as they reproduce an analogous version of the growing tyranny they preach against.

They become just as violent in their own way as those whom they accuse (perhaps on a smaller scale at first) while asserting that they're actually doing something else, something altogether different—that they're even driven by completely contrary values and intentions.

But it's just a redundant blaming of the same old and familiar *otherness* which spills out of their loud accusations, isn't it? Simply dressed up in different tribal clothing, nothing else.

And they actually deceive themselves into imagining that they're superior to and separate from the ones they project their hostility upon.

It's what they see reflected back from the same tribal glass which they've borrowed or stolen from their adversaries, from the diabolical ones whom they attack and condemn—yet whom they regularly imitate.

And there really is no *them*, is there? You are always them.

But you already know that by now, don't you?

Regardless of how much you pretend not to.

CHAPTER 22

Babble in Paradise

THE WALLS OF tribal containment gradually close in upon you, cutting you off from any and all *otherness*, secluding you, preventing you from waking up and from allowing the unified *Self* to come forth.

Darkness fills up the container, depleting individual imagination, confining it to uniform logic, to its estrangement—to the alienation of the *only-mind*.

Members are admonished and even forbidden from acknowledging anything of value outside the tribe's tightly scripted preset conclusions.

Each separate container convenes in an isolated vacuum, plotting out its own contentious strategy, bewitched in its zeal to try to seize and confiscate *That which is beyond confiscation*.

Splintered groups of followers climb up and into one tower of confused babble after another, leaving a disconnected wasteland behind, dotted with fields full of barren towers, each one stuffed with piles of its own incoherent tribal gibberish.

But that which you seek (you must eventually come to realize) is only accessible and apprehended on its own terms.

As *Being Its-Self.*

As pure relationship.

Not as an object to capture or claim as your own nor as a mere concept to fix a frozen name upon—whether in your mind or in your hand or from up in the sky somewhere.

It is forever too alive to be appropriated as if it was just one more of the many commodities in your *disjoined* collection, merely existing to award you with another assumed tribal identity.

Never static, it breathes in and out on its own, never to hold its breath in any one place for anyone, or under any one endorsement, or from any earthly say so, or behind any one imprimatur, or inside of any clever sales pitch; never allowing itself to freeze or to suffocate, or to be bought or sold, or to even temporarily stop moving or to stop breathing.

It is participatory, in a changeless relationship with all of *Creation*.

It gives and it receives, forever inviting you into its immutable *Self*—just as it invites *It-Self* into you.

It is in the *I*.

In the *We*.

And in the *You*.

It is in *It* and *That*.

In *Everything* and *Nothing*.

Everywhere yet *Nowhere*.

It cannot disunite from *It-Self* nor from any of its creations nor from any of its cocreative children.

Cultivate the spirit of surrender to his will, inside you and outside you, until you have completely surrendered up your ego sense and have known that he is in all, he is all, and you and he are one [sic], wrote the wise Swami Ramdas.[1]

The indivisible *Self* can never be controlled. It cannot be pinned down to any one location nor precisely measured, even though many of you continue to persist in trying to do just that with your limiting definitions or with your overexplanations and especially with the exclusionary tribal names you so often assign to it—which is (again) so dispiriting, yet so understandable.

But the best you can really hope to do is to feel it wandering around in and out of you at will, even playfully escaping and returning as you try to imagine capturing it with your tongue, while you breathe it in . . . and then breathe it out.

But your tongue will never catch or confine it no matter what it pronounces about it or with whatever it tries to tag it with. It can only help to move it along your journey or to move you along its journey . . . within you.

And as some of you may have guessed (but have little to no idea of how to express it), there is in the end only the *One Breath* which forever breathes through all of you, the *One Perception* which is always available, even though to so many of you it seems so unavailable most of the time, the *One Savoring* which manifests itself in so many feelings, flavors, tones, and contours.

And the two most faithful and accurate ways to name *That which is always becoming* are by not naming it at all . . . but instead, by permitting it to name you or by simply allowing it as many names as there are ways which it allows *It-Self* to appear in the various cultural and historical contexts which it arises, accepting each one as a partial perspective, as an incomplete uncovering of the whole, as a portal into a singular vision of completeness from a uniquely revealed incarnation of its entirety but still being a genuine expression of and an entrance into and an unveiling of the sacred wholeness *It-Self.*

The partial reveals the whole because the whole is fully revealed in every expression of *It-Self.*

God is not only seated within you but you and every bit of *Creation* consists entirely of God-stuff; nothing else. No part can be separated from the whole. It's impossible, no matter how much the divisive tribal *only-mind* keeps trying to convince you otherwise.

So in a very real sense, each partial tone includes the entire composition, which exposes the paradox. Doesn't it? Can you fit that image into your head and heart? That all partiality reveals the same fullness? That they are simply separate (but conjoined) *fingers pointing to the same moon*, as the wise Buddhist metaphor keeps insisting?

The separate becomes unified by seeing clearly through each entrance and through each perspective, through each visage or face, and through each unique incarnation.

Yet we're talking about a partiality which is revealed from and through the actual whole . . . from its actual portals; the partial views from within reality itself, into the true *Self;* way above, below, and beyond the boundaries of the tribal surface which you've been so used to standing upon.

Nothing of great depth or expanse is ever revealed or transformed through any of your ego inducements or through any of your memorized precepts or sectarian systems of convention by themselves, as accommodating as they may often seem to be to your day-to-day sense of security and comfort or to your undergrown and immature phases of individual or collective (spiritual and psychological) development.

Although we do realize that they can be of some practical assistance sometimes while you struggle to cope with current events, situations, and circumstances.

But on their own, they can't be much more than that, can they? Until they're allowed to let go of themselves or until they are allowed to be let go of. Then they can transform. Then they can begin to liberate you from the *disjoining* clutches of the *only-mind.* But not until then.

MICHAEL J. GAJDA

Water can never flow as long as it's kept frozen, can it?

The ice is kept alive. But it will never be released into the stream of life . . . into actually interacting with and relating to the rest of the creative cosmos.

While it remains frozen, it can never return back to its *Source*. Can it? From where all of life emerges and from where it awakens and evolves.

There's a great thawing out that needs to take place first, don't you see?

But most of your human-made systems and structures (which includes most of you within their reach) won't let go of themselves, will they?

There's a tight holding on and a fear of allowance which constricts compassion while it contracts the heart. Even though the cleansing little secret is that by letting go and reaching out . . . you become more of who you already are. You become one with the *Other* (which is no *other*).

But it's far more accurate to say that you awaken to who you are, isn't it? Because you really can't become who you already are. That doesn't make much sense. Does it?

But you know that.

And it's impossible to unlearn what is forever known. Isn't it?

Even though that doesn't exclude or deny the layers of awareness which the power of even one cloud of unknowing can uncover, does it?

You can still keep what you've got. Life only gets deeper and more expansive. And that's usually when it reveals to you that there's really nothing to hold on to or to keep in the first (or even in the last) place. Because what you think you've got . . . you don't.

The paradox is revealed once again and forever.

You even get to hold onto and keep more of yourselves by letting go. Because what you've been holding on to is not *You*. And it's not yours.

It's quite liberating actually, to you and to everyone else around you, whether human or *other* than human.

The clothes you've been wearing to protect yourselves come right off. And there you stand—naked but emancipated.

It's so powerfully strange, isn't it? And curious (yet true) but hard to grasp until you let go of it. And it's hard to let go of until you grasp it.

So many pieces to so many puzzles . . . eh?. Not so, say we. There's really only one puzzle to play with.

But so many of you in the invited group to be face launched tomorrow morning, resist the freedom to play. Don't you? You prefer instead to just plant yourselves down somewhere, absorbed into your tribal assumptions, which assume an end-all and be-all place for you to dig yourselves into and which you do, with great relief and with such resolve and with such tribal zealotry and dissociation.

But then of course you've got to keep those supplies coming in, don't you?

And you've got to put up your defensive walls and then make all those rules to abide by.

And you've got to have those enrollment and membership requirements and those tests of allegiance printed up.

You've got to mark clear boundaries and put up guards and draw up maps.

And then of course you end up with enemies who've planted themselves down somewhere nearby, too close to your tribal comfort zone . . . with different kinds of ideas about how things should be done and run, but with the same basic game plan and relative mind-set as yours.

Traitors, criminals, doubters, and weak-links of all kind are created from this mess. And they come and they go.

And tons of questions and dissensions begin to pop up as the population grows and history moves swiftly by . . . shifting through various imitations of itself, which you resist or deny, as generations continue to die off just to be reborn all over again into the same cyclical process.

And then you've got to make up a lot of resolutions and punishments to try to keep things in check and to hold to tribal tradition, don't you?

And you've got to have more weapons and laws to defend yourselves with, to keep everyone in line, as internal strife and ever-changing outside adversaries keep showing up on your doorstep to replace last week's antagonists—antagonists who look very much like you do, to them.

Then you've got to have your casualties and your heroes, don't you?

And you can't allow them to be forgotten—generically speaking, of course. Can you? Or to use an overly exploited and often empty cliché of yours . . . you can't allow them to *die in vain*.

So you've got to build your walls even higher and thicker and make your weapons bigger and more sophisticated.

And you've got to talk louder and with more conviction about how it is that you've come to occupy such a foremost and chosen place in the world with the truest of all tribal truths, supported by an unassailable and unerring tradition and by officially sanctioned ways and means which are always worth even sacrificing your own children for. Aren't they? Yet rarely (it seems) is it worth being very critical or discerning of any of its nonnegotiable tribal rules and conventions. Is it? Or of any of the overly treasured golden calves of the tribe in question.

And then you seem to draw even more enemies and threats your way. Don't you? Which only reinforces your continued justifications to stay in your defensive mode—which is usually more offensive than defensive, much like how some of your most prestigious tribal war machines are overseen by the likes of a *Defense Department.*

And violence continues to grow into your sentiments and across your borders as many of your own children suffer and die while they hide, defend, or attack from the fixed positions and perspectives you've passed along to them—which is all they really are, just perspectives. But you've made them sacrosanct, haven't you?

And almost all of you eventually get intruded upon at some level by some opposing tribe along the way, just as you violate or conquer a perpetual collection of alternating enemies yourselves.

And you invade, fight, and kill over food, water, and oil and over land and religion, over competing economic systems, and over natural and unnatural (so-called) resources.

Have you ever paused (for even one lonely second) to contemplate how the earth, water, air, plants, animals, and fish, and all the *other* species feel about being diminished to becoming mere *resources* for you humans to exploit and to clash over and to cash in on at your arrogant and anthropocentric leisure, as you bicker and battle over strategic geographic regions or over political influence or over military advantage, even over insults which you often label as treason or blasphemy—which are quickly coming to mean the same thing to many of you, as you wrap your gods into your flags and render your nationalistic anthems into religious hymns of pious praise.

When fascism comes to America, it will be wrapped in the flag and carrying the cross, said the wise Sinclair Lewis.[2]

And then you write history books from your one-sided points of view, don't you? To make the ground you walk upon even more adhesive.

And most of you describe your version of this mirrored sameness as something unique or even as exceptional, while each separate tribe uses its own specific vocabulary of tribe-defending words . . . words comparable to ones like *freedom, fatherland, sacred honor, national sovereignty, vital interests, homeland security, proud nation, historic sacrifice,* and *for God and country* (as if they were the same thing)—praising the tribe's revered way of life while always indicating a need to be fearful and on guard against an ever-changing specific threat to the tribe's containment . . . from an outside tribal *otherness,* while slipping in obvious nods to the recognized gods of tribal habit or to an occasional idolized name of an acknowledged tribal hero which you can drop into the lexicon to emphasize proof of your loyalty, while (along the way) elevating a certain group of key tribe-enhancing words or phrases of which you eventually expect everyone else in your enclosed encampment to be able to repeat when asked to identify themselves . . . simply to demonstrate their knowledge of and adherence to the sanctioned vocabulary of the group, while occasionally even picking out and reciting frozen excerpts and references from the tribe's sanctified documents to punctuate the evidence of your absolute and unqualified allegiance.

And the longer you sit and speak in the language of the overly contained tribal herd, the more you begin to smell just like the herd does (just like the container does) and the more you then begin to defend its aroma even as you deny what it actually reeks of or even that it carries a certain odor to it at all. Some of you even claim that questioning or criticizing any part of its tribal fragrance is actually demonic or seditious just in itself.

Whistle-blowers, truth-saying prophets, and the noncooperative are mocked and disgraced or imprisoned and tortured—or they quietly disappear.

And everyone in your culturally conditioned camp is expected to stand and salute or to bow down in literal or figurative but harmonious supplication to the tribal signs and symbols while each tribe remains on high alert for any dissenting or reactivated silence or disregarding stillness, both having risen to the top of the list of suspected *otherness.*

Tribal alarm systems are put into place to trigger loud warnings to the loyal flock, for whenever any incoming anxieties or critiques begin to drift in or for whenever the beginnings of a whispering mist of *otherness* threaten to pour down, even a mist of barely audible words, anything that feels and smells a little too much like a myth-shattering storm may be moving in—so that the flock can take immediate cover. Because if it doesn't securely shelter itself, then there's always the chance that a tiny drop of mistrust or apprehension might sprinkle or splash into someone's middle or inner ear and then get itself trapped inside the ear canal. And a pestering bead of uncertainty might begin to roll around in there and keep rolling down and even circulate into the rest of the listening system and then out into the tribal container itself. And it might spread out into the population. And somehow it might gradually begin to take over. And then the tribe could lose everything, couldn't it?

The tribe's actual survival could be at stake—or so goes the all-too-familiar (fear-driven) mythological (and disingenuous) teachings.

But most of you should be able to recognize such familiar and habitual stretching of the tribal imagination by now.

Shouldn't you?

CHAPTER 23

Lethal Forms of Language

THE ISOLATED TRIBAL imagination constantly forewarns itself of impending invasion, doesn't it? With fanatical fantasies full of ungodly attacks upon its sacred seclusion, of an encroaching army of *otherness* . . . imagined to be squirming toward the tribal container like a legion of hungry, sinful serpents.

But it's just more of the same old *disjoined* shadow play, isn't it? More shouts of tribal distraction intended to protect the *only-mind* from awakening to its own false witness.

Because if it wakes up, it will die. And it knows that.

Don't you see?

The tribe will then be released from its spiritual imprisonment.

The *Self* will resurrect and unlock the gated depths into the unknown.

And it's the liberation and the unknowing of that cloud of *otherness* which the *only-mind* fears most of all. Isn't it?

So you remain hypervigilant, don't you? While constructing even more walls of alarm around yourselves.

And your dogged watchfulness is quite impressive (we must admit), even while so much of it is held up to abstract notions of who you are.

We often wonder how you can keep trying to secure yourselves to something that isn't real, when there's really nothing there of depth and significance to adhere to.

But there's lots of form though, isn't there? Lots of noise-making tribal form, framing a thick yet fragile shield around the self-worshiping *only-mind*—blinding it of its own myopia.

But (much like silence and truth) *That which lasts* doesn't need much in the way of proof or explanation or of overzealous self-justification, does it?

It just is.

A thing of substance isn't afraid of uncertainty (let alone of being still) or of freeing up its own perceptual awareness.

The eternal core of *That which is always becoming* remains forever changeless and free of any constricting formula which may try to chain it up and contain it. It doesn't blow away in a storm of criticism or with the threat of attack or even with an evolutionary shift in its physical shape and density.

But anything which physically materializes is transitory, isn't it? And for good reason.

One's internal or external form may change, yet it doesn't really matter. Because it's always changing.

It may even change beyond recognition.

Everything is forever changing. Don't you see? Sometimes for the better and sometimes for the worse, either through time and wear and tear, or by way of human imperfection and often through human mischief.

Yet one's physical incarnation is never really separate from its fundamental core—from its essence, is it?

Each form of physical embodiment is there to be realized and to learn from, to incarnate, to model and to be molded from, to enter into and to explore, to be grateful for, to take care of and to cooperate with, to be respectful of and yet to be playful with, and to eventually let go of itself with compassionate detachment, not to be turned into an idyllic object of tribal adoration or into just another conjured-up devil of *otherness* to be disdained or disregarded.

But many of you among the invited have been marching to just such a violent tribal learning curve, haven't you? While doing your loyal best to divide up *That which is* from its very *Self.*

But you're about to enter into a unique (if not unusual) phase of instruction.

The formless does not change. It cannot be divided up. So there's no need to be afraid of being exposed to it. *That which is always becoming* is all there is.

And in its essence (beyond and beneath its apparent physical structure), each and every thing of *Creation* is immutable.

So (as we've already noted) nothing can actually be destroyed or can even be wounded, don't you see?

You can't wound or destroy what is beyond grasping. Can you? Or what is beyond what you can imagine as being eternal.

And yet many of you have convinced yourselves that your physical embodiment is your supreme essence . . . that it is the full extent of what you are and of what you can become.

You've defined and memorized your tribe-specific words in order to put a final explanation onto tribe-specific forms. You've rehearsed it all for years, to try to force significance into those words beyond whatever they're capable of meaning, to make the words mean something more than words, to force your words into becoming an extension of that same form, to make them stick, with your self-reverential and repetitious tribal wordplay.

But even the best of words in any real or imagined universe can only represent something more than what they are.

They can only point.

They can only be a doorway or a sign or a symbol.

They can never be what's behind the door, can they? Or even what's indicated by the sign, or what's inside the symbol, or what light is radiated out from the incarnated or evolving form itself.

Yet many of you have come to believe that certain words (and hence certain tribal forms) should actually be revered, that they should be held up so high as to be perceived as more sacred than life itself sometimes. Mere words! Along with the tribal forms which you consider to be absolute and final in themselves and beyond any question or doubt, locked into an unchangeable tribal interpretation, immovable and static, valued and praised for leading you to a safe and secure dead end of allegiance—to an absolute and indisputable world full of lifeless paragraphs and of figurines of permanent deliverance.

And by trying to freeze your words into one frozen place of distinction, by trying to replace essence with cold, culturally conditioned, and condescending forms, you've not only killed off the words themselves by freezing them to death, but you've suppressed the hidden *Self* inside and beyond those words . . . inside and beyond any and all words and into the patronizing forms of tribal worship and allegiance which you indulge.

And you readily defend those concretized forms to the death, don't you? To the very death of anyone who would dare to challenge or question your venerable *disjoined* constructions or of anyone who would venerate or merely show respect for a different form of *otherness* . . . for any combination of forms *other* than those which have been sanctioned by your tribe of deference, or of anyone who does not stand and pledge their loyalty to your tribe's specific forms of attachment and addiction, of anyone who would dare to walk through a different doorway, or of anyone who is able to respectfully let go of any and all formulated concepts in order to bathe in the presence of the formless (which is changeless) . . . and which paradoxically remains *That which is always becoming* (even while not being this and not being that . . . and not being one yet not being two).

And so many of you continue to strain and stretch to keep adding even more words to your pronouncements, to cause them to mean something even more intentionally exact and literal, to try to keep yourselves from forgetting why you were saying them in the first place.

But the more you repeat those words, the more you seem to be trying to convince yourselves that the act of repetition alone will bring them into a fixed form of tribal meaning . . . that it will somehow make them real, that it will make them come true like dreams so often seem to be—until you wake up from them.

Yet most of your virtuous tribal words and your devout, formal, and *disjoined* sentences aren't really repeated with the intention of drawing out more wisdom or compassion or of evoking more loving-kindness and truth into your lives, are they? Or even to pull you into a deeper state of awakened awareness or into a higher level of conscious development.

Instead they're merely verbal arrangements that you restate and emphasize in order to try to magically turn them into permanent shrines of security which you can then offer sacrifice to (human or *other* than human), or that you can try to substitute in for the infinite *Self,* or which you can reverently sit and wait in front of for further tribal instructions.

And eventually the correct pronunciation of the words themselves becomes even more important than clinging to them as objects of desire and adoration. And they become even more important than the amount of words you elevate which soon becomes more important than their meanings. And as we've noted earlier . . . loud barking abstractions tend to overrule and replace the calm silence of unmediated experience in much of your world, don't they?

Your pronunciations are even more important (based upon the value which you've been conditioned to derive from them) than how you interact or respond to real-life situations with real and alive sentient beings. The many bitter masks of your frozen language have replaced the sweetness of the human face, haven't they? Behind the distorted shapes, sounds, and abstractions which you've laced or injected your tribal tongues with.

What you verbally pronounce has finally come to trump what you actually do.

Pronunciation trumps doing. It even trumps being, doesn't it?

The more tribally correct the pronouncement is . . . then all the more prestige, power, and influence there is that gets bestowed upon the one doing the pronouncing.

And as long as you can say the right words, in the most precise way, then there's always something to live, to die, and even to kill for, isn't there? There's always something to feel stiffly proud of.

So it's become obvious that you find much if not all of your tribal purpose and direction in the spoken word as it's been passed down to you—which isn't in itself a bad thing, is it?

We like words. They have their place and their importance. We know that.

But then your hierarchy of elevated words and precise pronunciation folds out into your written language too, doesn't it? Into your documents and into your shallow traditions . . . even into your gang graffiti and into your religious or political talking points, into your loyalty oaths and into what you expect and even demand to be read, written, and heard by everyone else who is enclosed within the same commonly occupied communal container.

Your actions become subordinate . . . almost as afterthoughts, don't they? They become impolite burps after stuffing yourselves with a big meal of tribal sound-bites. The menu of *disjoined* speech and language only serves up recipes made of spiel.

What you say, write down, or are given to read or listen to as the established words of your established tribal order are what matter most, aren't they?

They're not necessarily intended to inspire *others* (or yourselves) to do good, but instead to be able to demonstrate your commitment to the specific trafficking of the words themselves.

Doing good (according to the cherry-picked ethics of the tribe) is still good. But saying or (better yet) directly quoting from what has been nailed-down as the tribal definition of good is so much better. Isn't it?

The doings are judged to be less significant than the enshrined sayings.

Good is no longer a value to be observed. Good is what the tribal incantation says it is.

And the strange thing is that words only seem to be important in relation to where you are born when you hear them . . . or when you were given the words, or by whom, or sometimes where you end up with them.

If you're born and raised over here, then these words are the true words, yes? And if you're born and raised over there, then those words are the true ones and not just the true words but the one-and-only, superior, and even the defend-to-the-death true words.

Just take any strict fundamentalist evangelical Christian from the southern United States or any strict fundamentalist Roman Catholic from Chicago, Northern Ireland, or Warsaw . . . or any strict fundamentalist Russian Orthodox believer from Moscow or Saint Petersburg. Then reincarnate and reintegrate their birth and upbringing into a fundamentalist Sunni Muslim family living in the isolated mountains of Pakistan. And then see what kind of language of tribal assumptions develops.

Or even reverse the experiment.

What do you think will happen to all of their overly contained tribal belief systems?

Do you think the fundamentalist Christians will keep idolizing those same familiar so-called superior words of truth (which they've become so used to adamantly espousing) from inside of their newly born-into fundamentalist environment of Islamic *otherness*, from inside of a completely different tribal indoctrination system?

What about the fundamentalist Muslim?

What about a fundamentalist atheist, for that matter (the scientific materialist who fundamentalistically refers to him/herself as a proud skeptic of any nonmaterial explanation of anything)?

It takes a very awake and courageous individual to break away from the tribal chains of religious or of antireligious egotism of any kind . . . and then to begin to trust *That which is always becoming*—to begin to trust the inmost and unifying *Self* in whatever language, religion, or culture of noise or silence you find it in (or that *It* finds you in).

Try the same experimental exchange of birth between a fundamentalist Jew from Israel and a fundamentalist Palestinian from the Gaza Strip or with a fundamentalist member of Hezbollah in Lebanon, or between a fundamentalist American (or global) Wall Street capitalist with a fundamentalist Chinese Maoist or a fundamentalist Cuban communist.

Heck, you can even attempt the same experiment between a fundamentalist New York Yankees fan and a fundamentalist Chicago Cubs fan.

You all know what would happen, don't you?

And as long as you sign on the dotted tribal line (to subscribe your unquestioning loyalty to them), then any words can be interpreted to justify just about any personal or collective pattern of thought or behavior—or of any violence practiced by just about any of the true-blue speakers, believers, and followers of those words.

And they are, aren't they?

It's happened millions of times. And it still does.

Just ask all of the dead and maimed who've been killed or tortured for expressing condemned or banned words, or for defending their meanings and pronunciations, or for being on the misguided end of the sword of some other tribe's pronouncement of words and sentences.

Just pick a war.

Pick a century or pick a country. Pick a neighborhood or pick a religion. Pick a translation. Or pick any hallowed or political document. There's plenty to choose from. No tribalized system of language is innocent of using its words to create suffering and destruction.

How often have words been used to defend, promote, and confirm the superiority of the group which claims to own them—or to suppress, exclude, and negate anyone who does not pronounce or wear them clearly, loudly, perfectly, quickly, and often enough?

It's incalculable, isn't it?

Most of you who partake in this fundamentalist tribal habit (with its dictatorship of words) mainly do it with your own inherited religion or nation-state or political persuasion . . . with their tribal language; with their hymns, anthems, oaths, and rituals; and especially with their sacred texts and hallowed heroes and idols.

And you so love to quote from your tribal texts, don't you? To justify your patterns of fearful and violent behavior, along with your tribal systems of belief—but even more so to condemn *others* and their beliefs and behaviors (and their texts).

So many of you are masters at fitting whatever words are needed into any circumstance you need to fit them into, not necessarily to enlighten the present but to control the past, and hence to contain the future— with jargon and gobbledygook and with tribal hocus-pocus.

Or so you assume and intend, don't you?

And your entrenched tribal blather has even spread out into and across all of your artificially created ethnic circles and racial boundary lines, hasn't it? It's spread out and into your history book influenced memories, even into your street-level chatter, and onto your highway wall writings; into your prison lingo, into your class or caste arrangements, and across your borders of geography, even into your body language and tattooed flesh; into your dialects and accents; and into any and all parts and methods of speech contained in any of your cults of tribal dependency and fear.

It's quite curious to observe that so many of your tribes have come up with such similar rigmarole (separately yet simultaneously). While no overly muzzled or tongue-confused tribe seems to be any less determined or inhibited in their linguistic plan of action than any other one.

The same kind of formulated tests of language allegiance rise up just about everywhere, don't they? Just different tests for different idioms of tribal mumbo jumbo.

To some are added the flags, salutes, and colors which simply supplement and reinforce the tribal verbiage—anything to expand the diction of control used by the tribe and especially by its dominator hierarchy. The more the addictive language spreads and infiltrates the tribe, the harder it is to remember how to speak or even how to think without it. And pretty soon . . . you can't.

Although not too many of your siblings on the fringe who'll be staying back tomorrow morning have been fooled or intimidated by this diversionary word game, have they?

Most of them play along with it though . . . simply to survive. But they don't buy into it. For most of them, it just costs too much. They live *in the* [tribal] *world, but not of it,* to borrow a phrase from the wise Sufi ideal.[1]

They keep their own inner texts from being overtaken.

As a matter of fact, most of them choose to be bilingual, or even multilingual when possible, and especially when necessary. But they're still able to return to the *Source* of all language within themselves (to that quiet *Self*) without being permanently noised out, sucked up, and absorbed into any of the artificial tribal terminology whose purpose seems to be (more often than not) to block communication across boundaries—or to become a boundary line itself.

And yet many of you still maintain (in such adamant terms) that you firmly believe in acting in accordance with the higher values found in certain elevated wisdom sayings and practices, embedded within the teachings of the ancient (Perennial) Traditions, don't you? Such as acting with love toward *others* (even your so-called enemies) . . . or not killing, not stealing, and not lying to or about *others*.

But actually engaging in the practice of those precepts doesn't seem to matter quite as much to most of you (among the invited) as does the memorization and the correct and loud repetition of the specific instructional phrases themselves, does it? And mainly for fellow devotees to hear so they can then assume that you know the right words to say and so you can then get the expected rewards and acknowledgments—as if getting recognized approval of your locution and nomenclature is the ticket and password that will get you into lingual heaven, the best way of fooling the gods of tribal vernacular (and their adoring groupies), where gaining *disjoined* acceptance seems to be equated more and more by so many of you to entering the golden gates of some kind of tribal paradise on Earth.

Many of you even seem to think that as long as you just keep talking the tribe's lingo, then they'll eventually have to let you in—simply because of your downright perseverance.

Following the ways of wisdom and compassion has become subordinate to correct and very public recitals of the pronounced and programmed tribal platitudes instead, hasn't it?

And most of you obviously do know the right words to repeat, don't you? To demonstrate your acceptable loyalty to whatever it is that's written on your side of the tribal walls.

And that's the kind of loyalty that counts, isn't it? The kind of loyalty that so often is accepted as being worth dying and killing for in your world, as we've already emphasized . . . and which you already know.

And that, ladies and gentlemen, is the story of the world which we intend to reface. Don't you see? Presented to you in one wide-angled snapshot description—which may seem to be a little oversimplified. But you get the point.

And as you know, so many of you humans have spent way too much of your time arguing and fighting over which is that one true finger that we keep referring to. So most of the time . . . you've actually missed the point, haven't you? And the pun is intended.

CHAPTER 24

The *Self* of Nonviolence

FROM THE BEGINNING and to the end, there will still always be just the one transcendent (yet imminent) *Self*, breathing inside and out of any and all of the manifold monikers you give to it—or that it has allowed itself to be given as its gift to you.

And whether you anoint it with a name or not is merely for your own convenience, isn't it?

It's simply a gift which is freely permitted . . . giving you a glimpse of the undefinable *Self*.

But you're neither the cause nor the refuge for its revelation. And you can never control how it's disclosed to you . . . or to anyone else, can you?

Nothing you can do, say, or conceive of (on your own) can make it any easier for you or for anyone else to realize what is beyond understanding. You enter that kingdom only by and through the uncontainable space (and grace) of divine presence and intercession.

Jesus spoke, lived, and died with the Jews—as a Jew, didn't he?

And Mohammed came to life and then left the Arab world—as an Arab.

Lao Tzu spoke his wisdom from inside the language and culture of the Chinese people.

While Gitche Manitou revealed *It-Self* in the surrounding natural world of the Algonquin—as the Great Spirit, connecting all of nature to *It-Self*.

Buddha woke up from his tribal sleep to the people of India—as one of them.

Krishna announced himself (even before that) into that same Indian culture and spiritual tradition.

The *Self* is only revealed and awakened in you in ways which you can comprehend. And (even then) many of you resist or remain asleep to the evolving revelation.

Yet once it is unconcealed (within any one specific tribe) it slowly unfolds out into the rest of the world, in a way which can gradually be retranslated and then freshly understood.

Unfortunately, many of you still try to push a frozen interpretation of what has been revealed to you onto yourselves and *others*—by way of force or tribal interrogation.

But the benevolent *Self* doesn't need to coerce or indoctrinate anyone—only you do.

So you often (and understandably) revert to using the pretense of conversion. Don't you? In order to fill the never-ending appetite of your ego-defending desires—which is why so much of your top-down religion looks and acts so confused and confusing, stuck in the mud of its own tribal fixations.

The spirit of *That which is always becoming* can only allow and include . . . following its own generous impulse to unfold and to unite (which is essentially what both the word *religion* and the word *yoga* point to—"to bind" or "to join").

Conversely, the disbound and *disjoined* ego of the *only-mind* is only capable of attempting to subvert what it cannot see—which is impossible, of course.

The inexhaustible *Self* cannot be undermined.

But that's exactly where so many of you get stuck in your confusion, isn't it?

You make the containment, control, and interpretation of *That which is beyond* your control . . . as your absolute goal.

Yet the name and face of the *Divine* is revealed to you in every being you come into contact with—human or *other* than human.

Every particle of the world is a mirror.
In each atom lies the blazing light of a thousand suns.
Cleave the heart of a raindrop,
A hundred pure oceans will flow forth.
Look closely at a grain of sand,
The seed of a thousand beings can be seen, wrote the wise Sufi poet Mahmud Shabestari.[1]

Meanwhile, you continue to reach for locked-in certainties instead, don't you? Or for the public humiliation or even the permanent destruction of *others* who may reject or ignore your desperate reaching.

And whatever results from the violence you dish out is quite predictable, isn't it?

It's quite certain that violence will follow when violence leads the way.

But (in the realm of *That which is always becoming*) what results from the use of deliberate nonviolence is not so foreseeable or even close to certain, is it?

Violence aims for mere victory, doesn't it? Somebody wins. Somebody loses. Someone's triumph is someone else's defeat.

While the intentional and disciplined use of (genuine) nonviolence doesn't aim for victory over anyone, not at all.

The aim is not to defeat but to transform, not to be triumphant but to transcend the temptations and illusions which insist (and even beg one to believe) that the *other* is actually more evil or less of a sacred treasure of divine creation than you are.

Instead, the genuine practice of nonviolence springs up organically or is brought forth through struggle (however clumsily) and from the *Self*-acknowledgment that everyone is complicit in whatever evil (or whatever good) germinates and evolves in your world. It springs up from the heart and mind, which imperfectly seeks but remains detached from a transcending and transformational outcome. It makes no awkward claims of superior certitudes. And it desires nothing more than to practice compassion (however flawed) in the name of faith, love, and justice—wherever that may imperfectly lead.

It's a difficult path to walk and a difficult path to trust . . . a geography where nobody wins and where nobody loses, where the intention always transcends and transforms whatever the desired outcome appears to be.

The practitioner of genuine (unpretentious) and all-embracing nonviolence follows the sacred heart of the sacred *Self.*

The practitioner of violence follows the despairing and disparaging laws of the *disjoined* tribal *only-mind.*

At its root . . . violence is head driven, calculated, and reactionary. It judges, plots, and attacks—for self-serving results, whereas the root of authentic nonviolence is heart driven and intuitive, awakened by love and compassion. It becomes its own result.

Most of you ridicule and run away from any intentional nonviolent reconciliation process as an approach to conflict resolution or even as a way of discussing differences—and especially as a way of life.

You tend to avoid or dismiss the use of gentler (yet firm) and more peaceful means altogether. And you especially avoid any direct nonviolent confrontation with evil when it's found to be growing within you or from within your own tribal systems and institutions, don't you?

Yet you're very willing to react against that same identifiable evil when it shows itself in *others* . . . or in *other* tribes, are you not?

But even then much of your reaction is vicious in its tone and temperament, whether you react verbally or even physically. You lack the awakened knowledge and skills (and hence the will and desire) to practice the difficult art of practical nonviolence. It just seems so impractical (even naïve) to most of you, doesn't it?

Again, it's quite disheartening and yet . . . still quite understandable, yes?

Nonviolence never starts from the outside with a personal or tribal agenda in mind.

It's not something you can calculate like a cold mathematical problem. Although pragmatic, it can also seem to be quite a paradoxical intervention.

It only develops as a result of interior transformation, which only evolves from the warmest of gifts—which only emerges from undeserving and unearned grace.

It's never about you or about what you can achieve or receive.

And yet it's always about *You*.

If it starts from the outside with a program or objective at the forefront, then it's only a temporary technique . . . a trickle-down trick introduced by the fragmenting logic of the *only-mind*.

And techniques always die young after running out of artificial steam, don't they? Just like so much of your *disjoined* tribal logic does, even if you continue to refuse to recognize or to acknowledge when it's dead.

But uncontainable grace can never die. It's the lifeblood of the universe. There's nothing to run out of because it's the only thing that expands and thrives. And the paradox which you resist is that it comes to you through your exposure to (and interaction with) the lives of *others*.

Most of you have come to believe that your fleeting (and migratory) identity is actually you—the permanent you. So you can't permit it to be tarnished or shaken, can you?

If your personal (overly contained) mask has come to represent an imperishable necessity in your mind, then it can't be allowed to be accused of being flawed, can it?

MICHAEL J. GAJDA

A flaw would cause the identity to crumble. Your conventional mind would flake away.

The mask would fall off.

That which is always becoming would be revealed in all of its wild yet welcoming glory.

There would be individual (and tribal) death and resurrection.

Scary stuff.

And the overly contained tribe's most common approach to any real or imaginary evil is that it must be reacted against with similar or greater evil.

So any real or imaginary violence then must be reacted against with similar or even greater violence, but only after you've made sure that none of the evil that you're acknowledging or reacting against in *others* can be traced back to your own tribal influence or involvement.

Yet even if it can be traced back to you then it must be justified, minimized, or excused, usually by blaming an outside force of *otherness* or by making it seem as if your tribe has suddenly become the accused victim of wrong-headed and misplaced blame itself, or by simply comparing your tribe with *other* tribes and exaggerating or even lying about the evidence of their corruption and violence . . . and of their threat to you and your tribe.

It's the old familiar reversal technique which rejects the grace being offered, isn't it? Of continually justifying your violent or corrupt actions by using the deceit of distraction, complaining that so many *others* are so much more dangerous and guilty of what you're being accused of—which you must loudly and frequently repeat to get it ingrained into the *only-mind*, as being an obvious assault upon your tribe's character and security, as an attack upon the tribe based on lies and exaggerations.

What else could it be to the self-serving ego of the tribal *only-mind*?

It keeps the accusatory heat pointed elsewhere, doesn't it? So you can then cancel out your own culpability by rationalizing that so many *others* are even more blameworthy than you are—which then somehow (in the disorienting logic of the tribal *only-mind*) makes you blameless.

The size of the lie is a definite factor in causing it to be believed, because the vast masses of a nation are in the depths of their hearts more easily deceived than they are consciously and intentionally bad, wrote the genocidal Adolf Hitler.[2]

We should never forget that everything Adolf Hitler did in Germany was legal, wrote the wise Martin Luther King Jr.[3]

And so then it must not really be evil (or even violent) when your tribe demonstrates similar behaviors as those of whom you accuse of worse corruption. Isn't that the rationale?

If the behavior on its own can't clearly (or easily) be justified, at least it can be made confusing by loudly and quickly changing the subject to the unfair and unequal justice being doled out against *you*—which somehow lessens your guilt and even proves your innocence and justifies your use of violence in defense of yourselves while elevating your own status when viewed through the lens of paranoid or narcissistic logic . . . to that of being unfairly singled out, to being purposely persecuted by a dangerous *otherness* out there (somewhere), which is separate from who you are and which is out to get you and is out to get your tribe, by an *otherness* which is intent on destroying you because of who you are and because of what you represent—because of your unique greatness.

And so you must always defend yourselves in order to survive in such a turbulent world that is full of such an evil and intangible *otherness*, an *otherness* which only exists in order to destroy the good guys who are almost always you . . . and your tribe, are they not?

Any deviation from that kind of perplexing logic is considered to be disloyal or naïve. It's simply dismissed as not being in touch with tribal reality or it's loudly ridiculed and accused of being contemptuous of the right to tribal self-defense—your tribal self-defense (of course).

And that seems to be the most commonly adhered-to tribal belief, doesn't it?

It's a belief which says that whatever the norm of corruption is, it can't be considered as corrupt or even worthy of specific blame when you partake in it . . . when your tribe does it.

If everybody isn't held accountable or clearly condemned for committing similar sins, to the extent that *others* may try to condemn your tribe for your analogous actions, then it must not be an inexcusable sin, especially when you commit it.

Or if it is actual sin (in the bizarre sense which the elite of most of your autocratic religions use that word), then your tribe should never be singled out for committing it. Because, if you are, then you're simply being used as a scapegoat because of what your tribe stands for—because of its culture or its gods, because of its superiority or its success, because *others* want to bring you down and take your place (which is considered to be an even greater sin than any violence or any evil that you've done to *others*).

The proof is right there in the *disjoined* pudding . . . right there in the most powerful tribes in your tiny world and in the shameful logic and norms which they employ to inflate themselves and which dominate the sanctimonious and chauvinistic *only-mind*—which is the (only) mind that most of your overly contained tribes seem capable or willing to think with.

And most of you among the invited have learned to use the same kind of tribal logic and intensity when justifying your own individual behaviors too, haven't you?

Even on a personal level, you avoid awakening to any struggle that even mildly moves you toward self-criticism, or toward taking full and personal responsibility for your bad or even your mildly flawed behavior, or that even moves you close to anything that looks like peaceful conflict resolution.

And almost all of you avoid practicing anything akin to the wise Mohandas Gandhi's approach of *satyagraha*—which (generally speaking) means . . . to use the force of truth through love and with right action,[4] whether you've ever heard of it or not.

The way of *satyagraha* is much too threatening to tribal concepts which are based upon the exaggerated lies and false promises of power and control, isn't it?

It's even too threatening to an individual's standing within the tribe, especially in a world that so often looks up to aggression and violence like a frightened child looks up to a bullying parent—not out of respect for the bully, but out of fear of the unknown violence which could suddenly intensify and burst open like a volcanic eruption, exploding out of the bully's need for power and out of its addiction to its own noise.

But the fire which *satyagraha* can ignite doesn't scare most of you just because it might awaken the bully, does it? Or even because it seeks the attainment of truth.

It frightens you because it seeks that attainment through courageous and loving means, through *ahimsa* (nonharming, lacking any desire to kill),[5] and because it demands the removal of violence not just from the social, political, religious, or economic tribal institutions (not just from the obvious bullies), but from within you first, from within your very own bullying heart, mind, words, and actions . . . which are the only channels of communication that can initiate the flow of its vital energy.

If you (only) love those who love you, what merit is there in that? asks the wise Nazarene.[6]

And it also scares most of you because it is uncompromising in its commitment to acknowledge and embrace *That which is in you* first—which it must be.

That's the part of it which must always take precedence.

It's the most difficult and most important element in the blazing process of *satyagraha*, in the practice of actual awakened nonviolence. Without it, you would never be able to acknowledge or embrace *That which is* in *others*.

The all-knowing and all-embracing *Self* must be acknowledged and embraced in yourselves first and foremost, or there is no such thing as love or compassion or courage or kindness or forgiveness—or *satyagraha*.

The only thing left would be that which is not . . . which is the draining and deceiving source of the dominant tribal logic, which leads to the continued reliance upon the execution of violence as the cure for whatever ails or frightens so many of you, which is the face that will begin to be unmasked starting tomorrow morning—first thing.

MICHAEL J. GAJDA

CHAPTER 25

The Doorkeepers of Desire

YOUR MASS MEDIA (whether filtered and controlled by an authoritarian nation-state, ordered and overly influenced by a monolithic religion, or bought and paid for by unlimited corporate dollars) rarely or even factually acknowledges the existence of the actual history and practice of nonviolence, let alone demonstrates any stirring or even curious investigative respect for it.

Does it?

But what exactly does it so often recognize, stir up, and even glorify? Care to take a guess?

Television Statistics. The following stats may be a few years old. But during those few years, have you honestly observed any tribe-transcending shift in the collective consciousness or in the collective behavior within any of your tribal containing systems? Or even a hint of evidence which may suggest even a moderate decrease of the hyped-up clout and tribalizing power of the media amalgamated (and thought deforming) *only-mind?*

According to the A. C. Nielsen Company, the average American watches more than four hours of TV each day (or twenty-eight hours per week, or two months of nonstop TV-watching per year).

In a sixty-five-year life, that person will have spent nine years glued to the tube.

Number of murders seen on TV by the time an average child finishes elementary school: 8,000.

Number of violent acts seen on TV by age eighteen: 200,000.

Number of thirty-second TV commercials seen in a year by an average child: 20,000.

Number of TV commercials seen by the average person by age sixty-five: 2 million.[1]

When the average person in North America watches over four hours of tribal television per day, who do you think is cruising (and controlling) the millions of neural highway miles which have been willfully deserted by so many of you, when you've simply vacated your vehicles of self-reflective awareness, after backing them into the huge containing garage of the *only-mind*—where you park and abandon them for safe and effective keeping?

Here's an easy experiment for all of you to try. It might give you a good indication of what the answer is to that string of questions (since we still have a little time left before we start to wrap things up).

So close your eyes.

Everyone.

Close . . . your . . . eyes!

Now . . . for the next five minutes try to think (only) of the word *one*. Sit as still as you can and close your eyes and just think of the word *one*—nothing else.

Whenever another thought or feeling comes to you . . . just gently go back to the word *one*. And don't try to fight off any invading sensations. Simply (but gently) return to the word *one*.

Understand?

Okay then. We'll let you know when your five minutes come to an end.

So let's do it. Shall we?

Ready? Ten . . . nine . . . eight . . . seven . . . six . . . five . . . four . . . three . . . two . . . one . . . and begin . . . .
. . . .
. . . .
. . . .
. . . .
. . . .
. . . .
. . . .
. . . .
. . . .
. . . .
. . . .

Okay. Time's up.

Now . . . slowly open your eyes.

It seemed to last much longer than you thought it would, didn't it?

But regardless of that simple finding . . . how did everyone do with the given task?

Well?

There's really no need to respond, is there? Since we observed so many of you giving up on the assignment well before it was even half begun.

We could feel the billions of agitational brain waves vibrating throughout the nonlocal atmosphere—even from way out here.

Your resistance to nonviolence may actually have more to do with your resistance to thinking your own thoughts, might it not? Or to feeling your own feelings.

It's so much easier when you can just let a herd of unruly characters (who happen to be dancing around in your head) do all of your thinking and feeling for you, isn't it?

Then all you have to do is to unconsciously follow their unruliness.

There's no need to concentrate or to make any intentional or discerning choices (on your part) at all.

It's just as easy as passively yet compulsively plugging yourselves into a trance-inducing TV network of uniform and repetitive images. Isn't it? Or into whatever else you plug into these days in order to fill yourselves up with whatever conforms to the tribal noise.

Nonviolence takes work, practice, concentration, and commitment—not to mention courage.

It means taking charge of your own thoughts and hence . . . your own life.

It's a discipline that demands much in the way of a patient and persistent use of skillful means,[2] rather than leaving it up to the arbitrary impulses and desires that so often result from being intravenously fed by the reactionary logic of conventional (tribal) wisdom.

It's hard enough to regularly resist those impulses and desires, even for many of those among the unconventional fringe dwellers whom we've referred to—even for them. Yes? Even for those who may actually be regular practitioners of some form or method of concentrated meditation . . . or of a contemplative or mindful practice of some kind, or for those practitioners of the simple but difficult habit of being grateful to the all-embracing *Self*. Even for them, it's hard enough . . .

even for those who've come to internalize and embody at least some of their practice into both the passive and active parts of their lives and even for those who try to keep themselves from being overly stimulated or from being overinfluenced by the surrounding tribal conditioning system and by its bombarding and boisterous (corporate) media.

Even for them it's no easy thing. Even for them it's difficult to try to remain in control of their own (God-given) head-quarters.

So we can easily understand why the rest of you succumb to your day-to-day conflicts and problems . . . in such violent and overreactive ways.

But to understand something doesn't mean to condone it, does it?

People try nonviolence for a week, and when it "doesn't work," they go back to violence, which hasn't worked for centuries, said the wise Theodore Roszak.[3]

But there are other factors too . . . besides it merely being a tough way to go.

Your resistance to the practice of an awakened nonviolence often stems from the self-gratifying yet impermanent perks which come from attaining even just a scratch of tribal power or tribal prestige, doesn't it? Which so many of you demonstrate such an obsession for (ever more so) by violently defending your tribal logic (subtle or nonphysical violence is still violence, isn't it?) and by your combative and unnaturally developed tribal nature which is triggered by your addiction to the *disjoined* thoughts which have taken hold in the *only-mind*, which is what most of you think with, or to be more precise, is *that* which mostly thinks *you*.

So you no longer actually ponder things, do you? Instead, you are pondered by them . . . by all of that which contains you.

And all of it is accomplished with a growing and habitual collaboration with a ubiquitous tribal media which you've purchased (and which has purchased you) for the cheap price of your own self-adulating pleasure—which steadily enslaves you in a codependent system of circular insanity. And it's a slavery which you've bought and sold yourselves into.

You've limited your vocabulary and your imagination to what your tribe allows, condones, or rewards—to what it has washed your brains and deadened your spirit with.

Thus your thoughts, words, actions, and desires become dependent upon the gatekeeper and the automatic pilot of the tribal *only-mind*.

And the pilot of your thoughts gradually becomes the custodian of your desires, doesn't it? Which gradually becomes the guardian of your words—and which eventually becomes the curator of your physical interactions with the rest of the cocreated world.

But if you're not the one who's consciously opening and closing the actual gate to your own intentions (to your own thoughts, words, actions, and desires) . . . then who is?

Or what is?

CHAPTER 26

Two Kinds of Warriors

T O DEVELOP AN authentic practice of self-inquiry.
To emanate a naked and unbridled childlike curiosity.

To allow for the unfolding emergence of the transformational *Self*.

To genuinely pursue common ground to stand upon (side by side) with enemies or opponents—with their so-called *otherness*.

With the downtrodden and the vulnerable.

With the mean and the powerful.

Or with like-minded *others* whom you're so used to separating yourselves from whenever they deviate at all from the dogmatic vision of the tribal *only-mind*.

To offer yourselves in charitable service for the greater good (moving beyond your *disjoined* and isolated desires) as most of your great prophets, sages, and saints have done.

To seek a more generous and compassionate understanding of those whom (from your remote tribal perspectives) you've feared for so long, as being so different and hence so unequally aberrant from yourselves.

These suggestions have all been derided as the naïve fantasies of do-gooders (at best), throughout much of your overly contained tribal histories, haven't they? By a *disjoined* worldview . . . constricted by incestuous logic and layered with centuries of tribal superstition.

Although we do admit that there's a gradual cost to going down the nonviolent path—which we are not only inviting you into without apology, but we also are proposing it to be the categorical and costly path that you will soon begin to take your first unacquainted steps upon—first thing tomorrow morning. And you can be damn sure of that.

Be patient. The path of self-discipline that leads to God-realization is not an easy path; obstacles and sufferings are on the path; the latter you must bear, the former overcome—all by his help. His help comes only through concentration. Repetition of God's name helps concentration [sic], wrote the wise Swami Ramdas.[1]

The path of the *bodhisattva* (one who is motivated, by compassion and love, to release not only himself/herself from suffering . . . and to attain enlightenment, but to do the same for all sentient beings) is not a lenient path to follow, is it?[2]

Perhaps that's why the prophets and sages are given those titles.

They've suffered and died along that path.

And it always takes a certain amount of courage and evolving self-knowledge to reach out beyond the violent conventional wisdom of the tribe, doesn't it? In order to demonstrate that boundaries and loyalties are designed to be crossed and broken and to be transcended in favor of unconditional justice and love . . . regardless of the risk and always in favor of *the least of these*, as the ever-so-wise crucified son of the carpenter (a true *bodhisattva*) more than once advised and demonstrated, along with the many other boundary-breaking transmissions he performed.[3]

Many of you almost seem repulsed by the idea of seeking to deepen and expand your own self-conscious awareness. So you stave off or quickly invalidate any inviting, unexpected, or unique moment of bliss which tempts you to wake up or which entices you to enter into the dark, cavernous, and danger-filled mystery of *That which is hidden* from your *disjoined* perception.

In its place you defend and praise the self-proclaimed supreme qualities of your objectified tribal gods and ideologies—which are always dependent upon their symbiotic relationship with a dictatorial tribal logic and with a cult of followers who are willing to embrace their ingrained loyalties with an unforgiving vengeance.

Hence, many of you feel an intense need to highlight your group's accomplishments, don't you? To anoint yourselves with the inbred rituals of the self-isolating tribe, rituals which are fashioned by an evangelical system of informational disguise and which are driven by the aristocratic desires of the ruling (inner and outer) elite—which extols and pretends to revere its recruited ranks of converted conscripts who willingly yet frantically defend the tribe's *disjoined* version of self-indulgent memory and morality, all of whom together personify patriotic tribal gods of greater and lesser extent and influence . . . who bless and justify any war made against any transgressing *otherness*, blessing and justifying any act of violence performed in defense of the glorified mission of the tribal *only-mind*.

And most of you wildly or passively approve of that hostile tribal agenda, don't you? Proudly or fearfully endorsing or even craving for more of the same cavalier violence which is so prevalent in an overly contained culture where every last straw of self-worshiping tribal publicity is collectively desired and automatically believed.

And you just can't seem to get enough of it, can you? Which may actually account for the fact that your global expenditure on all of that tribal *defense* (which is one of your favorite euphemisms—more accurately defined as massive profiteering by way of organized murder) has crossed the 1.7 billion U.S. dollar mark . . .[4] and is still rising. While your own United Nations reports that a mere speck of that amount (a $40 billion increase in funding)[5] could feed and clothe and educate the entire globe. But you don't do it. You don't even pay much attention to it, do you?

But let's get back to the warrior-worship thing for a moment, shall we? And to all that it seems to excite and elicit in so many of you.

According to a 2001 study done by your highly regarded International Committee of the Red Cross, the civilian-to-soldier death ratio in wars fought since the midtwentieth century has been 10:1—meaning ten civilian deaths for every soldier death.[6] We don't see that anything much has changed since then, do you?

And this is what gets you so worked up and aroused? This is what soldiers are trained for? This produces admirable warriors? This is what they consist of? This is what they're supposed to do?

This is a good thing?

This is why all of your military parades proudly show off all those big smiling priapic weapons?

The blood and suffering of curled-up and destroyed children is the symbol and result of tribal virility? Is that what you're saying?

The slaughtering of innocents defines a higher moral ground and purpose?

This is what your tribal gods and religions so proudly bless and solemnly justify?

But this is no joke, is it? Even while you simply turn your poorly disguised pronouncements of violence into doctrines of distraction and allegiance, without blinking an eye of embarrassment or remorse about what they really represent.

It's been like that throughout so much of your contemptuous patrilineal history, hasn't it?

Your group identifications, your flags, and your altar cloths have become security blankets and idols of worship in themselves—to kill, to torture, and to lie for.

No one group has ever been able to honestly and completely escape that pattern of *Self*-fragmentation (and the accompanying *Self*-denial).

But a sprinkling of courageous wisdom figures have. Haven't they?

Our bodies don't have just one part. They have many parts. Suppose a foot says, "I'm not a hand, and so I'm not part of the body." Wouldn't the foot still belong to the body? Or suppose an ear says, "I'm not an eye, and so I'm not part of the body." Wouldn't the ear still belong to the body? If our bodies were only an eye, we couldn't hear a thing. And if they were only an ear, we couldn't smell a thing . . . A body isn't really a body, unless there is more than one part. It takes many parts to make a single body. That's why the eyes cannot say they don't need the hands. That's also why the head cannot say it doesn't need the feet. In fact, we cannot get along without the parts of the body that seem to be the weakest . . . If one part of our body hurts, we hurt all over. If one part of our body is honored, the whole body will be happy, wrote the wise Paul of Tarsus.[7]

CHAPTER 27

Resistance to Celebration

N OW BASED ON your own best available scientific measurements, the universe itself first came into being approximately 13.7 billion years ago . . . with what many of you refer to as the big bang.[1] And modern human beings (along with the beginnings of modern human language) entered the arena somewhere between fifty thousand and one hundred thousand years ago.

Quite a gap there. Wouldn't you agree? From when it all got started and to when modern humankind finally began to manifest beside the rest of creation (which was already settled in and evolving).

Earliest human picture writing symbols arrived somewhere near 6,600 BC.

Earliest writing systems . . . somewhere near 3,400 to 3,200 BC.

Earliest coherent texts . . . somewhere near 2,600 BC.

The late wise scientist Carl Sagan developed something that he called the *Cosmic Calendar* in order to help to explain this (quite interesting) history of the universe. So let's, very briefly, explore a few things with it. Shall we?[2]

If you were to compress the entire history of the universe into one year, with each month representing a little over a billion years, you human beings would have shown up at about 10:30 p.m. on December 31—on the last day of the year.

The Earth itself wouldn't have been formed until September 14.

Life on Earth? September 25.

Sex would not be invented until November 1—by microorganisms.

Now let's move quickly forward to December 31 again . . . to the last day of the Cosmic Year.

Cave paintings show up about 11:59 p.m.

The invention of the alphabet? About 11:59:51 p.m.

The birth of Siddhartha Gautama Buddha? About 11:59:55.

The birth of Jesus of Nazareth? About 11:59:56.

That which is always becoming began to be given a name by you Homo sapiens pretty late in the tribal game, don't you think?

After all, you just got here only a few cosmic seconds ago, didn't you? Unless, of course, you're in the addicted group of big bang and evolution deniers. But then you won't be able to hear any of what we've been saying until tomorrow morning anyway. And unfortunately you'll then be getting a late start, doing most of your initial listening through your first new face with its new ears, which may take a few more faces and several more pairs of ears than you could ever presently imagine . . . in order to get to the deeper listening.

But for those of you who are able to hear clear enough right now, does that mean that the unifying and infinite *Self* didn't exist before you came up with a name for it, with your many names for it? Or that it didn't exist before it manifested and revealed itself to you, in the many ways that it has, which has led so many of you to bring forth a way to try to name and to call out to it, to somehow try to capture it?

Ask, and it will be given to you, search, and you will find, knock, and the door will be opened to you, emphasized the wise Jesus to his disciples.[3]

So does that mean that once a door is opened to you that you're supposed to then stop asking questions? And are you then required to stop seeking? To stop knocking? Are you even obliged to stop evolving? To stop creating?

Does that mean that once a door is unlocked that you are then duty bound to hastily walk through it? And then to quickly shut it behind yourselves? And to secure yourselves in that one tribal room for the rest of your entire life?

Is that what he was getting at? A game of finders keepers, losers weepers? And then that's the end of it? That life just stops right there in its tribal tracks? That there's nothing left to see or to become aware of after you open that first door? That there's no compassionate loving-kindness which can be deepened or expanded upon? That Jesus, and his words (like so many *others*), becomes just another lifeless and idolized statue, to lock up and protect in a tightly controlled and contained tribal storage room (and isn't that what many of your church buildings have become)? And that his teachings become stillborn, finite, and self-enclosed? Packed away safely beneath piles of tribal language and ritual? Never again allowed to breathe? That the only asking, seeking, and knocking which is then allowed anymore is within the confines of the tribal container? The one which you happen to find yourselves locked inside of? That any asking, seeking, or knocking is only permitted within its established and isolated tribal boundaries of interpretation? Is that what he meant?

What was the unifying and boundless *Self* doing all those billions of years before you entered the picture anyway? What was it doing before the universe existed? Was it not observing? And not speaking? And not breathing? And not being present anywhere? And not *It-Self* emerging and evolving until you got here?

Who was it that was fighting over and demanding the strict adherence to territorial boundaries (or to superior religious and political belief systems) before you arrived?

Nobody was.

They didn't exist until you made them up . . . when soon after you gradually allowed yourselves to get stuffed and stuck inside and behind their containing walls.

Many of you seem to base the existence and reality of the inmost *Self* (as you claim to believe in it and name it) on your own meager existence and experience. Are you then saying that if no human being ever existed in order to name *That which is always becoming* (or to experience it) that it would not exist? None of it? That it didn't exist before you existed? Before you could name it?

Did you not exist until you were named?

Did Christ consciousness (or the consciousness of Christ) not exist before Jesus so fully embodied and illuminated it?

Did Buddhahood not exist before Siddhartha Gautama so fully embodied and illuminated it?

Did the theory of relativity not exist before Albert Einstein imagined and then discovered it?[4]

Did the Earth remain flat as a card table until Hellenistic astronomy first established the fact of a spherical planet?[5]

Does the changeless and abiding *Self* not exist before it can be embodied and illuminated? Or before it can be named? By you? Only by you? Not as anyone else may experience it?

Is the boundless *Self* so small, fatigued, and inhibited that it will only speak the truth through you? Or more specifically . . . only through your tribe? Or even more specifically . . . only to and through your official tribal mouthpiece?

The epithet may change, alter, be replaced, or be retranslated. It may sound different, depending on the language spoken or the person hearing it. The name may disappear, be forgotten, or cease to continue to be relevant or meaningful to many in your world. It may even be ridiculed, turned into an object of idolatry, warred over, manipulated, misused, or banned.

But the reality of the *Great* hidden *Self* will still be there—as it always has been and as it always will be.

You do not control it by claiming to have exclusive rights to its name or even to its namelessness or to the entrance into any special room which you've constructed to keep it contained and defined by the image and likeness which you've trapped it in through the narrow perception of the tribal *only-mind*.

But the paradoxical equation also includes this, yes? That the *Great Self* is revealed and expressed through its emergence out of what it embodies. And what it embodies becomes its cocreator and its corevealer, its cocelebrant and its coevolutionist.

Yet the tribal *only-mind* still persists in its self-delusions, doesn't it? In its chronic and futile attempts to find some way to destroy *That which is always emerging* by continuing to maximize the pressure of its constricting containment.

But it can't be done, can it?

The uncontainable *Self* can never be destroyed nor can it ever be confined . . . as the last 13.7 billion years have clearly shown.

It can only be denied.

The universe must be experienced as the Great Self. Each is fulfilled in the other: the Great Self is fulfilled in the individual self, the individual self is fulfilled in the Great Self. Alienation is overcome as soon as we experience this surge of energy from the source that has brought the universe through the centuries. New fields of energy become available to support the human venture. These new energies find expression and support in celebration. For in the end the universe can only be explained in terms of celebration. It is all an exuberant expression of existence itself, wrote the wise Thomas Berry.[6]

Let us make humankind in our image, to be like us. Let them be stewards of the fish in the sea, the birds of the air, the cattle, the wild animals, and everything that crawls on the ground. Humankind was created as God's reflection: in the divine image God created them; female and male, God made them, spoke the wise voice from the Hebrew scriptures.[7]

In the beginning there was the Word; the Word was in God's presence, and the Word was God. The Word was present to God from the beginning. Through the Word all things came into being, and apart from the Word nothing came into being that has come into being. In the Word was life, and that life was humanity's light—Light that shines in the darkness, a Light that the darkness has never overtaken, spoke the wise voice from the New Testament.[8]

O mankind! We created you from a single soul, male and female, and made you into nations and tribes, so that you may come to know one another. Truly, the most honored of you in God's sight is the greatest of you in piety, spoke the wise voice from the Q'uran.[9]

And while I stood there I saw more than I can tell and I understood more than I saw; for I was seeing in a sacred manner the shapes of all things in the spirit, and the shape of all shapes as they must live together like one being, spoke the wise Black Elk, Holy Man of the Oglala Lakota (Sioux)[10]

Yet many of you keep feeding your spiritual tongue with poisonous tribal pap, as you keep breathing poisonous tribal fumes into your spiritual lungs . . . while keeping a blinded watch, closing your eyes to the *One cosmic perception,* holding your breath against the *One changeless inspiration,* and sealing your mouth off from the *One unifying taste.*

You attempt to block your spiritual passageways with as many *disjoining* concoctions as you can get away with, to keep gorging on the tribal formulas which you've become so addicted to and of which you've allowed yourselves to be consumed by.

Much of it is what you call religion or patriotism or a worldview or an ethnic group . . . even family. You even fragment your blood ties into rankings of worthiness—of distorted tribal shapes and colors.

So much of it is eating you alive, and yet you still fail to recognize not only what you're being swallowed up by . . . but that you're being swallowed up at all.

Instead, you stigmatize and condescend with exaggerated assertions that you make to and about each *other,* claiming that your tribe owns the only honest-to-god interpretations of what is true in your diminutive world, hoisting up your banner of tribal separation along with its symbols of opposition and its fading tint of tyrannical tribal belief, attempting to undo any trace of a unifying *Ground of Universal Being* (without which nothing would exist).

You seem to have more self-deceptive ways than you can shake a tribal stick at (to borrow a colloquial phrase), don't you? While trying so desperately hard to mislead and contain yourselves (and *others*, of course).

And it's quite amazing to watch.

It really is.

Your arms never even seem to get a bit tired either from all of that constant shaking.

And you never run out of sticks.

It really is quite amazing to watch.

It really is.

CHAPTER 28

Either/Or and *Both/And*

MANY OF YOU automatically denigrate anyone who even reluctantly confesses to waking up into *That which is always evolving*, don't you? As some kind of nontribal outlander, or as a defiant alien who leans too dangerously forward into the heretical realm of noncompliant *otherness*, or as an uninvited guest who embraces a disparaged new-age superstition of some kind, as a foreigner who intrudes from well beyond the walls of tribal orthodoxy, a trespasser too unconventional to allow within the container of your exclusionary tribal belief systems.

So whenever you do come into contact with any such unbearable visitors, you tend to either deny their existence or to demonize them, don't you? Or to quickly shift your tribal attention back to the language of your chosen and frozen orthodoxy.

Is any of this sounding at all familiar?

But what is pronounced to be orthodox doesn't automatically come right out of the freezer like a newborn, does it? Someone has to put it in there first, don't they? And it's usually the one who owns and controls the appliances, isn't it? And what is authorized as a truism must first and foremost serve the needs of the tribe that empowers it, yes?

If it doesn't, then it loses its cozy, comfortable little corner in the orthodox freezer right behind the sanctioned tray of tribal ice cubes, doesn't it?

The same thing can be said of citizenship or even of marriage and friendship sometimes, or of an all-consuming economic system like predatory capitalism or stultifying communism, can't it? Any lopsided relationship or membership in a tribe of more than one can usually adapt these rules to their own selfish desires with even the most rudimentary use of tribal logic and manipulation.

Whoever owns and controls the tribal appliances most always has the upper hand when it comes to making the rules about who to freeze out or who to freeze in, don't they?

So here's our advice. The less you depend on appliances the better—period. And there's actually a way to not only survive, but even to prosper without being overly dependent upon them. Although certain Earthly contraptions are not entirely unnecessary while you continue carrying on as planet inhabitants. We'll give you that.

Yet most things usually don't need to be frozen, do they? They do just fine out in the open air and under the cleansing light and heat of the sun, where they're allowed to grow or to be seen for what they really are—not for what you've frozen them into.

But whenever you do favor the freeze in or freeze-out approach to things, you tend to circle the wagons, don't you? And then you tend to increase the intensity and hostility of your tribal tone of voice—which seems to be a rather common mode to automatically fall into, doesn't it? Especially when you're faced with a little too strong of an unforseen dose of *That which is always unfolding*. The *disjoined* tribal *only-mind* can't seem to respond calmly enough to such surprises, not without lashing out at something that it can quickly sink its sharp and violent teeth into.

The more monkeys that dance inside and even outside your head, the less you have to feel or to deal with any of that vital life force which resonates out of the ubiquitous *Self*—which is life *It-Self,* of course.

But then there are still plenty of you who just dismiss *That which is uncontainable* as nothing spiritual or mysterious at all, aren't there? As something which has no real presence but instead is interpreted as something related to brain frequencies or to occasional chemical misfirings, or to naturally occurring phenomena connected to one's internal physiological or neurological wiring, or as merely the result of unmet psychological or emotional needs.

Despite the imperfect evidence.

Despite the imperfect (diverse) yet parallel practices which emerge from within what has been called the *Perennial Philosophy* by the wise Aldous Huxley, among many others[1]—which exude with repeated and reconfirming evidence of the unity and inclusion of all things, of individuals and of whole communities, inviting them into direct (evolutionary) experience, into the imperfect practice of extending and enfolding themselves with compassion, kindness, and forgiveness.

Despite the observed imperfect examples of individual clarity and transformation, of imperfect stillness and silence, of joyous and grateful presence and of imperfect dedication, of imperfect practitioners and seers, and of discipline and wisdom passed down from imperfect elders.

Despite the imperfect reports of revelation and wonder from those who've immersed themselves into the goodness and truth and beauty of the natural world.

Despite the imperfect evidence of shamanic wisdom and intuitive healing powers found everywhere from Siberia to Yangon and from Arizona to Ecuador.[2]

Despite the imperfect narratives and the revelatory rites of passage experienced and described by so many among the Native American tribes who have passed through the awakening *vision quest.*[3]

Despite the imperfect stories told of the *Dreamtime* myths, of the mystical travels and of the demonstrated psychic powers of the Australian aboriginal people (the Koori).[4]

Despite the enlightened teachings and imperfectly inspired and transformed lives of the saints, sages, and prophetic wisdom figures found in all of your world's most grounded yet imperfect Wisdom Traditions.

Despite centuries of divinely inspired imperfect poetry and art and exploration and music; and of literature, dance, athletics, and theater; and of the unfolding enchantment of *That which is beheld* through spontaneous scientific discovery.

Despite the spiritual energy and direction which has driven so many into their imperfect works of compassion and mercy and into their imperfect acts of sacrificial love while embracing (social, economic, political, and environmental) works of justice.

Despite the many trained and untrained but imperfect individuals who've attested to having endured a state of nondual (enlightened) awareness; or an aha moment or two of blissful revelation; or of divine union; to moving through higher, deeper, and more expansive levels of progressive awakening—into unrepressed waves of unconditional love for *others*; for *other* human beings and for *other* than human beings; and for *That which is the all-embracing Self.*

Despite the development of imperfect spiritual disciplines which have awakened, inspired, and liberated the hearts of so many throughout the millennia . . . through a wise and discerning ancestry of imperfect yet dedicated souls.

Despite the imperfect faith, hope, and love of millions of (loud to quiet) men and women who discern that there is *That which is beyond knowing* (but which somehow knows)—within all things, visible and invisible.

MICHAEL J. GAJDA

Despite all the imperfect yet verifiable testimonies accumulated through personal observation and experience by so many persistent fringe dwellers in so many varied ways, to the ever-present interweaving reality of *That which is all loving*.

Despite all the imperfect evidence presented . . . there are still those who tend to clump *That which points* to the inmost and unifying *Self* together with that which does not—together with that which points instead to the *disjoined* one.[2]

They clump together *That which points* to authentic inner (and outer) harmony . . . with fraudulent religious sideshows, or with bloodthirsty extremists, with self-adoring religiosity, and with vengeful hijackers of Tradition (which is especially evident in the Abrahamic Tradition)— who loudly plead with their tribal gods for public validation and for (always more) perishable rewards, including a materialistic vision of an afterlife, and who even pray for violent victories over unconverted enemies of *otherness*.

They clump together *That which is beyond complete understanding* . . . with humorless and closed-off (fundamentalist) thinking, with co-opted and power-hungry religious hierarchies and with cults of comfortable religious conformity.

They clump together *That which includes everything* (without exception) together . . . with a religious status quo that defends and gives its blessing to the prevailing motives and desires of whatever tribal nation-state it finds itself protected by or overidentified with; with the avoidance and lies which dismiss and detest honest religious institutional self-criticism; and with hostile defenders of rigid self-virtuous dogma over and against charitable love, fairness, and reason.

They clump together *That which is embodied as an awakening presence* . . . with the adoration of idols, with the demeaning of intelligence and common sense, with magical thinking, with a god conceptualized as a magician (as a god of tricks), with guilt and shame mongers, with cult-leader worship, and with institutionalized and organized cults of tribal abnormality.

They clump together *That which is grounded in goodness, truth, and beauty* . . . with escapist flights from reality; with churchiness and public piety; with the elevation of attendance; and with the robotic following of rules over and against justice, mercy, and compassion.

They clump together *That which practices nonviolent and compassionate loving-kindness* . . . with the unashamed cover-up of clerical or guru sexual abuse of young men, women, and children (for hundreds of years) and with the suppression of the wholeness of women (for hundreds of years).

They clump together *That which is gratefully hope filled and patient* . . . with radio and TV money changers of sensation, with the organizers of contemporary hate-filled tribal religion, and with deniers of science and of facts and of experience and of the discerning intellect.

They clump together *That which is courageously still and silent* . . . with the fear of and blind obedience to self-appointed religious authorities, with the images of a violent god; with justified war, with patriarchal gods of separation, with religions of exclusion and arrogance, and with the self-righteous emphasis on outer appearances.

They clump together *That which cocreates and coevolves* . . . with false gods of stolen wealth, of tribal divisiveness, and of retribution.

And many of you just join right in with the clumping, don't you? Clumping together all of *That which is beyond understanding* (yet is always becoming) with that which is not, clumping it all together as one big brain-dead heap of conjured-up mush—without distinction.

But is there really no worldly or spiritual difference between the likes of Badshah Khan of Afghanistan,[5] with his demonstrated bravery, leadership, and guidance of a truly nonviolent army, and the vengeful and cowardly religious violence of Osama Bin Laden?[6]

Between the dedication and humanitarian work of Albert Schwietzer[7] and the violent antigovernment militia religion of Timothy McVeigh?[8]

Between the beauty brought into the world by the genius and creativity of Hildegard of Bingen[9] and the priestly, violent, and ugly oratory of Father Charles Coughlin?[10]

Between the moral conscience and courageous wisdom of Rabbi Abraham Heschel[11] and the robed, hooded, and gutless violence embedded in the burning cross of the Ku Klux Klan?[12]

Between the audacious and planet healing work of Wangari Maathai[13] and the spineless child abduction and terrorizing brutality of Joseph Kony of the Lord's Resistance Army?[14]

Between the intelligence, benevolence, and forgiveness shown by His Holiness the Dalai Lama[15] and the misogynist cruelty and proud religious ignorance of the Taliban?[16]

Between the compassionate spread of unity consciousness demonstrated by Paramahansa Yogananda[17] and the harsh, ideological, and dictatorial oppression of Mao Tse Tung?[18] (Communism, or Maoism, like capitalism, has often been followed and revered by so many of you as just another overly contained tribal religion, has it not?)

Between the dedicated and empowering work with the developmentally disabled by Jean Vanier and the L'Arche community[19] and the white-collared criminal violence of mercantile religion, which worships beneath the flag of its jingoistic greed—where it shields, rationalizes, and excuses the fraudulent crimes of impunity committed by the ordained clergy of Wall Street?[20]

Is this all just one big interchangeable clump of Tweedledum and Tweedledee?

We think not.

Are there not multiple perspectives to see and act from? Some with more depth? Some with more expanse? Some stuck? And some deepening and widening? Some open? And some closed? Some exploring? Some refusing to look? Some freeing up? Some tightening down? Some being present to *That which actually is*? And some trapped in their own heap of tribal noise?

Is it just about who can best manipulate the mental objects floating around in your heads? Inside the tribal *only-mind*?

Is that what it is?

Or is it about trying to point to and experience the marriage of the human with the divine, to the mystery of *That which is everywhere* and which is always evolving (yet is paradoxically changeless), and to the incomprehensible and inexpressible unity within and of all things?

But it's so much easier to simply conceptualize the *Self*, isn't it? To nail it down somehow to your tribal liking, to wrap it up into an airtight philosophical theory or into a final anthropological or cultural interpretation, into a supremely revealed theology or into an incontestable scientific conclusion, into a simple-minded doctrine of obedience or into an arrogant and superior claim of incredulity—instead of staying open to *Its* ever-present light from wherever it shines . . . whether it be through science, culture, or religion; or through animals, plants, or humans; or through spousal or parental love; or through friendship, community, or work; or through exploration, art, or poetry; or through silence or noise; or through light or darkness; or through touch, smell, or taste.

To be able to see.

To be gratefully aware.

To be present and to be awake.

It forever tests the powers of discernment, doesn't it? To have the courage to wander along those uncertain edges and to stroll up next to the paradoxical, the ineffable, and the harmonious . . . as they all stand there beside each other in perfect yet incomprehensible unity, to walk between inclusion and exclusion, between up and down and in and out and there and not there, between what is and what is not, between the obvious and the obscure.

To balance your stride between the worldly and the spiritual, between the experiential and the unexplainable, between the confounding and the clear, between the letting go and the keeping, between the engaged and the withdrawn, between sinister shadows and illuminating light, between suffering and freedom.

To move cautiously between knowledge, the unknown, and the unknowing; and between deep dreamless sleep, the symbolic and lucid dream world, and the clarity of waking up.

To navigate the path that never seems to end, but can only deepen and widen into *That which is always becoming*.

But to experience what is real, you must let go of the unreal. Isn't that so? But not just in your observed and reproducible external experiments (which are of great scientific and aesthetic value), but also in what you can watch and repeat from within your own inner laboratory, in your own daily living and in what you see, create, and experience for yourselves.

They work hand in hand actually, don't they? In mind and heart and in thought and no thought, in the mind that is still . . . and in the heart that is unclouded.

It's never to be found in any of your either/or disputes, which merely keep you chained to your own fabricated tribal assumptions—which leads to even more discord and isolation and which only makes it more difficult to liberate yourselves from the glue of tribal logic while trying to prevent any uncorrupted beginner's mind from emerging.

In the beginner's mind there are many possibilities; in the expert's mind there are few, wrote the wise Suzuki Roshi.[21]

Although we do acknowledge that evidence of either/or properties plainly exists in your macroscopic universe.

We know that they do.

The world of Newtonian physics makes that very clear,[22] doesn't it? The law of gravity is necessarily real. You need to know and follow certain observable laws of physical science in order to physically survive, don't you? Any human being who tries to jump off the ledge of a skyscraper or out the door of an airplane (without a working parachute) will not be able to fly. That's a nonsuperman fact. So don't try it. If you ignore the law of gravity, it may very well be your last act of daredevil ignorance.

But the reality of an either/or dimension is not a closed-ended absolute condition covering all of existence, is it? Newtonian concepts and realities do not fit well into the quantum realm or in the invisible realm of the spirit, or in the realm which is beyond material observation (beyond complete understanding).

That which is always becoming is inexhaustible, remember? It exceeds yet includes the world of the either/or, expanding and deepening into an infinite and integrated (both/and) fusion of release . . . of exploration and of integral acceptance, which will soon lead us into our discussion of the necessity of a disciplined practice (of seeing, of living, and of being)—which is actually another promise that we can assure you of.

But either way, starting tomorrow morning, you will all be dealt a rarely used and mixed deck of select experience to participate in.

And whether you play the hand that your dealt (or not) will still be your own choice, as always.

You can count on it.

CHAPTER 29

That Which Cannot Be Captured

WHAT YOU ARE soon to be presented with is a tough thing to suddenly consider, let alone to realize and take part in without adequate and proper preparation—which in so many words is what we are now endeavoring to introduce and furnish you with.

You will just have to trust us on that as we move the endeavor along.

But we're not here to protect you from yourselves.

Far from it.

We'll try to highlight the paradoxical vistas as they emerge throughout our presentation. But even then, you may not even recognize or actually see what we're pointing to. That's apparently why they're normally (and sparingly) given in glimpses.

They can be quite alarming to behold in their full essence, especially when so many of you have spent so much of your lives choosing to (consciously or unconsciously) confine or even entomb them behind your outer impersonations.

Almost all of you have been trained and conditioned to lay eyes upon so little of what is real, haven't you? Instead you spend much of your invested energy trying to prove that only one part of it (your particular part) is by itself the only proof of existing intelligence and of evidential experience which is even necessary. And as we've already emphasized, you've mistaken the road for the destination, the path for the endpoint.

But we have to admit that you've built and maintained some well-fortified roads and some real hazardous and narrow ones too, haven't you?

And so . . . whenever you've happened upon a sporadic spark or even a full electrifying current of *That which is always becoming* (which you've done periodically), it's usually been by stumbling upon it, hasn't it? By forgetting to cling to the tribal *only-mind* for one split (nondistracted) second and then by abruptly letting go of it without even realizing what you've done, by being unprepared for what it was that you were falling into you, when you may have suddenly felt the unexpected heat left upon your skin by grace, love, or suffering (the trio of internal and external shock troops) which usually sneaks up on you . . . just like that, surprising any desired capacity that you may have for egoic control or prediction, blinding you into a quick forgetfulness and from any lasting apprehension of how, why, or who it is that just arrived into your conscious view—even while for that one split second you thought you may have recognized who you actually were.

But that's what makes them such worthy shock troops. Don't you see? They don't force their remembrance upon anyone. They leave it up to your own paradoxical discovery.

But many of you become so easily confused (and even panicked) by the surprising lack of tribal exactness found in the approximate *Self*, don't you? Confused by its feel of indefinable permanence . . . beneath and beyond the impermanent playing field, which is where most of you perform and compete from, where you pose as if you're the only players that really matter, while holding tight to all of your tribal attachments so as not to be peeled away from them, readying yourselves to quickly latch back onto the tribal *only-mind*—if and when worse comes to worse.

You've so often tried to nail the *Self* down ahead of time, which, as you know (but make believe not to know), just doesn't work. Its lack of a specified method of arrival or of mental hoop-jumping logic has nothing solid which will hold nails to it or for nails to hold down—which is a hint of an explanation to what resurrection is all about.

But we're sure you can recall some of those spare moments of wonderment that have come to you without explanation and which you knew held something real to themselves, those moments which can't be captured or restrained (try as you might)—even as you so quickly escape them.

You'll never find *That which is always becoming* by trying to force fit it into laws or doctrines or by gymnastically intellectualizing yourselves there. But most of you among the invited haven't abandoned that tribal strategy yet, have you?

Much of this you will just have to struggle through for however long it takes, just like the eventually wise Jonah did . . . trapped and then spit out from within the wisdom trip he reluctantly stomached, from inside the whale who may have been more surprised than Jonah himself was by the whole ordeal.[1]

Meanwhile, we'll try to provide you with the appropriate and cautionary clues relevant to your task.

But you can't see what you won't see, can you? That's an indisputable fact.

Your eyes will only open up when you have enough faith behind them, when your heart unties itself in the depth of your being, enough to begin to take on the task of realizing who you really are, not who you're supposed to be or who you want to be, or who you think you are or who you act like or imitate, or who others say you are, or even who you remember yourselves to be.

But who you really are.

Beyond name and form; beyond the senses; inexhaustible; without beginning; without end; beyond time, space, or causality; eternal; immutable, repeats the wise Katha Upanishad.[2]

That's when the uncovering will begin to unravel your disorder, when you'll be awakened by your own inmost witness, and when you'll begin to see just how stuck you really were before the unraveling began.

But like poorly disguised attempts to appear as though one has ascended into adulthood (by simply completing a checklist of tribal requirements), merely dressing yourselves up in what you hope to be a correct enough costume (or even in the razzle-dazzle wisdom of Solomon himself) won't ever get you to realize *That which is always becoming,*[3] will it?

It doesn't happen from the outside in, but rather from the inexpressible concurrence with the inside-out—as you already know.

First clean the inside of the cup and the plate, that the outside also may be clean, summoned the wise Nazarene.[4]

CHAPTER 30

The Loss of the In-Between

WHEN THE OUTER is cut off from the inner, when one is split from the *other*, when this separates from that . . . an illusive wall of divide goes up, splitting you wide open . . . one by one and then into tribal divisions, unhinging perception into dualistic extremes—between stark colors of black and white.

Gray vanishes. Doubt is held in solitary confinement. And all you're left with are tribal certitudes to defend and to substantiate. It's all you can see. There are no shades or gradations. There is no middle ground. And there is no in-between. There is only this or that, us or them.

Black and white becomes either/or while either/or becomes all or nothing, rejecting the mystery of self-inquiry and of actual and unmediated (evolutionary) experience, rejecting the mystery in the *other*.

Cardboard loyalties are propped up at opposite ends of the field with oversimplifications, leading to easy violence, to rationalized retributions sanctioned by the tribal logic of the either/or nature (and *disjoined* personality) of the *only-mind.*

And without nuance there's no enlightening uncertainty to enter into, is there?

There's no instructive ambiguity to ponder.

There's no protective compassion for the so-called *other.*

There's no empathic boundary to prevent you from crossing over into the realm of violence.

There's no genuine or expansive curiosity.

There's no liberating *Self*-realization.

There's no ocean of wonder to immerse yourselves into.

There's no unconditional love to exchange.

Instead . . . love becomes contingent, doesn't it?

The capacity for violence expands . . . spreading easily, becoming almost effortless to justify.

Illusion rises up and is amplified by the easing, producing even more attachment to the frozen logic of tribal certainties.

With more certainties to defend, more victims are chopped down in defense of the illusion.

The value of the *other* diminishes even more.

The mystery of doubt is solved by the addiction to the tribal drug of choice.

To the logic of the either/or.

To the black or white.

To the all or nothing.

To this or that.

To the logic of separation.

To either you're with us—or you're with them.

The inability to identify with others was unquestionably the most important psychological condition for the fact that something like Auschwitz could have occurred in the midst of more or less civilized and innocent people, wrote the wise Theodor Adorno.[1]

CHAPTER 31

The Fallacy of Perfection

IMITATION DOES NOT equal transformation.

It merely equals imitation (until you let go of it), if it was indeed needed as a kick-start in the first place, as it sometimes is—which is quite okay, for starters.

But even a kick-ass kick-start still leaves it up to you to put it into gear, doesn't it? And to then begin to move in one direction or another instead of languishing while waiting for extraneous permission or to be psychologically strong-armed into a comforting and comfortable obedience.

It seems to be an obvious and ultimately dangerous waste of time and energy to rely upon just sitting there, doesn't it? While revving up your spiritual engine and stalling out in neutral until you simply run out of gas—as you wait to be rescued or to be given orders for what to do next.

Yet so many of you seem to do just *that*, don't you? Until you find something or someone else to copy or conform to, when predictably even they eventually gas out for you too, in the long haul . . . or even in the short run of it.

Even so, many of you just continue to stay put . . . fastened to your overly contained tribal machinations, pretending that you're still cruising along on your own accord, like nobody's business, until some externalized authority figure gives you the okay sign to proceed—which you've come to internalize as something which you must patiently wait upon, after months or even years of conforming to tribal expectations.

And only then do you cautiously move . . . but usually just to a different spot on the same frozen topography, inside the same cultural space that you remain embedded in. And the more you get used to it, the smaller the map of your whereabouts seems to get—and the more compressed the tribal view becomes.

After a while you don't even need to turn the ignition key, do you? You've found perfect pleasure in staying right where you are—perfectly fed, protected, and contained.

Meanwhile, we can assume (without risking too much) that even a microscopic increase of compassionate, kind, and empathic behavior couldn't hurt, could it?

But it's got very little to do with impressing anybody else with an impeccable outer reflection, of which well-connected tribal adherents may loudly approve of . . . or may even want to associate themselves with.

The perfect is the enemy of the good, reminds the wise François-Marie Arouet de Voltaire.[1]

CHAPTER 32

The Art of Paying Attention

GOD'S WORD IS this. He who strives never perishes. I have implicit faith in that promise, wrote the wise Mahatma Gandhi.[1]

Disciplined, passionate, and intentional practice (paying attention) could have helped you immensely before it had to come down to tomorrow morning's facial rite of passage.

And it can still help to move the process of transformation along—which can appear to be contradictory when it really isn't; hence the paradox.

Genuine practice of the kind we're talking about has nothing to do with accessing the ostensible holy trinity in your world—of power, prestige, and possessions. It's got nothing to do with that kind of tribal conditioning and duty which you've become so accustomed to and where you've generally appeased some likely combination of that profane troika of addictions, which has become your sacred triad of attraction and arousal . . . determining how and where you move inside the tribal milieu while cementing itself into the centerfold of your psychological and spiritual universe.

This will soon become evident, but gradually . . . as we move the conversation along.

And when you are eventually able to realize *That which is always becoming* . . . well, then you will simply wake up enough to clearly see who you've wrongly perceived as the *other*.

You will realize then that there really is no *other* (whether human or *other* than human) . . . as we will continue to suggest.

All is one, as it always has been. Don't you see? Yet it is *not* one either, is it?

But (currently) most of you are quite removed from that paradoxical realization, aren't you?

And until you get there, it may feel and sound like you're just another dinged-and-scratched pinball being paddled about in some disorienting *other* world, similar to how it often feels now, for many of you.

But this is not a game, is it? As we'll keep reminding you.

And there will be plenty of work for you to do, starting tomorrow morning. Although you won't have to fill out any job applications for any of it. There will be no tribal unemployment lines.

Everyone is hired, right on the spot. No face will be turned away.

So you can have at it, as you will.

You'll be presented with loads of opportunities to reawaken and sharpen up any of your hibernating skills of *Self*-knowledge or of any repressed compassion for the vast kingdom of creatures who share your small planet (among *other* surprises)—once you get to the other side.

In any event, we sincerely wish you the best of luck, from this moment forward. And we really do mean that. You have our blessings, no matter how you may assess or respond to what we're attempting to flesh out for your instructional benefit.

Our goal is to immerse you into the relevant and necessary information (gradually and responsibly), which will lead you up to and into the targeted event. If we can do that in good order, we will have done our job.

And even though the past is the past (as they say), disquieting and even disturbing stuff will likely still rise up inside of you as we disclose the ways and means of what has led you to this point of arduous departure and of what you can expect to run into when the floodgates finally open up tomorrow morning.

So just be aware of that.

Okay?

CHAPTER 33

Watchfulness

YOU MAY BEGIN to remember things, the many things that you've stuffed away for what may seem like very practical reasons, but perhaps not for the intrinsic and abiding nourishment of yourselves or for much of the rest of the planet either . . . for that matter.

And when memories do arise during our presentation (and they will), don't worry about them. But don't merely remember them either. Watch them. Allow them to be absorbed. And then gently let them go . . . while you slowly come back to paying attention to what we're trying to prepare you for.

This practice will be invaluable in steering you toward a successful transition back into your unique (but interrelated) reembodiments.

Whatever you have difficulty letting go of (in the watching) will suggest a possible and problematic inner struggle, involving shadowy egoic forces vying for control of your internal command center—which you're more than likely to encounter when you wake up into your arrival on the other side.

And the less you're able to let go of what you see (once you get there), the more probable it is that it will become a recurring and vexing pattern—which will undoubtedly hinder you from making steady gains in the process of reawakening and in the reintegration into your real and authentic *Self*.

Again, it's very similar to the way things work on this side of things, yes?

At the very root of most of your habituated opinions, perspectives, and related behaviors are the miscellaneous thoughts and emotions which assume majority control of your operational system, convincing you that they are really you and that you (in unwitting cahoots with them) are the actual causal agent who fashions your very own independent appraisals of what you choose to think, feel, and even desire.

It's a very effective trick.

It works on almost everybody and on almost all levels of intellectual and creative sophistication of the tribal ego, who is (of course) *not* you but who *is* the *disjoined* one—who so often outmaneuvers you for control of your own conspicuous center of discernment.

Quite paradoxical.

Wouldn't you say?

Genius, in truth, means little more than the faculty of perceiving in an inhabitual way, wrote the wise William James.[1]

But we're scarcely beginning to sketch in the edges and the outline of the bigger picture here.

Aren't we?

So we advise you (again) to just patiently listen.

And begin to pick out and practice what seems to be most pertinent to you, from the contents and guidance of our message . . . without discounting any truth, goodness, or beauty which may still be hidden inside the broken space between the spoken word, as it gradually unfolds and begins to reveal itself—starting with your all-important watchfulness and with the letting go.

Beginning right now.

CHAPTER 34

Who's in Charge?

WHEN YOU DO begin to engage in the practice of patiently observing, you'll quickly see who or what has actually been in charge and how difficult it is to let go of their *disjoining* dominance.

But first . . . you'll have to jut yourselves out there (somewhere), won't you? So it might as well be from where you can start to grasp your primal circumstance, which is best begun with a discriminating and disciplined practice of observance . . . even though it will have to be exercised and initiated from within the inelastic fabric of your tribal memory banks.

And what we're talking about here is the urgent need to rearrange the network and the hierarchy of the see-through circuits running through the control system of your internal landscape while making sure not to repress or deny the intermingling influence of the tribal container with all of its spaghetti-like cables of attachments and determinants which have (for the most part) kept you tangled up in a vast *Self*-alienating and alluring paradise full of trivial and transitory desires—which most of you have sadly come to be transfixed and even spiritually impaired by while coming to depend upon them as psychological and social necessities, plopping yourselves down into a fleeting and shallow range of lightweight and quick-to-evaporate emotional states, unrelated to anything even mildly akin to a genuine experience of equanimity, clinging to the addictive and compulsive extremes of the either/or tribal mindset, to the magnetic poles which pull you back and forth in slingshot fashion, keeping the middle range of your interior domain empty and deserted . . . as one vast uninhabited and uninhabitable desert (which we will get to shortly).

So for most of you, right now . . . well . . . let's just say this: You're not in charge.

You never were or have rarely been . . . in actual charge.

You cannot be in charge of what you're scarcely aware of, can you? Or of what you focus so little concentration or attention on.

But remember this: You still can't go back.

We're sure you've heard that before. Yet it remains true.

And the only way forward is . . . well . . . forward, isn't it?

Although we're not talking about a linear or one-dimensional direction here.

This has little or nothing to do with climbing ladders of acquisition or achievement . . . or of accomplishment or attainment, or even of accurately adhering to a particular belief system, which so many of you have put so much energy into . . . epitomized by your habits of calculated speech, and by how you've come to rigidly evaluate and chastise yourselves (but especially each *other*).

Perhaps a better descriptive word or two of what we're trying to convey here would be to describe it as the practice of exploring and scrutinizing the spaciousness of your perceptual realm, in order to shake up and awaken the lethargic grasp that it has of its own capacity for *Self*-awareness, or maybe as that of indulging in that old standby practice of letting go of unnecessary psychological and emotional luggage, or of simply being exactly where and when (and hence who) you are, of returning to your creative center, of paying strict attention (as we've tried to emphasize), or of just trying to wake yourselves up from your spiritual sleep apnea and from its accompanying symptoms, of slowly freeing yourselves up from all of that jitterbugging tribal hyperactivity which tends to dominate the terrain of your already-overcrowded inner dance floor.

You're really not going anywhere, don't you see?

Changing your location, title, clothes, religion, or occupation will affect nothing in particular. Will it? Except to change your location, title, clothes, religion, or occupation.

The same person will still be that same person no matter what exterior alterations he or she may attempt to mask the inmost *Self* with. Isn't that obvious by now?

But dare we propose the practice of . . . surrendering?

Or perhaps there is no word for it.

Perhaps it just is.

Perhaps you'll just know it when you see it, when you become aware that you are it—that you are *That which is always becoming.*

But the only doorway that will get you there is directly through the present. Don't you see?

So lean forward and look for it tomorrow morning. It will be there, available for you to enter into. Don't pretend anymore that it doesn't exist. That hasn't done you any good either, has it?

The sporadic wandering of all of that tribal logic must be reeled in from its vacationary lifestyle.

It travels constantly to all kinds of (pleasurable and not-so-pleasurable) loud and overly contained hot spots, doesn't it? In order to distract you from your own genuine interior condition and from your own harmonious sense and presence of *Self*, from your essential duties—which are always and only to your own interconnected heart. Remember?

So you must stop chasing after it if you are to return home.

And you must make the return a hero's pilgrimage. You must make it a courageous journey of (self) transformation. And of (*Self*) realization.

It will be just such a pilgrim's journey which you will begin to wake up into tomorrow morning, even though it's a pilgrimage that really doesn't go anywhere.

It's not a journey of distance or divergence, but one of renewal and rebirth instead—a journey of *metanoia*.[1]

CHAPTER 35

The Hero's Odyssey

A HERO IS *someone who has given his or her life to something bigger than oneself,* wrote the wise Joseph Campbell.[1]

We would like to add this to Joseph's words: *A hero is also someone who has given his or her life to something bigger than one's particular tribe too.*

Some of your tribes (of family, vocation, or religion; and of ethnicity or peer group; or of corporation or nation-state) which have had sufficient means to do so, have sometimes been quite instrumental in pulling you up and widening your horizons, haven't they? From within their limited and limiting but fundamentally efficient use of space and time and of material substance.

But they've just as often been your biggest stumbling blocks to waking you up and out of the overly contained and cramped boundaries of the tribe, and out of its collapsing perspectives, in which you've long been Rip Van Winkling yourselves.[2]

The heroic work is always found in moving beyond yourselves, isn't it? Beyond your identifiable tribal confines and beyond your secure place in them, in order to return to your original and actual *Self*—which excludes nothing and no one.

There is nowhere that your *Self* is not, remember?

Yet the authentic work is reached for (most often) in a person's intentional and recurring (but difficult and distinctive) individual odysseys, from moment to moment, which the wise Homer wrote so eloquently about only a few thousand years ago. It's available to all of you (again and again) each and every time you wake up with fresh (yet untested) eyes, or into an unspoiled and reinvigorating experience.[3]

Odysseus and Penelope and Telemachus and Athena and all the rest—they wait impatiently inside all of you for the next courageous and visionary adventure.[4]

Although within so many of you, they're just left there to sit in fixed positions . . . slowly getting worn out with the wait.

They've grown bored with your loud interior rituals, so often replicated in your ceremonial lives, overlaid by tribal veneer, with all of its customary pomp and show. And so they just grow more sedentary and old, fat, and flabby, covering their ears as they wait.

They can't even look out through a window at the horizon.

You've pulled down the shades and cut off the power, simply to make certain that no horizon reveals itself beyond your conventional tribal narratives.

And yet an abrupt surprise can sometimes feel very much like a mini revelation, can it not? It can dare you to stretch your imagination beyond the boundaries of your *disjoined* awareness. And most of you do your loyal best not to allow any such moments of actual awe to accumulate. Don't you?

If sudden epiphanies become all too common, then what will become of your addiction to orthodox certitudes? Or to your holy tribal nap time?

If the indwelling (*Holy*) *Spirit* of the inexhaustible *Self* is real, then what eventually becomes of an outer god which insists upon being shackled to the logic of the self-worshiping *only-mind* (and to its logic of separation)—which keeps its captivated followers feeling safe and secure in their tribal paralysis?

But come tomorrow morning a brand new wake-up call will replace all of that tribal noise. It'll be an undiluted harmonic opportunity, permitting you to hear and to observe the universal hammer as it hits the impersonal nail right on the proverbial head.

It may sound and look Greek to you now (unless you're already Greek . . . then it may sound and look English, French, Spanish, or Chinese) or even when you first land on the shore of the other side. But there will be no language or tribal barrier there to hold you back anymore. You are the only ones who can do that, just like it's always been. Ακριβώς όπως ήταν πάντα.

But you already know that, don't you?

CHAPTER 36

Wise Foolishness

*M*AN IS LEAST *himself when he talks in his own person. Give him a mask, and he will tell you the truth*, wrote the wise Oscar Wilde.[1]

Maybe so.

But Oscar's truth is most often and obviously revealed in the discomforting and deceptive frolic of the holy fools and of the tricksters who romp among you.[2, 3] Isn't it? From along those disturbing edges, inside the rim of your walled-in tribal worlds, where they whistle and sing and where they jest and rhyme, where they toy with and dramatize and self-deprecate and divert, where they disrupt and expose . . . and where they pratfall and tap dance across all of your see-through disguises and atop all of your delirious quests for power and possessive self-importance—as if it was child's play.

Yet as clever as they've been at integrating the foolish with the wisdom of the wise, very few of you have been awake enough or even curious enough to discern or detect their wizardry. Have you? The chemistry of tribal self-absorption is just such a powerful and desensitizing drug, isn't it? Especially when overdosing on it becomes the norm.

All genuine holy fools and authentic tricksters will keep their own face tomorrow morning.

And we're hopeful that most of you among the invited will openly accept our invitation (early on in the unmasking process) in order to allow yourselves to freely enter into similar wisdom—disguised as foolishness.

We'll provide you with the doable means for such transcendent travel and with enough space and time to allow you the privilege of entering into this unfamiliar territory, filled with its boundless stories—which have always been there for the retelling and for the relistening. They're endless, but only because they arise out of the infinite. They arise out of *That which is always being told.*

But it will still be left up to you as to how or even if you will choose to enter into that portion of the announcement, just as it always has been.

But you already know that much by now.

CHAPTER 37

Begin to Understand

B EGIN TO UNDERSTAND that it's never been just a one-shot deal.

A hero's work is never done, is it?

Once you jump up to another level or discover a broader world beyond your current gravitas, there's a widening and a deepening of vision which accompanies each jump.

An infinite depth and expanse of possibilities immediately becomes available for further surrendering exploration and for heroic transcending—if only you can keep leaning forward long enough, with your eyes and heart wide open.

It's not easy work for those of you who aren't used to it. We'll grant you that.

And each jump up also contains its possible dark side, doesn't it? Where the expansion and deepening process can regrettably dissociate rather than differentiate, where it can split off instead of integrate, leading you to step up and over and to create artificial gaps, to exclude natural struggles in the organic flow of your own process of renewal—instead of transcending what's no longer beneficial while including what still is.[1]

It leads you to deny what you actually observe and even that which you intimately feel. It persuades you to controvert your own possibilities . . . your own actuality, to argue against your own transitional or instant awakening, even as the awakening rises up inside you—even while it's being paradoxically revealed in the face of *others* who can only be a mirror of *That which is always becoming*, don't you see? Just as you can only reflect the unifying *Self* right back to them.

And your quick and easy denial often comes in the form of easy blame or of knee-jerk pigeonholing, doesn't it? Where you try to discredit or even eliminate whatever you can't understand or contain, positioning each bull's-eye in your nullifying sites for easy tribal target practice.

It's just so much harder to hit a moving target of *otherness* than one which you can simply tie up to the tribal execution post, isn't it?

And for so many of you it allows life to become much less complicated than you fear that it might actually be, simply by rejecting this and accepting that in yourselves and in *others*, instead of rejecting nothing and accepting it all for what it is—as the essential ingredients in the uncontainable cosmic melting pot.

It's become a full-blown mechanical reaction for many of you, hasn't it? As you imagine and insist that your tribal version of heaven and hell, and even of the world in which you physically reside, are geographically separate domains isolated from and opposed to each other. You vigorously deny that they are both/and all of the same stream of consciousness . . . of the same void of potentiality, interconnected in the same field of energy, within the same mix of endless *Creation* and of the same spirit, rising up out of the same cosmic ocean, including all of *That which is*, blending the inside with the outside of you and of everyone else, human and *other* than human—right along with the air you breathe.

Deny it if you still must, but you can only breathe in unifying wholeness.

You cannot breathe in separate and isolated parts.

You breathe it in . . . all of it, whatever the quality and whatever the mixture, through whatever portal is available.

Yet it's really how you breathe it back out that completes the story, isn't it?

Listen, and take this to heart. It's not what you swallow that pollutes your life, but what you vomit up, spoke the wise Jesus.[2]

Breathe in and accept *That which is.*

Breathe out and accept *That which is always becoming.*

That's the practice which you've so avoided—the daily practice of death and resurrection and of surrender and renewal.

They are both one and in the same *Self.*

Are they not?

There can be no breathing in which is separate from the breathing out, can there?

There exists within you an inseparable sea of inexhaustible mercy and forgiveness, continuously renewing *It-Self* with each cosmic inhalation and exhalation, within each and every rhythmic cycle of death and rebirth.

How can *That which is indivisible* be split apart without leading to a death which denies its own resurrection? It's impossible, isn't it? How can this exist without that? How can one exist without the *other*? How can the breath be cut off from itself and yet still breathe?

If any of you can claim (without embarrassment) to be able to locate and observe a dividing line of disunity or of cosmic estrangement anywhere in the actual fabric of *Creation* . . . then where is it?

Just try breathing in without breathing out for a while. See how long that lasts.

Or try the reverse.

Either way, you'll be forced to let go, won't you? And to surrender up to the realization of your own illusions of permanence. Because the breath of life will always clarify who is in charge.

It is always in charge. Not you.

The immeasurable *Self* is forever undivided . . . integrating everything, even though you still try to carve it up into diminished tribal bits and pieces in a futile attempt to dismember it—which is impossible, of course. There is no resurrection without death. And there is no life-giving death without resurrection.

But your only real requirement is to trust your own indwelling *Spirit* (which you sometimes refer to as intuition) and to carry it along with a disciplined practice of intention . . . and of perceiving what actually is, instead of replacing what you perceive with conventionalized and clung-to tribal agendas.

It's the same old story that so many of you just can't seem to let go of—which can't hurt repeating, can it?

And among so many of you, there's an ever-present pull back to the days of nostalgic glory, isn't there? To what so many of you sentimentalize as the traditional utopian days—which is usually translated and reemphasized that way by those who've rarely or ever experienced the actual bad side of those glory days.

Yet the nontraditionalists and the flatland thinkers among you would also like to pull the whole shooting match back to zero. Wouldn't they? Into their own cave of dystopia.

There's a real battle of worldviews going on, isn't there? Mainly between the three most prevalent tribal divisions . . . each one claiming to contain not only the superior but the exclusive, final, and *only* valid way of rendering what is true or untrue and of what is good or bad, of what is wrong or right and of what is beautiful or repulsive, of what is sacred or profane and of what is real or unreal.

Listen closely to the following synonyms for the word fundamentalism, for the fundamentalist way of thinking and reacting to things—hidden within each synonymous word.[3]

Sabbatarianism, bibliolatry, bigotry, dogmatism, evangelicalism, firmness, hardness, hideboundness, hyperorthodoxy, impliability, inexorability, inflexibility, literalism, obduracy, obdurateness, obstinacy, orthodoxy, precisianism, purism, puritanicalness, puritanism, relentlessness, rigorousness, sabbatism, scripturalism, staunchness, relentlessness, rigidity, rigidness, rigor, stiff-neckedness, stiffness, straitlacedness, strict interpretation, strictness, stubbornness, unbendingness, uncompromisingness, unrelentingness, unyieldingness.

Quite interesting words, don't you think?

Do any of them align with your own way of thinking about or of reacting to *otherness* . . . whenever you cross paths with it?

Is it possible that most of you have submitted your almost total allegiance to the logic of one quarreling mentality among the many? To a mind-set which constantly competes to be the most dominant and holy chosen one? To one that claims to be the all-exclusive and unequaled *only-mind*—the only tribal ballerina left to dance around the idols of its own making?

You bet it is.

The most traditional of the quarrelsome divisions (the premodern mentality) proclaims and assumes the absolute truth and authority of its pre-established tribal ways, doesn't it? The way things were always meant and believed to be, not the way they're proven or shown to be, or the way they may feel or can be interpreted to be, nor how they may evolve to be better understood or experienced—but how they are always supposed to be, according to the rule of established and unchangeable tribal law and of inherited belief, or of ancient (and usually socially, culturally, politically, or religiously isolated) tradition—which is generally dismissive of any reasonable or rational argument, isn't it? Or of any newly discovered factual evidence, or of any direct or intimate personal observation or acquaintance, or of any evolving interpretation or experience which may put the entrenched (so-called traditional) way into question.

Meanwhile, the more modern (nontraditional) division generally proclaims and assumes the absolute truth and authority of objective facts and analytical reason—of material evidence, doesn't it? The way things are observed to be; not the way they were traditionally established, practiced, or passed down, nor the way they may intuitively feel, nor how they may be reinterpreted or subjectively experienced to be, but how they are determinately proven or physically shown to be . . . according to the laws of literal observation, through the reductionary rules of hard scientism, reducing all evidence to material evidence, all subjects to objects—which is generally dismissive of any established or long-comforting tradition, or of any nonlinear or nonmaterial (or even any translinear, transmaterial, or transrational) interpretation, or of any intimate, creative, intuitive, or interior experience which may put the rule of (patho)logical reason or of fact-driven material objectivity and of (patho)linear observation and analysis into question.

Then there's the third or postmodern (flatland) division which generally assumes the absolute truth and authority of horizontal (relativistic) interpretation, doesn't it? Of direct (but not necessarily demonstrable or reproducible) experience, of the way things subjectively feel, of how they're personally sensed, or how they're freely interpreted to be, not the way they were traditionally established and passed on or were meant to be, nor how they're objectively or materially verified (or scientifically or even peer reviewed) to be, but solely how they are perceived or intuited or even spontaneously concluded to be. It's the rule of personal and subjective interpretation and of experiential desire— which is generally dismissive of any established or strictly followed tradition of belief, or of carefully adhered-to clinical reasoning, or of any collection of observable evidence which may put personal interpretation, subjective opinion, or relativistic perception into question—especially by any hierarchy of authority, no matter how natural, healthy, and compassionate the hierarchy may be. And (from within this mind-set) personal experience, intuition, and subjective opinion are given equal or even more weight than any historic and evolving Wisdom Tradition (or lineage). Yet it's quite interesting to note that this peculiar tribal *only-mind* (which seems to credit all views as relative and therefore as relatively relevant and hence relatively credible . . . depending on who's doing the interpreting) actually establishes its tribal division as superior to the *others*—hence affirming an absolutist hierarchy of its own invention, mirroring the vertical worldviews which it claims to oppose.

So there it is, the existing state of mental stuckness in your world, of the pervasive and fundamental opposition of the three most dominant tribal divisions, which is what many of your mainstream observers label as the culture wars—which is a very delicate way of putting it, isn't it?

A superficial way to describe all of the hatred and venom stirred up and projected out from all of that adverse, hostile, and frozen tribal logic?

It's a self-convincing logic which can only see itself as superior, even as flawless and beyond reproach and which refuses to see much if any truth, goodness, or beauty in any *other* vision besides its own. It's the logic of the fundamentalist and of the narcissist.

Each of the prevailing divisions remains encased and barricaded behind the walls of its own glass house of illusion, each one vindicating itself with its own idyllic version of the *disjoined only-mind*, each willing to defend its myopia to the death, to the death of the *other*—to the final elimination of all *otherness*.[4]

But most of you can see what's really going on here, can't you? Even if it's only through the lens of whichever cult-like perspective you're beholden to.

And yet . . . all three of these overly contained tribal mentalities still have the capacity to embrace compassionate loving-kindness from within their own walls, don't they? But only if they choose to do so, just like every other tribe of human beings which has come and gone. Because unsentimental (transtribal) love and compassion, by whatever name you call it, is not only timeless and changeless, but it can penetrate and transcend any fortress of sentimental self-adulation that any tribe can erect in its vain attempt to keep it out.

That which is always becoming It-Self (through all of *That which it manifests*) is the one and only unifying yet paradoxical and absolute filter of truth, don't you see?

It is omnipresent yet omniabsent in its silence and should-less yet full of revelation, hidden behind and beneath the masks of all the worldly wannabes who try so hard to force their restrictions onto *That which is* . . . by attempting to possess it only for themselves; to contain and constrict it inside of tribal time, space, and ideology; to keep it locked up inside of one self-serving cage of prepossessed logic.

Yet the heroic *bodhisattva* craft, which is always accessible to all of you, of dying to yourselves and to your tribe, to be reborn for the sake of a wider and deeper purpose . . . for and with all sentient beings, stands open ended and never ending, eternally beyond any fantasized version of a shrinking *Self* which you can ever conceive of or which you can ever attempt to confine.

It forever invites you in with open arms.

Even so, the ultimate mystery of it all remains beyond your egoic reach.

Doesn't it?

CHAPTER 38

Another Piece of the Puzzle

AND SO ENTERS another piece of the puzzle.

The present is the only reality that has ever existed; as we've tried to emphasize.

There will be no brightly lit red exit signs to point and lead you to an escape hatch anymore. You've spent too much time there already, opening and slamming the doors of the past and of the future into (not only your own face, but) the face of many *others* along the way, just to avoid the *Self* that's always been there in the existing moment, the real one—which will be the key to your reentry back into yourselves beginning tomorrow morning, along with your diligent watchfulness and your deliberate *letting of the gos*. So to speak.

There will be enough practical information and tools of application coming your way to keep you sufficiently in tune for an adequate and critical preparation, no matter how many times you drift into and then back away from the watching of memories that surface.

We promise.

CHAPTER 39

Hold On

S O PLEASE?
Allow us now to carefully but clearly begin to elaborate upon the substance of what we intend, to begin to slowly break it down for you, to begin to be more precise while being reasonably thorough, to introduce you to the curious but inescapable crux of it all.

Our aim is to lead you toward a promise beyond but within yourselves and to what it will exact of you as you consider and act upon it.

So you just might want to hold on to something.

We'll be doing our very best not to pull any punches. And we'll be using lots of big words and lengthy sentences of which you may already notice yourselves trying to resist the understanding of.

But we've arranged it so that there will be nothing left to be misunderstood or confusing for you when we're finished with our monologue—which is way beyond the point of simple suggestion anymore.

The refacings will transpire and materialize.

So you can forget about playing dumb. We've taken that out of your repertoire for the time being.

You can have it all back after we've finished, if you still want it.

CHAPTER 40

To Start With

TO BEGIN WITH.
It won't actually be unused merchandise that you'll be squeezing yourselves into when you first open up your eyes tomorrow morning.

Instead, you'll just be relocating and repersonalizing yourselves behind and inside the facial attributes of someone else, as you borrow and temporarily assume their outward visual appearance, minus the tribal shrink wrap, of course.

All the while, you'll still continue to maintain your own essential awareness of reality. But it'll be integrated along with and into the being whose face you'll be occupying.

You just might find yourselves waking up to a whole new set of likes and dislikes, filled with different habits and routines—which may seem awkwardly familiar and yet foreign to you at the same time. It may even feel a bit disorienting at first. But you'll soon come to realize how essential these new ingredients will be to the facial readjustment process.

We know that this may all seem oddly sudden to you. But the strategy we've come up with is that having too much time to ponder this unusual intervention might impede the collective change of state from proceeding seamlessly—or from stepping out on the right foot with the new face.

And so here you are.

We again suggest that you pay very close attention, starting right now . . . or even before now, if you can reach back a little.

Every present moment has some degree of elasticity to it, doesn't it? From backward to forward and then back again. As a matter of fact, it stretches out equitably into all six directions, to give you a little wiggle room, just enough to be able to move around and get a genuine feel for it, for where you actually are, to locate your existent and fluid purpose . . . your point and flow of being.

No present moment is identical to any other one. But each one is also not unrelated to or disconnected from any other piece of the here-and-now cosmic puzzle, or from any of its multidimensional qualities.

So just keep that in mind without holding it or anything else too tightly.

The present isn't a constricted or limiting capacity at all. It is both particle and wave (to steal a little from the wise language of quantum mechanics).[1] It is movement and stability, dancing within each individual process of creative growth and development, within each unique being—within *Being* itself.

There is actually nothing which is disunited from anything else—not in time, space, or anything beyond them. Everything is interdependent yet simultaneously able to freelance, nonsymbiotically . . . from within the same roaring, strangely balanced, and paradoxical universe.

Regrettably though, the fragmentation most of you so frequently experience begins with your own light-deficient vision, muddied up by your persistent resistance to intellectual discrimination and to practitioner discipline.

You've developed a historic and collective tendency to neglect and subvert your own infinite source of creative energy, your own latent inner luminosity, by way of simple but proficient cognitive and experiential laziness—at the front end.

Many of you (among the invited) rarely if ever consider any of the following: reading about, discussing, listening to, interacting with, seriously observing, even chewing over empirical data related to, or attempting to understand any part of any world outside of your own mental or experiential habits.

Instead, you tend to think that you actually occupy separate tribal galaxies, don't you? Within encapsulated clusters of floating bubble worlds, isolated with just enough dividing space between yourselves and *others*, protecting your territorial mind-set from any possible incoming contamination which could cause your clustered awareness to expand . . . and thus, your see-through and thinly veiled bubble to burst.

You like to refer to this piece of tribal logic as normal—within the context of tribal addiction and allegiance, that is. Well, don't you? Or with some other comparable word meant to signify your not-so-exceptional sameness, exposing the fact that much of your thinking and experience and even your behavior and language is not your own. Yet you insist that it is, with unreflective self-deception . . . while rarely if ever taking an unpermitted peek beyond the horizon of your overly contained tribal logic.

And as we've already noted, you continue to maintain a clenched sense of superiority when comparing yourselves to *others*. Don't you? *Others* whom you not only do not know, but whom you scarcely know anything about—while pretending or convincing yourselves that you do.

Perhaps that would be referred to as normalized tribal logic in your world.

It's how you define yourselves, isn't it? Which cuts you off from the whole, from *That which is always becoming* in its totality, shutting yourselves in and down, against all possibility of knowing not only who the *other* is—but who you are.

Even so, your insistence upon separation is only equaled by your tribal hubris, isn't it?

But come tomorrow morning (and if you watch closely enough) you'll soon be exposed to *That which might surprise you*, even without any of our clues and suggestions. So remember to keep yourselves as open as you can. Can you do that?

There will be no withdrawal or retreat from the field and domain of *now* once you get there, which is where you always are already anyway, as we've been trying to drive through to your stiff and inflexible tribal psyche.

Deniability of any kind will fall away like a sun-begrudged shadow, especially the plausible kind, for any of you who may still be pondering the inclusion of that old trick.

The face-lifting will be well lit. But the illumination which you'll be entering into will cast no shadows of its own.

Nothing will be hidden.

Everything will be brought out and into the boundless light of *That which is beyond* any radiance that you will easily recognize.

CHAPTER 41

Brace Yourselves

WE'LL TRY TO keep all of this as simple yet as intellectually stimulating and as lucid as possible as we unfold the particulars. But our attempt to convey what you're about to enter into will be a tad more spacious and convoluted than any nutshell you may have encountered or climbed into before this one.

So please . . . do brace yourselves. We don't want anyone's face to be slammed through any psychic or spiritual windshields.

We're about to provide you with a somewhat dreamlike (yet demythologized) heads up, into what is soon to transform and to retranslate the way you're used to experiencing just about everything you've been so used to experiencing.

We want to do this thing as safely as we can, within reasonable but impelling guidelines. It'll be a bit of a tightrope walk between the requirement of a safe landing and the pursuit of a potent reawakening.

But a helpful heads up often emerges through the heart, doesn't it?

So you just might want to consider placing all cynical (and physical) knees and elbows more toward the back of the line. They're the ones who've misled and hardened so many of you along much of the way here, yes? Blocking your inner doorways of depth and perception—which has led to the necessity of this restarting gate, don't you see?

But what you're about to hear and feel won't be too easy to swallow, even if you're used to eating or drinking up much of your accumulated information through your ears.

You'll be very tempted to tune it all out.

But we're afraid that won't be possible.

It's too late for that now.

CHAPTER 42

Violence Disguised,
Violence Denied

YOU WILL EACH be exchanging your present persona for an *other* one—almost every one of you. There will be no exceptions made for anyone who's on the invitational list. If you've been summoned, then you're going.

But as we've already said, it won't be an unworn face that you'll be sliding into. It'll just be one that was previously inhabited by someone else who will probably be going through a very similar repositioning procedure themselves—if they've been invited.

Many of you will also undergo the unique experience of being depeopled (so to speak), of having the mask of the humanoid replaced with the face of an *other*-than-human being, in one or more of your facial transactions—if you're scheduled for more than one. But we'll get into that a little later on in the announcement.

And as for everyone who's been chosen for this illuminating ordeal?

No backroom sweet deals will be made . . . as you've probably discerned by now.

There's no such thing as a partial surrender when it comes to matters of the heart, is there? And in the end, it will solely be up to you to complete your own circle of return. We can't do it for you.

The time has come for something this pivotal (yet innovative) to take place—nothing less. Because nothing else has been able to slow things down or shake things up enough, has it? Nothing else has been able to put an effective pause or even a second-rate dent into the infantile and adolescent fixations which overfeed the intestinal track of each overly contained tribe (with so much enmity and waste)—clogging up the bowels of the *only-mind* with enough tribe-against-tribe turbulence to convince most of its captivated followers that it will somehow remain unmoved and untouched by *That which is always becoming.*

Yet we know that the vast majority of you are quite capable of demonstrating noble and compassionate interactions with and toward *others*. We've observed it. We want to be clear on that point.

So hear us out.

The refacing procedure will not remove or do any damage to any of your already civilized and humane qualities.

It will not eliminate any progress you may have made in reducing the frequency or percentage of direct physical violence which you still participate in . . . even if the reduction is only on the surface of things and even if the rumored decline in violent behaviors could be slightly misleading. For it implies a very narrow definition of violence, doesn't it?

It seems to ignore where all violence ultimately resides . . . which is in the heart, isn't it? None of it can ever fully be captured on paper or by computer or by any statistical analysis (coming from any part of the *only-mind*) that we know of. The heart is much too deep and vast to be stolen with analysis or penetrated by mere statistics, while all too often still being pierced by sharp and indifferent tribal violence, never itself indifferent nor insensitive to the type or degree of force or coercion which is so generously applied—even as so many of you try to project an image of nonchalant hardness to so much of the violence which bullies and stabs its way into the inner chambers of your own pulsating affections.

And heart-stabbing violence does show up in all kinds of undisguised ways, doesn't it?

After all, what is felt more intensely by a human being? A quick gunshot wound to the head? Or institutionalized suppression of speech and movement?

What about disappearing opportunities for jobs with livable wages?

Where does starvation fall in? And how about forced labor? Or human slavery?

What about sex, drug, or child trafficking?

How about having no access to clean drinkable water? Or being pushed off your land and out of your home so a predatory corporation or government (or both) can strip it of its minerals or of other sacred gifts hidden between the layers of earthly wealth (gifts which were meant to be shared and used wisely by all of your world's inhabitants, human or *other* than human)?

What about the savage devastation done to rain forests and to all of the interconnected species which depend upon those forests (and upon each other) for survival?

How about drug running? Or dog and cock fighting?

Or consider the culturally (and religiously) approved-of domestic abuse and suppression of women? How about macho-misogynist song and rap lyrics? Or the prevalence of degrading and violent pornography?

How does the desolation of the ozone layer fit into the calculations of violence? Or the heating up of the planet? The melting of the polar ice caps and glaciers? The rising of the sea levels? The loss of habitat for wildlife (from polar bears to caribou)? The shrinking of islands? The destruction of the traditional way of life of many indigenous groups of people due to the changing landscapes and rising temperatures, all by way of your obsessive and wasteful consumption . . . to the overreliance on fossil fuels which feeds your obsession and to the ravaging of woodlands which are replaced with vast empty fields for cattle to innocently graze (by obscenely rich corporations)—to eventually feed the privileged addiction of the overly fed and strung-out meat-eating tribes who are too often led by the nose and palate of shallow affluence and callous disregard?

And what about ranting radio hate speech? Or hate crimes aimed at human beings who happen to be of a certain race or who hold a certain belief? Or happen to be of a certain sexual orientation or of a certain religious or political persuasion? Or of a certain gender, culture, or ethnicity? Or of any particularly hated (but mostly feared) characteristic of *otherness* of which you choose to target and attack?

How about the duration and intensity of the violence? Does that matter?

Is the emotional and psychological degradation of a child within the secret confines of a private home by psychoneurotic and manipulative so-called adults (who wear the public mask of upstanding and responsible parents while deceiving the rest of the head-in-the-sand community) too small or perhaps all too common an occurrence of tribal dysfunction to be considered an example of life-destroying violence?

What about the terror instilled from a multitude of repeated rapes committed by roaming, unrestrained, and cowardly mercenaries . . . executed upon groups of abandoned and unprotected women and children?

Should we include the lack of any consistent, available, affordable, or adequate health care for so many in your world?

What about a discarded or fatherless child? Or a tortured or forgotten prisoner?

Are forty-four million premature and intentionally induced deaths per year of unborn (and unwanted yet conceived) children really so easy to dismiss and to forget and to quickly bury as mere abstractions? Is it really that cut-and-dry simple and so effortless to disconnect from any other act of premeditated violence? Is it really so easy to dissociate the destruction of any actual or potential life from the pervasive violence perpetrated against so many mothers and daughters and sisters and against so many children who were *allowed* to be born? Or against so many actual women who've been refused medical treatment or have even been accused of murder when undergoing an actual and natural miscarriage by those who dare to decide for everyone else when life actually begins and which life is most important and that physical life somehow trumps all other aspects of actual life in all circumstances, even if it means killing the soul in order to allow the body to survive for a few more years, hours, minutes, or even seconds?[1]

It all penetrates the indivisible heart, doesn't it?

And doesn't it also depend on the weariness of the heart being penetrated? Of the heart divided?

Too many of you still revert to tribal and individual violence when it suits your convenience or your impulsive and selfish desires—which you can't quite stop clinging to or to cease holding in reserve, can you? You seem to need to keep your finger on the trigger of violence just in case you feel the need to reup and retreat back into it, as you plug yourselves back into the false sense of power and security that it gives you—which even the threat of using it has pretended to protect you with, if and whenever push comes to shoving back, especially if and when an external or troublesome *otherness* shows up too close to your real or imaginary doorstep.

Some of your mainline institutional religions (which claim to preach the love of one's enemy) even have justifications for violence (justifications for premeditated war) written into their moral codes and religious doctrines.

Imagine that.

Thou shall not kill, but . . . you will be granted dispensation for the following list of approved-of exemptions . . .

Is that what that ancient commandment really said?

Did the god of Abraham actually include attached footnotes and clauses of immunity to the command against killing?

Maybe Moses just didn't notice the clarifying addenda which were carved into the fine print at the bottom of those stone tablets. Or maybe chunks of tablet just broke off into lost or trampled upon pieces before he could haul them down to the bottom of the mountain. Tablets can be pretty heavy, you understand. Maybe he dropped them. Who really knows? Apparently the rule makers in the upper echelon of your revered religions and their collaborative gun-toting governments do. Or at least they pretend to. And most of you go right along with the organized pretense, don't you?

But no one on your little planet really seems to be exempt from the excuse of using violence as a means to an end when it comes to sustaining their *disjoining* desires, their comforts and luxuries, or their long-held addictions, do they? Or from defending the tribal trance which contains so many of them.

Some of you may have publicly denounced, reduced, repressed, or obscured the more stark patterns of intentionally aimed physical violence toward *others*. But those tendencies still haven't vacated your trigger-happy tribal logic, have they?

They still persist in your collective psyche as internal security measures . . . blanketing your thoughts and speech, standing guard over your fear-laden imagination and your dehumanizing language, waiting to be dispersed and spread out on the beach of retaliation, if and when it becomes necessary to call up the troops, blocking the tribal door, preventing any lasting movement or any actual representative of genuine and practical nonviolence from walking through that hostile doorway unharmed—at least anytime soon.

Hopefully tomorrow morning will speed up the necessary redirection. There's still way too many precious humans and *other* than humans who live, suffer, and die by the sword . . . and way too many of the vulnerable and powerless who do most of the suffering and most of the premature dying—no matter how deceptively inconspicuous you try to wear the tribal sheath or scabbard.

Our intent is not to supplant but to complement and rehabilitate what needs complementing or rehabilitating.

But actually . . . *transform* may be a more precise word than *rehabilitate*.

And like any good surgeon will tell you . . . first we must be as honest as we can be with our diagnosis before cautiously proceeding with the surgery.

But the patient's response to it all is one of the most important if not *the* most important part of the healing and recovery process, isn't it?

There will be pain and discomfort . . . physical, emotional, and even spiritual affliction. And there is no magical or quick-fix cure for anything.

There never has been.

Affliction comes to all not to make us sad, but sober, not to make us sorry, but wise; not to make us despondent, but its darkness to refresh us, as the night refreshes the day; not to impoverish, but to enrich, as the plow enriches the field, wrote the wise Henry Ward Beecher.[2]

My business is to comfort the afflicted, and afflict the comfortable, proclaimed the wise Mother Mary Jones.[3]

CHAPTER 43

A Brave Initial Lending

B UT FIRST, BEFORE we continue, we'll let you take a brief listening tour of an aroused memory . . . just now coming to the surface, from one who will be making the delicate crossover with most of you tomorrow morning. So listen carefully.

Well . . . I'm back to church . . . and . . . it's been a while . . . before this return. I'm ready to try it out again, to experience a change. I walk in. Genuflect. Then slide across the pew into the land of "no one else is here and that is good." I'm early. I enjoy the silence. I smell the incense. I shake hands at the time of the greeting. I hear a very good homily. Love, compassion, forgiveness . . .

The Mass is ended . . . go in peace. I walk out into the parking lot . . . feeling reimbursed if not respirited. I feel better. Maybe this will work for me this time.

I'm not a rich person. But a poor person is wandering in the parking lot, asking questions. He looks embarrassed and ashamed. Humiliated. All of the more experienced parishioners are walking right by him, in some kind of slow-motion agreement, not even acknowledging him . . . while at the same time quickly ushering their children back to their locked cars, talking cheerfully to the others who also just left the church service . . . all ignoring, or shushing away the elderly, bearded, and slightly ragged man with the questions.

He keeps it humble. And keeps asking. "Hello, sir, I'm wondering . . . I need . . . a ride . . . just up the street . . . to my AA meeting . . . I'll pay for the gas . . ."

It's a very cold and windy winter morning.

He catches me, at the door of my car . . . and I say, "Sorry."

That's it. I never look him in the eye except to condescend.

And I get in my car and drive away. He looks straight through me. He knows.

I am not afraid of him. I am afraid of them. The attending parishioners. We are all afraid of each other.

All of us, the respectably dressed, in our clean cars . . . we refuse him . . . the Jesus man . . .

Right after the talk on love your neighbor as yourselves. Right after the prayers for peace, the handshakes, the reception of Christ . . . who favors the poor, the downtrodden . . . as it is sometimes but not often enough reminded . . . and is more often quickly forgotten in parking lots, pulpits, and on the streets . . . in the entertainment news . . . in the moneyed and pretentious exchanges of the day.

Sunday morning. Feels possible. I feel saved for a few minutes . . . until that guy comes out of nowhere and spoils the moment. Brings it into real life. I feel ashamed. But I don't turn around. I hide it.

He's someone whom I mistake; who is sent.

Watching now, it seems so obvious.

I'll wear his face. This time. I'm ready . . . I hope . . . goddammit anyway. I'm so tired of this selfish . . . this cowardly bullshit.

Excellent!

Well done.

A very brave initial lending with some apparent integrity from one of your memory-watching peers. We hope you were all attentive to his heartfelt observations.

His parking lot holy man is probably just an indication of similar faces which he may (additionally) be reentering. Or perhaps, if he wears this one with honor and respect, he'll advance rather quickly to another facial category to work in. But he's on the right track.

A good observational beginning.

But we caution you to be careful of retaining any reliance upon (or looking for some kind of paradoxical comfort from) being a boarding house for guilt. It's a definite transformational stopper.

Watch it when it comes up, just like the memories. Then let it go . . . gently but promptly. Just let it go. It'll help to keep the actual organic flow from shutting down.

When a wound or revelation begins to obsess, it's usually just another trick sent up from below by the *disjoined* one . . . who as we've already indicated seems to see the demonic or even the devil itself under every foreign or alien bed.

It likes to maneuver for control of your steering wheel, to distract you from allowing changes to naturally arise or to gently manifest.

Instead of keeping the doors open and the channels fluid with possibility, it tends to curl you up and to batten down the interior hatches, doesn't it? To shield and prevent awareness from expanding or from flowing freely, to close up the heart shop and to tighten up the chest, and to stifle breathing and to blur the vision of your inner (or third) eye.

So just be advised of that.

CHAPTER 44

A Sloppy Adventure

NOW FOR THE rest of you.
As you've just witnessed, watchable memories are already beginning to emerge and to circulate among you. It doesn't take much triggering, does it? So continue to keep your eyes and ears open.

That was just a first sharing of a specific example. We may occasionally permit more of these to be passed on to all of you . . . to borrow and observe throughout our elaboration, prior to your journey of individual and collective realizations, to allow you to see the variance in facial adjustments which you might become intimate with tomorrow morning.

From time to time, we may even put a pause in our presentation for a few moments, to admit a short vignette of someone's emerging memory into your consciousness, to be taken in, intercommunicated, and then to be let go of by the whole group.

And then gently but promptly, we'll redirect your attention back to our message of facial redeliverance.

We're determined to prepare you well for this experience.

Practice may not make perfect—which is a delusional goal in any event, for any genuinely desired movement toward wholeness and integrity, isn't it?

Simply put . . . evolution is a rather sloppy adventure. There aren't too many straight lines involved, even while so many of you spend much of your lives trying to straighten, sort, separate, and organize reality into some kind of worldly perfected explanation—to try to make what is real stand up to your anal-retentive tribal attention.

But practice can help to turn around and to balance the bad and the worse into coequal siblings with the good and the better.

And eventually it can help you to realize that pleasure and pain branch out from the same tree of life. They share the same roots. Neither is to be discarded or exalted. Both are to be eaten in their wholeness—together because neither is capable of changing your essential and changeless

Self. Neither is a threat to or a reward for who you really are, unless you project too much importance upon them, which many of you have spent much of your lives doing—which blocks the transformational process from returning home.

Practice can help you to avoid taking either of them too seriously. It begins to clear a path toward spacious equanimity.

So try to begin to realize that this will be a process of unlearning the habits which try so hard to separate the bitter from the sweet (the chaff from the wheat)—that this will be a process of unlearning all that is habitual.

When facial reunification is eventually arrived at and reestablished, there will no longer be a need for habits of any kind. The habitual will no longer survive since it only exists to separate and divide.

So when separation disappears so will all of its fixations—all of its divisive masks. You will all finally realize that you have no face to save or to defend anymore. You never have. The face of the inmost *Self* needs no saving.

And examples are often the best teachers after all.

Wouldn't you agree?

So.

Let's move on then.

Shall we?

CHAPTER 45

The List Goes On

BUT THAT WAS a very good first illustration of what many of you may be facing, from the recollected view on a smaller scale from within the larger group—of just one individual.

And those perspectives are important, aren't they?

We have no desire to diminish the significance of any individual act or its consequences, even though this illustration may be one of the less complicated and more commonplace refacings which will be encountered by many of you.

But they all add up, don't they?

They reveal the various complexities and struggles for control within each individual's interior order, sometimes even revealing the struggles between the inner and outer tribal schemes of control—in this case between the ambivalent compassion felt by one perplexed individual and the uniform and confident sterility routine of a specific group of parishioners (the local tribe), whose group identity and sense of security seems to derive at least partially from maintaining a germ-free appearance.

Group purity beat out sympathy for the immigrant with this one— once again, while the group justified its actions with its own protective sympathy for itself.

Please allow me to introduce myself, I'm a man of wealth and taste . . . Pleased to meet you . . . Won't you guess my name, wrote the wise Mick Jagger and Keith Richards.[1]

It can get pretty layered, can't it? Even devilishly musical sometimes.

As a matter of fact the individual examples not only add up, but they expand and intertwine (exponentially) into codependent realms and eventually out into their extremes where so many of you have allowed the controlling agents to gather, as if a huge hidden magnet exists out there somewhere, reining in scattered metal shavings disguised as a collection of logical or wise human beings, who attempt to fool themselves into believing that clinging to and glorifying in a static and stationary tribal logic is sensible—even illuminating.

And it works.

It's hard to comprehend it, we know. But somehow, it works.

And there's been a plague of sorts, hasn't there? Especially within the past few decades, resulting in violent reactionary responses to the shifts and even to the occasional leaps of consciousness that have been trying to free themselves from the forceful pull of that tyrannical magnetic field—which is something we will be expanding upon with assorted examples as we turn through the various instructional phases of our presentation.

But for now?

Well, allow us to recite some trigger words and phrases, in order to revive and redirect your attention to several of the recent controversies of change which most of you have been witness to—at least at some conscious or subconscious level of awareness.

It's been a bit of a bumpy ride, hasn't it?

But change never arrives via nicely swept carpets or perfectly paved roads, does it?

There's generally a lot of debris to remove, to wind through and to wheel around, to keep things moving—which includes a lot of wrong turns and U-turns, major fender benders and worse, not much of it being free of its own growing pains or from the resistance of opposing tribal traffic; most of it being driven by its contrary mandates or by those who remain stuck in the compulsive traffic of selfish desires—and to addictions of tribal belief.

So we offer the following list as a memorandum of the contentious changes you've undergone and even subscribed to—for your simple consideration. And you might want to try listening to this rambling roll call as a detached spectator, so as not to be so quick to take immediate sides—as you seem to like to do.

But either way . . . here we go with it:

Increased racial and gender acceptance and the emergence (in certain regions of your world) of greater equality and justice in those relational categories.

Expanded religious freedom and of its expression outside the control of the traditionally dominant institutions.

Mobilized challenges to the centers and sources of power.

Increased (intelligent) ecological awareness and action.

The rediscovery of experiential spiritual practice and of respectful interfaith dialogue. East meets West. North meets South.

The diminishing of traditional energy resources and the violent and desperate clinging to them as they disintegrate. And the threat and promise of green technology.

Universal and isolating home entertainment and the expanding lure and abundance of physical conveniences.

Worldwide (ever-present and) visually driven consumer-targeted propaganda. Subliminal and in-your-face corporate advertising. The rise and expansion of the power and influence and the self-identity sought after and misplaced in material craving and excess.

An accumulation of anthropological, archeological, and paleontological discoveries and an evolving apprehension of the history of your planet and its inhabitants.

Information explosion and the sense of overload. The flourishing of higher and faster technologies. The global mind change brought about by the Internet.

Greater understanding and compassionate attempts to enforce the rights and protection of various groups of humans and *other* species. The increased recognition that all animals and all plants and every drop of rain and each and every speck and particle of the manifest world coequally inhabit and are inhabited by the same spirit of divine *Creation* (no different than humans).

The slow but steady empowerment of women, of respective minorities, of the historically oppressed, and of the discriminated against.

Scientific revelations and inventions of all kinds which extend and deepen the conscious view of the universe.

Cross-cultural exchanges and increased travel. Massive immigration of the poor into the territories of the rich . . . of the darker-skinned people into the territory previously populated almost exclusively by the lighter-skinned people.

Birth control and greater sexual freedom . . . involving both intimate and caring relationships and *disjoined* and arbitrary ones. The lessening of sexual and gender stigmatizing. Decreased homophobia and the slow increase in the acceptance of LGBT human beings as having the same and equal inherent rights as anybody else.

Globalization of just about everything.

The sense that time is speeding up and that the planet is shrinking.

The overcrowding and exploitation of the global and even of the spatial environment by humans and their covetous corporations of overindulgence.

The acceleration of change.

The paradigm transforming theory of the big bang. The Hubble and Kepler telescopes and the discovery of billions of galaxies. The expansion in the reach and understanding of the origin and interconnectedness of life in the expanding universe. Space exploration and its science of awe.[2]

The loss or lessening of reliance upon the entrenched religious, cultural, and societal traditions (with a small *t*). Increased interest and practice in the deeper, more mindful, and contemplative spiritual practices. A slow returning to the Wisdom Traditions of the Perennial Philosophy (with a big *T*). The rediscovery, increase, and spread of nondual awareness (the awareness of mystery) while still having to navigate through the phenomenological world with all of its shades of gross and even subtle polarities.[3]

Nuclear, robotic, and chemical weapons. Cell phones and satellites. Drone weaponry.

The extinction of thousands of species of plants and animals and of whole indigenous tribes of people.[4]

The increase of noise and distraction. The loss of (and the need for) solitude.

The effects of creeping climate change and extreme changes in weather. The thawing of the polar ice caps. The rising of sea levels. The melting away of glaciers. The shrinking and slow disappearance of island communities. The increasing world temperatures (all of which we've already mentioned but bear repeating). The corporate and ideological resistance to ecological realities.

The exponential shortening of the human attention span.

The disappearance of a multitude of ancient languages and cultures.

The decrease of automatic deference or submission to authoritarianism. The spreading of the ideal and intent of individual and group liberty engaged in for the common good (the Zapatista Movement in Mexico, the Saffron Revolution in Burma, the Arab Spring, the Occupy Movement . . . before it was infiltrated, hijacked, and marginalized, etc.). The increased exposure to independence of thought, behavior, and lifestyle colliding with the opposing and reactionary increase and pulling back into individual and collective self-absorption and conformity (Islamic extremism; Christian fundamentalism; the polarizing politics of self-righteousness; the antiscience, anti-intellectual, and antimetaphysical movements, etc.).

The breaking down of language and of communication barriers. The corporate impediments to a flow of free and necessary information from within mass media and from collaborating governments.

The slow dissolution of recent and traditional dictatorships, empires, and so-called superpowers.

The relaxation and increased acceptance of interracial and interethnic socialization and marriage.

Organ transplants. DNA. Surrogate motherhood. Sperm banks. Cloning.

The widening of the gap between the rich and powerful . . . and the poor and the powerless.

E-books, iPads, iPhones, and iPods. Twitter and Facebook. And the expansion and integration of social media into the psychology and interactions of the planet's human inhabitants.

The increased use and abuse of various legal (and, of course, illegal) drugs. The immense failure of the cynical, phony, and moralistic *war on drugs.*

The epidemic of obesity (from fast, easy, cheap, unhealthy, and massive food production and distribution) while millions hunger and thirst and even starve to death from the lack of having enough basic nutrients (or even enough water) to survive.

The lack of outrage and the creeping sense of normality (and even acceptance) bestowed upon the criminal activity wreaked (by the few upon the many) from within the confederation of corporate (financial, military, political, and religious) entities—and the contrived excuses made for their duplicitous actions. The outright cover-ups of those crimes and the routine immunity that's automatically given to the well-heeled and well-protected perpetrators of ideological or greed-induced institutionalized evil.

The epidemic of AIDS and the search for a cure. The incredible advances which have been made in the field of medicine and pharmacology. The increased human life span within the population of the rich nations . . . and among the richest people in the poorer nations. The continued attempts made to suppress and marginalize alternative health-care methods and therapies.

The evolving characterization and understanding of who and of what God is, from that of a static, distant, and externalized God of mental belief—to that of a relational God of nearness, presence, experience, and incarnation.

The billions of truly (nonfictional) *left behind* children caught in the midst of tribal and power-grabbing wars and between unnatural catastrophes and foreign exploitations.

The millions without refuge from economic or (institutional) physical violence.

The increased domination and control of world resources (including food and water) by the despotic few. The buying up of local cropland by foreign powers and by governmental control centers, by fewer and fewer of the world-tentacled corporations and the benefacting bureaucratic rulers—along with their local cronies.

And let's not ignore all of the reactionary opposition to so much of these recent convulsions, as well as the predictable counterreactions at almost every level of resisted change . . . against each of the near-frozen opposing tribal paradigms.

Add your own examples and et ceteras to the overflowing list if you wish.

It grows out of its own accord as we speak, doesn't it?

The list of change and the list of resistance to change.

And the resistance to the resistance.

The list of exploitation and adversity and the list of resistance to exploitation and adversity.

And the resistance to the resistance.

The list of deniers and the list of truth seekers.

The list of imbalance and the list of those trying to bring balance.

The list of problems and the list of attempts at solution.

But why go on?

You already know the extent of the lists. And it never seems to be approaching an end, does it?

But we'll stop here for now nonetheless, if you don't mind.

It's such a tiresome list. Yes? Especially when so much of the allegiance or opposition to so many parts of it seems to favor the hunkering down of the either/or mind-set over and against anything which could lead to the actual transcendence of the divisive (and relative) *only-mind* . . . a hunkering down which accommodates the same old violent correctives instead (for what it intends to rectify or eliminate) and a likewise belittling of the hope and guidance which an active practice of compassionate nonviolence could provide—which would reduce and exclude nothing from *That which is always becoming.*

Because it can't be done.

Can it?

CHAPTER 46

Pressure Makes Diamonds

HERE MIGHT BE a good place to acknowledge the growing number of human beings who are beginning to emerge from a cutting edge of uncaptured practice and experience but who still dwell on the fringe, the ones who seem to be able to keep a vigorous psychological distance between themselves and much of the reactionary fray which seems to dominate the overly contained layers of belief in your world.

Most of these precocious souls of minimal (but expanding) influence will not be taking the trip with you tomorrow morning. They'll be among the many who'll be left to hold down the fort, so to speak—waiting to embrace the rest of you when you eventually return from your collective and individual facial expeditions.

And they've remained rather inconspicuous. Haven't they? Even self-effacing and almost bashful of the gifts they've been given while still being able to function beyond the commonly prescribed (and restrictive) capacities of human conformity—which demand so much *disjoined* tribal attention. And they've done it in ways which have slid a new twist into the emerging ball game, haven't they?

They've discovered that they can watch themselves transform, even while they keep moving beyond each uneven shift in the transformational process; even while moving beyond themselves. And they don't feel the need to reject or demean any particular function or part of themselves, or of any *other* sentient (or even nonsentient) being either.

They've experienced varying degrees of a rare freedom that only the very few have so far been able to glimpse . . . up until the last few decades anyway, when an unassuming band of unsuspecting fringe dwellers began to slowly emerge and inhabit a new height and depth of awareness—which has largely gone unnoticed by the majority of you.

They're the ones who've been willing (yet still almost always surprised) to be able to see while looking out from their original face (with its invisible eyes) and from within its inexhaustible spaciousness, where the origin and capacity of the indivisible *Self* resides—held together in one continuous flow. And it's from within that all-embracing continuum that they're often able to see only a wholeness, in and of itself, coming into and out of itself—simultaneously.

It's as though they have no choice in the matter.

And it's from within that spacious and awakened continuity where they can clearly see that they are infinitely faceless.

Just as you are.

But most of you aren't able to realize that yet, are you? Because as we've been trying to demonstrate, most of you remain so overly identified with the tribal face which you've been assigned to that you refuse to give it up. You even flinch at letting it fall off on its own—even for a few moments of comforting respite. You seem to believe that if it disappears then you will disappear, don't you?

But you can't disappear!

The *Self* can never disappear!

Yet the face can disappear. Can't it? And the body can disappear (and it will). Even your attachment to the masks you've been wearing, which so many of you have spent your whole lives bringing forth and proudly showing off and clinging to—even it can (and will) disappear, which may shock and frighten many of you.

The tribal trance can (and will) melt away. We guarantee it.

But what is never born can never die.

And a thing that isn't can't be a thing that was.

Can it?

If you look closely, you can plainly see the paradoxical landscape which includes everything and everyone, human or *other* than human. It includes the masked (false) self. And it includes the relative and embodied (yet genuine) self as well. And it includes the infinite and faceless (Absolute) *Self.*

Yet it still takes much practice in the ways of dying in order to undo the intense tribal conditioning to which you've been infused, doesn't it?

You've all come into the world with childlike vision, able to see that what is real is unified—and that it is changeless. You don't even think about it. It just is. Isn't it?

But then you're soon taught and told over and over again that what is real is not actually real, that instead reality is what you're instructed to believe it is . . . by your culture, or by your religion, or by your parents; by your status, or by your grasp of power; by your peer group, or by your possessions; by what you look like, or by how you appear to others; by your sense of worthiness;, or by where you were born—and by what you were born into.

Reality becomes what the tribe says it is and by what the tribal mirror reflects (of its own image) back to you.

Reality becomes separated from itself.

Childlike becomes childish.

Selfless becomes compulsively self-absorbed.

The changeless becomes subject to ever-changing and ever-competing tribal logic—which is how so many of you have come to lose your original face and your original sight, into the various masks which generously bestow their *disjoined* confusion upon you.

The faceless ones are covered over with facial simulations of the containing *only-mind*.

Character actors replace human beings . . . rehearsing their inherited lines of self-containment, pretending that they're not really pretending at all (to be who they are).

But there's a slow growing number of (even more) *others* joining the nontribal fringe-dwelling group all the time, joining in on the seeing at varying speeds and along various channels and through various wrinkles of coincidence—and by invitations of grace or sometimes just all-of-a-sudden and out of nowhere (which is everywhere), conjoined in one instance of seeing for the very first time, even though what many of them are beginning to finally see has been forever within their range of sight.

But a certain amount of waking up is always necessary for clear and even sane vision to come about—which can even extend into a lucid and awakened dream state while actually sleeping. Can it not?

These fringe dwellers whom we speak of have been able to slowly flourish and mature, accepting and bringing along what is true, good, and beautiful from previous experience; leaving behind what's no longer useful, appropriate, or nourishing to them or to the life around them, as they move about and within their own interconnected journey of awareness.

They don't reject their past. But they don't live in it either. They imperfectly move beyond it and out of it . . . little by little, and often unevenly. But they do it. And the deeper they look the more they see with clarity into the vast and spacious present moment, as it continues to lean forward into *That which is always becoming*.

And the more often that they look with committed concentration and intent, the more they can actually see.

The more they can actually see!

But it's not a quantitative *more.* The inexhaustible and eternal *Self* has no material or spiritual quantity which can be measured.

And these seers on the fringe seem to recognize that some of their past ways of relating, which they've been gradually shedding and leaving behind, may have been quite necessary. They may have been the prerequisite lessons which were required in order to get to where they are now in their ongoing spiritual evolution.

But now . . . they can let them go. They must let them go.

They've come to a place of no choice (and no place), where *That which is always becoming* becomes the chooser and where *the disjoined* tribal *only-mind* slowly disappears . . . shrinking into the uncontainable background along with conscious contrivance and with the selfish will of the individual and with any compulsive need to be right or to worry about (con)temporary outcomes, which will eventually die off and disappear—as all outcomes in your impermanent world do. Because those needs and worries only exist in the shadowy illusion of separateness, in the illusion that deceives you into imagining that it's possible to be separate from the unifying *Self*—which excludes no one and nothing and includes each and every bit of *otherness* (even your own).

To behold the ineffable is actually what is trusted most by these fringe seers. It allows for everything to come forth out of *That which always is.* Conscious choice is replenished by trust in the boundless *Self,* by melting into the ocean of *That which is revealing It-Self into Being,* in every moment of *now*—in every bit of evolving *Creation.*

Yet everyone's skin sheds differently, doesn't it?

Getting to a place of beholding *That which is real* is quite a unique event, every time . . . and for everyone. So one sure way to waste a lot of momentum is to try to exactly imitate any *other* person's messy path to awareness. And it can be a very messy path, can it not?

But if it's not your path then you will not even be welcomed. You will get your delusional ass kicked instead—every time. But if that's what you need . . . well then . . . maybe a certain amount of delusional ass kicking is part of your particular path. Who's to say? No one knows . . . but you.

Yet we digress.

It's not only what they take with them which fuels these seers forward. It's also what they leave behind. It's especially what they let go of and leave behind. It's one of those sweetly hidden secrets that you will hopefully soon discover, that spiritual vision is awakened by the alarm clock of subtraction—by the peeling away of the tribal mask.

And while acknowledging this transcendent process of surrender and inclusion in themselves, these observers also recognize that it's a path without an end and that the same untidy process is necessary for any further expansion of goodness, truth, and beauty to continue (in themselves . . . and in the rest of you), within and alongside all of what appears to be separate and idiosyncratic—while still integrating all journeys into one unifying journey.

The continual voice of paradox never stops revealing previously hidden windows or previously hidden doors to look or to walk through, don't you see?

Nothing of *That which is* (nothing of the unifying *Self*) can be separated nor hidden by tribal illusions forever.

These seers don't seem to need to condemn what they've already spent of themselves anymore either . . . in order to accept their own awakening presence or vision.

And you'll find it very difficult to antagonize any of them into an oppositional or contentious argument. Although they don't deny that evil and deceit do exist and that they need to be called out and confronted when necessary and disavowed their power whenever possible, and that the fallible and difficult vigilance and practice of resisting evil and exposing lies, wherever evil and deceitful invention may be found to be hiding (or even pretending to be something other than what they are) never ends.

Yet these are not perfect human beings we're talking about by any means.

Or perhaps another way of putting it is that they are perfect in their imperfections.

They are not immune to regress. It happens. It's still one step forward and . . . well . . . maybe not quite as many steps backward for many of them as there used to be.

But there's always the danger of getting stuck in some regression lane along the way, isn't there? They're still tempted to fall back into habitual behavioral patterns and responses which they were taught to become accustomed to just like the rest of you. They too have their own demons of tribal conditioning that sneak up on them when they're not looking out from their own face, which in reality (as we've said) is faceless because its true nature is not of a specific face which can separate itself from anything else at all. That would be impossible, but not impossible for the false nature of tribal *disjoined* self-deception.

Hence, there have been some within the ranks of the seers who will be accompanying the rest of you on tomorrow's facial journey. Regrettably, they've regressed too far or too corruptly in some areas of their lives to be left safely behind. They didn't pay enough attention to the whole . . . to their holonic responsibilities, to being interdependent beings in a continuous and vital relationship with the larger *Self* nor to being independent beings of wholeness themselves . . . carrying and being nourished by their own interrelated ecology of unified parts.

They thought they could outsmart their relationship to *That which is* with a few well-played hands of facial aloofness. But things don't separate out like that, at least not in very real ways. There's always a blind spot that can creep up on you if you allow it to—as it did for them.

A holon is something that is simultaneously a whole and a part, according to the wise observations of Arthur Koestler.[1]

Those seers who may have regressed also forgot that being overly attached to power or status, or to spiritual and material circumstances, is not a harmless psychological act . . . if left to its own devices (as we've previously discussed). It can take over as quickly as you can keep saying yes to its compulsive desires. And it's good at doing just that.

A genuine holonic being can only evolve or wake up if his or her interconnected environment remains operative and awake to its inherent unity.

Dysfunctional atoms make for dysfunctional molecules.

A dysfunctional liver, kidney, or heart makes for a dysfunctional physical body.

A hate-filled or self-righteous and violent mote of belief, or bits and pieces of selfish, jealous, or bigoted behaviors make for afflicted bodies—gross, subtle, or even causal, do they not?

Take a fresh drink of a cold and clean glass of artesian spring water. Then drop a speck of feces in it. Then take another drink. One bad apple; that's all it takes sometimes.

But fortunately, the majority of this minority has been awake enough to be able to catch enough tailwind of truth along with enough goodness and beauty to recognize that there's no inherent division in any of it.

MICHAEL J. GAJDA

There's only one howling universal wind. And no one superincumbent tribe or any intensely charismatic individual can lay claim to any part of it as their own.

And these human seers that we're speaking so highly of? They still have plenty left to wake up to and transcend—which makes the whole thing worthwhile and exciting. Wouldn't you agree?

Every time they open a door, they find another door behind that door . . . and then another one behind that one, until somewhere down the road there are no more doors to open or to walk through. There's only the *Self.* There's only *That which is* . . . which is when and where liberation suddenly transcends realization, which itself had just gradually moved beyond mere understanding, and which just prior to that had finally shed and overcome most its own remnants of tribal ignorance.

And whenever anyone will eventually enter into that infinite space of liberation (that ultimate resting place beyond death and resurrection) is beyond knowing. Because *That which is always becoming* is beyond place and beyond time and beyond space and beyond cause and effect. It's even beyond shape or form and beyond any of the trap doors or false windows which are hidden and confined inside the tribal imagination.

But the difference between most of these seers and most of you is that they seem to know that every being represents a partial piece of the truth. Nobody has it all. A wave is not the ocean (as it has often been said). But it consists only and completely of ocean stuff. If separated from the ocean it dries up and evaporates, doesn't it? Which, of course, is impossible. Because separateness is impossible. And once again, the wily blessings of paradox expose and peel away another layer of that blinding and sticky tribal mask of ignorance.

And these seers know that being human is being imperfect and fallible. So they still use what works. And they still make human mistakes, plenty of them. But they have no turf to stand upon and defend (neither physical, spiritual, nor experiential). *That which is always becoming* is *That which is always becoming.* So they know that they can never own it. The whole universe is theirs, to learn and to grow from and to respond to and participate in—but not to own. Nothing is attached to or fastened down so tightly that it can't reach out or be reached for with higher, deeper, or wider compassion or with more self-forgiveness, or that cannot be let go of—if that's what's called for.

Probably the most common characteristic which most of the seers share is that they continue to reach . . . and that they continue to be able to let go. To be self-satisfied is not a goal of theirs. But it's often an essential component in the big bag of tricks offered up by the *disjoined* one, isn't it?

And the more that anyone is able to establish themselves in an actual stream of progressive awakening, the more they're able to release themselves from the bondage of thinking that one can (or already has) finally figured it all out. And subsequently (or even simultaneously) the more they're able to release themselves from the bondage of an overreliance on thinking itself—which tends to cut things up into tribal calculations. And then of course, the more they're even able to release themselves from the bondage of seeking guaranteed or permanent security of any kind or from wallowing in all of that tribal arrogance and addiction.

And when you mix a little too much of any one of those self-deceptions with any other one, or carry around too big of a load of any one of them, or hold a dependency upon any one of them as an exterior shadow to project upon . . . it almost always leads to violence, doesn't it? Whether it's spiritual, physical, or psychological violence—it leads to death and destruction of some kind.

It leads to more *disjoining* rituals and decrees, which almost always lead to the scapegoating of some alien *otherness* or of some *other* group or of some convenient or expendable individual . . . human or *other* than human.

But you already know all of that. Don't you?

So this group of seers (who will be holding down the planet for the rest of you) are a work in progress just like you are. And most of them seem to know it.

There is struggle. They know that. There is always struggle. It's part of the process, part of the practice.

But pressure makes diamonds.

Doesn't it?

CHAPTER 47

Prophets of *Otherness*

HAVEN'T THERE ALWAYS been individuals who've discovered how to be able to keep themselves above the fray of ignorance and suspicion? And out of the grasping fists of fear and violence? Away from joining the cults of greed and compulsive acquisition? From being too self-absorbed? From overidentifying with any particular tribe or with any seductive level of tribal status?

Haven't there always been individuals who've been able to do that?

Of course there have been.

But not without coming up against resistance from within the tribal milieu, or even from within themselves—not without experiencing inner conflict and outer struggle.

But the historic evidence suggests that most human beings who've unshackled themselves from the chains of tribal thinking (before this recent revival began) were rare spiritual mutants. Doesn't it? They usually stood up alone or in very small numbers, standing out among the assemblage of mass conformity so dominant within all spiritual slave-holding communities—which have always been in place at various levels of strength and number throughout your so often (purposefully or unconsciously) forgotten tribal histories.

Many of those freedom lovers were willing to risk their own physical lives for the sake of that love and for the sake of seeing clearly, for the sake of living out their lives according to what they could see—not for the sake of what the tribe tried to convince (or even tried to intimidate or force) them to look for.

Yet (now) many of those same (long-dead and) courageous human beings are proclaimed to be sages, prophets, saints, or martyrs, aren't they? To be wise mystics, to be awakened or anointed ones; to be avatars or incarnations; to be messiahs, heroes, or guardians of the faith; even to be repossessed and redefined guardians of nation-states, which always seem to need mythological heroes to build upon in order to justify their systems of uneven justice and violence, don't they? Nation-states that are usually backed up by a collaborating (unofficial or official) religion to give themselves the appearance of being chosen by the formally acknowledged (and renovated) god of tribal habit.

Many of the currently honored whom you've now placed upon your tribal pedestals were rarely acknowledged or even considered to be anything close to being revered by the vast majority of their contemporaries . . . when they were still alive and breathing. Were they? Especially not by the established political and religious status quo of their tribal place and time.

And the irony is that now many of them are reclaimed and adulated by your present-day (dominant) political and religious institutions, by the established tribes which still cling to the same ancestral addictions and fears which condemned and rejected those prophets and sages whom they now exalt . . . the prophets and sages who were once condemned and rejected for spreading their troublesome love . . . for resisting tribal lies and for trying to replace those lies with simple truth, goodness, or beauty, or for just asking questions that the powers which were in place at the time didn't want asked—which is pretty much the same reasoning which accounts for the condemnation of your present-day prophets and sages whom you reject, isn't it?

But when hearing the call . . . well . . . genuine prophets just can't seem to stop themselves, can they?

Although the gift of prophecy that's bestowed upon them (of telling and living out their truth) is a tortuous one, isn't it? And it can't be returned or exchanged for a different or less demanding one either. Because once you've got it . . . it's yours. You become it. And it becomes you. And you always die to the masked self because of it—and then get resurrected by (and right back into and through) the genuine self, and then reunited into the Great *Self.* And sometimes you're actually killed off because of it, aren't you? Usually by the institution or tribal system within which you hear your prophetic calling.

Prophets tell the truth. They live and die to speak truth to the *disjoined* powers of the *only-mind.* But first and always, they must tell the truth to themselves.

They don't lie about who they are or about who they've been. And they don't predict the future. They tell the truth. They tell the truth to political and religious institutions and to economic and social systems, to all *disjoined* fixtures of tribal power—which is what always sends them into internal or external exile and which gets them rejected, excommunicated, tortured, or even put to death by (officially staged) public execution or by cowardly character (or even physical) assassination.

Generally speaking, overly contained tribal institutions don't even like hearing about the truth, let alone hearing it directly told to them. They've already claimed it as their own, to control and loom over others. It's where they sustain their sense of power, their self-elevated prestige, and their hoarded possessions.

Real truth (not partisan or sectarian truth) unhinges that kind of racketeering.

And there are of course plenty of marginalized prophets alive today who (when they're dead and gone) will be renovated and turned into saints and sages by your descendants. Don't you see? By those same rejecting tribal authorities, just like the image and reputation of truth sayers have always been rigged to the advantage of whatever *disjoined* tribal institution can most benefit from their reinvention.

These prophets and truth sayers still walk among you as we speak, just as they always have.

And just as the gifted and suffering ones before them, they remain mostly nameless or censured, rejected by the time and place they were born into, by the culture and religion and politics of their times, by the temporal powers that call the temporal shots, and by those who anoint themselves as the official interpreting agents of the *only-mind*.

It's quite a predictable cycle of chronicled human behavior, not isolated to any one culture or religion or to any one segment or divide of ideological or political history.

A prophet is only despised in his own country, among his own relations and in his own house, spoke the wise Jesus, just before the people in his own house murdered him.[1]

Socrates: Poisoned.[2]
Al-Hallaj: Tortured and executed.[3]
Akiva ben Joseph: Tortured and executed.[4]
John of the Cross: Tortured and imprisoned.[5]
Teresa of Avila: Exiled and silenced.[6]
Jesus: Tortured and executed.[7]
Francis of Assisi: Ridiculed and thought to be a raving madman.[8]
Dietrich Boenhoffer: Imprisoned and executed.[9]
Keila Esther Berrio Almanza: Threatened and assassinated.[10]

Mahatma Gandhi: Imprisoned and assassinated.[11]
Malcolm X: Marginalized and assassinated.[12]
Franz Jagerstatter: Marginalized, arrested, and executed.[13]
Martin Luther King Jr.: Imprisoned, rejected, and assassinated.[14]
Giordano Bruno: Condemned and burned at the stake.[15]
Nelson Mandela: Tortured and imprisoned.[16]
Khan Abdul Ghaffar Khan: Imprisoned and exiled.[17]
Ken Saro-Wiwa: Marginalized, arrested, and executed.[18]
Oscar Romero: Threatened and assassinated.[19]
Medgar Evers: Threatened and assassinated.[20]
Dorothy Stang: Threatened and assassinated.[21]
Benigno Aquino: Imprisoned, exiled, and assassinated.[22]
Crazy Horse: Hunted down, imprisoned, and assassinated.[23]
Thich Quang Duc: Persecuted and burned to self-sacrificial death.[24]
Digna Ochoa: Threatened, abducted, and murdered.[25]

All of them were feared and hated and outcast and distrusted by the archetypal tribal powers of their place and time. All of them sacrificed themselves for the sake of the whole or for the sake of the wholeness within themselves.

But these are just a few among the many of the more renowned who fit the bill of being despised or dreaded during their lifetime, by the reigning political or religious tribal forces and by their criminal, military, or corporate allies, later to be honored and sometimes even idolized by so many of those same forces after they've died or have been murdered or after they've outlasted their persecutors—which is frequently just another way of trying to soften or strip away their humanity and to deny their essential and difficult message, isn't it?

We put Jesus on a pedestal in order to keep him safely at a distance. It is easier to worship Jesus than to follow him, wrote the wise Brian C. Taylor.[26]

And if that same Jesus were to show up today in your world with his same message of *agape* (of unconditional selfless love for all),[27] with his uncompromising ways of nonviolently challenging tribal hypocrisy and injustice . . . especially when he saw it in the prototypical religious and political authorities of his time and place, there's about a 100 percent chance that he'd be sold out and strung up all over again, isn't there? By many from the same crowd who currently claim to worship him, led by those at the top of the political worship chain . . . where they wield their politicized religious power and influence over others in his name and where they teach and often do almost exactly the reverse of what Jesus taught and did—in his name.

His life and message of nonviolence and simplicity, of forgiveness and inclusivity, and of speaking truth to power is just as threatening to the present-day religious and political imposters and tribal hypocrites and to the peddling empires of violence as they were then.

But instead of a cross, they'd use a bullet or a noose or a needle or a chair to try to shut him up and make him go away, just as they're currently trying to silence any of the prophetic voices in their own present-day flocks who threaten their crumbling and corrupt mechanical power hierarchies.

And the same fate could probably be predicted for Moses, Jeremiah, or Mohammed,[28] for that matter, among so many other dead and renowned prophets and sages, if they returned to their own present-day neck of the woods.

They'd be seen as similar threats for the same feeble but fearful tribal reasons by many of those same people who currently claim them as their own sacred prophets, led by those at the top of the claim chain—where they wield their violent influence along with their sanctimonious and hollow rituals of suppression.

Claiming and worshiping is always the easier route to go when compared with actually transforming the way one thinks, acts, and lives . . . especially if it requires unconditional love of the *other* or unconditional trust of *That which is the Self*—which includes everyone, human and *other* than human.

Belief (especially strict and unbending fundamentalist belief) is a much safer and easier road to travel than one which requires that you directly experience *That which is beyond* tribal perception—where the practice of faith, justice, and compassion are the difficult requirements, not the cowardly comfort of self-certainty, judgment, and vengeance.

But just think of all the thousands . . . no! . . . the millions of unknown or unheralded human beings who were treated in the same despicable way or even worse during their lifetimes but who now are just forgotten dust beneath piles of tribal history and lies, their lives too simple or small to be remembered because they were just too powerless or too different or because they ignored or refused the tribal systems of *disjoined* conformism or the oppressive orthodoxy which was in place at the time of their persecution.

I was hungry but you would not feed me, thirsty but you would not give me a drink; I was a stranger but you would not welcome me in your homes, naked but you would not clothe me; I was sick and in prison but you would not take care of me, was the wise reminder which Jesus gave of his true identity.[29]

And he wasn't just referring to his own tribe of Jewish neighbors from Nazareth or Galilee either, was he? He was speaking of the great *I Am*—which includes everyone, human or *other* than human.

Keep remembering this: there is no *other*. There never was.

But there are martyrs confirmed by history. And there are martyrs confirmed by the precarious institutional powers of the moment—for purposes of propaganda and control. Unfortunately many of you still have difficulty recognizing that distinction, don't you?

Let us all be brave enough to die the death of a martyr, but let no one lust for martyrdom, said the wise Mohandas Gandhi.[30]

Men do not accept their prophets and [so they] *slay them, but they love their martyrs and worship those whom they have tortured to death*, wrote the wise Fyodor Dostoevsky.[31]

All spiritual journeys are martyrdoms, said the wise Jean Cocteau.[32]

A thing is not necessarily true because a man dies for it, wrote the wise Oscar Wilde.[33]

CHAPTER 48

The *Otherness* of Change

BUT LET US briefly return to our list of controversies and ponder them with you just a bit further, shall we?

A good deal has changed in your rather neonate world over a very short and recent period of time, hasn't it? And at a tremendously quick pace. And it hasn't been slowing down much either, has it?

Sizable earthquakes have jolted the fragile fault lines of knowledge which you thought had been firmly set into stone, by assuming that you could simply think or believe them into permanence.

There have been a multitude of such recent realignments. Haven't there? Of reenvisioning and of reinterpretation, of reevaluating and of redefinition, and of reconstructing and of deconstruction—all of it shaking up the long-held opinions and beliefs which you've clung to for so long, the relied-upon presumptions that have kept you from falling off the wagon of your tribal tendencies.

Much of the shake-up has accumulated (and accelerated) in just the last several decades, while many of you simply continue to cling to business as usual—hibernating in your long-established condition of tribal sleepwalking.

And these changes not only came up on you fast but with the assistance, power, and speed of the very technologies discovered and relied upon within the occurrences themselves—which enhanced the effect.

It's been a lot to handle and to digest for many of you who would have preferred not to touch or eat any of it, hasn't it?

If you didn't always appreciate and respect the way things were (the way you imagined them to be or the way you thought they should be), at least you felt reassured by the custom-made signs and symbols embedded in the conventional routines and traditions which you've invented and attached to them.

Accordingly, you haven't shown much enthusiasm for any likelihood that would arrange for the inmost *Self* to even begin to mildly wake up and then expand into your conscious awareness, have you? Not by any stretch of your overly contained imagination, no matter how enlightening the chips could possibly fall, especially if they were to bump up against any of your vulnerable beams of tribal stability . . . the nuts and bolts that have been holding up and bracing the floors and walls of your mansions of despair and delusion for so long, decorating your interior life with their *disjoined* components—which so many of you reminisce about and rely upon, from within your one-dimensional memorized accounts of what your lives were like in the good old days.

Yet it doesn't really matter whether or not they were actual lives which were being lived or which you've been longing to return to, does it?

Longing to be where you've never fully been present and never intend to be or especially for where you are *not* (from right here and now) is a waste of creative time and energy, isn't it?

It's even a waste of the illusion of tribal continuance which you insist upon clinging to . . . in your vain attempt to constrain it. Don't you see?

You can never fully appreciate what you're unable (or refuse) to let go of—which is what most longing does to the present moment, doesn't it?

It deadens it.

Because most longing in your world is a materialistic hunger for that which doesn't last . . . which is why most of it is mere addiction, even though you try to mask it up in the clothes of spiritual desire or in the language of a romanticized tribal ideology or in the drowning tears of sentimental allegiance.

If you can't even imagine removing your tribal clothing or becoming visible, open, and present to the nakedness of the divine and compassionate *Self*, then you've become an addict to your own disguise, haven't you? No matter how well-dressed you are in your inherited tribal camouflage or how well versed you are in your inherited tribal jargon.

The mask is not and never can be the face of what is real. And the clothes are not and never can be the skin of what is true.

Yet you still remain ready and willing to use bare-skinned violence to defend your overidentified-with tribe, don't you? Against any of the transformational changes coming at you.

The *otherness* of change (which you constantly guard against) threatens to soften and disrupt your hardened perspectives, don't you see? Perspectives which are maintained by the mundane memories and assumptions which you've embodied for so long.

So in alliance with your reactionary habits of tribal violence you've joined forces with the epidemic rise of hoarding, haven't you? With armies of hoarders—hunkering down into your own little claustrophobic and separate tribal units, no matter how big and airy you imagine them to be, in order to fend off for as long as you can any of that unwelcome change—which you fear much more than you despise.

CHAPTER 49

The Hoarding

HAVEN'T YOU EVEN begun to notice the many thousands of storage facilities that are rising up all around you like instant villages of containment?

They appear to cover even more ground than your burgeoning colonies of gated affluence do, don't they? Providing you with safe and secure domiciles for all of your unused objects of surplus desire, of which you can't seem to be able to keep from accumulating or from even knowing what to do with anymore—but which you refuse to get rid of just the same, even though you have no practical or worthwhile use for much of what you hoard.

Many of you can't even remember or describe most of what you've packed away once you've pulled the storage unit door down upon it all, can you?

And you rarely even think about any of it either. Do you? Except to vaguely wonder if it's all still there . . . or if someone may have stolen or damaged any of it, or if a family of mice may have built a comfortable nest for themselves among the ruins of your ruthless overconsumption.

Yet you do peek in on it, yes? Periodically . . . just to make sure that it all still exists, that it's all still yours, and that it's still safe and secure.

The periodic peeking allows you that quick and blissful hormonal fix of secreted adrenaline which you so look forward to, doesn't it? Lustfully reminding you of why you still impound such an overabundance of long-forsaken objects of such short-lived psychological pleasure and of such fleeting physical gratification.

But you don't stack up and stockpile all of those coveted perishables merely to protect them, do you? No. You don't. Instead, you're driven by a domesticated desire to keep feeding the addictive tribal habit with the chronic and collective act of hoarding itself—even though you never seem to be able to satisfy the habitual urge which drives you to amass so much discarded waste in the first place.

And what a paradoxical addiction it is, isn't it?

There exist millions of dispossessed and homeless human beings (and even more abandoned and abused dogs and cats) roaming the jungled streets and back roads of your world. They drift and wander in search of their own safe and secure nook and cranny where they can curl up and sleep for a peaceful moment or two or where they can temporarily rest their tired and hungry bones in a quiet and undiscovered cubbyhole for a while, knowing that there's not exactly an overabundance of gracious and hospitable villages or of inviting and safe shelters or even of welcoming warm homes rising up for their physical protection and security—not even of the ungated variety.

With one obvious and growing exception.

And that exception is found in the plenitude of tribal fears which forever disturb and overexcite you to subsidize and expand upon your plunderbund of bloated prison colonies, where you collect, classify, and contain the undesirables of your species—which isn't exactly an expression of preventive social medicine, nor is it a compassionate gesture of protection for the most vulnerable among you on your part, is it?

And it certainly doesn't create harmonious environments for the squeezed-in and overcrowded ones who reside in those isolated colonies, does it?

No. It doesn't.

Not for those who must sleep, eat, and try to hold out there. Not for the mostly poor, developmentally disabled, illiterate, abused, marginalized, physically addicted, and often mentally ill residents who tend to occupy much if not most of the space in those violent containers of abandoned human storage. Not for those or any other discarded, doomed, and tribe-forgotten human beings.[1]

But it does seem to give many of you who live outside and far enough away from those human confinement facilities a calming rush of sedation. Doesn't it? One not so dissimilar from the adrenaline surge you get when you think of all of that other stuff that you've safely secured inside all of those other depositories of overindulgence.

Locking stuff up seems to be a convenient solution for so many of you, doesn't it? And for so much of what confounds you. It's the reliable yet forever temporary fix for your addiction to excess—which takes up so much space inside of the tribal psyche, doesn't it? And which needs to be emptied out at regular intervals in order to make room for more of the same so you can keep on dancing to the tribal storage rhythms that pound the *disjoining* drum inside the head of the *only-mind* . . . to one habitual percussion pattern, filling it up and emptying it out and then refilling it back up again, with whatever fearful fixation that you seek relief from but rarely if ever let go of—squeezing as much into each unit as you possibly can.

Empty space scares so many of you, doesn't it? Just like silence or stillness does. And needing to fill it up is quite a paradoxical preoccupation of yours, isn't it?

Space becomes much more valuable to you the more it's inhabited. Its worth actually increases the more the space itself diminishes.

It's such interesting tribal logic, isn't it?

The more the space is occupied, the more it outvalues whatever occupies the space.

But your wasteful extravagance almost always overtakes the area needed to contain it all, doesn't it?

So your solution is to just build more and more holding units for more and more things (human or *other* than human) to stuff into them.

Whenever there's too much accumulation of which you don't know what to do with anymore, you simply squeeze the excess into one of your many newly constructed storage containers, which then provides you with more space outside of each new installation, to which you can then return to filling back up again with more of the eventually unwanted accrual, which you will, in time, squeeze into future storage just like all of that other stuff which you've already packed away.

You just keep tossing out and locking up more objects of obsession, replacing them with new ones to fill up the space of emptiness which you occupy—which never seems to have enough in it to feel completely full.

It may feel overstuffed at times. But it never feels quite full, does it?

Meanwhile, your *disjoined* addictions remain loyal subjects of the tribe's core of overly contained influence, which is what motivates and inspires your constant craving, isn't it? You forever crave to fill up every inch of empty tribal space because spaciousness tends to create problems of equanimity, doesn't it? Which naturally collides with the prevailing imbalance of the *only-mind*. Equanimity tends to patiently reveal and then remove all tribal masks while quieting the surrounding noise with surprising patience and with unabashed transparency, leaving you face-to-face with who you are—with *That which is always becoming* and with that of the faceless and indivisible *Self.*

MICHAEL J. GAJDA

I neither am my body nor in it. On the contrary, it—along with the rest of my world—is in me, wrote the wise Douglas Harding.[2]

And yet somehow you always seem to be able to build or find enough enclosed space to contain all of your glut, don't you?

But is that really what the wise Nazarene was talking about when he encouraged his listeners to give shelter to the homeless, to feed the hungry, and to clothe the naked?[3]

To give shelter to the homeless couch and tables? To give shelter to unwanted furniture? Or to bicycles and bookshelves? To old records and picture frames or lawn mowers? To chairs and rugs? To silverware and golf clubs? To band saws and the broken toys of grown-up children? To board games and books and electronics and exercise equipment? To extra windows and doors? To feed and then overfeed the tribal ideologies? And to clothe them all with rituals of fear?

Is that the kind of shelter and protection he was talking about when regarding the poor, the illiterate, or the mentally ill? Or the abused, the hopeless, and the frightened? Or the angry and the unjustly treated? The unconventional and the outcast? Or even your most dangerous brothers and sisters?

Is that what he was talking about? That kind of shelter? That kind of feeding frenzy? That kind of covering up of naked truths?

Well then?

At least you're helping out the tribal economy, aren't you? By buying up or capturing all of that overabundance and then paying someone else to lock it up and to keep a close watch on all of it for you so that nothing gets stolen or escapes from the space you fill up with it all.

There always seems to be a silver lining to be found somewhere, doesn't there? Which is so frequently found in someone's lucratively lined pockets.

And desperately locking up the so-called dangerous ones is a lot easier than asking yourselves what makes them so much more treacherous than anybody else or more irredeemable than you—if they really are. It's much easier than asking how they got that way, Isn't it? Or if that even matters. It's a growing business, after all—and quite a profitable one too.

And it does seem that it doesn't really matter much (if at all) to most of you, doesn't it? Not if you can just pay government and corporate enterprises to routinely lock them up so you can then forget that they're there—just like the rest of your trifled away objects of overindulgence.

And yet it doesn't really seem to matter that it doesn't seem to matter. Does it?

Nevertheless, we've often wondered why you haven't tried to confine and contain other forms of misspent lavishness, which could add quite substantially to your collection of squandered discards, like any of your modern or advanced collections of war-making weaponry for instance— or even some of your war-making weapons manufacturers themselves, for that matter.

They seem to be compulsively dangerous. And you seem to be excessively obsessed with their growth and preservation.

And they sure do fill up a lot of space. Don't they?

They also tend to destroy a lot of what's inside of that space while they're at it, creating evermore empty expanse to fill up all over again . . . with their *disjoined* tribal magic which claims that it can turn bullets and guns into bread and butter.

And they've sure seemed to break into and break up way more space (while they overly contain it) than any of that *other* human or *other*-than-human stuff which you've been locking up and storing away like gangbusters, haven't they?

And they even seem to multiply much faster than your most overly hoarded and discarded desires do, don't they? Even faster than your most frightening wrongdoers and misfits—in actual number and in actual amount of devastation of previously undevastated or safely inhabited space.

Just ask the hundred million or so human beings who were murdered in all of those immense tribal wars which you've so willingly subsidized, with all of your implements and experiments of systemic destruction, especially during much of the previous century . . . not to mention the millions who were physically or emotionally maimed for life by those same weapon systems, or the millions of *other*-than-human beings that got in the way and were slaughtered in those huge waves of normalized and premeditated tribal violence.

And what about all the victims mutilated or murdered in civil and religious strife, within your disputing tribal territories? What about them? Or in your ethnic or racial conflicts? And in your blood feuds? Or in your genocidal uprisings? In your fanatical terrorist crimes? Or from your ideological insurrections? Or inside your political prisons or torture chambers? Is that where all that bread and butter is supposed to come from?

And it still goes on, doesn't it? Your officially sanctioned institutional violence hasn't let up on those mostly directly affected by it, has it?

Most of the mangled and exterminated victims of the merchants of brutal weaponry have themselves been locked up and abandoned in a different kind of storage space, haven't they? Enclosed by realistic (as opposed to richly imagined) fear . . . and tightly packed in by the walls of poverty, drought, hunger, or destitution; surrounded and locked into geographical dungeons too dangerously overwhelmed, chaotic, clogged-up and violent to escape from; overly contained in their own spatial pockets of powerlessness and of neglect and abandonment—while war-mongering weapons of physical and spiritual destruction continue to be invented, overproduced, and politically or religiously justified in their use.

And then of course new alibis for their repeated use must continue to be refashioned and rationalized, don't they? Just to make sure that the retargeted use of weapons comes to be passively accepted as a tribal norm. Because each newly invented weapon (or weapon system) needs to be tested on real life targets, whether human or *other* than human, just to make sure that it works efficiently enough. But if it doesn't, that's okay too. Because inefficiency creates just another excuse to invent, merchandise, and then test even more weapons on *other* real life bull's-eyes, doesn't it? And for only one profiteering purpose—to terrorize and to devastate.

But you already know that.

So enough about space already.

It can never be completely filled up and contained anyway.

Can it?

No matter how much of whatever (or whoever) you lock up or destroy.

So let's move on.

Shall we?

There's still a lot of ground to cover and a lot to expose to the light which has for so long been hidden behind all of that tribal darkness.

Although we don't pretend to be able to fill in all of the missing pieces for you.

We would surely be contradicting ourselves if we did.

Wouldn't we?

MICHAEL J. GAJDA

CHAPTER 50

The Merry-Go-Round of Indispensable Enemies

THERE'S BEEN A burgeoning occurrence of resentment, distrust, and refusal when it comes to even minimal give-and-take dialogue in your world, hasn't there? And the growing animosity hasn't just been limited to a loathing resistance between separate tribes either, has it?

It's even infected the way that subordinates within each tribe communicate with one another, or to be more precise, the way communication is stifled and blocked between individual human beings within each of your isolated tribal containers.

And the intensity and degree of suspicion and ill will which is spread so widely and so thoroughly among you is no mere accident, is it? It's plain and deliberate, executed and enforced by the well-established pitchmen and provocateurs of each tribal enclave, by the orchestrators of hatred and fear who tend to benefit the most and by far and who not only intentionally instigate the antagonisms but then just sit back and watch (from behind the scenes) while quietly applauding themselves whenever another wave of bitterness and hostility begins to ferment between competing tribes or between schooled and manipulated tribal subjects or even between and within the walls of an individual's habituated thought process and its overly contained contents of tribal overidentification—where the *disjoined* ego so often runs the emotional and cognitive show.

The well-studied practice and discipline of deception provides the peddlers of distrust with plenty of Machiavellian[1] elbow room, doesn't it? Especially when it comes to crafting their disharmonious tribal (mis)direction and logic—which not-so surprisingly leads to an almost complete absence of any spiritually enlightened or politically well-informed opposition rising up from among the invited ones . . . from among the huddled, hornswoggled, and xenophobic masses.

Most, if not all, of the incriminating heat simply slides off the Teflon back of the surreptitious upper crust of conspirators, along with most of its chicanery . . . like beads of cheap and hot bacon grease zealously splashing the blame outward and onto *others*, spilling it around the tribal board of artful accusation with cloak-and-dagger expertise, fanning any flames of resentment and distress well away from the well-protected and shadowy hucksters themselves, and away from the adulated tribal system of corruption—which they embody and defend.

And with little, if any, serious suspicion aroused among the indiscriminately loyal rank and file, the *only-mind* of the tribe is kept perpetually occupied and entranced with itself, isn't it? No matter where or how often the mania of fear, blame, and confusion is dispersed and then driven into the constipated bowels of the tribal container.

It doesn't even matter if the projected oversupply of blame seems unwarranted or even if it's crystal clear that it's utterly baseless, does it?

If a lie gets repeated loudly and often enough, it seems to convince most of you among the invited that it must be true, especially if it's something that the *only-mind* of the tribe is obsessed with needing to believe about its target of incrimination. And a lie always seems more credible when it's spiked and seasoned with bits and pieces of truth taken out of context, doesn't it? Or when it's officially condoned by the political or religious establishment of the tribe, so often in cahoots with the collaborating machinery of a corporate (or government) controlled media, whose mission is to persuade a passive audience of the upright character and dutiful message of those at the top of the tribal pyramid, by reflecting back (to its listeners and viewers) a spitting but fragmented image of themselves—as perceived through a house of tribal mirrors.

It takes one to know one . . . as so many of you unconsciously assume. Or does it?

Nevertheless, whenever a group of wide-eyed but *disjoined* onlookers sees itself as inhabiting an upright vision, mirrored to those at the top of the tribal heap, it quickly concludes that it knows the truth when it sees it (or hears it) being broadcast on the tribal network—even when that knowledge is built upon a false equation.

It's a masterful way to disseminate a communicable disease, wouldn't you agree?

And yet it's so beautifully simple, isn't it? Spread around as easy as jelly on toast; especially if the tribal citizenry can be magically distracted by each knifelike move, enough so to be mobilized into projecting their full attention of organized angst and violence against whatever demonic *otherness* is suddenly being marked for attack by the tribal curia.

It becomes most effective when a growing number within the body politic can be convinced that certain trivial issues are no longer trivial . . . that they've suddenly become important and even urgent, that previously nonexistent or insignificant threats to the health and welfare of the tribe (or to individual, psychological, or physical safety) can be blown out of proportion into horror stories involving questions of ultimate concern or into horrific hallucinations which predict the loss of tribal security, even into exaggerated matters of life, death, and survival, especially when the contrived threat is imagined to be aimed at the pandered-to sanctioned religion or at the economic or political nucleus of idolized tribal power.

And any previously ignored (yet conveniently available) *otherness* can easily be redefined and elevated into becoming today's newly feared and targeted enemy, can it not?

If the tribal center of influence and control needs to create a newfound foe or an ascendant devil to replace a previous one which may have somehow worn out its usefulness or which may not be quite as accessible or effective or as economically lucrative . . . or as fear-producing of an enemy as it once was; all that needs to be done is to stir up the pot of anxiety in a new direction, toward a fresh-faced enemy target whom the tribe can easily turn against and which it can then be effectively unified around—with a full-blown orchestra of againstness.

Whether there's any reality to the stirring up or not doesn't really matter much, does it?

A half truth works just as well as no truth at all, don't you see?

And as a rule, most of your sworn into "so help me God" testimony, which is done in defense of your tribal gibberish . . . is committed to while unconsciously holding a handful of fingers (tightly crossed) behind your back.

And it's an amazingly simple strategy, isn't it?

Just look at the recent history of indispensable enemies which the power-broking elite of your most sprawling and dominant present-day global empire (the USA) has been able to whip up (essentially unhindered) on a moment's notice, whenever they've needed to . . . over the past several decades or so.

The evil Soviet Empire which falls apart is suddenly replaced by Islamofascists . . . in the blink of a military-industrial eye. The evil of its *otherness* is simply transferred into a different account—as easy as making a tribal bank transaction.[2]

Evil over here is merely withdrawn and then deposited over there.

International communism becomes international terrorism—just like that.[3]

It's simply too obvious to ignore, isn't it?

Just take a quick tour of the historic, most generous, and well-distributed adversary alterations made by just this one contemporary empire and its affiliates. It's quite revealing.

The center of evil *otherness* can be shifted around the enemy control board of the tribe quite effectively, in a series of smooth maneuvers . . . without ever being acknowledged by the vast majority of you, yes?

It's almost become a tribal tradition of hide-and-seek, hasn't it? Some tribes are simply more advanced and experienced in the tradition than others.

And it's really not very hard to do, is it?

For example: The evil *otherness* of Vietnam is easily transferred and then turned into Chile, when it becomes necessary . . . or when it's simply useful to do so (Ho Chi Minh turns right into Salvador Allende—in the blink of a tribal eye),[4] which can then turn into Angola,[5] which suddenly turns into Iran,[6] which can then turn into Nicaragua,[7] which turns into Grenada,[8] and then smoothly into Panama,[9] which can turn into North Korea,[10] which then turns into Iraq,[11] which can easily turn right into Al-Qaeda,[12] which can turn into Afghanistan,[13] and then smack-dab into the Taliban, which can turn back into Iran, which can then turn into Somalia,[14] which can turn back around into Serbia,[15] which can always turn into China or Russia, and even back into Vietnam . . . when digging up old wounds may be useful, which can then even turn inward and outward at the same time . . . into traitorous American socialists or secularists, which can then turn toward the southern border into waves of immigrant *otherness*, which can then turn into Mexican drug cartels (this one's almost too easy . . . isn't it?),[16] then with a hop, skip, and a jump, it can turn right into Venezuela, which can then easily turn into Bolivia or Ecuador,[17] which can turn all the way around again . . . right back into North Korea or Iran or even into Syria or Libya,[18] and then with just a whisper of a move, it turns right into Hamas or Hezbollah.[19] *Voila!*

Oh, that reminds us . . . and let's not forget how all of that angst can suddenly turn toward and then right into the French for some irrational reason.

And it can all be routinely turned (with great intensity) into Cuba,[20] can't it?

Old reliable Cuba. The hot Latin target which seems to always be available if *disjoined* American fear and hatred needs to redirect itself, in order to replace the diminishing heat of any other enemy agent of *otherness* which may be fading away or simply cooling off.

Although with Mr. Castro getting up there in years (and he may even be dead by the time you hear this), the newest enemy upstart of *international terrorism* could become an indispensable stand-in, couldn't it? For whenever the need to fall back onto a quick and surefire replacement arises.[21]

You just can't beat a forever war full of ubiquitous, often invisible, and even homeless terrorists for its indispensability, can you?

And if and when Fidel finally does die, who knows how long Cuba will be able to hold on to its top spot?

And don't forget about the accusatorial addendum that's been proudly inserted into this rest assured strategy either: The wire pullers of the western nation-states have just about guaranteed the endless existence of an indispensable and violent war, one declared upon worldwide acts of terror which haven't even occurred yet, and upon acts of terror committed by people who may not yet even be aware that they're going to carry out any of those devastating acts which they're being predicted to commit, or upon devastating acts of terror predicted to be committed by people who aren't even born yet.

The prediction seems to almost be one of wishful thinking, doesn't it? We wonder. Who among you could benefit the most and even greatly profit from a guaranteed war like that? *Hmmm.* Do any multinational corporations, military industries, power-hungry politicians, media conglomerates, or diamond-wearing preachers of apocalypse come to mind?

So anyway, there you go, one big solid enemy in the bank . . . guaranteed for a long-term deposit. And now that very same so-called enemy is looking through that very same lens itself, isn't it? But only from the opposite end of it, predicting similar acts of terror from an opposing empire of *otherness*—against *it*. They too have gained an indispensable enemy to aim their fear and violence at.

And how convenient . . . for all those so disposed and addicted to the *disjoined* frenzy.

Meanwhile, not a whole lot of effort (from either side of the lens) is being put toward trying to address any of the underlying issues behind this whole mess, is there? Including issues related to economic injustice and greed; the excessive and growing presence of unwanted foreign military bases; cultural chauvinism; suppression of personal and political freedom; lack of jobs; the stealing the wasting and the destruction of life-sustaing natural resources; gender inequality; religious fundamentalism and bigotry; the continued outside military and economic support of dictatorships; the deception, abuse, and torture of the citizenry by those in power; the attempts to diminish and censor free speech and the free access to information; the lasting effects of historical foreign imperialism; the intentional instigation of hatred between religious or ethnic tribes; the assassination or overthrow of elected officials who don't play ball with the corporate big boys; the sorry lack of any real courageous and honest leadership; the scarcity of mature and wise elders; the refusal to make any real attempts at nonviolent conflict resolution; the absence of a universal truth and reconciliation process (such as in South Africa); the pretense of real democracy; and the obvious hypocritical foreign and domestic policies, based on local and global greed and hegemony . . . among so many other things which have led to so much of the fear, confusion, and vulnerability which has driven so many of God's undeniable and innocent children into becoming angry, cynical, and hopeless adults, so angry and lacking in hope so as to even blow themselves up, along with a multitude of completely innocent and precious *others—others* who may be looking through the other side of the notorious lens but who are also God's undeniable and innocent children.

Tragically, most of your efforts have been invested in putting out smaller fires with larger fires . . . by just making the fire bigger and hotter, rather than trying to figure out and to then address why the fires keep getting lit in the first place and why they continue to spread . . . even while they're so paradoxically predictable.

But again, we digress.

It somehow pays to have the feared *otherness* depicted and portrayed as the devil incarnate. Doesn't it?

It pays to have an evil figurehead with a recognizable face, especially if it's the face of a different cultural experience and expression . . . with antithetic or unfamiliar ways of articulating itself, which Mr. Castro has so generously provided for so long for the U.S. upper echelon of power and influence, and for the tribe's collaborating media machine.

Thank god for that untamed beard and those long ranting speeches, eh?

But there's plenty of *other* available devils waiting in the wings to replace him, aren't there? Even some fairly qualified ones . . . which makes it even more convenient for Fidel's dominant evil *otherness* to simply be transferred and awarded to any one of them once he's out of the proverbial picture, doesn't it?

If history proves anything, it's that there will always be rising enemy stars moving up the long ladder of scared-up (and so often contrived, psychologically projected, or exaggerated) evil.

And we're confident of that statement, even with your most recent and quite unfortunate loss by vengeful execution of a triad of genuine satanic tyrants: Saddam Hussein, Osama Bin Laden, and Moammar Gadhafi.[22]

You've lost some real good *bad ones* there, haven't you?

But it didn't leave a real big vacuum to fill, did it?

Just listen to this short list of currently targeted archetypal devils in disguise: the Supreme Leader of Iran, Daniel Ortega, Mohammed Omar, Kim Jong-il and now Kim Jong-un, Hugo Chavez (oops, just lost him), Mahmoud Ahmadinejad (another oops, just term limited out of office), Evo Morales, Bashar al-Assad, Khaled Mashaal, Hassan Nasrallah, Vladimir Putin, and the up-and-coming Rafael Correa.[23]

But let us not forget the dangerous whistle-blowing of Bradley (now Chelsea) Manning and Julian Assange.

And look at how circumstances can so quickly change. Here comes Edward Snowden with his own brand-new whistle . . . as a brand-new recruited enemy replacement for those recent losses.[24]

Heck, you still have Manuel Noriega locked up to fill in a quick space of fear-driven memories if the need arises.[25]

And as we've already said, you don't really have to have an authentic evil representative of *otherness* to stand up and be counted. You only have to have one whom you can depict that way . . . or whom you can turn into one, for the benefit of overcrowding the easily distracted *only-mind* of just about any *disjoined* tribe that you're trying to manipulate and persuade.

Although the genuine article of depravity and corruption always helps to make the selling a whole lot easier, doesn't it?

And there are some genuinely depraved articles out there, aren't there? No doubt about it.

But as we've already indicated in various ways, throughout the course of our announcement—perception is always more real than reality.

Reality is only as good as far as it goes, as far as it can actually penetrate the overly contained realm of the *only-mind*—which isn't very far if perception refuses to follow, is it?

But the continued spread of confusion and fear sure does the job when it comes to contracting and distorting tribal perceptual experience, doesn't it?

It always has, especially if the targeted audience has been trained well enough to forbid themselves from questioning those who have been put in charge of spreading the motivation.

That's why the training and installation of automatic and unquestioning allegiance into the tribe is so important, especially allegiance to the tribal power hierarchy and to a revered (even idolized) and sealed-tight tradition . . . along with its ever-expanding mythology. It gives a big and necessary boost to the *only-mind* when you're trying to firmly establish and maintain its *disjoining* strength—which is also why creating and maintaining outside enemies is so critical to fostering tribal conformity.

Although inside enemies are often just as persuasive, aren't they?

Just think of how the members on the following list of indispensable internal enemies (within the USA) have been used (historically) as effective distractions away from *That which is always becoming* while one looming (sacred cow) archetype of the *only-mind* has been constantly propped up in order to maintain its mythological image, likeness, and meaning.

Take a good look at it. You'll see some very familiar faces.

Communists and socialists; beatniks and hippies; homosexuals; the always-offensive (especially when visible) homeless; beggars (*too lazy* to work) . . . or street people in general; flag burners (all three of them); welfare moochers and frauds (excluding big banks, stock-market manipulators, and too-big-to-fail corporations . . . of course); Muslims, Jews, and wayward Christians; *radical* feminists (whatever that means); Mormons; African Americans and Mexican Americans; atheists; any political protest coming from an alternative perspective—which may threaten the tribe's customary power base; generic radicals (which can describe whatever you want it to describe); third (political) parties; taxes (except for those which contribute to the making of more war machinery to use or to sell, or for making perpetual war, for that matter); big government (in the abstract); nameless homegrown terrorists; immigrants (of a certain shade and color); job-stealing foreigners; speaking and reading in foreign languages; *radical* environmentalists (whatever that means); (pointy-headed?) intellectuals; hot-shot investigative reporters; and any science which doesn't line up with the power elite's political, financial, religious, social, or economic ideology and interests . . . or with its overly contained and *disjoined* tribal desires.

And sex and drugs have always been pretty reliable and easily demonized distractions too, haven't they?

And what about the distorted and disquieting (cherry-picked and exaggerated) examples which point out the inherent evils of jazz and of rock 'n' roll or of hip-hop?

How about the visual decadence of Hollywood? Or the freedom-diminishing plot to take away all of the tribal guns (even as the gun laws become less restrictive and almost nonexistent)? Or the unholy, so-called liberal-leaning media (even as the mainstream of American broadcasting becomes more of an accommodating mouthpiece for the corporate *only-mind* . . . which owns and absorbs almost all of it, and even as an extreme fundamentalist right-wing shouting-machine dominates, infiltrates, and expands across the public airways by leaps and bounds)?

Or how about the East and West Coast demonic elite, the accused (without evidence) who are all supposedly members of a conspiratorial club which secretly rules the world?

Even Santa Claus, Halloween, and the Easter Bunny have become the occasional whipping boys of tribal misdirection, haven't they? Targeted (seasonally) by the tribe's very influential religious extremists, moving the *disjoined only-mind* further and further away from the possibility of perceiving *That which* (actually) *is*.

So there you have it . . . several of the obvious and usual suspects who've made regular enemy guest appearances on one very powerful tribal shit list over the years.

Unfortunately, the strange yet predictable and disheartening thing is that several of those same enemy targets who've been attached to this one specific database of evil *otherness* tend to retarget and project their own shit onto plenty of *others* themselves, don't they? Upon their own similarly preyed-upon and abused but quite indispensable enemies.

Well, they do . . . don't they?

There's no sense in denying it.

Disjoined tribal logic is quite egalitarian in that way, isn't it? Especially when it comes to who can join in the convenient, almost mandatory, or at least conventional . . . and often groundless assault on *otherness*.

The more that any overly contained tribal *only-mind* is able to exaggerate the treachery and threat which the targeted enemy may pose, the stronger and more effective the impact of its own distractions and of its self-deceptions will have on its own *disjoined* logic.

And we'll remind you once again to please continue to keep the following statement in your head . . . which can never be overemphasized.

Reality always takes a backseat to perception.

Unless, of course, you've been able to transform yourself enough into becoming one of the fringe dwellers whom we've earlier tried to characterize and describe for you. But then you would already realize that you've been able to evolve and to liberate yourself beyond the complete grasp and influence of any *disjoined* perception . . . irrespective of the size and shape of its tribal containment. Wouldn't you?

But have you not noticed a particular and quite predictable pattern of blame and defamation showing up in almost all of the anticipated places? With almost all of the usual (slandered and reviled) suspects popping up so conveniently whenever your tribe needs to test its brand-new weapon systems? Or whenever it needs to reconsolidate its troops? Or to advance its culture war? Or to justify and protect the expanse of its tribal reach?

How many so-called scientists and media manipulators became the highly vocal hired guns for your tobacco companies (for instance), simply to assert (as fraudulent fact) that cigarette smoking was relatively if not completely safe, as they besmirched and blamed those of whom they labeled as scare tacticians . . . for spreading all of that cancer hullabaloo around while disparaging real (peer-reviewed, corroborated, and validated) science by repeatedly calling it junk science, and convincing so many of you to believe it . . . and to keep on smoking, and to laugh sarcastically at the death threats, and then to suffer and die by the ignorant hand of your own co-opted allegiance?

How many of those same slandering pseudoscientific gunslingers were called upon to deny the dangers of acid rain, and that American and Canadian industry had nothing to do with causing it . . . even when they were finally forced to admit that it was toxic to the life on your planet?

How many of them pulled out their slanderous artillery (of defamation, blame, and confusion) again . . . with the discovery of the hole in the ozone? And against the effects of Agent Orange on civilians and combatants in Vietnam? Or on the reality of PTSD?

How many of those same recruited propagandists of false claims, mud slinging, and accusation are loudly making the same kind of inflammatory pitch of denial about the cause and effect of climate change and the growing weirdness of global weather patterns? Or even (still) about secondhand smoke?[26]

When it comes to threats against the tribal ideology or against the profiteering centers of power and control, the weapons of mass distraction (of outright lying, of repetitive slurs, and of loud and constant bad-mouthing) will be drawn and used. They always have been.

And publicly refusing to dialogue with the accused target of vituperation is money in the tribal war chest. Isn't it?

Warfare can start on a dime when you take that kind of stubborn stance, can't it?

And then it can go on forever and just about anywhere—just like it has, hasn't it? As long as you simply restrict or deny any real communication with the *other*.

Fear, confusion, and distrust can just keep building up . . . when you allow it to. Don't you see?

And then . . . whammo! You've got yourself a war . . . physical, political, or cultural—whichever you prefer.

It's as simple as that.

That's why your vague, vast, and endless war on terrorism, like your war on drugs and like the growing war on sex and body-related issues within some of your self-identified so-called traditional tribes is such a win-win way to go . . . for the mercantile, religious, and political establishment. Don't you see?

Truth can be reinvented and reshaped into anything you'd like it to be, rather easily manipulated through intentional fear peddling and energized by broad demeaning and repeated statements about any accused *otherness* of your choosing . . . especially by statements that go unchallenged, by statements based solely on the need to make them— but especially on the need to hear them confirm the predetermined worldview of your tribal containing system.

As we've said, not much in the way of concrete evidence is actually necessary.

Just continue to broadcast and repeat the scripted message of bewildered fear and revilement of a specific or even of an abstract *otherness* . . . along with an opposing and unquestioning tribal allegiance.

And do it through your most provocative and entertaining carnival barkers. It's a formula that can't miss. It's been proven . . . over and over again, hasn't it?

All you need is one loud-mouthed, tribe-authorized marketeer. And the rest will follow, as long as there's enough money backing it up and enough bread to be baked and consumed from inside the tribe's ideological oven—or enough *disjoining* clout and prestige to maintain or to go after.

The more mammon juice you've got flowing in to sanction the tribal message, the louder and more hypnotizing the noise becomes, doesn't it?

So if you want to make war (of any kind), you just go to your drawer full of dots and take out the ones you need . . . and then proceed to connect them. Got it? The same way that it goes if you want to sell fraudulent mortgages . . . or if you want to needlessly raise the cost of health insurance or prescription drugs, or even if you want to increase the dependency on oil and coal companies, or if you want to invade a faraway country or spy on your own people, or if you want to raise the cost of living for working and poor people or discredit legitimate labor unions, or if you want to eliminate the taxes and expand and increase the subsidies for the super-rich, or even if you want to diminish the right of habeas corpus,[27] or if you want to do just about anything where you can envision the power and control or profiteering possibilities—even if you want to make the nauseating and moronic claim that Jesus himself backs up and symbolizes the image, actions, and the imperial ideals of unfettered capitalistic greed and might, which is so proudly displayed by the tycoons of *disjoined* tribal excess . . . and that he even would say so himself, were he alive to talk about it today.

We're quite sure that you can extract enough cherry-picked and out-of-context *disjoined* Bible passages to prove that point (or any other point) if you wanted to. The tribal *only-mind* does it all the time, doesn't it?

Simply go to the magic drawer and make the magic disconnection and then sell it . . . just like church raffle tickets or far-flung tribal fantasies.

If it's the violence of war that you're selling, then more sophisticated weapons and weapon systems will have to be built and distributed by the tribal weapons manufacturers, won't they?

Tribal armies and corporate mercenaries will have to be recruited and paid for.

Large profit margins will have to be made and then paid off to tribal investors . . . in steep and regular returns.

The dots connect in all directions, don't they?

A tribal run media will have to emphasize the tribe's corporate and political side of the story while setting up a pretense of debate. And that same media will have to be made to be afraid to tell the truth to or even about the tribal centers of power and influence (at all costs) . . . especially to or about those in charge of the banks; or to or about the dominant global corporations; or to or about the conventional keepers of political and religious language; or to or about the energy centers that foster tribal dependency; or to or about the weapon makers and the military establishment's hierarchy; or to or about all those who provide the necessary funding and ingredients which make war so easy to enter into; or to or about any board members from the tribal old boys and girls network who compromise, deceive, and provide the tribal media with their best insider information and profitable payoffs, along with access to future can't-miss stories . . . in order to keep injecting the tribal angst into the rest of the *disjoined only-mind*, to keep the empire's reach and modus operandi in favorable strategic position, aim, and direction.

And once you've got all those moving parts trapped and in place inside the spinning carousel of containment—nobody can leave. Don't you see?

You can't get off the tribal merry-go-round unless you want to jump—or unless you're pushed off.

But for most of you, jumping off is just too risky and too costly, isn't it? You know that the likelihood of bouncing back up without any near-fatal wounds (or worse) is pretty slim. You've gone past the point of no return. So you might as well just get good at marching to the tribal goose step. It's the safe and smart way to go, isn't it? Tribally speaking.

Corporate talking points made up of official-sounding information will have to be quoted as if there's always some truth to them and then attributed directly to sources rung high on the distributing ladder of disinformation, assured to have come from somewhere deep in the belly of an important office of an elite expert or esteemed executive of some kind . . . or from within a rich, mainstreamed think tank, where the narcissistic ascendance of tribal admiration for polarizing logic climbs all over itself for attention and recognition, for more and more emphasis of either/or and "us against them" thinking.

The result of all this (as most of you know by now) is the perpetual pigeonholing and disparagement of a routinely denigrated and accused *otherness,* whenever it becomes necessary or simply useful to do so, combined with a vigilant contempt for (and resistance to) building bridges of understanding between yourselves and *other* tribes, or within tribes, or even between yourselves—as we've already alluded to.

Intellectual considerations beyond a fixed tribal terminus must be forbidden . . . restricting debate to within the compressed and narrow informational norms of the overly contained tribe; rejecting and condemning any experience of unauthorized *otherness*, denying any of the tribe's past deviations from the strict tribal norm it now upholds, and in truth . . . denying its past in order to reject its own promise of intellectual or spiritual integrity or of *Self*-discovery, taking the expansible here and now and turning it into a slab of tribal cement.

And unless there's a crack in the slab, not even an isolated weed of creativity or dissent will have an easy or likely way to get out from under it.

So much of your available awareness is wrapped up and tied down like a corpse in the dumb-downed logic of the *only-mind*, to make sure it stays forever dead . . . or at least unconscious, to prevent even the slightest possibility of a collective and revived self-reflective perception from resurrecting.

And as we've said, it's all quite understandable.

Dispiriting? Yes. Yet still quite understandable.

But you can't see or understand what you won't even allow yourselves to imagine, can you?

To raise new questions, new possibilities, to regard old problems from a new angle, requires creative imagination and marks real advance in science . . . Logic will get you from A to B, imagination will take you everywhere, wrote the wise Albert Einstein.[28]

No pessimist ever discovered the secret of the stars, or sailed to an uncharted land, or opened a new doorway for the human spirit, wrote the wise Helen Keller.[29]

The soul should always stand ajar, ready to welcome the ecstatic experience, wrote the wise Emily Dickinson.[30]

The man who has no imagination has no wings, said the wise Muhammad Ali.[31]

CHAPTER 51

Awakening Will Happen

I T'S NOT ONLY change that takes place, but transformation does. There's an awakening process which proceeds with or without your permission. It moves well beyond simple revision or adjustment, beyond the mere exchange of masks—empowered and sustained by the evolving and unstoppable energy of the indivisible *Self.*

And it will continue to awaken *It-Self* through *That which it manifests* and through *That in which it is embodied* . . . no matter how many bombs you drop on it, or how many hours of redundant language or distorted tribal images you pump out into your overcrowded containers, from any *disjoined* segment of your loud and lopsided media, or from any of your sensational and rancorous websites—or from anywhere inside of your frequently paranoid blogosphere with its narcissistic rants and incestuous tribal opinions.

It will happen no matter how many politicians you bribe or how many destitute and desperate people you trap, confuse, or indoctrinate . . . or how much you extol and deify your own way of perceiving and believing as being tyrannically superior to the way *others* perceive and believe.

It will happen no matter how many assassins you hire or how many vacations you take into the land of guilt and shame, or how much hate speech with its imagery of fear that you batter and bathe yourselves in—or how many men and women of good conscience whom you can scapegoat, imprison, torture, or execute.

It will happen no matter how many more North Koreas, Myanmars,[1] or Al-Qaedas come and go . . . or how many criminal or violent (drug, oil, political, religious, military, economic, or banking) cartels try to control the flow of wealth and power or of values, belief, and information.

It will happen no matter how many more Roman, Christian, Islamic, Spanish, British, French, Mongol, Soviet, Japanese, Ottoman, Nazi, Dutch, Chinese, Portuguese, or American empires are built or fall apart.[2]

It will happen no matter how many governments or social movements are infiltrated, bought off, or overthrown by whatever amount of tribal greed, envy, or zealotry you may throw out there as bait.

It will happen no matter how many or what kind of tyrants of absolutism are elevated into whatever positions of power and coercion you desire.

It will happen no matter how many Joe McCarthys or Joe Stalins or any other Joe Blow dictator of thought or behavior rises up into a reign of destructive influence.[3]

Transformation will happen.

Awakening will happen.

It always has. And it always will.

We're just trying to push it along a little . . . while trying to include a whole lot more of you. That's all.

But you already know that by now, don't you?

MICHAEL J. GAJDA

CHAPTER 52

The Blaming of *Otherness*

LET'S TAKE A closer look into the repetitive reality of your violent tribal histories. Shall we?

Millions have been murdered and silenced or enslaved and imprisoned . . . tortured and discredited, especially (and to an incredible degree) in your twentieth century; the century whose proud yet extremely divided citizenry likes to take exclusive yet *disjoined* credit for either having established and exemplified traditional and virtuous values, for launching and accelerating modern medical and scientific innovations and advances, or for developing a postmodern pluralism with insights and breakthroughs into higher levels of mental, social, and spiritual understanding and experience.

Yet paradoxical alternatives of conversion still continue to emerge, don't they? Regardless of the polarizing and violent divisiveness which digs itself even deeper into the delusional ditch of the either/or logic of the *only-mind*.

And an unexpected and remarkable rebirth often follows, doesn't it? Sometimes it even leads, moving right through and beyond all of the physical bloodshed and right through and beyond all of the psychological torment, both of which strive to smother out any and all remnants of undesirable *otherness*.

Consider this:

First came Hitler and the gas chambers. Then came the imperfect state of Israel and a Germany at peace with the world—for more than sixty-five years.[1]

First came the Western Christian Church's (its institutional hierarchy's) religious silencing of the astronomical and so-called blasphemous discoveries of Copernicus and Galileo.[2]

Then came quantum mechanics, the theory of relativity, and the sacred science of evolution;[3] the landings on the moon and even on Mars; international space stations; the discovery of black holes and of billions of previously unknown galaxies; even the creation of the

Pontifical Academy of Sciences[4] and of the Islamic World Academy of Sciences.[5]

First came the crime of apartheid. Then came President Nelson Mandela.[6]

First came the terrorism of hundreds of years of African slavery, a violent civil war, and evil Jim Crow laws. Then came Martin Luther King Jr., the Civil Rights Act, the Voting Rights Act, and an African American president of the United States.[7]

First came oppressive monarchies and dictatorships. Then came democracies.

First came the papal-approved inquisitional burning of witches and so-called heretics by fundamentalist and heretical clergy. Then came the curative and sane conceptual separation of church from state,[8] the growth of a compassionate secular humanism,[9] Vatican II,[10] a slowly maturing and humane people of interfaith dialogue and prayer,[11] a growing movement toward interspirituality,[12] and a slow awakening into the reality of Interbeing.[13]

First came the forced labor and exploitation of children. Then came child labor laws to protect them.[14]

First came the culture of patriarchy and the mistreating of women at almost every societal and cultural level across the globe. Then came Prime Minister Indira Gandhi of India, Golda Meir of Israel, Margaret Thatcher of Great Britain, Benazir Bhutto of Pakistan, Khaleda Zia of Bangladesh, and Helen Clark of New Zealand; President Michelle Bachelet of Chile, Megawati Sukarnoputri of Indonesia, Mary Robinson of Ireland; Ellen Johnson-Sirleaf of Liberia, Maria Corazon Aquino of the Philippines, and Park Geun-hye of South Korea; Chief Wilma Pearl Mankiller of the Cherokee Nation; and Chancellor Angela Merkel of Germany,[15] among many others.

Yet conspicuously missing from the list of these sometimes-heralded women leaders are any names from three of your largest and most powerful nation-states—the United States of America, the Union of the Soviet Socialist Republics, or the Soviet Union (recently shrunk to the Russian Federation), and the People's Republic of China.

And let's not forget to observe the same obvious and intentional absence of influential leadership roles for women still at large in some of the most powerful and patriarchal religious institutions in your world—systems and sects which include the Roman Catholic Church, the Orthodox Churches, most of fundamentalist Christianity, and most of Islam . . . for example.[16]

Do you even wonder at all what that might say about how power and gender is perceived and implemented by those *disjoined* tribes which have so much cult-like, concentrated, and institutional power to defend, to justify, and to cling to?

But here comes the paradoxical and tragic twist again. Are you ready?

First came the Crusades and then came more and more Crusades, even returning now into your own present day . . . in freshly twisted forms and disguises, with new technologies of divisiveness . . . hundreds of years later, from both sides (many sides really), so-called Christian against so-called Muslim against so-called Jew, the new pornographers and manipulators of religion, even Christian against Christian and Muslim against Muslim and Jew against Jew.[17]

And as most of you know, the word *Christianity* means many different things to many different people, doesn't it? Even within that wide and often contradictory tradition itself . . . of faith and human experience.

But the same can be said of the word *Islam*, can't it? Or of *Judaism*; or the same with the words *socialism* or *capitalism*; and the same with *peace, freedom,* and *justice*; or *love* and *loyalty*; or *God* and *honor*—and so on and so on.

It often just depends on who's in charge of the distribution of words and images, doesn't it? Or on who's holding the microphone, or on who sits at the centers of operational power and informational control, or from where and how much one is currently awake and aware on the transformational pathway . . . or along any of the individual and collective lines of diverse human growth and development.

And for many of those in charge, it simply depends on how many hapless dependents they can count on to be unconsciously or even consciously manipulated, doesn't it? Dependents who keep looking for black-and-white solutions to a rainbow of perceived problems . . . and often of unperceived opportunities, who can be fooled or intimidated into abiding by and collaborating with their heavily vetted tribal definitions and with their repeatedly justified tribal acts of violence . . . perpetrated against the feared and thus hated *otherness*—which they can spot almost anywhere, especially when times are tough. Because that's when scapegoats come in so handy, don't they? For the tribal *only-mind* to point to and to blame and then vilify.

Just (for example) take a close look at any historical or contemporary downturn in any particular powerhouse tribal economy. Fingers of blame rise up everywhere, don't they? Like submarine periscopes looking to attack, but not only to attack individuals, but entire groups—entire political or economic philosophies, or even entire religions, entire cultures or entire races, entire castes or classes, chastising and typecasting entire groups of categorized human beings because after all—something or someone (or a group of someone's) created this economic mess, didn't they? And it couldn't have been the worshiped (as god-like) economic system of the tribe in question, could it? Instead, it must have been an invasion or a corruption of the system itself. Because the tribal system is always defended for it superiority, if not for its perfection. And you're taught to always remember that, aren't you? That the tribal system is not responsible. That it is never at fault. So it can't ever be blamed for its own flaws, can it? Since it has no flaws. Any flaws which it may appear to own have instead been brought in from the outside or from the edges of the inside by infiltrating evil forces, contaminating and then draining the tribal god system of its inherent supremacy.

Isn't that what blindly loyal and *disjoined* tribal thinking insists upon?

So then there has to be a specific villain to cast blame upon, Doesn't there? A satanic force from somewhere peripheral to the tribal norm, some easy fall guy or fall group to distract the collective *only-mind* away from the reality of life's unanswerable complexities, away from the reality of reality itself and away from its mystery, away from the vast unknown, and away from any inkling of uncertainty (especially when pertaining to itself) which may expose any obvious or hidden tribal blemish or deficiency.

If there's some sacrificial lamb that can be identified and blamed and offered up to the deity of tribal narcissism, then it simplifies and even reinforces the materialistic logic of the *only-mind*, doesn't it? The tribe can then be reassured of its unique greatness and of its guiltless arrogance—of its rationalized superiority complex. Sacrificial blame so pleases the hovering god object of the *only-mind*, yes?

Yet there are endless opportunities for being able to see clearly, are there not?

They're right there in front of you all the time, interspersed throughout the *hidden wholeness* of the inexhaustible and indivisible *Self* (to borrow a timeless metaphor from the ever-evolving words and vision of the wise Thomas Merton).[18]

But you have to look . . . in order to see, don't you?

CHAPTER 53

The Spirit That Empties the Law

I T'S BEEN RATHER amazing, hasn't it? And yet it's been quite discomforting for us, as we watch the throngs of tribal enthusiasts who continue to champion their versions of so-called absolute truth—which can never actually exist in your impermanent and evolving world. It can't exist in a world which is always in a constant state of inconstancy and of spinning relativity.

Yet there are those among you who adamantly claim to have sole possession of the one-and-only true religion, aren't there? Or who claim to possess the one-and-only correct political message, or the one-and-only fair and just economic theory, or the one-and-only heritage of unparalleled morality, or any of the unquestionable tribal absolutes which are sought after and conformed to by so many of you who content yourselves with a one-and-only abstract god, which is imagined to be confined to being a material object of worship of some kind, isn't it? A god which can be made into either a religious or a political object or into an economic or moral object . . . but an object of worship just the same, something that can be physically photographed through the blind believing eye of the *only-mind*, a god-object which most often is imagined to be a supernatural male human being, a god-object with male testicles, a separate objectified physical being of some kind . . . hovering over your planet like a supreme spaceship, floating around somewhere up in the tribal sky, a large and powerful god object of reciprocal allegiance who only takes the side of whoever believes that *he* actually exists in the exact tribal way prescribed and that *he* is even willing to be a violent god or at least encouraging of violence, which *he* willingly casts down upon the enemies of the one-and-only tribe which claims to have been granted exclusive rights and privileges by *him* because of its elite status among competing tribes . . . of being the one-and-only true container, full of true believers in the one-and-only true divine object—which is to be worshiped and feared.

Yet it all has to do with sheer mental belief, doesn't it? And with the manipulation of tribal words.

Somehow if you think and say the right words, then in some odd way that in fact seems to trump everything else, doesn't it? And then the only thing that truly matters is what you say about what you think and about what you believe, that it's all just a cognitive and verbal exercise which literally makes up so-called true religion—whether it's religious religion, or political religion, or economic religion, or cultural religion, or scientific religion . . . or even the religion of opinion, and that it's not so much about how you treat or interact with *others* that's important, or even what you personally experience that really counts . . . or even what actually *is* which indeed matters, is it?

And under this type of tribal reasoning the value of goodness, truth, or beauty is often diminished or is completely dismissed altogether—especially if it's not proudly and clearly accompanied by the one-and-only true belief object of the tribe. Because if it doesn't have the correct address of god attached to it, then it must be godless—which is usually translated as being bad or wrong or at least ignorant, or even as the devil's evil messenger itself . . . depending on the context and extent of the belief in question.

And a godless goodness is not a real goodness at all, just as a godless truth is not a real truth. And a godless thing of beauty is not a real thing of beauty. Because it can't be, can it?

You've got to have the precise object of tribal adoration attached to it, don't you? In order to cut the distinguishing ice of the tribe into acceptable proportions.

And it's somehow assumed that if you put enough coins into the tribal god object's slot machine of a mouth, then even shinier coins of reward will come falling down into your waiting lap, proving that your singular version of Object Almighty is the only and authentic image of god among all the *other* objects of worship—all of which are likewise frantically competing for sole and supreme authenticity, but in their own presumptuous and objectifying way.

They just have a slightly different brand or collection of tribal slot machines, that's all.

And if you want to ascend up to a permanent afterlife and settle into an actual geographic and eternal celestial territory, or if you want to apprehend a sense of heaven-blessed permanence on Earth, then you better demonstrate an indisputable allegiance to the superior and unflinching belief system of the tribe and to the anthropomorphic image of its tribe-certified god of magic and desire, as well as to the tribe's self-exalting interpretation of its message and meaning—to the god object which idolizes itself through the words and rituals projected upon it by the tribe.

Because you know what the wise Moses, Jesus, Buddha, Mohammad, and Krishna all said about how essential it is to idolize, don't you?

Nothing. Nothing at all. Except for this: Don't do it.

Why do you see the speck that is in your brother's eye, but do not notice the log that is in your own eye? asked the wise Jesus.[1]

Better than a thousand hollow words is one that brings peace, said the wise Buddha.[2]

Do you love your creator? Love your fellow beings first, said the wise Mohammad.[3]

Just as a reservoir is of little use to people when the country is flooded all around, so the scriptures are of little use to the illumined man or woman, who sees the Lord everywhere, said the wise Krishna.[4]

But it's really not all that amusing, is it?

More violence has grown out of the opposing idolatrous words which pour out of the mouths of the ideologues than has ever been triggered from actual events and circumstances.

Events and circumstances are often just the convenient props rigged and manipulated by the tribal power elite in order to make its case to the naive and to the gullible, to the intentionally ignorant or to the confused—and to the self-serving and the fearful.

And as we've already overemphasized and demonstrated, the actual is always secondary to the perceived in any world full of competing yet transient facsimiles of reality, especially when the facsimiles are forged into tribal truisms which end up as factional laws or doctrines—with the weight of those laws pushing down hardest on those at the bottom of the tribal food chain.

And who needs the simple unfolding of truth when you've got tribal libraries full of ancient law books and piles upon piles of legal documents written and reinforced by the political, religious, corporate, and cultural kingpins (and king makers) of the tribe; when you've got recorded texts which the tribe readily accepts as being verbatim sacred testimony to be interpreted literally and acted upon as such and without deviation and which do the legal and reductionist bidding of the *only-mind*; the tribal archives which you insist are not and have never been intended to be construed as if they were living and breathing documents of evolving wisdom.

Instead, you proudly pronounce them dead, don't you? And then you worship the dead as if they were still alive and as if they were put in divinely appointed charge of the tribal soul.

Such strange and spiritually paralyzing logic.

Is it not?

Follow me, and leave the dead to bury their dead, urged the wise Nazarene.[4]

So you don't really have to trust your own experience then, do you?

You just have to be able to read from the restricted but shiny tribal menu which never changes. Or you just have to follow the person in front of you in the tribal cafeteria line—which always serves the same indigestible food made from the same antiquated and mundane recipes.

Yet there are laws which are still actually available for receiving and for interpreting and for applying with open, gentle, and wise guidance, aren't there? Even though they may be quite hard to detect and discern from within an overcrowded tribal container of overly coerced sameness.

But you all know that.

We refer here to the unspoken and unwritten laws which apply themselves through the release and revealing of the spirit of *That which is always becoming*, which paradoxically conceals *It-Self* within the invisible stillness of those laws and which forever surrounds yet indwells you, always moving freely beyond its own secret hiding place of quietude . . . the breathing spirit of the *Great Guidance,* which whispers through each evolving particle of life with unspoken and unwritten words of truth and of love, of fairness and forgiveness, and of justice and compassion—with things like that, with things which are not things, but which are always in the process of opening up, of inviting in, and of becoming one *with*— of returning to the indivisible and inexhaustible *Ground of Being.*

But that same hidden spirit is so often covered up or rebuked, isn't it? By the *disjoined* logic of the *only-mind*, by tribal rulings which are frozen in time to be tightly contained and adhered to, the ones which so many of you cling to and rely upon for security and safety sake, the laws concocted to hand out rewards when correctly followed and to hand out punishment when they're not—which is better known as the rule of the letter of the law, frozen in illusion and in time and in obedience by its own anesthetizing tribal jargon.

And you all know the difference between the two types of legal applications, don't you?

Most of you among the invited anxiously apply the letter while ignoring the spirit. Do you not? Narrowly interpreting and applying the objectified and idolized words more than you ever experience or even acknowledge the space between them, even though the space between has been left there purposely for you to explore.

The space is where the spirit lives and breathes, where it plays its liberating and musical game of hide-and-seek. Don't you see?

Your interaction with the vocabulary of tribal law has been restricted and reduced to the worship of its terminology, has it not? Along with the customary condemnation of those who may actually be caught communicating in a taboo language . . . speaking in the tongue of an unrecognizable *otherness* or of those who may reject or ignore your scribbled tribal scripts and symbols which sanctify your containment.

And so much of your blood-shedding aggression is provoked by your *disjoined* dedication to the survival and dominance of the tribal lexicon, isn't it?

The overly contained tribe is forced to either defend the honor of its precarious dogma or to choke on its own words. And the tribes which are most resistant to expanding their linguistic horizons are the ones which are most willing to inflict acts of violence upon *others*, aren't they? Especially when the ultimate intent is to forever shut them up.

The fossilized letters of the *only-mind* begin by closing ranks. And then they slowly solidify into harsh words, then into even harsher sentences, which then crystallize into symbols and images of attack, and then harden into sharp and deadly weapons, and then stiffen and extend into merciless acts of havoc and into ever-expanding destruction, wildly rising out from behind the cross or the crescent or from behind the swastika or the hammer and sickle, from behind a favorite color or an unmistakable visual pattern, from behind the hypnotic waving of the tribal flag, or from behind hate speech in the guise of free speech, even from behind terminally ill and dehumanizing humor, from behind all of the frozen-into-adolescence and drug-like symbols and images repeatedly used by all of the tribal pied pipers in your world,[5] who've led so many of you (zombie-like) into recurrent letter-protecting tribal mayhem, at the mere drop of a word, behind signs and mastheads and emblems and doctrines, from behind commandments and anthems, or from behind superiority creeds and political strategies, behind thought police lines and sacred land claims and slogans, behind false promises and lies made by tribal high priests, even from behind memorized theme songs with insipid words rhyming you to sleep, even though you still imagine that you're actually awake—while tightly snuggled and contained inside the isolated tribal dream of the unawakened *only-mind*.

It's simply amazing, isn't it?

Eyes wide shut is a description many of you could easily claim as your own (borrowing a title from the late wise filmmaker Stanley Kubrick).[6]

But none of your tribal violence in defense of the letter of the law has ever been able to completely stop all *others* from waking up, has it?

Although you could have been co-inhabiting your planet with much gentler and kinder cooperation, yes? And with much less loss, with much less pain and much less grief, much more peacefully, and with much less habitual distress than you've burdened yourselves with.

Your reverence for and addiction to letter-defending violence is not only woeful and tragic, but it's self-defeating—to the tribal core. Don't you see?

There's not a whole lot which you haven't tried to divide up and conquer, is there? For the sake of merely demonstrating your loyalty to the tribal book of facts—which contains and controls you and enforces your inherited legal servitude.

Is there anyone or anything (anywhere) that has not been violated in some way by the wrath of your tribal bondage?

Territory and influence? Information and resources? Land, animals, or people? Religion or science? Finance and media? Opinions and facts? Politics and governance? Actual events of history? Even life's beginnings? It's living modes? Or even the end of life itself?

Most of you mechanically defend your tribal terminology without question behind whichever mask it wears, don't you? Sticking to the tribal agenda in support of its tone-deaf documents . . . and at whatever the cost.

But now it's time to remove those masks and to tally up.

It's time to reinterpret those restricting letters and words by widening the space between and even inside them—which holds everything together.

Without releasing yourselves into that pure spacious energy, the letters themselves will merely conform to the archaic and uniform script of the tribe, becoming ever more lifeless inside—and ever more deadly outside.

And until you can penetrate that space, you'll just continue to cling to your tribal vocabulary as if it was your life raft to an insular and sectarian heaven.

The paradox is that the letters exist only to point you to the space which surrounds and indwells them, where the ghosts of truth, beauty, and goodness live and breathe . . . but which can never be fully or finally defined or possessed. Don't you see?

The very nature of that spaciousness is evolutionary. It is spiritual and liberating.

Spirit's very nature is to keep dancing, to dance beyond the complete grasp of your limited human understanding, into the space between and beyond all relative knowledge, inviting you to forever reach and stretch beyond who you think you are, into the realm of the indwelling *Self*—into *That which is always becoming.*

But you already know that by now.

Yes?

CHAPTER 54

Returning to Before

J UST LISTEN TO some of the loud tribal madness which still sends tremors of violence out from the deranged and *disjoined only-mind.*

During and after the establishment of Israel came extreme Zionism, resurgent anti-Semitism, Cold War interference and manipulation, Islamophobia, the desperate suffering of the Palestinians, tribal warfare, state and individual terrorism, and the assassination of tribe-transcending peacemakers . . . by their very own people.[1]

After the slow victories of the American Civil Rights Movement and the end of South African apartheid, and even after the election of the politically conventional and middle-of-the-road Barack Obama, came the revived rise of angry, violent, and racist energy, conspired by the masked merchants of white privilege and by a corporately cooked up and infectious fear of *otherness* and of change—even of minimal change.

After women came into national (and global) leadership positions of shared prominence and power . . . came assassinations, the resurgence of misogynist and repressive tribal religion, and the retooling of reactionary patriarchal culture.

After children were protected from exploitative working conditions . . . came child soldiering, child slavery and trafficking, the epidemic of physical and sexual abuse, and an ever-expanding industry of child pornography.

After Rhodesia became liberated into Zimbabwe . . . came the deconstructive and cruel reign of Robert Mugabe and his gang of thug followers.[2]

After the hope and faith which the campesinos found in Latin American Liberation Theology . . . came the murder of Archbishop Oscar Romero;[3] the slaying and torture of prophetic nuns, priests, and peasants; more corporate funding of and collusion with brutal dictatorships; continued training of mercenary armies and police death squads by the U.S. Army School of the Americas,[4] which pleased the United Fruit Company, among other corporate tribes of documented greed and influence (and have you even wondered why they recently changed the name of the school?),[5] while the tribal hierarchy of the local Roman Catholic Church just quietly stood by and watched, sipping brandy with generals . . . securely relaxed in its comfortable, cowardly, and compromised gospel.

After the crime of Pearl Harbor . . . came the crimes of Dresden, of Hiroshima and Nagasaki, death and destruction in Berlin, then Korea, Vietnam, Laos, and Cambodia.

After the crime of the Twin Towers . . . came the crime of invasion, the destruction of Iraq, the occupation of Afghanistan, the disgrace of Guantanamo, a surreal war of revenge proclaiming itself infinite, supplying the justification for billions more to be spent on instruments of death instead of on the sustaining of actual life and on the needs of the living—while lavishly funding the Pentagon and the corpulent manufacturers and profiteers of perpetual bloodletting.

After the peaceful return of the Panama Canal came the invasion and overthrow of the puppet dictator who turned against his American paymaster.

After the occupied and carved-up nations of Africa and Arabia became free of direct European colonial rule . . . came tribal war; CIA and KGB Cold War instigations; installed dictatorships of oppression and greed; corporate theft of oil, land, copper, and diamonds . . . and of bioresources (among so much else); then came stateless nations and ocean piracy.[6]

After the breakup and fall of the brutal empire of the Soviet Union . . . came unrepentant massacres in Serbia, Croatia, and Kosovo, then in Chechnya and Kyrgyzstan.[7]

After the end of the horrific Chinese Civil War . . . came the brutalities and massacres of the cultural revolution, the carnage of Tibet, and the slaughter in Tienanmen Square.[8]

After great improvements in food and agricultural technologies and hope for the world's hungry . . . came food used as a weapon: the sanctioned and starved, the thirsting of millions, the growing power of Big Agra over the world's food supply, the control and patenting of seed genetics by Monsanto,[9] the virtual slow extinction of small farms, land grabbing by nation-states and corporations, collaborating with tribal dictators . . . from Ethiopia to South Asia to South America, and the exiling of millions from their land, food, and culture.[10]

After the Great War to end all wars . . . came a century of continuous and exceedingly profitable war making with the blood-shedding revenue filling the pockets of the fomenting few.

After the genius and spread of democracy . . . came corporate dominance, mercantile politics, liberty for sale, an unrestrained and worshiped capitalism merged with gorging tribal ambitions . . . and with a fervid and jingoistic religiosity.

And the reversing trends still continue. Don't they?

Much of it is rationalized with glamorous and bogus evidence, hidden by the suppression of facts and information, sidetracked by false historical accounts and by memorized tribal beliefs, by the abolition of critical thinking, by an ever name-changing villainous *otherness* to defend against, corrupted by tribal name callers, distracted and confused by a multiplicity of imaginary demons, warned to be always just over the horizon—which somehow vindicates all of the violence and sorrow as being necessary.

So the blood just keeps getting wiped clean, doesn't it? With the same old rag of death which never seems to dry up from lack of use.

And then there's this:

As reported in 2006 by the United Nations News Center, the richest 2 percent of people in the world own more than half of all household wealth while the poorer half of the global population control just 1 percent, according to a study released by the United Nations University (UNU).[11]

Much of the wealth is concentrated in North America, Europe and rich Asia-Pacific nations such as Japan, Australia, and the Republic of Korea, despite their comparatively small population when measured against Africa and countries such as China and India.

We don't see that much has changed in the last few years—except that others (within that 2 percent) are now competing for a bigger share of the unsustainable pie.

And many of you still refuse to see, don't you? As you blame the destitute for their own destitution while overidentifying yourselves with tribal vocabulary . . . which predetermines your tone of voice and language, parroting the arrogant and isolated assertion that easy opportunities are available everywhere and for everyone . . . just for the taking, reverting to survival-of-the-fittest philosophies, hunkering down even deeper in the deception of the *only-mind*, trapping yourselves behind your own small pile of temporal accumulation and security—drooling for even more.

And many of you simply act as if "So what . . . we have ours, even though it may have once upon a time been yours."

And so you do, don't you?

Yet it never seems to be enough, does it?

You brag and complain about what you possess and about what you lack but wish for—all in the same sentence.

It's a bewildering world in which you constantly overconsume, bombarded by media-exaggerated objects of anxiety and desire. You breathe all of it in as normal intake, even as sustenance. And much of it is just so arbitrary, isn't it? And clearly unjust for so many. But you already know that.

Yet it still seems to be so paradoxically understandable, doesn't it?

When there's no compassion saved up for *others* in your heart, little sympathy gets evoked for what you refuse to see or for what you even refuse to imagine.

And so many of the defenseless and vulnerable *others* (the untouchables whom you reject as unrelated to yourselves . . . as not really God's children) have less and less energy to plead for mercy anymore. Don't you see?

And so many of you in the so-called middle have simply allowed critical reasoning and a sense of justice to be replaced by a cold tribal reactionary stance, frozen into tribal law by a tribal logic which worships at the altar of an overly contained allegiance to itself.

So the puzzle gets solved, doesn't it?

The ruling fat cats of each tribe toss a few pleasure bones your way to keep you *disjoined*, which keeps you in the loop of blaming those at the bottom of your heap . . . or of blaming those at the bottom of any heap. After all, any one particular bottom of a heap is as good as any *other*, isn't it?

And the blame and the brutality trickle-down like a shower of sharp knives, piercing down and hard upon *the least of these*—upon those at the bottom of the bottom who have nowhere to go and nowhere to stop the bleeding, nowhere to trickle-down their own honed confusion and fear. So it just accumulates and sharply expands sideways.

The few among the wealthy who demonstrate bold acts of charity and truth telling are even ridiculed and condemned for going public with their extensive or even minimal philanthropy or for their encouragement of the same from their super-rich peers.

What seems to be regularly sanctioned and so often yet so awkwardly expressed by so many of your rich and super-rich (and by the wannabe rich) is that doing good is actually doing bad somehow, yes? Especially when you operate outside of or seem to compete with the controlling influence of the tribal bigwigs and their narrowly defined, easily corrupted, and fiercely enforced closed system of profit and finance, or if you stand out even slightly from its ever-growing congregation of compliant devotees and especially if you resist its rigid rules of operation which are rigged in favor of legalized money laundering for a few select members of an elite and well-insulated cross-tribal club, with its cult-like worshiping of an unhinged globalized capitalism, and of the whole fiscally *disjoined* process itself—of free-market collectivism for the tribal rich and social Darwinism for most everyone else.[12]

The majority of the overly contained have been convinced to submit to and even to worship and then defend the materialistic system of top-down economics, as an unimpeachable and sacred symbol of irresistible power and of worldly stature, and of the possibilities of endless accumulation of which they imagine themselves getting a hefty share of someday and which the privileged few who already have more than enough . . . especially of their (unfair) share . . . have become so used to banking on in order to extend and hoard even more of their exhaustive control of the buying and selling of perishables, which not so surprisingly have come to be seen as necessities by most of those among the invited—as projected through the indoctrinating lens of the *only-mind.*

But examples of unashamed generosity create an uneasy feeling among the overaccumulated, don't they? They fear those who appear to be overly generous . . . more than they fear natural catastrophes, it seems. They fear what it may lead to. Too much generosity or compassion could expose the cracks in the *disjoined* ideological facade which purports to desire a level playing field with free, open, and fair competition and which pretends that that kind of balance and justice not only exists but prevails, with uncontained opportunities for all. It's a very realistic fear—from a very lopsided and self-serving point of view.

And it all appears to be so upside down, doesn't it? So insane really, so much so that it hurts beyond words—as it should.

Although it's still so goddamn understandable, isn't it?

But understanding by itself doesn't ease the pain of anyone very much, does it? Unless there's some compassionate action that's standing up right behind it.

But most of you already know that. Right?

CHAPTER 55

The Loss of Collective Attention

I F IT'S OKAY with you, we're going to take a short break here . . . a brief pause in our presentation.

We're beginning to sense an acceleration in the loss of your collective attention, a gradual rise of resistance, and a looming and widespread fear emanating from below—which may indicate that several of you might start to lose some of your visible composure (if we don't allow for a little downtime) in response to what you've heard so far and from the distaste and resentment that you've been savoring and which you now seem to be brooding over.

It appears that some of you are even feeling a bit nauseous, which could actually be a good sign. We're not quite sure.

But we'll remove ourselves just the same, temporarily . . . to let things settle a bit. It'll provide you with a brief opportunity for some silence and some stillness, for some contemplative self-reflection.

And (so far) we're not at all surprised by your resistant reaction. It's to be expected.

It's basically following the same pattern of response many of you have had to anything that attempts to pull you out of your collective trance.

So some quieting down might help. But if not, we'll still be returning to continue our presentation.

We promise not to cut significantly into your preparation time.

This intermission period might be a good opportunity for many of you to practice some prevention techniques, to prevent yourselves from quickly escaping back into the vacuum of your favorite tribal noise.

And as usual, we ask only for your patience and for your honest intention to see.

CHAPTER 56

A Brief Intermission

CHAPTER 57

The Power and
Expanse of Each Decision

O KAY. WE'RE BACK.
So let's just move ahead with things then, shall we?

We do appreciate your understanding and patience, even if it's a bit of a charade . . . and despite the fact that right now you may not be feeling very patient with us or even if you're still trying to pretend that you're not receiving or that you just don't understand the message being transmitted to you.

We acknowledge your reluctance.

But we're quite sure that you'll eventually get to a place of necessary fortitude, if not to a place of slowly accepting the situation at hand for what it is.

You'll have to, in order to make a genuine and safe (transformational) turnaround.

But anyway. Where were we?

Oh, yes . . . here we go.

It takes a while for any kind of satisfactory phenomenon to arise or then to even survive . . . from the smoldering ashes of fear and greed, doesn't it? Or from the *disjoined* depths of despair and hatred, or from the overreactive and terror-stricken pattern of punishing *others* in order to relieve yourselves of punishment, or from a longstanding trepidation and resistance to any incoming sense of actual transformation, or from the ferocious dread of losing any real or imagined self-importance, even if that self-importance is misplaced or misguided by mechanically deferring one's belief system to the prevailing tribal logic—by disregarding and discounting one's own unmediated experience and heart-expanding *Self*-knowledge.

Thoughts, words, and actions have consequences which don't disappear too easily. Do they not?

Just listen to this:

Acid rain is blown in from Midwestern factories in the United States, creating hundreds of dead lakes and dying forests, along with their native inhabitants . . . in the Northeastern states and in Southeastern Canada, from corporate carelessness and from a lack of thoughtful, serious, or practical regulation, along with an emphasis and desire to put extravagant profits above the health and welfare of the natural environment . . . and of actual people. Does it matter?[1]

Then there's this:

Hundreds of thousands of human beings are slaughtered, raped, abandoned, and abused after months of daily hate speech is widely broadcast (repeatedly) through government sponsored radio and television outlets in Rwanda and in the former Yugoslavia.[2]

The broadcasts start out with some subtlety under the cover of political speech and from behind distorted tribal accusations claiming that abstract injustices are being done. Then they gradually move into the blunt hatred of *others*, often labeling them as cockroaches and worse . . . to complete the dehumanizing process.

Machetes, liquor, and bullets are passed out. The genocide begins.

Does anything in your present-day local or regional tribal environment sound vaguely similar to this? Are any familiar sounds of fear and hatred coming out of *your* radios, televisions, cell phones, and computers? From *your* pervasive tribal media? Even from *your* elected officials? Is any of it being barked at you now, but only with different targets of accusation? With distinct tribal allusions? Voiced with various levels of inflammatory unraveling? Merely from a different tribal echo chamber? And are you a passive and neutral collaborator or even an enthusiastic supporter of the hatred and blame which you're being entertained with . . . and implored to listen to?

How about this:

So-called professional or superior athletes pour drugs into their bodies to win championships, excessive salaries, and fame by cheating and lying . . . sending the message to so many of you (who tend to hero worship and idolize your tribal sports figures) that the materialistic ends of prestige, power, and possessions can justify any means of getting there—especially when seeking affirmation or adulation from the rest of the tribe.

Can you recognize this kind of lying? This kind of exaggerating? This presenting of a false image of respectability? While covering it all up with more of the same deception? Is it being similarly mirrored in your present-day political, religious, corporate, media, and cultural spheres of influence? Or even in your personal lives?

We'll let you take the quiz on your own. It's an open-book test. So there's no way to cheat or even to fail unless you choose to lie to yourselves.

We suggest that you deeply consider these few telling examples and inquiries. Ponder them seriously, on this side or on the other side—preferably both. They're only among the many illustrations you could have been facing up to on a regular basis and with much more courage and integrity than you've demonstrated up until now.

But if the questions can't even be asked without fear of retribution or rejection from your tribe of allegiance, or from the fear of feeling disloyal or of maybe even having to slightly adjust your perspective in relationship to *others*—then what does that tell you about the powerful influence that the tribal *only-mind* has over you?

Try to gather up enough bravery within yourselves so you can take these questions along with you to the *other* side. Okay? They can only help to clarify and speed up the transitional process.

And ask yourselves this:

Just how many notorious or simply well-known CEOs or representatives . . . or judges, politicians, or bureaucrats . . . or ministers, bishops, or generals . . . or any other powerful overseer of any persuasion from any of your most prosperous and influential tribal institutions ever volunteer to be openly questioned or criticized, either directly or indirectly . . . especially by those from within their own immediate flock?

Or even dare to ask yourselves this:

How many of you personally try to block yourselves from hearing any criticism or from asking any critical questions of any kind about any of your sacred tribal cows?

What does that tell you about you? Or about the fragile and fear-driven insecurity which infects the *only-mind* of each overly contained tribe.

Even so . . . good, true, and beautiful substance and form still manages to break through . . . and to climb up and out of it all somehow, doesn't it? Somehow, through all of that rubble, it still rises up out of your repeated regressions in order to keep reclaiming and reaffirming your humanity.

And yet right alongside your many breakthroughs, and running neck and neck with them, come your predictable reversals which give it all away again . . . over and over again.

If you look back honestly over your contradictory and confounding tribal history, of *disjoined* back and forths . . . it certainly looks as though you haven't been able to make up your collective mind about who you really are as a species, doesn't it?

Very often (as you know) only more fear, hatred, and despair has built up and come out of any previous wave of fear, hatred, and despair . . . before something good, true, or beautiful has been able to reintegrate and take hold again after the violent dust finally settles.

But every action has multiple and expansive effects, doesn't it? Some sooner and some later.

First comes death. Then comes resurrection . . . of some kind.

Over and over again.

Still there have never been any easy or uncomplicated resurrections resulting from your violent ideas, have there? Or from your violent language. Or from any of your collective violent acts over the centuries.

Some part of *Creation* always suffers from the blunt of it, doesn't it? Either from the direct or immediate vibrational blows or from the aftershocks, like so many oblivious dominoes waiting in line to be struck down just because they're in the interconnected vicinity, in the wrong violent place at the wrong violent time. It's what so many of you leisurely and euphemistically label as *collateral damage*. Isn't it?[3]

And how does one mourn for or resurrect from collateral damage?

It's just one more old-fashioned tribal paradox, isn't it? Real human beings are being redefined into something you've been taught and told to rename as collateral—no longer seen as being in God's image and likeness, as some of your religious traditions claim that human beings are molded into.

Instead, they're moved outside the prayer tent—while heartless, soulless, and nonbreathing autocratic corporations move in to take their place, corporate bodies which are redefined as embodying the identities of real people.

Have your tribal institutions actually become the newly crowned exemplars of what you now consider to be the real and essential image and likeness of the *Divine?* Have they become the revered representatives of your tribal gods?

Is that what you're trying to say?

Is that the secret trade-off?

Millions of innocents continue to be buried and forgotten in collateral burial grounds. It doesn't seem to stop in your world, does it?

And there appears to be no end in sight. The long lines of dominoes are interminable.

There's a little breakthrough of compassion, enlightenment, and liberation over here. Then there's a sudden surge back into fear-driven tribal selfishness and into more hatred and violence over there.

But now the continual return to this violence could end up being permanently fatal. Couldn't it? For the whole human race and for much of the rest of *Creation* too (not just for you)—and once and for all.

Much of it resists and even refuses its own resurrection.

Change comes. It's never easy. Transformation unfolds. It's never effortless. But you needn't create artificial suffering. There's enough of the real stuff to go around already, isn't there? Just from the bare everyday imperfections arising and evolving naturally out of the interactions and complexities of simply being human and alive, in an impermanent and imperfect world where death and suffering are a daily raw occurrence.

Yet you keep going back, don't you?

If you don't figure out a way to reenvision these things soon, then the only thing that may resurrect after a while will be the dust and muck you'll be turning the planet into.

But you're already doing a lot of that now to a growing portion of the globe, aren't you? A brief and direct look at the oil contaminated Gulf of Mexico or at the Kalamazoo River in Michigan will tell you that.

Or just take a look at the desecrated rainforests of Indonesia or the Brazilian Amazon, or at the moon-scape mountaintops and soil-filled valleys of West Virginia or eastern Kentucky, or the years of sequestered oil spillage in the Niger Delta . . . or in Peru and Ecuador, or the millions of internal and external refugees all over the Earth . . . fleeing for their lives.[4]

Did you know that Iceland and Greenland are the only two countries in your present-day world where confirmed human slavery cannot be found?

We're talking about today—not hundreds of years ago.

There are over twenty-seven million slaves trapped or traded for—all over the planet. Today![5]

And the main inducement for this continued slavery is continued profit making. Nothing else even comes close. Slavery is profitable enough for a whole lot of people to stay in the business in order to make sure it continues. A whole lot of them are. Which means that a whole lot of you are too, even while you go on denying that you are—refusing to even consider that you might be contributing to that deplorable business.

Do you ever ask yourselves any of the following questions?

Who makes these physical objects that I purchase? What are the working conditions like for those real, live human beings who do the work to make these things? Who profits and who gains from this? And who suffers and who loses from this? Where does the money that I spend go? Into whose hands and pockets? And does it matter? Who made this T-shirt? These dress shoes or sneakers? Do they matter? What about the diamond in my wedding ring? How about the components in my computer or smartphone? Am I supporting the violence of slavery along with slave wages and inhumane working conditions through my desire for tribal (and hence, personal) comfort, security, and convenience? Is that possible?

You may find that there is no good, clear, or easy answer to any of this—until you begin to ask the question.

But there is at least—the question, isn't there?

And many humans and *other* living beings are significantly affected by whether you ask it or not.

And they're impacted by how you ask it too (and who you ask it of), aren't they? Whether it's with compassion in defense of life . . . or if the subject is merely brought up to flaunt your knowledge of statistics, without any real sense of concern beyond the numbers you memorize or the tribal logic you defend, or whether you simply ignore it altogether and just keep moving yourselves up the line of the materialistic food chain, closer to those material rewards at the material checkout counter where so many of you seem to check yourselves out even before you get there.

Again, these are just a few obvious examples among so many . . . from off the top of our head. And it really does hurt to think too much about this stuff. We do understand that. Believe us. We do.

Yet at the same time, there's significant and substantial pain and suffering that's continually being reinforced from thinking too little or not at all about it, isn't there?

Is any of that pain and suffering really any less grievous just because it's not your pain? Just because it's not you who personally suffers? Or because it's not your tribe which is wounded?

The choice is and has always been yours.

And it will still be yours tomorrow morning.

We're just trying to provide you with some informational clues to hopefully take into serious consideration beforehand.

It might help to quicken the transitional process. It might even lessen the collective angst and agony a little. It might even begin to wake you up from your separation from the *Self*, from *That which is always becoming*—which excludes no one and nothing.

But either way, all of your decisions will still remain in your hands and in your heart.

Whether you like it or not. Won't they?

CHAPTER 58

To Be Grateful and Generous Is Good, *Isn't It?*

MANY OF YOU seem quite willing to accept the one pervasive falsehood which somehow deceives you into believing that the sacred Earth and all of its inhabitants are something separate from who you are. Don't you?

So you revert to recruiting your version of god and his leading spokesmen . . . into being your principal accomplice in proclaiming your separation principles. And it's usually that same old male god whom you keep recruiting, isn't it? Along with his paternalistic mouthpiece of either gender—whether it's the god of religion, or otherwise.

Do you still refuse to acknowledge any of this?

Just try to compare the amount of energy you put into asserting your supremacy over (and your separation from) *others* to the amount of energy you put into being grateful for who you are and for who *others* are—or to the amount of energy you put into being grateful for the gifts and grace of each evolving present moment. It's really no contest, is it?

And let's get a few things cleared up here, shall we? Tribal arrogance along with its condescending pride, which tries to hide behind the window dressing of righteous *disjoined* piety, is a bankrupt substitute for heartfelt humility or for unashamed gratitude.

How can so many of you who have so much still have so little to be thankful for anyway, while continuing to collect so much residue of worry, of anxious and insecure self-promotion, and of bitter animosity (toward *others*) in your bones?

There really is no time to waste here. Is there?

How did your lust for security and status, for a guaranteed afterlife salvation for your earthbound ego, and for unrestrained material accumulation rise so high and fast (and so emphatically) to the top of your charts of tribal ambition?

How does clinging to the fantasy of personal perfection and to tribal certitudes take precedence over extending compassionate loving-kindness to yourselves and to *others?*

How does vengeance and retribution so often smother out forgiveness and understanding, restorative justice and mercy, and even peaceful coexistence?

How do your presumptions of preordained tribal superiority and your assumed entitlements (usually gained by force, luck, connivance, or intimidation) so regularly outstrip the balanced and reasonable sharing of the necessary basics (of even minimal comfort and survival) with *others* who are in regular and genuine need?

How does closefisted selfishness so easily trump the parceling out to the unfortunate or to the destitute of most if not all of what you wastefully compile and store up?

How does immediate and fleeting self-indulgence edge so easily ahead to replace all of the slow beauty which the Earth provides and which you could be leaving behind untarnished for future generations to savor if you had the will and desire to do it?

How does the want and worship of office and title and of perishable objects of arousal come to outweigh a deep respect and reverence for the universal and unifying goodness found in all of *Creation?*

You cannot plow two rows at once, cultivate two minds in meditation, or follow two different rays back to Unity.

You will either turn away from one light, like the moon waning, and shine from the depths toward the other, like the radiant sun.

Or you will take up the weight of one work, honoring the burdens that come, and neglect that of the other, considering it a worthless punishment.

You cannot work for Unity, without being unified.

You cannot cultivate the depths and simultaneously pile things up on the surface of life, observed the wise Jesus.[1]

We'll simply repeat that it's all still quite understandable to us . . . considering the historic path of tribal containment you've restricted yourselves to. Even though it's still beyond difficult to sympathize with it at the same time.

Is it understandable? Yes. But it's also indefensible.

The conundrum continues.

But it continues to be predictably dangerous too, doesn't it?

The most obvious evidence is in how you allow your tribal extremes to not only be your loudest and most dominant voice, but also how you proudly encourage them to enlist so many of your children into their *disjoined* ranks.

CHAPTER 59

The Excluding *Only-Mind*

YOU'VE FALLEN DOWN . . . into sentimental romance with the dead, with the death of anything outside the grasp and control of your suffocating tribal logic.

A necromania has taken hold, spreading itself out into conscious thought—with deadly and deliberate behavior.

Eros deforms into Thanatos—depriving the tribal heart of its capacity to love *others* without condition.

The vital force within you which transmits passionate and mischievous love is undermined (or so you seem to wish), remasked and captured by tribal hordes, which chant . . . "Death to all *otherness* and to the love of any outside *other*! And death to the inmost *Self* and to *That which shall never become!* Death to the inexpressible God of Love who includes too much!"

Thanatic excitement is aroused. Eros is repressed and refabricated into yet another of your substitutional demons, commodified into just another piece of tribal consumption—to use up and to throw away.

And every toxic word which you pronounce is just one more reinforcing ego ejaculation, isn't it?

Aging tribal myths are shaken. Old ways of understanding are purposely forgotten. Tribal horns are locked against any unfamiliar upstart of *otherness* that appears on the scene.

It's the same old *disjoined* story, yes?

We've grieved over it for all of you. Yet it hasn't done much good.

But filling up more of the divisive picture frame is just about anyone who has the means to obtain the price of just one eight by ten potential photo of ample devastation with their name on it, to fit inside the tribal container, to hang on their mother's wall, to make a famous name for themselves, to be immortalized, envisioning themselves sitting on the right hand of their wrong god—looking down at all those *others* left far behind.

The insolence is almost as striking as the delusion, is it not?

Your growing despair is borne out of the fear of losing what you don't even possess.

But the indoctrinated desire for what will never last is strong enough to take matters into its own hands, isn't it? Filling you up with illusions of bravely defending that which only exists in the hallucinatory world of the tribal *only-mind.*

Some of you are so addicted to your desperate allegiance and to the material meaning that it gives you, that you invent visions of mourners weeping over your framed portrait. You watch them as they lay afterlife accolades upon the masked memory of your deceased body.

Your fantasies of being idolized through an act of tribal martyrdom are worth more to you than the life and love of a child walking innocently to school or to that of a busload of mothers and fathers faithfully going to work.

And it doesn't really matter whether you develop your photos of self-adoration from behind the wheel of a bomb-loaded truck or while wearing a suicide vest of murderous intent, or if you do it from behind the machismo site of a high-powered gun or grenade launcher, or if you're seated atop a bomb ready to be dropped from inside of an empire's corporate high-tech jet . . . thousands of feet up in the air, or if you send your message of death from behind an anonymous and secluded desk in a quiet and cozy Arizona room, thousands of miles away from your undisclosed target . . . while drinking coffee and giving orders or pushing buttons to control human or mechanical drones, delivering their demise to complete strangers on the *other* side of the world.

It's all bad death, leading to more and more bad resurrections, isn't it? And yet you still pretend to be shocked and puzzled by yet another lone gunman who calmly walks into yet another public building and tragically murders yet another dozen or more beautiful and blameless schoolchildren . . . right before taking his own pathetically desperate life.

Lots of reawakening needs to be done.

And it soon will be. We promise.

A major objective of the refacing intervention will be to pull your *disjoined* containers down from the altars of smugness which shelter and safeguard so much of your religious and political violence, where so many of you reverently place your masks of tribal worship—which blind you from seeing *That which is forever unified.*

And as we will continue to repeat . . . *That which unifies* excludes no one, neither human nor *other* than human.

CHAPTER 60

No Allowance

ONE OF THE functions which we've been able to integrate into the *other* side of the facial exchange is that there will be no chance to end it all . . . or to actually instigate any more violence. And the exchange will automatically monitor these temptations until they gradually dissolve and eventually disappear from your tribal repository.

No escalations or reinventions of any type of cruelty or aggression will be permitted. But there will be the necessary reenactments of course, for pedagogical purposes . . . meant to stimulate and encourage the unmasking process. But no extra or recruited violence will be added into the mix at all.

And if anyone attempts to push or extend those limits, if any of you go too far with it into your replacement reactions on the *other* side . . . well then . . . you'll just be about-faced, spun around to start all over again.

There will be no added death camps or world wars and no further terrorist attacks. No additional drug, domestic, sexual, or gang-related violence will be tolerated. Nor will any rationalized or stirred-up form of patriotic or pulpit-pounding hatred be permitted to be aroused or directed at anyone. Not even an added fistfight will be allowed to show its pubescent face.

Not another violent word will be put up with.

Any deviation from that mean and the switch will be immediately flipped. And you'll get to start all over again . . . with another face fitting.

As soon as even the beginning thought of committing an additional act of violence of any kind begins to come forth, you'll be beamed right back to the initial launching pad to repeat your steps . . . faster than a deadly bullet. Do you understand?

Any extra fragrance of violence at all, and it doesn't matter—the train will stop dead right there on the tribal tracks.

Even if you commit a superfluous violent act of omission—it makes no difference. It will be automatic. *Boom.* New face.

And you will never run out of chances to try again.

Hope will be kept on hand as it always has been, able to be viewed through an eternal window . . . just as it is now on this side of things. We're just trying to make it a bit more obvious to you. We're going to make sure that the glass remains clean enough to keep putting it right back in your face—literally.

So there should be no real surprises, should there?

We do trust by now that you're at least starting to understand the urgency of our intervention and the necessity for expeditious and large scale transformation.

Come tomorrow morning, it will all be up to you . . . just as it always has been.

It's paradoxical, isn't it?

It's still understandable yet paradoxical.

Tricky stuff.

CHAPTER 61

The Transience of Tribes

FOR MOST OF your brief human history, you've clustered yourselves inside separate, isolated, and competing tribes, haven't you? You've huddled into sequestered groups of birth, adoption, or desire . . . and quite understandably so. There's no paradox there.

There's safety in numbers . . . after all. Isn't that so?

And each of your overly contained tribes insists on trying to extend its carrying capacity over time, doesn't it? Unless it gets absorbed into an even larger or more powerful vehicle . . . through cross-fertilization; or if another tribe diminishes its tribal numbers through genocidal violence (euphemistically referred to as *ethnic cleansing*), or if a plague hits, or if a major natural disaster of some kind interrupts the tribe's growth curve, or if the tribe loses so many members through natural or unnatural attrition that the remaining members either die off alone or are absorbed into another tribe's influence—or for any number of other reasons.

Take the famous American Indian, Ishi, as an example.[1] Remember him? He was the last remaining member of the Yahi (an otherwise-extinct tribe) who was studied and then taught the ways of the white tribe which found him. Although it's unclear whether he ever truly internalized their tribal ways and logic.

And then, of course, there's the federation of tribes which were contained inside the Soviet Union, which no longer exists . . . except in the mind and logic of a dwindling and aging minority of former tribe members.

The baseball tribe of the Brooklyn Dodgers has no surviving active members. Does it?

How about the tribe of silent-movie watchers? They've long moved on to the talkies, haven't they?

The tribe of the horse and carriage is found only in very independent fringe-dwelling groups like the Amish and is otherwise almost nonexistent in your so-called developed world, which has long been dominated by the tribe of the automobile.[2]

The tribe of cigarette smokers in some parts of your world has greatly diminished . . . mostly due to education, social stigmatizing, and millions of early deaths.

While the tribe of prescription drug users (and abusers) has steadily risen, has it not?

The tribe of postcard and letter writers has basically been replaced by the tribe of e-mailers and texters.

And the tribe of small farmers is on its way to extinction. Isn't it? Rapidly being replaced by the overextending global tribe of corporate agribusiness—by Big Daddy Agra.[3]

Tribes do tend to come and go.

But while they're still alive and kicking, most of them also tend to act as if they're never going anywhere, don't they? As if things will always remain just as they are and as they've always been, even though there is nothing that has *always been,* except for the eternal *Self*—except for *That which is always becoming.*

But again, it's all quite understandable, isn't it?

After all, who really looks forward to their own demise or to any kind of major interruption, for that matter, even if the interruption is necessary or if it may even be for the evolving benefit of the common good?

Transformation is never easy, as we've already acknowledged and have tried to illustrate. And neither is dying to the superficial image of one's self . . . which has been rigorously adhered to, or to a clung-to tribal image which includes all of its customs, traditions, and habits as well as its established and routine belief system—which might help you to see why most of you resist change so much, almost any kind of change.

But if you take a quick look into the long view, back and then forward, it might give you a better sense and perspective of how you got to where most of you seem to be stuck at right now.

For the most part, the very first real tribes that were formed were hunter-gatherers (or foragers) who roamed the Earth for their food and survival. They eventually began to decline and disappear into larger stationary tribes who settled themselves into more permanent agrarian communities of planters, farmers, and ranchers, which then gave way to industrial tribes who migrated into overcrowded cities and who worked together in large numbers in huge factories, mass-producing modern objects of utility, pleasure, or convenience . . . objects made from the Earth's vast accumulation of raw materials.

But beginning very recently, most of your larger tribal societies have been moving quickly into a postindustrial phase, haven't they? Moving out of the manufacturing realm of the industrialized and citified tribe, evolving into tribal associations based on the provision of service, information, innovation, and finance.

The increased globalization of just about everything has interrupted and transformed just about every interconnected system of human interaction on the planet, hasn't it? Including how to make a survivable and dependable living.

Automation and technology have also added to the transforming interruptions, haven't they? Slowly replacing, reducing, or redistributing manual labor . . . replacing humans with mechanization and replacing the tangible and seemingly permanent workplace with the virtual or temporary one, moving from the storefront to the cyberfront, from a stable place of (often only imagined) secure employment to a worldwide market of profit mobility, of job dispersal, and of frequent relocation, much like when the massive manufacturing tribes replaced the less-concentrated agrarian tribes which had replaced the much-smaller foraging and mostly mobile tribes who had been wandering the Earth in small groups most of their lives, gathering the necessary food they needed just to survive—well before the big ball of societal and cultural change started to really get itself rolling.

And now, in a peculiar and destabilizing way for many in your postindustrial era, tribes and tribal members have been slowly forced to return to a unique form of foraging for survival all over again, haven't they? Just like many in the destitute and even in the very poor communities of human beings have always had to do.

Progress has rolled itself all the way around the globe, completing the circle, right back to the beginning, hasn't it? But the circle continues to spin just like it always has. It just spins a whole lot faster than it used to. At least it seems to, doesn't it?

And most of the present-day spinning is generated and contained by the overreaching, virtually invisible, and ever-expanding empire of the global *only-mind*, isn't it? By an (economic, military and political) empire of conjoined tribal religion which has come to dominate most, if not all, of the world's anxiously *disjoined* traffic and logic—in its chaotic entirety.

Don't you see?

CHAPTER 62

Clusters of Containment

B UT MOST OF your major clusters of containment do change over time, don't they?

And very few of your species have ever fully escaped the effects of the larger waves of transformation; even though there still is that minority who we've already spoken of who are willing to live on the edge of tribal jurisdiction, by choice and by disciplined practice . . . or through the mystery of grace, who still refrain from being *of* it, not allowing themselves to be overly contained by any prevailing or hypnotic tribal logic or circumstance, no matter how much the pressure to adapt and conform to the *only-mind* weighs in upon them.

Yet most of you among the invited have willingly gravitated and clung to the inner circles of your overcrowded tribal containers, haven't you? Becoming the metabolic nuts and bolts of each and every mechanized cluster of tribal machinery.

You've unwittingly come to perceive yourselves as less than you are . . . through the gradual process of tribal osmosis, as each of you metabolize your reactions more and more into that of an accommodating automaton, personifying the same programmed personality of the tribe which contains you.

Each system of tribal containment overrides but includes each specific cluster held within itself, unconsciously interacting and overlapping with several *other* ones while still clinging to its own specific and separate collection of individual human beings.

But sooner or later all clusters (paradoxically) interchange most of their parts and much of their information, don't they? As well as their contradictory values and their tribe-bridled knowledge and experience . . . along with any leftover or overlapping history which they reluctantly or unintentionally reveal to each other.

And the interchange is both vertical and horizontal . . . up, down, and sideways; with varying degrees of regularity and extent, enmeshed in the shared DNA of all those who've allowed themselves to be ensnared in the web of the *only-mind*—tangled up together like wingless and paralyzed flies.

You can admit to recognizing at least that much . . . can't you?

Or maybe not just yet.

Even so, there's no end to the messy process of cross-tribal invasion and exchange, is there? The process can seem to move from conflict to cooperation in an instant, or, when proceeding in the *other* direction, from assimilation to division—which often leads to what seems like complete but only apparent separateness, doesn't it?

Even so, you remain enmeshed in the adhesive web of the *only-mind*.

Meanwhile, you've gradually become less valuable to your own containers somehow because of this polarizing entanglement. And many of you have felt that loss deeply . . . and at a very personal level.

Haven't you?

The more that you're entwined together in the terrestrial mix (full of opposing tribal containers) the more it conceals who you are in the depth and span of the sacred (but hidden) wholeness, doesn't it? Obscuring any sense of being part of an indivisible *Self* which unifies—conforming you instead to the delible fiber of the divisive *only-mind*.

And there lies the fatal trap.

Each separate tribe of allegiance may display it own unique coat of arms. But each still wears the same competing armor of conformity (beneath its pretentious coat).

The intent is to suppress.

The unified *Self* is uniformly renounced by antithetical yet collaborative forces which blame each *other* for the very entanglement which they deny.

So as you've grown in number and in the intensity which you've overidentified with the globalized system of tribal containment, you've come to feel diminished in your own necessity and importance, don't you see?

This explains (at least partially) how so many of you have come to revere your tribal masks of allegiance and their *disjoined* facial expressions over and above the individuals who wear them—including yourselves.

Perhaps for many of you some things are simply too evident to see, yes? Yet just noticeable enough to deny.

You've come to idolize the facades of your nation and of your religion, of your color, of your language, of your family, of your culture and ethnicity, even of your short-lived traditions. You've strategically affixed yourselves to each tribal facade (as a convenient necessity) in order to avoid the open embrace of *That which is always becoming It-Self*.

Haven't you?

Loyally staring into the tribal mirror has devolved into your most chosen way to perceive and interpret reality . . . preventing yourselves from entering into the well and wonder of any unmediated spiritual experience.

It's become your favorite tribal fig leaf, hasn't it? Shamelessly used to cover up the nakedness of *That which is*.

And the more of you who can pose together while dutifully squeezing yourselves into the group portrait of denial, the more tightly packed and proud each mirrored image of the tribal container becomes, doesn't it? Filling up each *disjoined* frame with the face of the entangled *only-mind*.

Rules of tribal compliance replace individual common sense, don't you see? Keeping so many of you tightly attached to a preconceptual logic, trapped in the cross-fertilizing mind field of *disjoined* but paradoxically codependent tribalism.

Yet overidentification with one's own ilk seems to happen for some very valid reasons sometimes, doesn't it? For reasons related to the legitimate need for a sense of belonging or for a sense of safety and of meaning . . . among other things.

Human beings seem to need containers which they can identify with and which they can carry around in their heads, just like honeybees need to retain the image of their queen when they're out buzzing around away from the hive.

And in order for any official representative of tribal royalty to convince itself that it can effectively control the swarm (of the loudly quiet and compliant masses), it needs to be able to contain enough minions to make it worth its while, doesn't it? To confirm its legitimate and worthy status among the competing communities of colonized (human) hives.

And that (at its most extreme) is what directly led to and even necessitated the infamous death camps of Hitler and Stalin, isn't it? And it's that which has continued to lead to so much narcissistic tribal propaganda to this very day—very similar to the fear-driven and addictive properties of containment fanatically fed into the acquiescent and *disjoined* minds and bodies which built and ran those death camps.

It always seems to come down to an extreme necessity, doesn't it? One sustained by tribal insecurity and by the pacifying stories that an overly contained persuasion somehow needs to believe about itself . . . often

MICHAEL J. GAJDA

leading to the creation of a mythology of preeminence which inflames an already paranoid tribal logic, frequently rearoused by one of the many bizarre versions of a tribe-redeeming last battle of Armageddon—always against (and in fear of) a nefarious force of apocryphal *otherness.*

So each overly contained human colony gradually becomes what more and more of you happen to depend upon as necessary (by default), through routine and docile allegiance or through habitual and overanxious submission—unless of course you reassign yourselves or are forced to leave the container for some disloyal reason. But then, most of you among the invited just take your impoverished loyalty and its abstract neediness with you . . . into another *disjoined* tribal configuration.

Do you not?

Your security and survival are derived from inside of whatever confinement you inhabit. So the inevitable objective is to keep the tribal seduction system closed off and well defended, even if it means that an increasing number of you are diminished even more by the seducement or even if you actually die in the process—physically or spiritually.

The survival of the containing system takes ultimate precedence over everything else. It has to, doesn't it? It's become the highest cause one can (and often feels that it must) surrender to.

Name any imperious or autocratic nation-state, any top-heavy or monopolizing corporation, or any overcentralized or magisterial house of religion anywhere. You'll witness the same cajolery, perhaps across different developmental levels of enticement or at varying degrees of imposing effectiveness—but you'll still witness it.

You can even name an overly contained sports team and get the same purview and effect.

Can't you?

The marketed team image outranks the goals or the needs of most individual players, doesn't it? Even though it may exempt the so-called superstars (of course) who so often become the dominant marketing symbol of the so-called team—until their individual star begins to fade and their stardom is no longer of exploitable use.

And the idealized image of an overly contained nationalism outranks the rights and freedoms of the average individual citizen, does it not? It even outranks the rights and freedoms of the average individual community infected by such zealotry.

Abstract but ingrained religious doctrine and self-ordained authority figures (along with tribal ritual and ceremony) outrank any reports of direct spiritual experience, of any enlightening personal or communal prayer, of any contemplative insight, and especially of any divine guidance or revelation which hasn't been preauthorized by a hovering hierarchy or by a self-censoring *only-mind.*

Party politics and political dockets outrank objective, thoughtful, or independent-minded party members or any political logic formed outside of or even slightly counter to that of the overly contained tribal agenda.

A generalizing but dogmatic ideology outranks the well-reasoned or specific idea, doesn't it? Even outranking peer-reviewed or repeatedly reconfirmed scientific evidence which conflicts with the tribal paradigm and program, as well as outranking any empirical data that hasn't been rubber stamped by the tribe's upper crust.

An idea, it seems, must first fit into the tribe's cerebral containing system before it can safely be exchanged inside the overcrowded quarters of the tribal zone of compliance. If not, then it's banished.

Out the container it goes.

At least for several years.

Or maybe even for a few hundred years.

That's how frozen in time and logic some tribal force fields can get. Can't they? Until they can figure out how to recapture and recontain the banished one without losing any of the tribe's schedule-setting dominance or control.

Just ask Joan of Arc or Copernicus, or Charles Darwin or Malcolm X, or Alexander Solzhenitsyn or Dorothy Day—or any of the blacklisted Hollywood writers, directors, and actors who were brought down by the communist witch hunts of the McCarthy era, during its reign of political terror . . .[1] among all of the many *other* historical scapegoats of paranoid tribal logic.

They'll tell you.

They were only let back into the fold and reapproved of when the elite of the tribe was ready to let them back in . . . after reinventing itself once again, or after the banished and blacklisted were dead-and-gone, or after those outcast *others* were themselves reinvented by the loyal functionaries of the tribe, only then to be adapted fully into the tribal contrivance of how things were to be played out . . . but only how they were to be played out according to tribal convention, not necessarily in line with any lasting or evolving truth, goodness, or beauty.

One of the best examples of this often-used strategy is when the Roman Emperor Constantine (after years of the empire's persecution of those who followed the *Way* of Jesus) suddenly legalized Christianity in AD 313 . . . and then became a benefactor of the newly institutionalized Church himself, giving it the power and influence of state patronage backed by the office of the emperor. This would eventually lead it to be declared the official religion of the Holy Roman Empire by a later emperor, Theodosius, in AD 381.

The followers and imitators of Jesus were gradually absorbed into this empire-legitimized alignment . . . of the Church with the state. And soon after, by Roman law, all citizens were strongly encouraged, if not persecuted, into becoming at least unofficial champions of the official Holy Roman Imperial Church . . . which joined forces with, while very closely imitating (and even outright impersonating) and following the hierarchical norms and structures of, the Holy Roman Empire and its emperor (whom most of the popes have since continued to consistently mirror and emulate).[2]

The message of the inclusive, nonviolent, approachable, simple-living, and selfless carpenter's son was soon watered down and reinvented by an aloof and aristocratic official institution full of sparkling gold and authoritarian glitter.

The liberating message of Jesus was recaptured, redefined, and replaced . . . hung on to a stained-glass wall by an often violent, exclusive, secretive, extravagant, self-absorbed, and imperial corporate entity. His tattered peasant robe and sandals were exchanged for gold embroidered vestments, crowns, and canes. His open and wandering homelessness was obscured, buried, and largely forgotten beneath a statue-filled basilica of power and secrecy . . . beneath the weight of property, of official statehood, and of arm-guarded governance.

Even the architectural design of the original Old Saint Peter's Basilica was that of a typical basilica of the Roman Empire.[3] It's amazing to us how so many courageous and enlightened saints, mystics, poets, priests, sisters, brothers, theologians, thinkers, lovers, peacemakers, anonymous parishioners, martyrs, prophets, and holy people of simple but compassionate faith and lifestyle have been able to embody the transcendent life and message of Jesus, by putting on the mind of *Christ* and entering into *Its* consciousness, even from inside the thick and *disjoined* layers of that one huge *only-mind* of empire and dominion.

But many of them have, haven't they?

So it just goes to show you how the unifying and indivisible strength of *That which is always becoming* cannot be denied. It cannot be buried and covered up forever, no matter how much top-down power, prescribed prestige, material wealth and possessions, or formalized rules and rituals you try to replace it with.

Even the vast tribal power and control of such a worldly and overly contained institution can't completely or forever redefine or compromise the universal *Self*, can it?

In many ways, throughout its history, the power hierarchy of the Roman Catholic Church itself (like many other tribal institutions, religious or otherwise) has been forced to reluctantly evolve, hasn't it? To catch up and surrender to the often kidnapped and suppressed message of the *Rejected One*—in order to survive its own self-deluding vertical distractions.

The True and Great Self will always remain an exception to the rules of containment. It can never be completely trapped inside of any apparently all-powerful version of the *only-mind* (when you can awaken to *Its* presence). And as is so evident in this example and as we've already shown, there is nowhere *Its* presence cannot be found, is there? No matter how much you try to redefine, restrict, or even supersede it.

But as long as a tribal containing system resists and tries to repress the awakening (or the evolution of awareness) of any of its members, the qualities of the indivisible *Self* have to be watered down. Don't they? At least enough to fit back into the frozen logic of the *only-mind*.

That's pretty much how it works in your world, isn't it? Pick any group which is controlled or dominated by the tribal *only-mind* . . . by any name. You'll get a similar result.

The abstract image and customs of the *disjoined* family too often nullify the values, beliefs, and experience of the individual family member.

The intangible assets and the expanding control of the *disjoined* global corporation too often override the daily, weekly, and monthly bills which need to be paid by the flesh-and-blood individual human being.

Quick and unlimited Wall Street investments and an unconstrained (and oxymoronic) free-market economy are too often disconnected from their effects upon real people and upon viable life on a finite planet.

And as it so frequently happens, the dangerous tendency along the way is to settle and dig into the extremes, isn't it? To move toward the goal of completely conforming to group thought, which usurps the flow of the individual conscience . . . and then to mask over the unifying *Self* with tribal talking points which point to nothing that can be freely explored outside the boundaries and logic of the *only-mind*.

But you already know that.

Don't you?

CHAPTER 63

Hidden Wisdom Figures

YOU'VE GRADUALLY ALLOWED a portrayal of superiority to define your most powerful tribal containers, haven't you? Lavishly bestowing upon them an elevated title and persona which magically transforms them into some kind of ultimate being, which you steadily submit to—while you willingly or unwittingly accord the title of persona non grata to your actual *Self.*

You've swapped and given away the value of your own relative (and even your *Absolute*) integrity, becoming ever more addicted to the concentrated power of these exalted terrestrial organisms, buckling under in the hope of enhancing your own individual relevance, rendering to each overly inflated Caesar that which does not merit the rendering of anything of worth.

It's led to a tidal wave of acquiescence, hasn't it? Wherein these elevated entities have come to embody conventional yet obligatory images of authority, unable to be seen or even imagined by most of you (among the invited) for what they truly are. But how could they be? When you're so busily consumed by the spinning imagery of the very thing through which your perception is so narrowly tethered?

Overcontainment (of any kind) never intends to gently guide and wean you from its protection and control. Instead, it steadily captivates and then absorbs you into its circulatory system. The more captivated you become, the more solidified the containment becomes . . . and the more you then fade into the background, becoming just another microscopic blood cell flowing through the veins and limbs of the *disjoined* anatomy of the *only-body* of the tribe.

You gradually diminish and dissolve into the container . . . as it expands and solidifies. But you have to. Don't you? There's only so much room to move about in. More and more of you are crowded together, squeezed ever more tightly into the tribal holding tank—shrinking instead of becoming, by the hour if not by the minute.

The value of the container continues to inflate until it becomes fused into the tribal psyche as something irreplaceable—as something near or even entirely omnipotent. While the value of each human being captured within it steadily dwindles, near or even entirely to the point of psychological evaporation.

And the only way to elevate one's social esteem in such a *disjoined* system is by trying to make a louder noise than anyone else—a noise projected outward in support and defense of your own confinement.

It's the same old-fashion head fake, isn't it? The squeaky wheel gets more of the container grease. The loudest and most rigid defender of the tribal logic accumulates more prestige, more power, and even more tribal privileges for their efforts—while all three of those craved-for rewards outrank whoever is awarded them.

It's so paradoxical, isn't it?

Your prized plaque on the tribal wall has come to embody you . . . more than even you do yourself.

It's so disheartening to observe, isn't it? Tribal acceptance has gradually come to eclipse personal meaning and purpose. Life in the *only-mind* is condensed into one big contest for evermore recognition. The value of the individual is reduced to mere status, to how much the face of an actual human being can mirror, reflect, and extol the overriding containing system . . . a system which you've come to assume to be more valuable than each of you are, by virtue of its size and accumulated component parts—which are always (and nothing but) you.

Remember?

Quantified tribal approval has come to overshadow individual quality of life. Form is separated from (and elevated above) substance— enough to conceal and to even disown the pure essence of *That which is.*

Many of you have simply encased yourselves inside of an assumed tribal identity, have you not? Epitomized by your rank and standing within the tribal pasture. You've come to be defined by whichever abstract grouping you've allowed to convert, to claim, or to classify you.

Overly enmeshed families and peer groups are no different in their essence than overly enclosed teams and organizations. Or than overly guarded corporations and institutions. Or than overly isolated cities, states, and nations. Or than overly defined philosophies and religions. Or than overly biased ideas about gender, race, and ethnicity. Or than an overly sheltered career or vocation. Or than an overly defended tribal history or political persuasion. Or than overly absorbed media imagery. Or than overly spoken tribal language.

You need only to name it for what it is in order to see it. And yet there appears to be no innate immunity from catching this overly contagious disease, is there?

Although there always seems to be enough available space within the tribal *only-mind* to be able to squeeze another one or two of you in, if the immune system has been weakened enough—and as long as you're willing to be squeezed, of course.

But some overly contained structures are less toxic than others, aren't they? Even though one infectious container of captivity isn't much different than any other one . . . when it comes right down to it.

The individual human molecules within each isolated system of containment are what feed and keep it growing. The more it's fed, the bigger and more dominant it becomes (in its *only-mind*).

Each bundle of confinement tends to grow into an even more confining one.

And over time, each overly confined tribal structure tends to fill itself up with smaller yet more numerous ones. The numerous become the multiplying nutrients which feed and sustain the ongoing expansion of tribal uniformity.

Growth at any and all cost has become the insistent, intoxicating, and sacred mantra of most of your (artificially created) tribal containing systems—which have actually come to be viewed as being alive, haven't they? Because wittingly or not, you've bestowed the personification of life upon them.

Abstract corporations (at least in the USA) are now being proclaimed to be real people—by supreme tribal law.

Have you let that one sink in yet?

And yet you just keep feeding the gluttony of confinement with your very selves, don't you?

The paradox is quite striking, is it not?

Even so, containing systems in themselves (as you already know) are not inherently evil, are they? Not at all. They're actually very natural and necessary extensions of the evolutionary life of the planet and of all of its inhabitants.

There really are such things as parent-led families which teach and guide their children to become independent (as opposed to codependent) and evolving people of conscience, aren't there?

And there actually are sage-led religious practices and Traditions which try to transmit that same wisdom to those who come to them for guidance. Are there not?

Aren't there even political and social activists and public servants who actually try to influence and guide public policies which benefit the most and the least among you . . . in fair and judicious ways? Of course there are.

Are there not tribal institutions which try to put people and the side effects from their business operations upon the rest of the planet, and upon *other* sentient beings, before excess profit and personal or corporate greed? Yes. There are.

And aren't there still some sincerely gifted and civil communicators who use the media to try to enhance the common good and its intelligence and try to bring people to a higher level of *Self*-consciousness and of compassionate understanding and of mutuality and interconnection and of cooperative involvement? Of course.

Are there not even some government and military leaders who actively look for and even find nonviolent solutions in the midst of tense and potentially slaughterous situations? Yes. They may be a rare breed, but yes.

And aren't there tribal elders among you who effectively lead *others* toward the discovery and experience of the integral *Self*? Toward the clarity of *That which is always becoming*? And toward your inherent capacity to behold the unified cosmos within yourselves?

Of course there are.

CHAPTER 64

Try These Experiments

S O MANY OF your tribal constructs are merely mechanical (hand-me-down) obligations. Aren't they? Sewn into and attached to your day to day interactions . . . huge and complicated, bureaucratic, stuck right where they are, interminable and alienating, and all-encompassing, so tightly interweaved into the collective psyche that you can't even seem to wield an understanding of their combined components or functions . . . at least not with any consistent or meaningful level of comprehension.

Although you can't safely envision a world without their overcontrolling presence either, can you? Even while most of you still refuse to acknowledge the addictive hold they have upon you, even in your most private moments—if only to yourselves.

Instead, you try to bury your awareness beneath a pretense of being autonomous, abandoning your own inherent capacity for contemplation—allowing your interior life to be compromised by relentless intrusions of tribal noise.

Disjoined preconceptions have come to so dominate your sense of reality that they've become your reality—your virtual reality, haven't they? So much so that their proliferation has gradually established an internal system of protection, one which is quite willing and determined to defend and preserve the purity of the tribal terrain (the terrain of the *only-mind*) at all costs, from the depths and center of its perceptual discretion . . . where it outwardly projects its hostilities from behind the heavily fortified perimeter of the *disjoined* persona which you collectively inhabit.

Your uniqueness has been displaced, hasn't it? Superimposed by the barricading face of the tribe. You've become an isolated replica of that which contains you.

But let us attempt to better illustrate what we mean with a few simple experiments in thought. And we'll need your open-minded and imaginative cooperation in order for the experiments to make any sense or to have any effective meaning. Because you'll need to perform the proposed exercises in your head for right now. There's just not enough time left to be able to carry them out concretely . . . in real time. Although that shouldn't be much of an impediment. We've found that the practice of visualization often works just as well as actual physical performance does, as long as you're being completely honest and open with *You-know-Who.*

So. First imagine that you're exiting off a typical highway ramp . . . somewhere in America. And then tell yourself what you see. Are the sights and sounds at the end of the ramp significantly different than what you might encounter if you were to exit onto a similar ramp somewhere else along any of your overly congested American highways? Who really owns your world anymore? Who tells you what to see and what to appreciate and desire? Who tells you what to eat? Do you eat it? Who tells you what gas to buy? Or where to shop (and even that you must shop)? And what to shop for? Or where to bank? How to invest? And whom to borrow from?

Next.

Imagine turning on your television set and surfing through the channels. Stop and watch only when you see and hear something which may have some genuine depth and unpredictability to it. This exercise may actually stretch your imagination more than you've been used to doing for a long while. It may even awaken you to a surprising sense of how disconnected you are from *That which is always becoming* . . . which includes everything and everyone, remember? Human and *other* than human.

How many times did you stop to watch? Who really owns your world anymore? Who tells you what to watch and what to listen to? Do you watch and listen to it? Do you ever question it? Or are you too overidentified with what you're watching and listening to to even to realize or admit to your own overidentification?

Here's a third experiment.

Think back (or ahead, if you prefer) and watch and listen to the reporting of (so-called) mainstream tribal news for one full week or (if you still read) read through several so-called mainstream newspapers for that same week.

And try to remember that what many of you tend to divide and call *conservative* or *liberal* doesn't really count for much anymore, does it? If it ever did. Most of those who are on either side of that synthetic political division are beholden to the same clandestine corporate fraternity, are they not? To the same overprivileged patricians who shamelessly grease the palms of both the captivated left and the mesmerized right; lubricating the entire (either/or) cognitive container and its spellbound yet overly enmeshed tribal polarities—applying the grease to wherever it can be most effectively spread.

Compare the lead stories or editorials about world, national, or local news for that one week. Make a list of any stories or editorials which either deviate from the norm, go into any investigative depth, challenge any of your common assumptions, or teach you anything new or affirmative about a part of culture, society, or about any group of people, or even of a perspective that you had very little or even no knowledge of.

How long is your list?

Who really owns your world anymore? Who tells you what is important and what to think and to believe? Or what you should know or not know (much of anything) about? Or who you should or shouldn't be compassionate toward? Do you think it and believe it? What do you really know?

And then last but not least.

In your thoughts, spend one full year fasting from so-called mainstream media of any kind (any form of tribal media counts). Totally avoid eating at any franchise or fast-food restaurant of any brand or category. Completely withdraw from shopping at any major corporate store of any type. Do not watch any television or listen to any radio at all. Do not read from any major corporate-owned newspaper of any sort. Do not visit any internet news or information websites that you feel strongly aligned with (politically, culturally, or religiously)—of any weight or influence. Sit in silence for at least thirty minutes each morning while just watching your thoughts (not thinking them, but watching them). And spend at least five minutes a day in sincere gratitude for whatever you can find yourself feeling grateful for.

At the end of a year (when the experiment ends) you're then free to do whatever you want, including returning to old patterns of ingrained and compulsive behaviors.

Would you be able to continue watching your thoughts and feelings? Would you trust them? Would you be patient enough to see where the space between them may lead you?

Or would you fall right back into the bottomless grooves carved into the *only-brain* by those same old *disjoined* tribal convictions . . . latching on to unimaginative collective certitudes, surrendering your trust to them, hoping that if you lower yourselves down and deep enough into them that you'll simply fall back into an abysmal confinement full of reliable absolutes, forever protected from any uncertain or unwelcome *otherness*, imagining yourselves to be free of all anxiety and fear and from all of the suffering weight that even a speck of ambiguity can deliver?

Would you be willing to leave the whimsical and mysterious *Self* behind? For the sake of your guaranteed addictions? For the sake of being able to keep hanging on to those fleeting fragments of tribal (false) security?

That's what most of you among the invited seem to be doing right now with your lives, isn't it?

Imagine that . . . if you can.

Most of you refuse to admit to being addicted to the *disjoined* habits which you embody and embrace and which you can't help but personify while clinging to the same old dubious logic which you readily inhale and then exhale into and then out of the mouth of the *only-mind*, caught up in the subtle bribery of its cleverly attached and convenient promises, with all of those recurrent pat answers to any critical question which may ask you to think outside of the tribal box . . . pat answers which you've come to heavily rely upon and to automatically defer to and to obediently parrot.

You've fallen into a subterranean and collapsing tribal mentality, have you not? A mind-set more capitulating than even we thought was possible, cast down into the spellbound channels and crawlways of the *only-mind* . . . and into the even more hypnotic fear of losing the voice of captivity from which you speak.

You're not merely subsumed by a tribal language anymore. Its jargon has actually extended its reach so far into your interior domain while squatting down and filling up the space inside you with tribal occupation, that it actually adjoins your inside with your outside—by adjoining that which it simultaneously *disjoins*.

You fear losing that which you deny ever having.

How's that for a paradox?

It's quite remarkable, isn't it?

You sacrifice your very selves (but usually *others* first) just to keep your abstract yet heavily enmeshed containing systems alive—even if those systems just lay there, motionless and flat, on their obvious and inevitable deathbeds.

Although witnessing the death of an abstraction doesn't seem to be possible, does it? How can something die which can't even breathe and which has no heart and soul?

Yet some of your dying empires of containment which you won't allow to pass away, even into an inescapable death, have had their moment in the sun, haven't they? Some have actually been of certain value for a while, even advancing things at earlier developmental stages in your individual or collective history. They've even helped to lift some of you up to higher levels of understanding or even to occasional temporary states which may have included a momentary but clearer awareness of things. That's true.

But at an earlier time period in many of your lives, the realization that *1 plus 2 equals 3* was a big advancement too. Wasn't it?

But you didn't stay stuck there, did you?

No. You didn't.

You moved on to higher mathematical skills (and understanding) . . . while not rejecting the truth of *1 plus 2*. Because *1 plus 2* still has something to offer, doesn't it? It's still a piece (a very small piece) of the ever-evolving puzzle. But it shouldn't stop you from learning how to multiply, subtract, or divide . . . or even from moving on to algebra, chemistry, or physics. Don't you see?

It shouldn't convince you to deny *other* calculations, should it? Or even *other* evidence that may include additional truths . . . truths which may be able to provide and reveal an even more expansive universe to you. It shouldn't cause you to treat each *other* possibility as a threat to your own knowledge and experience of *1 plus 2*, should it?

Yet that's exactly what you've tried to do with so much of what tries to organically emerge and develop through the process of being alive, isn't it? Especially in much of your tribal politics and in so much of your tribal religion.

You try to prevent any chance of an organic or spontaneous emergence from occurring by freezing things up at the level of *1 plus 2*. And you even kill, die, or indoctrinate . . . build armies, churches, and doctrines . . . and bury yourselves in nations, in frozen ideologies, and in loyalty oaths . . . surrounding the so-called truisms of your peculiar tribal version of (ideological) *1 plus 2*—simply in order to protect and defend it from losing any of its frozen influence or any of its containing dominance in your lives,

You turn it into your imagined life-support system while you try to breathe the force and energy of your individual lives into it, to keep it where it is and to keep it from moving or from ever exploring anything beyond its artificial boundaries . . . boundaries which are conjured up by you.

It's become your central fantasy of meaning and your altar of holy sacrifice, hasn't it? *1 plus 2* . . . in all of its many reinventions and in all of its *disjoining* absolutes, found in the mathematically stunted depths of an *only-mind* which constantly closes in upon you, an *only-mind* which has relegated so many of you to exist as eternal children . . . never to grow up, but to remain as perpetual dependents, defending your inherited tribal logic to the very end, denying *That which is beyond* any tribal confinement—while renouncing what you're unwilling to see.

Take language, again . . . as a specifically overly contained example. Some of you actually try to convince yourselves that there's a designated hierarchy of tribal language, don't you? Not of effective communication skills . . . or of developmental sophistication and not of intelligent linguistic processing or of compassionate and caring voice tone, not of respectful body language or of verbal expression, not even of contextual appropriateness . . . but of one group's ideological or dominant terminology and nomenclature over another—no matter what the context and no matter what the considerations, no matter what communication may be beneficial to enhance human compassion or cooperation, or even peace between and among tribes.

Take language in the United States of America . . . as a specific example within the example.

Many of you who protest against the tyranny of the so-called politically correct language police are the same accusers who not only hypocritically insist that everyone be compelled to (only) communicate through the same official language of English, preferably American English, and preferably your own specific regional and ethnic brand of American English . . . but you even resent any *other* so-called foreign language from being spoken, don't you? Even if only in private conversation . . . and especially if in earshot of you at all.

How strange it is that a culture which brags about being built on the backs and languages of foreign immigrants, not only attempts to constrain many of its own citizens but encourages them to deny and suppress their own complex and diverse (even if overmythologized) past, especially when it comes to accepting present-day newcomers as human equals . . . for the lame sake of propping up a reconstructed and constricting image of the tribal face.

Although most of you already know that all of your noisy warnings to halt the wave of so-called *illegals* from crossing over into your tribal promised land are simply red herrings, don't you? That they're merely rhetorical reinforcements, preached and spread by the apostles and missionaries of the disembodied *only-mind*, used to convince themselves of the righteousness of their intolerant cause, with the aim of keeping any amount of unwanted *otherness* from entering the tribal container.

The words *foreigner* and *immigrant* have simply become tribal code words, haven't they? Used to identify and target out the usual suspects, the darker-skinned and newly-crowned *others* whom you evangelize against.

The caretakers of your euphemistic tribal imagery are especially resentful of any dialects spoken by the *other* than white and by the *other* than (a certain type of fundamentalist) Christian, or by those with *other* than Northern European ancestry, aren't they? While their use of such tribal logic is essentially driven by the *disjoined* (even if unconscious) intention to spread more bigotry and more hatred . . . more fear and more ignorance. But you all know that.

And in their most extreme expressions they're even willing to encourage and participate in (or actively or passively support) acts of irrational violence, are they not? Meanwhile, they carry around their very own hierarchy of correct speech and language, which they deny doing . . . but which they try to enforce upon *others* nonetheless.

Yet those pockets of violence and denial that are full of so much divisive oration and which hunker down in their isolated and often privileged clusters . . . from within the specific borders of the North American *only-mind* are just a few of the obvious yet typical examples found among the many linguistic prisons which are being erected throughout your container-filled world, aren't they?

Give me your tired, your poor, your huddled masses yearning to breathe free; The wretched refuse of your teeming shore, Send these, the homeless, Tempest-tossed to me; I lift my lamp beside the golden door! reads the wise inscription on the still yet standing Statue of Liberty.

And if you were to actually take an honest and clear look at the many hostile and violent scatterings and cavities of fundamentalist Islamic culture . . . with its resurgent desperate language of holy war, or at the animosity filled and loveless fundamentalism rising out of a certain type of desperately contrived Judaism or out of a certain type of desperately contrived Hinduism, or from greed-and-angst-filled and unrestrained fundamentalist capitalism and its sadly contrived consumerism for that matter, or even from the remaining remnants of the perversions of actual communism in any of the shrinking pockets of containment still left standing . . . it would tell you that much. Wouldn't it?

The extremes of speech and language have hijacked much of the public and even private discourse in your divided world. A growing wave of tribal intolerance, among and between its various cloned factions, constantly competes with its own mirror image for full semantic control of the tribal tongue.

And many of you try to marginalize or even eradicate any unconstrained verbal artistry from the tribal tone of voice . . . frantically replacing those creative elements with sterile and repressive rules of order, uncritically advocating for the exclusion of any combination of words which haven't been formally approved of by the official mouthkeepers of the tribal *only-voice*.

And that kind of grammatical arrogance is spreading nearly everywhere, isn't it? Into almost every tribal containing system . . . from left to right and from top to bottom, as a pandemic solution for heading off an imaginary tribal apocalypse—which quickly and violently comes to the forefront whenever too much freedom of thought and speech has snuck out into the tribal container and then dared to express itself.

The in-between does not even exist for many of you anymore, does it?

Compromise and compassion? Dialogue and negotiation? Or even a little give and take? Learning from differences? Finding beauty, truth, or goodness in the *other*? They all seem like ancient and even nonsensical words and ideas, don't they? Reduced and dismissed as naïve and heretical concepts by so many of you.

Just observe any tribe or individual in the world which won't allow for occasionally poking a little fun at itself or for even lightly criticizing any of its idiosyncratic assumptions. Then back up and watch out. Because here comes some reactionary violence. Here comes some real tribal knee-jerk insecurity to be distressed about.

But as you can probably recognize by now, most of what we've been summarizing has been the story of self-inflicted wounds, hasn't it?

You've anthropomorphized your tribal containing systems just like you've done with your gods. You've convinced yourselves that they're not just containers but that they're living organisms and not just human-like . . . but human plus. And in the process you've relinquished much of your distinct humanity to the whims and habits of the *only-mind*, as you dehumanize *other* tribal expressions in the process.

You know something's wrong, so you attempt to project your anxiety onto the disparate o*therness* . . . to try to make it disappear.

But it doesn't disappear.

Does it?

CHAPTER 65

Globalese, the Language of Empire

B Y NOW, YOU must be able to sense (to at least some extent) the ubiquitous reach and effect of the dictatorial *only-mind*, yes? You must be able to sense the gradual magnification of its size and scope or at least be able to recognize some of its most obvious means and methods of control and consolidation.

You can surely sense (for instance) the arbitrary callousness so evident in the mercenary culture of your globalized system of finance and trade, can't you? And the proliferation of economic codependency which it bankrolls and which spreads so much uneven (and greed-driven) misery around the terrestrial game board.

You are able to acknowledge at least some of this. No?

Unfortunately, it's clear to us that most of you are not.

Somehow the expanding and addictive grasp of the economic *only-mind* has become almost imperceptible to you, hasn't it? Even as it includes ever more of you within its paradoxical containment, splitting you up and spitting you out to its convenient advantage—especially if it comes down to either you or it.

Just take an honest and realistic look at the worldwide numeric game of musical chairs which so many of you have been (and are still being) subjected to . . . as jobs are moved out of Detroit (for example) to other parts of the United States or to Mexico and to China, or to the Philippines or to India, or to wherever—and then sometimes even back again whenever it becomes commercially expedient to do so for those at the very top of the material food chain.[1]

The ambiguous voice of the global corporation (the preeminent archetype of the *only-mind*) forgoes any speech that may seem to imply a clear and committed purpose. Does it not? It avoids speaking through any one coherent mouthpiece. It doesn't even commit itself to being loyal to any particular human work force of which its policies and plans may greatly affect or even to any particular tribal container of which it may effectively control.

Although it does expect the reverse, doesn't it?

The official sounding words of the corporate *only-mind* can only enunciate themselves inside of non-committal and unintelligible sentences. They can only be spoken through a forked idiom of vague and dubious interpretation, pronouncing themselves through guarded dialects, murked up and held back by the materialistic mother tongue of the *only-mouth* from which it makes its muddled sounds.

And the obscure language being poured out of that discursive tribal pie hole is Globalese. The language of empire and incoherence—but of incoherence with a purpose.

And it's not that difficult to predict when the next *disjoining* opportunity to stop the music will again present itself, is it? Nor is it naive to expect that another factory, bank, business, or labor pool will soon (gradually, or even suddenly) be pulled out of the tribal line of livable means, especially if an aloof and disconnected gang of officially anointed tribal accountants can (just maybe) make an extra quick dime or two by closing it all down . . . or by moving the current operations to another expendable location, at the mere hint of a better tax break for the benefit of those who patrol and administer the inequitable distribution of power, or if a cheaper workforce from another tribe can be recruited, bought off, and exploited—or if it appears to be slightly more profitable (even though not urgent or even essential) to change localities.

Meanwhile, it's quietly understood that each resettlement is only temporary, isn't it? Just until the next whiff of excess earnings tickles the nose hairs of the tribal upper crust, enough to then move on again to another slightly more lucrative venue.

And the mercantile machine often moves with very little warning, doesn't it? Leaving empty buildings, jobless job hunters, and even homeless human beings behind . . . at the drop of a last paycheck, until the next empty chair is eventually pulled out from under the next assortment of bewildered former breadwinners and their bread-eating children, in favor of another unprotected and soon-to-be subjugated workforce from someplace else on the interwoven field of tribal containment, where the sport of bourgeois connivance and bureaucratic greed is played for keeps—and where the outcome is always the same because the corporate fix is sure to be in.

So the story being retold in almost every spoken language is that job-seeking human beings all over the world are conveniently pitted against one another, isn't it? Just as they are (even) in their own surrounding local communities . . . everyone hoping that the globalized industry which employs so many of them won't suddenly take their business someplace else, to a neighboring (opportunistic) state for instance, as soon as an open chance to stretch their earnings or to deepen their pockets presents itself, even if it's only for the unpredictable short term—and sometimes even if it's only for a mere pittance of an increased profit margin coming out of another profiteering scheme.

So it's not that hard to see why so many of you are filled with such anxiety when it comes to matters of dollars and cents, is it? Or why you're so driven and overburdened by a lingering and worried desire for strict and reliable guarantees for your material security and for impossible assurances of permanent bodily safety. You've become aimless servants . . . addicted to the survival and stability of your fickle economic overseers and to their arbitrary use of power and mobility, psychologically shackled to tribal containing systems which play you like an out-of-tune piano, as they exhaust the Earth of its sustenance while searching for even more exhaustible riches to gorge themselves upon, demanding your undying but only as-needed allegiance and dependency—as you anxiously forage for your own piece of the shrinking and crumbling tribal pie.

Yet even as you're so often left to hold and carry the empty bag of unkept promises, those same overseers are still able to persuade you that their survival is essential to your security, aren't they? That their survival is indispensable . . . that it's for your own good, and for the good of your soul, and for your community—for your personal economic (and even spiritual) salvation, for the good of your nation or for your family, for your children, for the sake of your traditions, for the good of your economy, for your health and welfare, for your disappearing pension and benefits, for your dwindling freedom, for your future, for your self-image, for your pleasure and profit, for your honor and pride, for your happiness, for your free and fair marketplace (even if it's only free and fair for the very privileged and illustrious few), and for your (tribal) god—even while the God within you and within every bit of *Creation* is laughing its celestial head off because *That which listens and sees and is* needs no defenders. It just continues to love and to embrace all of its accusers—not because they're so comically dishonest, but because most of which passes for truth among the overly contained doesn't even come close to what it's trying not to aim at anyway, does it?

It (most foolishly) does not.

And yet you still clearly feel yourselves and much of the world around you as being diminished, don't you? As you lose more and more concrete control over your own isolated circumstances.

But you keep playing along anyway . . . often blaming *other* workers and whole *other* tribes of human beings on the *other* side of the planet or from *other* cultures, who speak *other* languages, who believe *other* things, who eat *other* kinds of food, and who physically appear *other* than you do (even while many of them work in sweatshop conditions which you subsidize with your consumer indifference).

And you do all of this without ever critically questioning the tribal proprietors whom you've surrendered your loyalties to.

It's just so much easier to blame your anonymous and equally (or even more often) mistreated human mirror image, isn't it? Especially when it comes down to simply targeting some faraway alien of accused *otherness*. It's just much less painful than it would be if you directly or even indirectly took on or separated yourselves from the prevailing tribal power structure itself, isn't it? Even while it stares right through your eyeballs—as if you had no real eye sockets of your own to look out of.

But that way you don't have to feel like such a patsy. Do you? For giving so much of your soul away . . . along with your sweat, or for being bought off with chump change by the tribal authorities—or for betraying your own spirited hopes and dreams with your own reckless loyalty.

Yet so many of you still refuse to even look at the built-in patrimonial hypocrisies. Don't you? Or even at the lies, or even at the shadows upon shadows hiding in the dark . . . in their contradictory corners of shame, clogging up the intestines of the containing bodies themselves.

Many of you still refuse to admit that you can see anything at all outside the box of tribal letters . . . out of which you speak your words of trapped allegiance.

Doublethink means the power of holding two contradictory beliefs in one's mind simultaneously, and accepting both of them, wrote the wise George Orwell.[2]

You routinely pretend to trust what your given tribal system tells you to trust, don't you?

And you act accordingly . . . which leads to so much animosity and even to war and desecration, exchanged between competing yet artificially created camps of enemies . . . in a *Self*-crucifying world, where you disregard the reality of your own independent perception, and of your own felt experience.

Instead, you habitually brush aside and replace your appreciation of that reality . . . even when it's adequately informed, with a frenzied pursuit of an exterior ancestral belief system, which you've inherited and attached yourselves to, spending much of your captured time defending it—trying to force-fit an image of yourselves into the mold of that which contains you.

Yet . . . it's not quite so easy to do anymore.

Is it?

CHAPTER 66

Celebrity Food

I T TAKES A lot of work to dismiss your own discernment—to muzzle your own evolving awareness, doesn't it?

Yet another of the many paradoxes which you'll soon come to recognize is that any tribal system which expects you to blindly nourish and defend it almost always outsurvives and outthrives its most intoxicated dependents.

The containment carries on with or without those who've willingly offered themselves up for the sake and survival of the dominant order. It proceeds as if your squandered offerings were never made, as if the ones who thought they were making an exceptional sacrifice never existed at all—as if *you* never existed.

Yet afterward, the surviving members . . . on the instructions of the privileged and powerful few at the top of each tribal heap, often prop up the previously sacrificed as revered tribal celebrities, don't they?

The self-sacrificed are raised (postmortem) into one-dimensional, flawless, and fictional beings . . . memorialized into luminaries who exemplify tribal uprightness, into nonhumans (nonbeings), into lifeless and safe picture postcards of themselves, to be viewed and collected reverently by the surviving admirers—to be mounted on a *disjoined* wall of tribal fame.

You've collectively celebritized your *disjoined* sense of what is important and worthwhile, upon the stage of who you wish or pretend to be, through whom you desire to emulate at the most enmeshed level of tribal logic—gradually becoming a loyal collection of wishful thinkers.

You've become vicarious . . . assuming a proud posture of self-importance whenever another interim celebrity is propped up by the tribe, imagining yourselves as being interchangeable objects of desire with those of whom you envy and revere, with those whom you've affixed to the rampart of tribal adoration—which always has qualities and dimensions of self-worship sewn into it, doesn't it? Which is what makes it so effectively appealing to so many of you.

Your wish is to become one of the renowned, one of the held up . . . one of them, another recognized famous one within a transposable system of celebrity invention.

It's your way of grasping for notoriety . . . no matter how fleeting, which is usually determined by how much imperfection can be removed from the immortalized, to clean them up for the viewing, for the idol-worshiping festivities packed full of collective self-flattery—allowing for even more lofty shadows to be cast down upon your fabrications of tribal ascent.

And the accolades of fame have become your most sought-after earthly rewards, haven't they? Even surpassing your vague cravings for an impossibly guaranteed security—which no amount of collective desperation can manifest.

You've left the *Self* behind (or so you think), having aligned yourselves with like-minded tribal facsimiles, colliding against those of whom you've typecast with your artificially imposed labels of *otherness*, who barely exist in the *disjoined* fantasies of the tribal imagination, as pigeonholed replacements for the lost enthusiasm you once had—but of which you deny being able to recall.

Any leftover space within the tribal container is quickly plugged into the noise of the tribe's hyperbolic media apparatus, which turns itself on by praising its own bluster—overloading your senses with its hostile exaggerations.

And all of it is simply *that*—melodramatic noise, distracting and convincing you with its camouflaged bravado, attempting to conceal the vacant soul of the tribal gods, overstating the importance of almost everything you've been taught to submit to, persuading you to stay put and to celebrate your own containment, to abstain from trusting your own discernible experience, to recoil from looking too deeply into anything, to withdraw from any inner struggle and from any and all curiosity—to avoid acknowledging anything that could be of value (at all) outside the tribal box of overplayed logic and blame.

CHAPTER 67

Bearing the Wait

W E'VE PUT TOGETHER what we believe to be a painstaking, if not airtight, plan of action, in order to prepare you for this unprecedented event and to hopefully prevent any unwelcome surprises from popping up out of nowhere. Although we do know that there will be surprises. There always are, aren't there? As long as you're still alive and breathing.

We don't intend for any of you to wake up into some kind of bland world of sameness tomorrow morning—which would merely replicate the *disjoined* monotony you'll be leaving behind.

What sense would that make?

Our purpose and strategy is driven and steered by years of intense research, verified by a vast accumulation of data which has been carefully analyzed and based upon closely examined empirical evidence and even upon some emerging discoveries in the postempirical realm—inside of many long hours of grueling observation and sorrow-filled scrutiny.

We're convinced from our findings that the actual facial conversions will adequately deliver the message we intend.

You'll just have to take our word on that, even while we acknowledge the difficulty of the logistics and in the massive planning and coordination that's involved.

How you receive and deal with the message and its deliverance is another matter altogether though, isn't it?

We know this won't be easy for most of you to conceptualize right away. So just bear with it for a while.

You'll catch on to much but probably not all of it as we move things along. But you'll at least get a good enough idea of what you might be in for to avoid being too surprised or from feeling like you've just been ambushed.

In any case, you really have no other option at the beginning of this event. But afterward, all the picking and choosing will return right back into your lap again.

So don't sweat that part of it . . . yet.

CHAPTER 68

It Could Be Anyone's Face, *Couldn't It?*

NOW.
These won't necessarily be direct facial trades you'll be making. But they will be reasonably recognizable—to all of you.

Your newly assigned appearance may not be a specific or intimate reincarnation of someone whom you'll know by name or whom you'll be able to identify through your own personal or social history—when you first stare back into your own glassy reflection. Yet that could happen.

You may look into the mirror tomorrow morning and be surprised to see Howard or Jolene from your high school days, whom you joined in putting down or even in beating up.

Or you might find yourself staring back at an anonymous person of a different ethnicity or of a different race or of another professed religion (or of a nonreligion), whom you harassed or whom you entered into harmful and bigoted or even hateful talk about . . . from in your (not-so-small-anymore) techno-connected country town or from in your (not-so-street-smart-anymore) wannabe-mainstream big inner city, or at your (not-so-truth-seeking-anymore) dogma-dominated place of worship, or even at your (not-so-welcoming-anymore) if-it-ever-was family gathering.

It may be the dog you kicked or tortured or the body of water you polluted and then lied about.

It could be someone whom you refused to show even minimal acts of compassion for, or for whom you refused to even consider giving a fair hearing to, standing firm in your refusal . . . from inside of an overly contained and rigid tribal preoccupation with opinionated correctness.

It might be some poor soul whom you condemned or excommunicated or even beheaded, out of twisted obedience to fear or to false promises or out of pious zealotry filled with delusions of grandeur. Or it may be one of the many *others* whom you gave the orders to lethally inject, or to stone or to lynch or to shoot or to electrocute, because you were duteous to the law of revenge written into the current mood of political or religious logic—in your particular neck of the electoral or tribal woods.

It could be the contagion of growing hatred incubating in your heart and infecting (oh so subtly) your words and actions, while portraying yourselves to be righteous . . . convincing and deceiving even yourselves and a lot of other tribal loyalists to participate in the wreaking of collective havoc.

Or it may simply be the stranger whom you passed by on the side of the road who could have used some good Samaritan help and assistance.

As you can see, we're giving plenty of latitude for the interpretation and use of the word *face*.

And let's face it. We can do that because we have to. Most of you among the invited have been involved in more than one type of injury or disservice done to the *other* along the way, haven't you? Either directly or indirectly—either physically, spiritually, politically, emotionally, or psychologically.

And the harm that you've done hasn't just been restricted to *other* human beings. Although you have done some pretty significant damage to *others* just from within your own unique branch of the anthropoid clan.

We'll give you that.

CHAPTER 69

The Accumulation of Names, or Fill in the Blanks

A S YOU KNOW, while your tribal technologies have become more refined, they've also become more diversified. And so have your objects of exploitation and violence.

You've gradually dispersed your organized patterns of inhumanity, over a relatively short period of time, to include a wider variety of unsuspecting objects of so-called *otherness*. Haven't you?

You've become addicted to blunt, reactionary, and unimaginative (yet more treacherous and sophisticated) forms and methods of tribal hatred. And it's that very addiction which drives you to justify your projected acts of cruelty. Isn't it? It's that addiction which compels you to absolve yourselves of those acts when attempting to solve real or imaginary problems. And it's that addiction which obliges you to exonerate your real attacks against real or imaginary enemies—which not only leads to an obvious escalation and an increased dependency upon that outward hostility, but also to the collective kneeling down to a tribe-against-tribe tradition of self-vindicating and irrational enmity toward *others,* doesn't it?

Just ask any of the ever-observant fringe dwellers. They'll tell you.

They can see what's happening the clearest, from their own special vantage point of sober yet marginalized awareness, just by standing wisely back . . . out of the violent and addictive fray.

They've struggled to maintain a calm yet circulating presence, usually dwelling along your outer edges . . . as we've already shown, but from where you can't seem to see them, even when they're right there in clear sight, dancing right in front of you . . . a community of the virtually unknown, the seldom-recognized practitioners who remain anonymous yet somehow discernible to each other, whose commonality exists in their intention and practice to find ways to realize and to deepen the expanse of their humanity . . . in their spirit as well as in their flesh, which they're increasingly unable to set apart within themselves. So they increasingly don't. Because they've gradually come to realize that the spirit is inseparable from the flesh, just as every bit of *Creation* is ultimately indivisible from *That which is always becoming* within all of you.

They move about detached but purposefully supported within *Self*-awakening and like-minded groups, prepared to learn from and to teach each *other* and themselves, acknowledging the diversity of gifts which paradoxically unite them, sharing the practice of what seem like esoteric exercises when observed through the narrow perception and judgment of the *only-mind*, but which are actually practical and Perennial disciplines which help to lead and to sustain them on their intricate journey into becoming who they already are—but only when the disciplines are applied with sincere effort and consistency, and with a growing unconditional trust and love for the *Self* within, of course.

They remain distinct from but not automatically adverse to, nor compulsorily disengaged from, your more formal tribal norms or from the coinciding exoteric rituals, even though they tend to recognize strength and unity where the *disjoining* logic of the *only-mind* can only seem to accuse *others* of weakness and separation.

They use the grist of daily living as the ingredients for their practice of seeing and of doing, delighting in any expansion of practical awareness wherever it comes from or to wherever it may lead, however much they acknowledge its scarcity—first and foremost in themselves.

Yet most tribal container walls are porous to them.

They pass unseen right through them, from tribe to tribe . . . like meandering ghosts, facelessly whispering clues into their own ears, following the previously left subtle traces in the air, which hint at where to look for and of how to see and then of how to connect to the unifying wholeness of *That which is always becoming*—which is always right there for the taking and for the entering into.

Dedication to their practice of seeing and of doing can lead (and has led) to an ongoing series of imperfect and modest although sometimes dramatic transformational shifts in their own consciousness, which can lead (and has led) to similar shifts in the conscious awareness of the human community as a whole—which is so often unaware of its own progressive and paradoxical awakening. It leads to a heartfelt compassion for *others* . . . including themselves, to a compassion extending to all creatures, human and *other* than human—well beyond the restrictions and circumscribed vision of even your least ruthless tribal containing systems.

And as we've said, you haven't recognized these imperfect seers very often, if at all. Have you? But when their presence is detected, they're usually and quickly dismissed or discredited, or piously and sometimes even criminally charged in some sped-up tribal fashion and response—or even worse, aren't they?

For the most part, they display no extraordinary, obvious, or loud appearance.

Although they do like to participate in the making of festive music. The people on the fringe tend to like to sing and dance. Don't you see?

They seem to know how to let their hair down without losing their head or their original face and purpose. And they appear to celebrate for the sake of celebration (nothing else)—while being able to simply let go of it all when it comes time to become quiet and still again or when it's time to get back to work.

They don't readily reject any part of themselves or pay much serious attention to what kind of response they get from others.

They seem to know that humility doesn't come from trying to outhumble anyone, that wisdom doesn't flow out of the loudest mouth, and that freedom to enjoy doesn't come from trying to outdance or outsing or to outtalk or outdistance themselves from anyone else. So they don't try to. Although they do like and thus tend to explore much of what's available to explore.

And being calm and quiet when it's time to shake it up doesn't make much sense to them either. They try to pay attention to the guidance of *That which is always awake* and then just let the chips of jubilation or of quiet bliss rise and fall when and where they may.

However, they do refuse to participate in any door-to-door or pew-to-pew attempts at winning anybody over.

They seem to appreciate that the only necessary and ultimate conversion is to the deathless *Self*, to *That which excludes nothing*, which in turn has given rise to many futile attempts made by the *only-mind* to apprehend its *Eternal Presence* and to limit its indivisibility . . . to try to attach a denominational name or sound to it, to use doctrinaire language or to perform exorcising rituals in order to magically capture and then harden it into a state of tribal intransigence, to try to kidnap and squeeze it into an airtight bottle of tribal precepts, and to view it only through one-dimensional formats of tribal belief which so often disregard, ridicule, and even condemn the qualities of love, compassion, and kindness (even forgiveness) if they appear to ignore or to discount the rule of tribal law in favor of the demands made by the inmost *Self*—which insists that to be loving and compassionate and kind and forgiving takes precedent over everything else . . . no matter what.

But tribal law is what trumps everything else in the hard view of the *only-mind*, isn't it? Which explains why it has put so much energy into hijacking the conscience, character, and conduct of much of what passes for tribal religious tradition in your world these days.

But contemplative attempts to behold (not to abduct) *That which is eternally present* are still being made by those on the fringe. Don't you see? Through the art of listening, of seeing, and of speaking, through paradox, poetry, and metaphor—and usually through the ear, the eyes, and the voice of the mischievous mystics and scientists of whom you may be vaguely familiar with.

We've compiled the following list of just a few of the names and sounds that have been heard, seen, and voiced by many of those same contemplative corroborators, by those who consent to be embraced and awakened by the inexhaustible *Life Force*—which beats in every heart and vibrates in every being.

As a group, the list represents a labyrinth of unified desire, a fascinating garden of diversity beyond anything that one name, sound, or fragrance can ever appropriate on its own—which is the ultimate revelation, isn't it? It can only be revealed in the tapestry, in the full interrelationship of all names and sounds and in the space within and between them, in the soil beneath and from the light above them, shining beyond and through all of you—through to infinity.

So we shall briefly recite the list for your listening pleasure.

If that's okay with you.

Some of the names may sound quite familiar to you. There may even be one or two in there which you'll want (or maybe even feel obsessed) to separate out . . . to stuff back into your tribal pockets of overidentification.

We understand the compulsion. It's a very common one.

But remember. These are just fingers which are simply pointing. Your tribe-induced compulsion to stare only at yourselves almost always blinds you from seeing the inexhaustible composition of the *Self*—to which the fingers aim their antennae. In fact, many of you almost seem to be in terror of looking anywhere beyond your own self-hypnotizing appendage. So instead, you often hold on to and wrap yourselves around it for dear life, with your eyes closed and with your heart and mind folded into the womb of the tribe. And so you miss the point altogether. Don't you see? You turn the finger into a paragon of *disjoined* tribal perfection, when it's simply a beacon shining a light toward the vast and spacious *Self*—toward *That which is always who you already are.* So listen closely.

Being, Wonder, Creation, God, Om, Aha!, the Great Mystery, Buddha Nature, the Eternal Presence, Krishna Consciousness, Allah, Brahman, Oneness, Higher Power, the Kingdom of Heaven, Creative Energy, the Great Spirit, the Holy Instant, Yahweh, the Unnamable, the Tao, Love, Universal Intelligence, the Transcendent, Our Father, the Vital Force, Nature, Shiva, the Unfolding Universe, the Ground of Being, the Divine Mother, the Absolute, Nondual Awareness, Interbeing, Cosmic Consciousness, the Great Guidance, Wholeness, the Inmost *Self,* the Underground Stream, the Cosmic Christ, the Anointed One, the Supreme *Self,* the Presence of God, Now, I Am, Emptiness, the Holy Spirit, Fullness, Gaia, the Creator, Gitche Manitou, Suchness, the Life Force, the Unknowable, Atman, the Holy Trinity, Isness, Aaaaahhhhh!, and of course . . . Silence. To name just a few.

To many or maybe to most of you this diverse collection of names and sounds might seem uninteresting or even frightening or irrelevant. Perhaps it seems too varied or too inclusive to even casually reflect upon or to even care about or to even consider a quick hearing of the list as worthy of your personal time and effort—as too far below the surface of where so many of you breathe, too far outside the familiarity of your own tribal containment.

To plunge in too deeply may lead to the risk of drowning. And to extend your gaze too wide may lead to the risk of seeing.

Might it not?

So many of you among the invited just continue to float along, atop the shallow waves of tribal water wherever they may take you, rarely to hazard even a quick peek below into the hidden depths or seldom daring to take a clear or expansive look around you at the endless horizon—which you've divided among yourselves for the sake of tribal identity.

You cling to your tribal logic and to your tribal names just like you would to a luxurious lifeboat.

And you imagine that anything beyond or below the surface of your ship of tribal separation can only be part of a perilous ocean of *otherness* full of deadly sea creatures and unimaginable danger.

But the fringe practitioners on the periphery have nothing to sell you that you don't already own, other than a wake-up call—which isn't for sale anyway. It's free, just like it always has been.

So there's no need for a high-pressure sales pitch then, is there?

You'll hear it when you're ready to hear it.

You'll see it when you do and not before.

But listening takes practice, doesn't it? Just as seeing takes practice and even as being takes practice.

And practice takes willingness—which always takes readiness.

There is no way to It, because It is the way, say the wise.

Most people don't see things as they ARE. They see things as THEY are, observes the wise Richard Rohr.[1]

The lamp of the body is the eye. If your eye is sound, your whole body will be filled with light; but if your eye is diseased, your whole body will be in darkness. And if the light inside you is darkness, how great that darkness will be! taught the wise Jesus.[2]

But we can try to nudge you some, starting tomorrow morning, can't we? To get you to pay a little more attention to the details which you tend to ignore. Then maybe you can begin to notice a clearing or a path which may be opening up for you—to show or to point you toward some additional and enlightening possibilities.

Those on the fringe (on the seeing edge of things) are going through just as many trials and tribulations as the rest of you, even though their trials and tribulations may be related slightly more to intention than to reaction; to expansion more than to constriction; more to the struggling search for a deeper authenticity than to the narcissistic seeking of tribal recognition, or than to those momentary payoffs sought out by the spiritual materialist.

They may not be included in tomorrow morning's commencement exercise, even with all of their remaining imperfections. But they're certainly not ignorant of the subject at hand or of the necessity of their particular efforts in the specific practice of seeing and doing.

They've had to endure the same reality as most of the rest of you have. They come from all corners of your round planet just like you do.

And . . . well . . . you all practice at something, don't you? Whether by habit . . . through conscious choice or in tribal conformance.

The seeing minority whom we briefly refer to here have chosen with fallible but significant measure and intent, for the benefit of all and to the exclusion of none, to apply themselves at something out of the ordinary.

Yet they are as distinct from what most of you might consider to be rebellious as they are from what you generally regard to be within the mainstream of your traditional extremes.

Your so-called tribal mainstreams are a lot more violent, confining, and restrictive than what most of you would like to imagine or pretend them to be, aren't they?

They tend to push and swim in one undeviating, constricting, and dominant direction. Don't they? Gravitating to the *disjoined* call of the *only-mind*.

And many of you are just pulled along by the noncurious and nonself-critical drift . . . by a nonseeing inwardness, showing little if any interest to investigate or even in becoming aware of any unique branch or tributary, or of any curious creek or hidden river, or of any incidental waterway, or of any deviation which may divert you away from the tribal drift or into any *other*wise fertile current of intrigue which can only be found outside the tribal stream of consciousness.

Only those very few *Self*-aware souls among you dare to swim against that stream.

Yet they don't choose to do so as a guiding principle for its own sake. What spiritual or humane sense would that make? They do it as a consequence of waking up into *That which is always becoming*, as they imperfectly know it to be . . . pulled along by the expanding flow of the integral *Self*, forever reawakened into and by its oceanic wholeness and love.

And most of your mislabeled mavericks and rebels are actually playing it pretty safe the majority of the time anyway, aren't they?

But you all know that.

They either burn out from lack of spiritual depth or from lack of self-discipline and commitment or they move on to more grasping and so-called *realistic* ventures, predictably shedding their pretense of rebellion to then join forces with any one of the many conventional transaction centers opened up and actively recruiting for tribal business, where they return to competing for the same old trophies of impermanence, for the perishable cargo of power and prestige and possessions, for the objects of their compulsive desire—objects which are scrapped and battled over from inside the belly of the sinking mother ship of the *only-mind*.

False dichotomies pop up and thrive just about everywhere, don't they? Like traveling carnival games taken too seriously.

But no offense is intended here to the *carnies* among you. We know it to be a most valuable and honorable way of life . . . wherein, by the way, quite a few of those seers who will be staying back tomorrow morning tend to rest invisibly in their quiet space along that part of the nomadic fringe.[3]

And we won't be addressing the destitute or even the most poor and powerless among you either, with any of our critiques and candor. They have it tough enough as it is, don't they?

We can also confirm that an honest survey taken of all of your *other*-than-human brothers and sisters would reveal that many of them are not only feeling crowded out by your numbers and by your endless pillaging of their surroundings, but also by your expanding condescension.

You seem to view yourselves as extraworthy in comparison to your *other*-than-human relatives, don't you? Even those of you who claim to be disgusted by the same sense of entitlement you observe from within your own ranks among your fellow (so-called) human beings, especially when it comes to who's entitled to what proportion of what's still left of the ransacked and *disjoined* tribal pie.

You don't do much consulting of *other* species though, do you? Nor do you consult much with the less powerful or the less propertied or those with less status among your own kind.

Is any of this starting to ring an inner doorbell yet?

Have a listen to this short list of questions, for a few more starters:

What does the massacring of prairie dogs, baby seals, and elephants mean to any of you? Or what about all of the overly bred, abandoned, or eventually put-down cats and dogs? Or the families of dolphins, apes, wild horses, and buffalo among so many others who are hunted down and murdered for the mere sport, profit, or negligence of it?

What about the intentional carnage of whole geographical areas of native plants, animals, and people to the point of their extinction? Does that scare up any compassion in you? Or how about overheating the shared atmosphere and overfishing the shared seas? Or ripping apart the earth, the waters, and the skies in delirious pursuit of riches, security, and dominance in the quest for overpriced, polluting, and unsustainable energy—and for tribal and selfish convenience?

MICHAEL J. GAJDA

What about keeping millions of pigs, cows, and chickens locked up in inhumane, overcrowded, and suffocating torture chambers inside of huge (corporate farming) concentration camps for most of their short lives, so that many of you can overstuff yourselves on the flesh of the survivors?[4] How does that taste and smell to you, in the depths of your true being?

How about giving little or no deep listening to the voices of so many of the unborn or already-born human children . . . or to many of their earthly mothers, when it comes to what should feel like heartrending considerations concerning their significance and promise and their suffering and existence, their meaning and contribution—beyond what's in it for you or for your intolerant competing dogmas of life and death?[5] Can any of their cries of desperation pry loose your clinging fingers from the fear-driven assumptions of the self-righteous *only-mind?*

What about the stealing of so much of the hidden treasures from the earth while spilling, wasting, mutilating, and bribing for control over them?

Or what of the injecting and spraying of poisonous chemicals into and onto almost anything that grows or that will be overconsumed by the overly fed and by the underinformed among you? Does any of that give you pause or concern?

How about when you use your so-called sacred political and religious texts to justify, spread, yet deny much of the ecological and human tragedy you practice? Does this stir anything up within you that could lead you to make different choices?

Those are just a few of the questions from our list which most of you among the invited have rarely if ever considered asking yourselves.

But you already know what's on most of this list. Don't you? Even as it keeps expanding and even as more and more of those who are on the list suffer and die for no God-given justifiable reason.

So just fill in the blanks with the rest of the questions yourselves when you feel honest and brave enough to do so. But not beforehand.

You don't really need any more wasteful noise pushing its way into your already-overcrowded and *disjoined* vision of reality.

Do you?

CHAPTER 70

Thinking Ahead

PERHAPS YOUR WORLD would be a different place if you would have applied the Great Law of the Iroquois and then considered (as they did) how the decisions you make today will benefit your children a full seven generations into the future.[1]

Maybe then there would have been a very different list to recite.

But so many of you rarely gaze beyond the impressions of the next moment. And even when you do, it's mostly limited to how things may impact upon you specifically, isn't it? Or upon the close-knit membership of your specific tribe of compliance and its ardent allies, especially those of you who already cling to so much above and beyond your portion of the planetary bread and butter, which you're so afraid of losing or which you're so afraid of sharing with those who have so little of it, even as you sit there . . . right across the table from them, watching them shrink away as you outgrow by leaps and bounds beyond anything close to whatever your fair share was meant to be. You've lost all sense of justice and proportion, haven't you?

You seem to think that too much on your side of the table is really not enough and that an empty plate on the other side that appears to be moving a little too close to yours is actually threatening your survival.

And we could go on for days . . . even years, couldn't we? But you all know how huge the historical database is. It's inexhaustible. You know it. We all know it. The relevant facts and information have been repeated so often and have been made so obvious in so many ways by the well intended that it's lost its meaning on many of you, hasn't it?

When it comes to the calling out of iniquities for your urgent attention and alleviation, repetition has become the mother and father of denial.

It's become *the more you see it, the more you don't* . . . or perhaps more accurately put—*the more you won't*. Which is often accompanied by the automatic and cynical silencing or targeted demise of the few prophets of hope and thunder who still speak any real truth to the mean and the manipulative, or to the most crookedly powerful among you—or to those most addicted to their own tribal containment.

Loyalty to petrified opinion never broke a chain or freed a human soul, observed the wise Mark Twain.[2]

A foolish consistency is the hobgoblin of little minds, wrote the wise Ralph Waldo Emerson.[3]

It is foolish to think that we will enter heaven without entering into ourselves, wrote the wise St. Teresa of Avila.[4]

CHAPTER 71

No Demonizing, No Sanitizing

S O WE'VE RELUCTANTLY decided to involve you in another way of seeing . . . and of doing.

And as we've been trying to make plain and clear to you, we've simply observed too much and for far too long of the same habitual, violent, and self-perpetuating patterns of behavior soaring out from your tribal addictions—which seem to us to have no end in sight.

The need for an immediate and effective intervention is not only undeniable but it's imperative—even urgent. Don't you see?

So you'll all be getting a new face to peer out from (or, for some of you . . . many new faces), each one generating one or more imported perspectives which you've methodically resisted, ignored, or denied due to being under the *disjoining* influence of the ever-intruding *only-mind*.

Each facial exchange will represent a group of faces which you're already familiar with, faces which you've become acquainted with by way of your interactions with specific individuals who typify the group . . . some *other* beings whom you fucked with in one of the many ways human beings have figured out how to fuck with *other* planet residents (to put it bluntly)—whether they be human or *other* than human.

Now . . . we can immediately sense that some of you want to make a big deal out of the use of a so-called *bad word*, don't you? So allow us to respond.

Just gently put a big, fat (but clean) sock into your pseudopious mouth.

Metaphorically speaking, of course.

A whole lot more damage has been done throughout the short stay of (so-called) human beings on your planet, by and through the pretense of respectability, than has ever been done by a few choice words which may need to be pronounced for the sake of clarity, honesty, or emphasis . . . or, as in this case, to shake loose some of that paralyzed tribal logic which seems to regularly dry up your *disjoined* perspectives and interactions with the world around you—into a thick and heartless cement.

Too often, and rather too obviously, you even try to demonize individual words, don't you? As a decoy—to try to silence the truth before it can break through to your brains (or god forbid, even through to your hearts).

Many of you would like to make it seem as though saying fuck is much worse on the scale of evil doings than subtle, evasive, or sophisticated hate-filled speech; or than financial or theocratic deceit; or than racial, religious, or ethnic bigotry; or than destructive mountaintop coal mining; or than giant oil spills; or than the assassination of foreign, national, or even local leaders who may have rocked the boat of a thin-skinned but powerful corporate elite; or than media and political hype and propaganda; or than institutional cover-ups of sexual abuse; or than lying to friends, children, the elderly, or to yourselves; or than ignoring the homeless and the hungry; or than any real suffering or evil which you've too often just shut your eyes to, or that you've even been directly involved in by encouraging it—or in perpetrating it yourselves.

I shouted out,
"Who killed the Kennedys?"
When after all
It was you and me, sang the wise and perceptive Mick Jagger.

So just give us a fricking break already. Will you please? Your next face landing should quickly clarify several ignored and forgotten human priorities for you.

But let's get this straight. We're not endorsing the coarsening of language here either.

We're quite aware that many of you paradoxically confuse vulgarity for truth telling. So don't give yourselves too much credit in that area, okay? Especially when it comes to your own habit of using low-brow language and behavior, which is often meant to circumvent honest and respectful human interactions by intentionally refraining from the use of intelligent dialogue or compassionate conversation.

You don't get smart or attain any wisdom or sharpen or expand anyone's intellect or deepen anyone's awareness or extend any goodwill or enlarge anyone's humanity through constant interruptions of what you disagree with . . . or with threats, ridicule, name calling, and intimidation or by talking dumb, derisively, and loud . . . or by pointlessly filling your paragraphs with four-letter words as so many of your lame stand-up comics do who seem to lack any real depth of humorous or enlightening storytelling ability . . . or from robotically hurling memorized religious passages (at *others*) like hand grenades to prove a tribal point or by compulsively repeating ideological affirmations or by echoing *disjoined* statements pulled out of official political playbooks just to try to prove that you can remember, pronounce, and obey any of those shallow and distracting tactics.

Adulthood isn't arrived at through precise appearances or through tribal conformity . . . as we've already tried to underscore and articulate, whether it's through bad-habit caricatures of risky or rebellious behaviors or through high-brow pretensions of cleanliness, morality, or public piety, or through any variant of self-congratulatory arrogance—as hard as some of you may try to force that bellied-up idea into fruition.

Although some of it has often worked to establish some pretty scary tribal dictatorships of violent proficiency, hasn't it? And at some very powerful levels of clustered and complex know-how and finesse.

Just for once, take an honest look into your collective history—if you can sprout enough backbone.

What do you honestly see?

As many of you may privately admit to yourselves (yet resist any overt acknowledgment of), a sincere and mature act of loyalty is not even a distant cousin to an irrational act of blind compliance—no matter what the lawfully affirmed tribal membership claims of itself. It's not even located in the same developmental mind zone, is it? Or even in a nearby evolutionary time-slot . . . whether it's anxiously claimed and declared in your street gang or in your religious denomination or in your place of employment or within your political party or in your family or in your ethnic group or in your race or gender or in your socioeconomic class— or especially in your nation-state . . . and all of which that implies.

We'll say it again, just in case you refused to hear it when it was expressed earlier. Uniformity is not the same as unity. But we do admit that it often makes for some memorable and hypnotic mass rallies and for some exceptionally choreographed and synchronized marches and even for some exquisitely harmonized sing-alongs—the kinds of things that tribalism is really good at doing to make sure that it can see how well the line is being towed.

But it never creates authentic communal harmony. Don't you see?

Intelligent discernment and discrimination and mature faith and trust do not rely upon the strict following of foregone conclusions—especially when what's being concluded is forever forbidden to evolve or from even stepping out of line.

Uniformity derives from and leads right back to itself, into an even deeper tribalism which leads to the death of *Self*-awareness and to the death and suffering of the *other* (to the death and suffering of God). While unity derives from and expands out into a unitive consciousness and to the liberation of all *otherness* (to the release and embrace of the indwelling and indivisible spirit within all of *Creation*).

It really is time to grow up, isn't it? To quit playing house, to take down all the masks hanging on your tribal walls, to remove the *disjoining* tattoos, inside and outside . . . and everywhere in between.

One of our intentions is to resurrect respect for the intelligent choice of words, which has nothing to do with demonizing or sanctifying any specific sound which may talk itself out of your mouth or with demonizing or sanctifying any particular look that may walk itself out of your front door—nor with demonizing or sanctifying any peculiar face hanging in your closet of faces, which you may reserve to wear with or without intent or disguise.

It has much more to do with speaking aboveboard . . . clear and wise, and with a passion for life (all life), by choosing your words like an owl to advance and fine-tune compassionate communication and understanding and by recognizing the importance of cultivating a genuine sense of humor—one that can cut through any (individual or tribal) bullshit which may take its own scent too seriously, if not too proudly.

We seek nothing less than the termination of the practice of allowing your words to choose you, to quit permitting words to be chosen for you by the various tribal warlords who contain your vocabulary, to cease the following of any dogma of tribal language meant to censor your genuine inner struggles or your inquisitive reasoning, to desist from following any school of tribal thought that inhibits the free expression of ideas . . . no matter how unsophisticated or countercultural or how unpopular or paradigm shattering or even how rudimentary the expressions may be.

No seed of thought is born a genius, is it? But its inborn intelligence cannot be ripened unless it's allowed to crawl, stumble, fall, and explore—regardless of how long it takes.

Wisdom always needs to scrape its knees before it can become even a little bit wise, doesn't it?

Our aim is to eliminate or at least to greatly diminish any further impediments to your innate (and always evolving) conscience and integrity . . . or to any path leading toward any genuine enlightenment, or to any intrinsic beauty of freed-up and creative speech and language.

We hope to inspire the spread of a spacious silence between your thoughts and your words, so that your language can breathe—so that it can emerge out of the sacred intuition which always inhabits that silence.

We are convinced that your facial regeneration will speed up and enhance the process of reclaiming who you are.

After all, impermanence is all you really have to work with, isn't it?

It's all you've ever had.

It's the only thing that's permanent in your world.

The refacing will be a valuable lesson in the practice of letting go . . . if you allow it to be.

To release your grip is one of the most effective and simplest ways to realize that you're already being held—by what is changelessly real. So you don't have to hold on so tightly anymore—to anything. It's already being done for you by a deeper *You* with an open hand, below the many layers of facial coverings which you've tried to disguise yourself with, by trying to build a wall of separation between your tribal self and *You* . . . between you and your inmost *Self*, in order to avoid any genuine meeting with the great *I Am*—which is another of the many paradoxes which you've unwisely kept hidden from your own view for so long.

You hold on and you are held by letting go. It's as simple as that. And this understanding and practice has always been available to you. But it takes faith and it takes practice, doesn't it? Yet many of you still place most if not all of your marbles of trust upon what you hope to be a sure thing instead. But there are no sure things, remember? Except for the poetic certainty of *That which is always becoming.*

But the idea of letting go has long been the one thing which you've had little or no difficulty letting go of, don't you see? In the meantime, you've tightly held on to just about everything else, haven't you? And this may account for all of that clutter which keeps distorting so much of your *disjoined* view of the cosmos, the cluttered-up view which you squabble over like desperate miners anxiously digging for what might lie hidden beneath the dirt below your feet—when there's really nothing there at all except for more dirt and more clutter.

Yet (speaking of paradox) your belief in a relative permanence, along with your addiction to clinging, is one of the most commonly combined causes of turmoil in your world, is it not?

Letting go of your face for a while may help you to see your reality through the eyes of *others* who (when they surrender their own face) will be able to see through and from that same reality themselves.

There will be a fundamental and widespread cleansing of sight.

Your view (of course) is never the only view. Can you even begin to comprehend that? It's never the true or only view of anything. It's always and only a partial view (*always* and *only*—two words which we never use lightly). And when it's held too firmly it's no longer a view of anything, is it? It's just another addiction which can only see itself and nothing else—and which can only desire and feed upon even more of the same addictive desires.

But when you actually do let go of it, little by little, and let it interact and interplay with how *others* perceive and experience things, it slowly unlocks itself and begins to crawl out of its internal incarceration, to reunite with the *Great Interweaving*—standing itself up and moving beyond its own narrow self-reference and beyond the choke hold of the tribal *only-mind*.

Becoming more whole, it then adjusts to a deeper and wider lens. And you're then more able to see that everything originates from the same indefinable *Source* and breathes through the same life-giving lungs and bathes in the same replenishing reservoir and that you all behold the same inexhaustible universe through the same eternal eye—whether you can actually see through it yet or not.

The problem has been that all of the tightly clenched hoarding you've done has blocked many of you from being able to see much of anything that's real. So an epidemic of tunnel vision has spread like wildfire.

Full of blind and burning spots.

Full of tightly clenched, blind, and burning spots.

The eye with which I see God is the same with which God sees me. My eye and God's eye is one eye, and one sight, and one knowledge, and one love, said the wise Meister Eckart.[1]

The most beautiful thing we can experience is the mysterious. It is the source of all true art and all science. He to whom this emotion is a stranger, who can no longer pause to wonder and stand rapt in awe, is as good as dead: his eyes are closed, said the wise Albert Einstein.[2]

So let's get back to it then . . . shall we?

CHAPTER 72

The Great Excuse

WE KNOW THAT a lot of your unkind and remote ways of responding to *others* is not always intentional.

But so what. They're still unkind. Yes?

And many of your harmful habits are purely reactionary, aren't they? Merely cloned and habitual responses that have been rehearsed and ingrained over time.

What once may have been consciously planned out is now internalized, sucked into the tribal black hole of an addictive knee-jerk reaction to *otherness*—whenever *otherness* shows its alien face on your tribal radar screen.

Many of you seem to accept it as just the way it is, as the way of the tribe, don't you? Which doesn't necessarily make an evil action more or even less evil than it already is. It just makes it seem more conventional (more tribe like), more satisfying and acceptable to the psyche of the collective, therefore quite justifiable—even fashionable.

Everybody does it, yes? Everybody, that is, who's enmeshed into your (big or little) tribal addiction—into its staunchly loyal and violent overreactions.

So then it must be okay to respond in those ways, right?

It might even be better than okay.

It might be a good thing—a tribe-approved good thing.

It might even be necessary.

"No harm intended, then no harm done," goes the reasoning. If you didn't mean to drop your flesh-shredding bombs onto those schoolchildren, then it's not an evil act at all. It's just part of war, isn't it? It's normalized. It's collateral. The cause and the intention were right. So that settles that.

If you didn't intend for that chemical plant to explode, burning and frying the lungs out of the local population, while slowly maiming and then finally destroying all those people . . . or for its toxins to leak into their drinking water from that poisonous chemical plant which you quietly built into the hidden neighborhoods of the poorest and most powerless . . . well . . . you didn't mean it, after all. You were even supplying jobs for some of them, weren't you? The cause and the intention were quite well-intended—and even profitable.

If you didn't mean to leave all of those land mines buried throughout the world's crop fields and forests, after your countless invasions and blood wars, allowing for several generations of descendants to eventually stumble across them, getting their feet and their hands and their faces blown off . . . well . . . if you didn't intend to do it, then it's not your show. Is it? The results were inadvertent and not premeditated—which makes the cause and the intention justified.

If you didn't mean for all those children to die so early from various kinds of cancerous disease, caused by the tons of toxic additives that you've put into the food system . . . well . . . you didn't know (for certain) that what you dumped into the mix or into the air and water would actually seep all of that bad stuff into the human bloodstream, did you? You meant for food to grow quicker and bigger and to increase profits—not to make it deadlier. It was good business after all. It grew the narrowly defined economy, didn't it? And you'll continue to do it until it can be proven otherwise, won't you? Behind your parade of high-powered tribal lawyers and your government and business lackeys and behind your bought-off media stooges.

The cause and the intention is for the sake of unfaltering economic progress (for a select few), for tribe-fixated financial and material expansion, and for the influence and control of unregulated capital.

If you didn't mean to contribute to racial, religious, political, gender, or other group-related slander and hatred (which has led to so much irrational yet rationalized terror, abuse, rape, murder, assassination, and war) by the constant use of the exaggerated *put-down*, by the dehumanizing language you employ . . . well . . . you were just talking, that's all. It was really no big deal. You were just blowing off some steam and just trying to be a little provocative and even a little entertaining, emphasizing some real justified anger and defending your tribal values. It's free speech, after all, isn't it? It's not your fault that somebody else took your words to heart and then got heartlessly violent with them, is it? The cause and the intention were your justifiable right to be heard, Right? Not to be accurate or conscientious.

If you didn't mean to insult and disgrace that defenseless child, then don't worry about it. They're just words. You didn't mean them to be destructive to the child's sense of being loved or of loving herself. Kids need to grow a thick skin early on anyway in your brutal world, don't they? It's a tough place to survive, after all. So throwing harsh insults at vulnerable children when they're still young might even be a good thing. It'll get them prepared for the real world—of your *disjoined* creation.

So there's no need to apologize.

The kid should be grateful for your thoughtfulness.

You didn't mean to hurt her anyway, did you?

You were just trying to toughen her up, isn't that right?

As long as you didn't mean it or intend it, just don't concern yourselves with it. Simply move your mouse to another website.

There's more unintended clicking to be done.

MICHAEL J. GAJDA

CHAPTER 73

The Eternal Presence

THERE'S AN OFTEN-OVERLOOKED and misread teaching in the ancient story of the burning bush.

You know the story, don't you? The one in which the wise prophet Moses heard something in the bush . . . speaking directly to him.[1]

But here's the misreading.

It was actually coming from within himself, not solely from somewhere outside.

The burning bush was the mask or the symbol of the common speech of the heart, which the wise and curious Moses discovered in his climb. And which he became available to. And then was able to open himself up to. Just as he was opened up from it. From someplace deep within himself. Where the divinity and unity within all beings dwells and arises. Where he recognized the authentic face beneath the one he was able to remove . . . in order to uncover, then reveal, and integrate into it. The one which is shared by all beings. The place where the fire burns inside all of *Creation*. Where there is no separation. Where there is no part to play that is separate from the whole . . . among the human or the *other* than human. Which is no mere exaggeration. And which is no different than it is now either.

It's the *Eternal Presence*.

And it still speaks through you. Through and to those who can hear. Beyond the overly forced and self-magnifying rattles of *disjoined* distraction which claim to be the sole arbiters of what is true, good, or beautiful. Which is the most common tribal facade, isn't it?

And it must be brought down.

Don't you see?

CHAPTER 74

The Paradoxical Prize

MANY OF YOU will have to work your way through several face adaptations and exchanges, in order to get back to your original face, where there really is no face to get back to—which in the long run is the ultimate paradoxical prize, isn't it?

You're the ones who've stumbled more than most in your mistreatment of *others*—either by intention or neglect. So you'll have a few more looks to work yourselves through. Maybe a whole lot more.

But we're not condemning anyone here. Let's get that clear. We're just stating the facts—with a little added color and repetition along the way for emphasis.

We're just trying to keep it real and clear so that no one gets too confused or complacent. The aim here is to bring you back to who you already are, remember? As contradictory as that may sound to you right now.

We do expect that there will be some unforeseen glitches though. So we're just trying to minimize them. We want everyone to start out with the same advantage. Justice and fairness are very important in giving this thing every possibility to work.

We're more than convinced that all of you will return transformed for the better . . . and awakened to an extent that will surprise even the most cynical among you.

We're almost sure of it.

But we can never be too sure about anything, can we?

But we can still hope and pray.

And so can you.

CHAPTER 75

The Shadows of Imperfection

WE DO ANTICIPATE that the vast majority of you (upon your return) will no longer be tempted to bury the face of your unintegrated interior life anymore either. At least not with such muscular denial.

Although most of you won't be blatantly showing it off either.

In fact, we expect that when you do eventually come home to yourselves that you'll be able to invite it out into the open and to calmly wear it with a smile and only as needed, without trying to exaggerate its power by attacking it or by running away from it, or by trying to stuff it back down into some secret prison inside yourselves so it can just keep trying to break out of its cell with the persistence of a dying man who's been falsely accused.

And you'll be able to name it too, maybe not with any great ease at first, but soon enough to bring it back to life as part of your wholeness, to use it in the service of *others* . . . as well as of yourselves, or at least to keep it from doing any more unnecessary damage, as it so often has . . . usually from being squeezed tightly between the cheeks of your overly clenched backsides, where so many of you have tried to stuff it and hide it, trying to present your unrelaxed selves (along with your tight-assed tribe) as some supreme model of shadowless perfection.

But what you've tried to bury and hide has often ended up projecting into and out of the back of one or more of your innocent and unsuspecting brothers and sisters (human or *other* than human), hasn't it? And most often of course out of the back of one or more of the always convenient and stationary targets of *otherness*.

The more that you've kept your accumulating shadows locked up and concealed from the outside world and from your own self-conscious awareness, the more violent the irruptions have been whenever they've exploded out of one your overcrowded inner dungeons.

And your world doesn't need any more conventional, polite, and especially nice boys and girls just waiting around to blow up in a rage or to be Dr. Jekyll'd into Mr. (or Ms.) Hyde.[1] Does it? It doesn't need any more cooped-up tribal inmates trying to escape from themselves (or from the oppressive *only-mind*) through the pain and suffering they transmit to *others.*

Just ask any of the grief-stricken friends and relatives of the victims of fervently brainwashed suicide bombers, or of the victims of repressed and sadistic military torturers, or of the victims of body-obsessed fire-and-brimstone religious leaders, or of the victims of the greedy and narcissistic corporate elite, or of any of those who've been bereaved by the violence which has been launched upon their loved ones from all of that protracted and confused mixture of political, religious, financial, and military butt clenching—which is the most common and most murderous kind, isn't it? The institutional kind—which so often calls for the clenching and constraint of *That which is spacious and free* and which frantically defends the *disjoined* logic of the overly squeezed gluteus maximus of the tribe.

It's the way it works in the overly compressed world of the *only-mind,* isn't it?

But as the wise Zen master Lin Ji has advised, *If you meet the Buddha on the road, kill him.*[2]

Anytime that you think you've found your one-and-only tribal savior or your one-and-only tribal truth machine . . . destroy it. Smash it into little pieces until it all disintegrates, before it destroys you, and before the *disjoined* tribal *only-mind* swoops it up and in.

It's not real anyway. So you'll only be destroying that which doesn't exist. And that which is nonexistent can never destroy anything that's real—including you, can it?

What's that word again?

Paradox—that's the word.

So when you break it all down, it's pretty much the same at all tribal levels, isn't it? The macro isn't that much different than the micro, until you get into some very interesting and arcane questions and observations related to your relatively recent discoveries in the world of quantum mechanics (not to mention string theory)[4] . . . which (to most of you) seems fairly irrelevant at this juncture, if not incomprehensible, doesn't it? But keep an open mind to it anyway. It just may show up on the other side of how you now perceive things.

A primary goal of the facial exchange is to help you to wake up with a receptive but concentrated mind, one which will be able to regularly discriminate between available choices—which for most of you will take some considerable and disciplined training, won't it? Especially since you've so often allowed your thoughts to wander and to soften and to so easily follow the prevalent and lazy patterns of addictive tribal thinking.

We're confident that your newly formed reincarnations will greatly help to accelerate the process of retraining and of strengthening you in the practice of becoming more mindfully aware of whatever you perceive . . . in each and every moment which presents itself to you.

And when you initially open your eyes tomorrow morning, you'll almost instantly become conscious of the sharpened details in your surroundings, sharper than you could have ever imagined them to be— and sharp enough that your eyes might even begin to feel like they're bleeding.

You'll wake up to a clarity that you've rarely perceived before, beyond those few coincidental moments of pointed awareness which some of you may have experienced accidentally and which you were surprised by—and which you soon abandoned with little interest, maybe once or twice in your life, if you were lucky.

The degree of the initial change in your ability to actually see will astound most of you when you first experience the visual transformation that will have taken place. And yet you could have attained that level of sharp attention with a daily disciplined practice well before this intervention . . . if you had chosen to. It's always been available.

But when tomorrow morning arrives, you'll quickly and quite noticeably move into a higher, and, maybe at first, even into an unfathomable level of alertness.

There will be a definite decrease in thought wandering. Your state of awareness will immediately intensify. But to be sustained, it will necessitate concentrated effort.

You may even begin to develop and feel muscles pulling in your intellect and heart and in your visual and imaginary conduits, which you've never felt before.

And as in any worthy exercise or discipline, there will be some accompanying soreness, which should indicate to you that you're just beginning to get into better shape . . . spiritually and psychologically speaking.

However, it may also at first develop into what feels like (and may actually be) what has rarely been recognized as being a Spiritual Emergency,[3] and which has so often been casually misdiagnosed as being psychotic or delusional behavior instead, hasn't it? By those who've been overly trained in the ways of conventional, Western, or modern thinking; or by a restriction of professional imagination; or by the habitual denial of the spiritual experience altogether . . . as even being a real experience at all; by the habitual denial of *Spirit* which is strongly adhered to in most of your established and elite (medical, psychological, and sociological) professions and institutions.

Although (paradoxically), a great amount of that denial is actually generated from within your more powerful religious institutions, isn't it? And among their controlling clerics.

But maybe it's not so paradoxical after all, since much of organized and institutional religion,when led by a dominator hierarchy, tends to contain and control the rules of spiritual engagement and development, doesn't it? While preferring to settle into and to even languish and violently defend the comfort and security of its long clung-to tribal characteristics, by which it often defines itself as separate from and superior to *others* . . . as opposed to how an (ideal) integral hierarchy tends to operate, when embodied and embraced in the spiritual dynamics and harmonic resonance of the entire flock, however imperfect that embrace may be.

It would take a virtual miracle to crack open the tabernacle windows wide enough in some of these overly contained churches, temples, and mosques to allow for the *Spirit* within each one of its devotees to breathe just enough life into their lungs to permit them to let go of themselves— which is what they're really holding on to, isn't it? Which is the image and duty they assume from the information fed to them through the visual cortex of the container of institutional (tribal) religion itself, isn't it?

But to let the *Spirit* in means you've got to let the dominant middlemen out. Don't you see?

And with no more blank checks of authority automatically handed out to autocratic gatekeepers then the whole institutional structure would have to change. Wouldn't it? What would happen to the overly contained world of any religious institution if authority was no longer solely inherited or ordained into existence from above, but had to be earned and authorized only through consultation with and by the voiced approval of the whole *Spirit*-led community? What if the dynamics of authority were no longer only vertical in emphasis, nature, or direction but were also integrated into a horizontal structure of leadership and disecernment?

After all, what would become of any unquestioned or even any so-called infallible top-down system of administration and control if an unannounced *Holy Spirit* (by whatever name it's called) was actually released and allowed to come down from the altar . . . where it's so often relegated and confined, and then allowed enough space to breathe freely and to mingle among and even beyond the congregation? It's a big question, isn't it? But only for rigid tribal hierarchies which make it their central and obvious mission (above all else) to retain and expand their power and control over property, principles, or people—and which not only rely upon but thrive upon how much of that power and control they can loom over *others*.

So there will be pain and confusion coming your way tomorrow morning. No doubt about it.

And disciplined awareness will be essential to getting through it all, in order to enter into the process of returning to who you are. So keep yourselves focused and committed.

Try to remember that.

But as always it will still be your choice when it comes down to when, at what pace, and how far into the pain and confusion that you're willing to face up to who you are (on the way to your deepest levels of *Self*-knowledge) as you enter into the vast and mysterious world of *That which is always becoming.*

CHAPTER 76

Wholeness, Not Completeness; Goodness, Not Perfection

THE AIM HERE is for wholeness . . . not completeness. For a movement toward goodness . . . not perfection.

You're already perfect just as you are.

It's just that so often you don't seem to know who that is, do you?

The goal is not to load up on more of the same but only different, nor to inject you with a tribal bias based on some *other* frozen or idiosyncratic worldview.

No. That is not the objective of this experiment.

If that's all we were aiming at we could have gone for wholesale lobotomies, couldn't we? And even though that would have made things far less complicated for all of us, it would have taken all the decision making right out of your hands—which many of you have already been doing to yourselves for quite some time, haven't you? Which has been so often and so proudly displayed through your idle and passive parroting of tribal habits of thought, and of speech, and of behavior.

So we reiterate. Pay close attention.

We will not have time to answer any lingering questions.

You will have to address all of your own conjecturing when you get to the other side. That will be your practice. That will be your way back. Although you can give yourselves a bit of a head start by beginning to think about your emerging speculations right now, can't you? And maybe even begin to visualize what your own specific responses to them might be.

It can't hurt.

Can it?

CHAPTER 77

The Personal Is Always Political

T HE FACES YOU'LL be acquiring will be recognizable right off the bat, but perhaps not specifically. Although the feel of the face and its discomforting self-awareness will be obvious to you, in your gut. Because you'll be putting on the face of someone who represents a certain population or who represents an individual or group characteristic or a certain theme or condition—all of which will be quite familiar to you.

And don't try to fool yourselves. This will all be very personal.

But as you know, the personal always extends into the body politic, doesn't it? The personal always becomes political. It always impacts others by and through every degree of involvement or withdrawal.

No one is an unaffected island. No one. Just ask any credible hermit or any non-oblivious social butterfly, for that matter.

So we repeat once again. There is no escape. Get used to that fact.

A visceral feeling of contempt, fear, anxiety, or even regret may arise within you when you wake up tomorrow morning. Because your new face will represent *them* . . . the *them* of your past and present facial life, the *others* whom you've failed to demonstrate much care or compassion for, those whom you've harshly ridiculed, the ones whom you've diminished and written off as subnormal or even as nonbeings, those whom you've tormented after accusing them of being unbelievers in your tribal tenets, those contemptible *others* whom you've stifled whenever you could . . . even trying to make them disappear, those tainted ones whom you've resented for their differences, those defective *others* whom you've ignored or brushed aside . . . pretending not to see them at all, rejecting them for who they are, turning away from their calls for assistance or for protection from being injured or abandoned . . . when you could have warned them away from impending danger or away from zones of bigotry, away from frightening or tortuous circumstances—away from the fear-obsessed or greed-driven tribal death traps.

The range of possibilities will depend on how well you've faced-up to crisis and opportunity in your individual and in your communal lives up to now.

And this has nothing to do with becoming a doormat for someone else to begin to step on. No. It's quite to the contrary.

There will be no reversing of roles. Perpetrators won't be turned into victims—or vice versa.

This is a practice meant to remove the doormat as an unnecessary feature of any and all human interaction once and for all, starting with each and every one of you and with how you begin to face up to your own crucial role and responsibility in the collective reawakening process.

So you must first stop being the doormat of your own thinking. Get it? Then (and only then) will you begin to recognize the benefits of properly cleaning your own shoes. And it will never again be with the face of *otherness*—any *otherness*.

The doormat swings both ways (in all directions, actually). But first you must stop it from swinging within, then from swinging back out at *others*. And only after that will it stop swinging back into your own face on the automatic rebound.

But we'll be getting into all the details and possibilities as we gradually move things along.

In fact, they will all begin to become more obvious to you as you travel through your specific (and sequential) stages of facial self-realization.

It will be a process of progressive awakening . . . as we've already indicated. So we advise you to avoid trying to rush through any of this.

It took time to accumulate and to be able to wear all of those masks, didn't it?

So guess what.

If you intend to bring your original face back to the head of the line, where it's meant to be . . . where it will return to its faceless spatial capacity once and for all, then it will take some time to remove all of the disguises.

Now doesn't that make sense?

CHAPTER 78

Collaborators

SOME OF YOU will be involved in what we will refer to as a collective facial exchange, due to the poor choices you've made in collaboration with those of your so-called *own kind*—against *others*.

So you may find yourselves looking out from behind the exact same face that thousands of *other* invited collaborators also end up wearing, or that perhaps a few dozen do, or that maybe just a few of them do—or that just one other of your fellow invitees does.

It will all depend on the extent and the type of crimes you engaged in with coconspirators, even if you had no conscious knowledge of your own involvement in any tribal conspiracy.

Augusto Pinochet[1] never directly conspired with Idi Amin[2] about anything, did he? Not that we know of. But both were brutal dictators. Both willfully took part in the same type of treachery which so many tyrants take part in, of violently suppressing the people within their own specific tribe. Their very own people! Especially those suspected of being in blunt opposition to the tyrannical power of the tribal *only-mind*.

So whether you deliberately or directly joined forces with *others* in any specific criminal actions or malicious behavior won't necessarily be what determines which facial category you may fall into.

Instead, the similarity of the crime, the type of negative energy you helped to feed, and the typology of the victim will be the most influential and deciding factors.

So if and when you end up coming face-to-face with any of your coconspirators, you may be quite astonished when you see them staring directly back at you . . . looking equally astonished, and through the very same eyes of the very same face which you'll be staring out of yourself . . . at the very same time. It should make for some very interesting bonding opportunities, don't you think?

And if you end up having to look at and feel the presence of hundreds of faces, including your own, which duplicate the face of a child who was sexually, physically, emotionally, or psychologically abused . . . you'll then know why, won't you?

That child, who may be representing all children, needs at least that much love and compassion repaid to him/her, doesn't s/he?

And all of you need to feel and experience the cleansing of that repayment, coming out from yourself to that child . . . and then right back to you again, in a continuing expansion and healing of the collective heart and of the collective mind, of the collective body and of the collective spirit—in a gradual rejuvenation of the interconnected and indivisible human soul. Do you understand?

It's all part of the same sacred process which you've forgotten—or which you've buried beneath the sacrilegious tribal disguise which you've been leading with.

And how you treat *others* has a simultaneous affect upon you, doesn't it? Although obviously not with identical or even equivalent tone and measure.

Yet everyone benefits from this rejuvenating process, don't you see? And that's the hidden beauty in the previously unearthed guidelines. You all get to return to your original face through the practice of advancing compassionate loving-kindness forward.

And there's the paradox.

The more you move things ahead, the closer you get to returning home.

Now how easy and uncomplicated is that?

But hopefully by now you're getting the idea of what this all entails and what it will demand of you. Yet if it was all that undemanding, we wouldn't be so thorough in preparing you. Would we? You would have already been there and back by now—without ever leaving.

So yes, we know this is hard work. And it will often feel impossible. But that's the nature of going up against the *disjoined* one, don't you see?

And that's why there have been so many corrective opportunities available to you all along the way—which you've simply and quite successfully avoided or ignored, up until now.

And understandably so.

CHAPTER 79

Never Give Up

B UT THE TIME for impersonations is over, isn't it? Which is just another one of the numerous ambiguities which we've integrated into this *experiment in truth*, permitting ourselves to once again steal (without embarrassment) an essential phrase from the liberating language of the brave and wise Mr. Gandhi, who happened to be an archetypal embodiment of someone who understood the power and necessity of realizing who one is . . . by facing up to *That which is always arising* from within one's *Self*.[1]

And just like many of the saints and sages still among you, he looked out at the world through a series of refocusing lenses (from behind a series of faces) throughout the many trials and tribulations which he endured during his own interdependent and experimental life, selflessly allowing each face to fall away when it was deemed necessary, sustaining himself through the power and grace of the *Divine Indwelling Spirit* which he aligned with and which is shared by all of you, and through the painful understanding which he acquired of himself . . . through his deep compassionate love for (and service to) *others*.

But yet . . . he never became perfect, did he? No. He didn't. He was actually quite imperfect. But he did rather well in the movement toward goodness, wouldn't you say? In the movement of spiritual face-lifting—which is the practice we seek to remind you of.

He would have been an obvious exception to the rule of tomorrow morning's event, wouldn't he? Because he allowed enough of his own inherited part of the tribal masquerade to simply decompose so that he could pursue a more expansive reality—just like any persistent scientist, seeker, or imperfect practitioner of truth would be predisposed to do.

And there have been and still are many *others* like him, yes?

We're not proposing an impossibility here. Quite to the contrary. We're presenting hope . . . and the spaciousness required for the joy and promise of how your very own life can be faced up to for what it is in its seed potential but which never comes without its hazards and risks or without its hidden structures of darkness—which always accompany the necessary peeling away of worldly attachments.

We're tough graders, which we'll admit to. But we're fair.

So we're providing you with the extraordinary chance and latitude to face the big embrace of a liberating sunrise—bright and early, tomorrow morning.

So take advantage of it.

It'll only be your last chance if you don't. But even then, it'll only be your last chance this time. Because we never give up—even if you do a million times over.

We'll still keep coming back.

Because we're always here.

Which isn't our whereabouts or even our inclination.

It's our calling.

And how many times should we forgive? *Seven times seventy-seven,* insists the wise Nazarene.[2]

But as you can see . . . it's not all that easy of a calling to live up to.

Is it?

CHAPTER 80

Disheartening Bullshit

W E REALLY DO get the sense that many of you, maybe even most of you, would rather just do your time . . . and then simply be done with it, wouldn't you? Instead of being faced with that beseeching wake-up call and all of the subsequent calls to awaken yourselves even further, as if the pressure of standing up in the batter's box tomorrow morning is just too much to bear (to borrow a baseball analogy).

Well, that may be.

But guess what. No batter up, then no wake up. And no wake up, then no crossing home plate. So you will be gradually taking the necessary swings (whether you like it or not). There's no getting around it, no matter how many facial changeups you end up fouling off or how many you may even completely whiff.

And yet in the long run, no one will be left stranded. We guarantee it.

So get your head in the game, and keep it there. And put on that old internal game face. A brand-new season is about to start. But this won't be your typical rivalry full of competitive desire—for anything or against anyone. But it will desire much from whom much has been given.

And we know that you all embody the necessary strengths and capabilities to make this thing happen, even to find it quite invigorating . . . if you so choose.

It's not just the face that we intend to transform. You understand? We're looking at the whole enchilada—the whole nest of being. That's the hope in this thing anyway.

And you'll soon have the opportunity to turn everything on its head by finally realizing that you're not separate from any *other* being in the nest.

So just think of the prospects here, the self-knowledge that you'll be uncovering and which you'll experience, the branches of wisdom that you'll be able to pick fresh fruit from for the very first time, throughout this unmasking experiment.

Yet it's still up to you to do whatever you will with it.

Isn't it?

And if you don't understand that by now, then you really don't understand much of anything.

Do you?

Or maybe you just don't want to understand much of anything.

Or maybe you're just still pretending. Maybe you're still relying upon some of that old-fashioned tribal bullshit to get you through all this.

That would be a little disheartening . . . but still quite understandable, wouldn't it, though?

CHAPTER 81

Facing the Music

B UT AS WE'VE tried to suggest, you won't necessarily get the face of anyone who gets yours.

It's a little more complicated than that.

There will be gradations of difficulty, of course. Don't forget, there are several billion of you, yes?

So some of you will have some major adjustments to make. And some of you will have much less to adjust to. And probably most of you will be in the middle somewhere.

But you'll all be part of the same facial mission, you understand? All playing your interdependent part.

It'll be an excellent opportunity to practice, won't it? To practice figuring out how to let go of all of that either/or thinking which you so love to cling to, and to eventually give it up altogether—and once and for all.

You'll be descending into a warm soup of *Self*-discovery, returning to a place where there is no real separation between cold and hot. And you'll be arriving and leaving with everyone else, where no exclusions will be allowed or even desired anymore, where you'll be plugged directly into a paradoxical but curative energy field which connects and surrenders up everything to the unifying and inmost *Self*—to *That which is who you are always becoming.*

The goal is for all of them to become one heart and mind—Just as you, Father, are in me and I in you, So they might be one heart and mind with us, prayed the wise Jesus.[1]

I am he as you are he as you are me as we are all together, sung the wise John Lennon.[2]

To be fair though, some of you (well, many of you) tried at times to be there for *others*, didn't you? Or even to see yourselves in them . . . enough to occasionally empathize with them.

We recognize and acknowledge that.

It's never been an all-or-nothing total failure on your part, has it? No. It hasn't. It isn't as though you somehow lack the heart to know how to commit a simple act of kindness or compassion. How ridiculous would that be? No one can actually embody or manifest a total lack or a total failure—of anything. It's just not possible. Even though many of you have had some difficulty in accepting or in even acknowledging your own occasional compassionate efforts yourselves, haven't you? Especially whenever those efforts happened to sneak up on you and then cross over and into one of those tribal no-fly zones . . . where you might have suddenly found yourselves committing a spontaneous act of kindness or compassion against someone *other* than those contained within your own tribe.

Yet as strong as the tribal pull has been and as much developmental damage as it's been able to do, it can never completely overcome the pull of the *Divine* which is entwined into every bit of your humanity. It can never completely overcome the pull of your essential *Self*, can it?

But many of you just keep forgetting that, don't you? Forgetting who you are and where you came from. Because you've allowed tribal logic to blur the internal memory cells, right along with everything else, haven't you? Causing you to forget that you're all in this together, all the time. Not just when it's easy and not just with your own tribe or only with those who seem to perceive or experience things the same way that you currently seem to. Not just when things are going your own way either—no matter whose face you think you may be wearing.

You're all traveling along your many different lines of individual development (cognitively, spiritually, kinesthetically, psychologically, aesthetically, physically, socially, ethically, spatially, affectively, relationally etc.) at your own individual, holonic pace. Remember? No one aligns perfectly with anyone else at any level along any one line for long . . . if ever. Everything is always in motion in every one. Even when it appears (or feels) that you're stuck along one of those lines.

But nothing remains stuck forever. *Creation* will always be an interwoven, dynamic tapestry of change. Unfortunately, many of you among the invited have too often resorted to violence to get rid of the apparent stuckness in *others* which so disturbs you, simply because they don't line up perfectly enough with the *disjoined* desires of the tribal *only-mind* which your *disjoined* thoughts inhabit.

But we're getting a little ahead of the game plan here again, aren't we?

And there's a little more to it than just changing into or remaining a compliant and codependent good little tribal boy or girl, isn't there? As we've already discussed.

And it'll demand a little more of you than just saying a few magic words meant to please or fool the tribal powers that be . . . as you may have begun to realize by now.

Exacting too much obedience to your tribal loyalties and illusions is what got you into this whole mess in the first place, isn't it?

And we know that forgetting or disregarding *others,* keeping them pinned down as abstractions, is an easy thing to do when you've locked yourselves and your revered tribal agendas into the prisons of selfish compulsion and self-attachment. Which as you know is another easy thing to get used to doing, even to get addicted to—which many of you are, aren't you?

It's been quite astonishing to us to observe how so many of you swear by the anthem that you were born into, even now, and without question . . . as you have for decades, even centuries, quarantined off from daring to even quietly recite, read, or listen to *other* compositions, with or without the accompanying music of that *otherness* which you so dread.

We're hoping that you will soon see the futility of dividing up so many sounds, beats, and rhythms of *Creation* into opposing pieces of tribal noise. Because, as we've already emphasized, all parts do reflect and participate in the whole orchestration, no matter how much you try to isolate them from one another. And it even makes for more interesting music, doesn't it? Especially when they begin to relax and to freely mingle with each *other* and to gradually or spontaneously harmonize.

So there's no need or purpose for any more tribal or territorial worship or for any relative allegiance at all . . . anywhere. Is there? No matter what the territory is made of. Because there's only one cosmic terrain to be concerned with. So get used to it already, will you?

You may find this hard to readily acknowledge, but tribal maps and lines of demarcation never existed until you so-called humans arrived on the planetary scene.

Well . . . did they?

And as we've already underlined and punctuated, a tremendous shortage of curiosity still resides in your *disjoined* and compressed perception of things. So it's no wonder that so many of your addictions proceed, purely out of the boredom and anxiety, which you often try to cover up or camouflage with antiquated tribal apologetics—or with hyperactive tribal hyperbole.

Perhaps your new faces will be able to trade in on enough genuine passion and curiosity to speed up and intensify the necessary turnaround. Those two qualities alone could cure you of much, if not all, of your fabricated arrogance . . . if you'd let them.

Couldn't they?

MICHAEL J. GAJDA

CHAPTER 82

The Hook

B UT THE FANTASIES of the *only-mind* continue to multiply and to expand, don't they? Beyond any reasonable limit—as you sink your eye teeth even deeper into the tribal mirage which somehow persuades you that it's yet another contaminated invasion of *otherness* which approaches, intent on stretching and accusing the tribal imagination of being a mere figment of itself.

Imagine that.

And then imagine this:

Hope that barely dangles in the hearts of the fatherless and scarred, in terrified children of absent adults, puffing out their chests and murdering each other . . . in Detroit and Flint, in Baghdad and São Paulo, in Glasgow and Johannesburg, in Kingston and Caracas, in Compton and Baltimore, in Belfast and Juarez, in Lagos, in the isolated villages of Uganda, among so many *others*, as it slowly edges even more into your fear-riddled and emotionally frozen neighborhoods now.

Then there's this:

Fathers and mothers of Mexico and of Honduras, from Guatemala, Nicaragua, and El Salvador, from the Congo and of Nigeria, from Somalia, from South Sudan, from Mali—they try to escape.

From the destitute and desperate south—they forever try to escape.

They roam the planet and look north for work and for food and for safety . . . to send home survival money to their children and siblings, even to their parents, desperate in their attempt to get out from under the boot heel of the local gun and out from under the greed of the gang bangers and *coyotes*, out from under the mercenary multinationals, and out from under merciless politicians, out from under the powers that hover over the poor and the destitute who get squeezed and demonized for surviving what has been stolen from them, unsettled in ever-increasing nomadic numbers, restless wanderers entering your insulated world—trying to make themselves visible and real to you.

But you would rather not see who they actually are, would you? So you call them names. You accuse them of being *illegal,* as if they come from a separate uncreated universe. You dismiss them as being the *other,* no longer precious sentient beings at all.

And this:

A wrinkled war veteran stands shivering with one hand stretched out, holding the equally wrinkled beggar's sign with the other hand which trembles in cold humiliation. The flimsy cardboard held between his numbed fingers is his only remaining and visible battle decoration. His sorrow-filled scars stand there with him, inside of him . . . on the corner in the chill of winter, a few feet outside and away from your warm-yet-insecure containment, from behind your shield of panhandler-proof car windows, protected by the push-button clunk of your quickly locked doors, sitting in a long line of hurried consumers—who just got their fix, wearing anxious and amnesiac faces behind their shopping-mall steering wheels, at the (much-too-long) red traffic light.

His hands look like your hands.

Your eyes stare straight ahead.

The flag that was waved for him when you cheered him off (from home to war) has been taken down.

He stands alone . . . homeless and flagless, until the tribe raises the flag back up again, when you then look through and from behind your protective glass one more time . . . for the next wave of returning sons and daughters, sent off to fight *others* again—*others* whom they do not even know.

The light turns green, and your car bumper speeds away, shamelessly wearing a yellow ribbon sticker, which reads:

Support Our Troops.

And much of it doesn't seem to exist with any reality for you, does it?

The window is a TV screen. The war veteran, a character actor. The mass of desperate wanderers—mere extras in a foreign movie depicting dangerous aliens.

Your attention is used up in a temporary suspension of disbelief.

So you change the channel or click on to another website and put another lock on the door or draw new and thick borders on your maps.

Where's the remote? I can't find the remote.

"I cannot save the world either," you say to yourselves. "I am only one person. I have to take care of my own. It is not my fault. I'm off the hook," you say.

But you don't even care about the hook.
"It's all too much. Nobody's perfect," you say.
But you do know that there's only one hook, right?
You do know that.
Don't you?

CHAPTER 83

Hitting the Ground

THIS EXPERIMENT WILL start to deliver the goods (the beginning shifts in awareness) right from the get-go—which is something else we'll guarantee. And it won't start out stuck to anything. Not to speed or place nor direction or time—especially not to time.

Stuckness will not be allowed to take charge or to sabotage the work at hand. You will hit the ground running. We've bet the farm on it.

Unfortunately, for you . . . it's your farm.

Or maybe it's fortunate. It just depends on how you look at things, doesn't it? And how you face up to them. Or how you begin to actually see them.

But none of what you will soon be facing up to can be nearly as painful in comparison to how so many of you have been denying yourselves (and each *other*) so much for all these years, can it?

At least we don't expect there to be any unmanageable physical pain involved, in the initial transformational phase anyway . . . unless for some reason the face you wake up with is too tight of a fit, or if it's just so much of a shock that it frightens you into an anxiety attack that goes psychosomatic on you—or if for some reason there's a mistake made and you're given the wrong face replacement.

But we're confident that most if not all possible obstructive issues have been looked into and have been taken care of ahead of time by our highly regarded research team and by our competent technicians.

Our understanding is that all the bugs have been worked out.

But we suppose anything's possible, isn't it?

This is (after all) a major shift in the rules of engagement.

And there's a little more involved here than just zooming up and then into a different temporal time zone, isn't there?

Jet lag will be the least of your worries. And there's no danger of a crash. You can be sure of that. But a soft face landing cannot be assured of either. And for that . . . we apologize in advance.

We'll keep an open eye out for any necessary recalls which may have to be implemented. We do have backup facial coverings in our inventory for almost everyone and for almost any contingency—when and if they're needed.

That's because so many of you seem to have multiple facing-ups to do.

So we do expect breakdowns to occur.

Once again, we're not trying to be too faultfinding or callous or even too cautious here.

We're just trying to prepare you.

It is what it is, after all, isn't it? Which is all it's ever been or even could be.

So accept it as our gift, from us to you.

But as an evolving gift, as a gift of expansion.

Try to make the most of it.

Won't you?

CHAPTER 84

The Two Rules

I N ANY EVENT, there's a brand-new rule which will take effect at dawn (the rule of the new face), as we've been trying to make as clear as we possibly can. It'll be applied to all who have too often abandoned the Golden Rule.

Most of you are well acquainted with that one, aren't you?

It goes something like this: *Do to others as you would have them do to you.*[1]

That's the one. Or maybe it's some similar version that you've heard yet have often ignored along the way . . . which, as we've said, more than likely will include just about every one of those who we've presented with our invitations.

But when we refer to you, of course, we mean those of you who are thoroughly familiar with the Golden Rule, in any shape or form or through any Tradition that it may have been revealed or handed down to you . . . consciously or even unconsciously. Naturally this will exclude all life-forms *other* than self-consciously aware adult human beings.

You're not going to see a dog wearing the face of a rhino tomorrow or a tree with a horse's face. The ocean isn't going to turn into an overcrowded center of a big city. Night won't empty itself of faraway stars, nor will the man in the moon be replaced by someone else. Air won't liquefy into hot lava. Oxygen won't transform into mercury. No plant will replace its leaves with hands or fingers or suddenly display *other* Homo sapien characteristics. The sun won't be wearing a handlebar mustache. No insect is going to be forced to carry and wear the oversized head of a human being. Birds won't start growing gills. Evolution will not stop.

No *other* species will wake up with a human face (or *other*wise) to work itself through. And no human child will be affected by this rule change either, nor will any adult who hasn't reached the level of self-reflection needed to comprehend the complexities of life on planet Earth, or the height and depth of awareness necessary to value and follow the ways of the Golden Rule . . . for the giving and the receiving of its revelatory gifts.

The balance of *Creation* and evolution will continue to thrive around you just as its real presence does now. Even with all of your previous intrusions upon it.

And *Creation* is such a surprising and forgiving place to hang your hat upon and to appreciate, isn't it? But that's only if you can just stay with it long enough to give it your full attention and if you can put your complete yet imperfect trust in it.

So let us remind you of what we've continued to emphasize: Practicing patience throughout this transition will help—but only if you pay attention.

We advise you to begin with the practice of breathing slowly, even slower than slowly. You may even want to try counting your breaths. It might help you to see with greater clarity. It may not only expand your lungs, it may even expand your generosity. Who knows?

But there's really only one way to find out.

Isn't there?

CHAPTER 85

The Party's Over

B UT THE CHILDREN of your planet, and the childlike adults
blessed with their own given lack of sophisticated awareness . . .
well . . . they already do as much as they can and as they should do
(to *others*) within their own capabilities, don't they? It's built into their
limitations. That's their gift . . . to (and of) themselves. So to speak.

And there's a reason why they are who they are, isn't there?

Each of them is just one more opportunity for the rest of you, to
remind yourselves of an important practice . . . the practice of becoming
more fully awake to your own divine yet indivisible humanity, each of
them being a suggestion of who you are, but always in relation to *others*,
to the rest of *That which is always becoming* all around you (human or
other than human)—which so many of you have kept yourselves from
entering into relationship with, with any consistent clarity or with any
depth of lasting compassion, haven't you?

Instead, you've tried to confuse things by turning *That which is* into
a collection of *disjoined* and competing tribal beliefs and allegiances,
with your particular tribe hovering above and condescending down
upon all those abstracted *others*—from its self-elevated perch.

Yet most of you (in your heart of hearts) don't much trust your own
remote tribal ways and means, do you? Which explains why you rely upon
the same old, tired strategies of using defensive spatial arrangements (and
tribal disguise) to insulate and protect yourselves, anxiously huddling
together inside the same old, tired jar of containment.

But that party is soon to be over. That road is soon to be closed. That
wall will soon come tumbling down—Humpty Dumpty style.[1]

Beginning tomorrow morning, all partisan party masks will be taken
off, turned in, and burned.

All roads leading back to the parochial *only-mind* will be blocked or
rerouted.

All walls of clannish separation will disintegrate before your naked
eyes.

Redemption will no longer be an inside tribal job . . . especially when done at the expense of *others*.

But if it starts to lean that way . . . well . . . then you'll just be sending yourselves that much deeper into the infinite realm of endless refacing—until you get it right.

You can count on it.

CHAPTER 86

Freedom from Circumstance

ONCE AGAIN, WE'RE not making any strident judgments here. We're just laying the cards on that old, familiar cosmic table which we referred to earlier.

Denial is just another ineffectual culprit which you've regularly employed, isn't it? Misleading you to this precipice, to where the masks must now be removed. It's been (for many of you) your front card. So don't go there. The ever-shifting front of the *only-mind* won't help you anymore.

And when you do get your first new face, try to remember that your full acceptance of it will be an essential part of the practice which aims toward returning you to your original *Self*, with its original face—to the faceless *One*, not to drop you into another tribal dressing room so you can just slip into another comfy suit of conventional disguise.

There's a much deeper and more unifying face within, remember? A universal indwelling expression of *That which is ultimately inexpressible . . .* a transcendental *Someone* who is not an object at all and who is not separate from you nor separate from anyone else (human or *other* than human), and who cannot be easily recognized by most of you. Because s/he is only revealed in all of her/his divine and paradoxical *Isness*—and *only to those who keep their mind* (and heart) *one-pointed on the Lord of Love*, as the wise Katha Upanishad states.[1]

And that's your ultimate goal, after all, isn't it? If you choose to work toward that end. And you will still have that option, won't you? Which we will continue to remind you of.

It's always your decision. There's no one else to blame anymore. There never was.

Although some decisions may be more difficult than others. We'll grant you that.

For instance, if, come tomorrow morning, your luck of the draw happens to have you living as a hungry and oppressed peasant in North Korea, then your everyday choices (even your every moment choices) are almost certainly going to be more difficult than if you were reborn into white-male skin somewhere inside the continental boundaries of either North or South America or into the enmeshed territory of most of Europe. Your more limited choices may involve risking your *Self*-denying tribal reputation . . . or even what little freedom that you're able to pretend to have. Or they may even involve risking your own physical life.

But it still always comes down to you, doesn't it? No one else.

Freedom is always a flame that burns outward—radiating from the center of the heart.

The exterior circumstances may determine the risks, the levels of difficulty, and the paradoxical opportunities. But freedom is always determined by the heart's response.

Between stimulus and response there is a space. In that space is our power to choose our response. In our response lies our growth and our freedom . . . Everything can be taken from a man or a woman but one thing: the last of human freedoms to choose one's attitude in any given set of circumstances, to choose one's own way, wrote the wise Victor Frankl.[2]

By the time you return from the other side . . . *blame* will be a forgotten word.

It will be an amusement, at best, as real as the belief in a flat planet or in an Earth-centered universe or in a geographical heaven and hell . . . or in the misleading and false tribal perception that your containing circumstance is indissoluble, that it is forever in absolute control of your inner freedoms and your outer choices.

Those lies will all dissolve and disappear into the faceless expansion of a joyous universe.

Into *That which is.*

CHAPTER 87

Too Much Face

WE'RE ASSUMING THAT some (or maybe even most) of you will decide that the work is too difficult and that you may just try to adjust to your new environment by countering with the same old monotonous and exhausted reactions, the ones which you've locked into for so long that you've even got them memorized—the ones which brought you into this unexpected wake-up call in the first place.

That may be your initial knee-jerk response.

And so be it.

It will just postpone your return and make the transition back that much more demanding . . . when and if you decide to change your mind. And you must change your *mind* in order to change your *actions*—in order to change your *face*. That's implanted in the rule.

But there's a derivation of that implant.

It goes like this: You must change your *actions* in order to change your *mind*—in order to change your *face*.

You must never lead with your *face* though. You either lead with *actions* or with *mind*—with disciplined and discriminating activity and behavior or with mindful and *Self*-discerning awareness.

Face should always be placed last in line . . . just the opposite of how you've been used to doing it so far.

You've tended to lead heavy with your exterior window dressing, forcing your *mind* and *actions* to follow—squeezing them in behind.

That's no good.

By doing that, you just keep chasing after appearances. Don't you see?

And because of that, they become disappearances. They become this: *no-face, no-mind, no-action*—which (paradoxically) is the goal.

But the living in process is what matters most, isn't it? The course of living action is what needs to transform in order to realize that goal. Or else you just completely miss the whole point and then jump right back into the loop of attempting to lead with your face again. And then *no-face, no-mind, no-action* turns right back into this: *much-face, much-mind, much-action.*

It doesn't work. It becomes overcrowded, polarized, and confused—which is something else to pay close attention to when you wake up tomorrow morning.

As the wise Lao Tzu once spoke, *The Tao is still, at rest, yet nothing is left undone.*[1]

CHAPTER 88

The Gift of Death

THESE CHILDREN AND these uniquely gifted and childlike adults that we speak of. And all the animals and plants. And the fish and the birds. And all the molecules, atoms, and quarks of creation. And all the gifts which they bring to the cosmic table. Well . . . they've all continued to evolve, to be just who they are, haven't they? Just who they always are. Nestled within the horizontal and vertical layers of *Creation*. Spread throughout and surrendered to *That which is always becoming* (within themselves). Which is all they ever can be, isn't it? Even if they can't really fathom who or what that is, even if they have no conscious hint of self-evolvement or of self-conscious awareness. Even if they have no inner need to know.

They merely have the need to be.

But you . . . on the other hand. You are the sole members of your (or any *other*) species who have conditioned yourselves to either displace or reject your own unique evolutionary gifts.

You've trained yourselves to conveniently forget or deny that you do know who you are, haven't you? Especially when it falsely appears to be advantageous for you to do so. You've even trained yourselves to forget or deny that you've actually ripened into becoming self-reflective human beings, that your own self-conscious awareness is the very price you must pay for the gift and grace of transcendence, and that the ultimate cost of your inheritance of that unique and bewildering way of knowing is *to be consciously aware that you are consciously aware*, and that as long as you can breathe, think, feel, and observe, then you will continue to be reawakened out of your habitual slumber—no matter how deeply you've been conditioned to enter into any of your overly congested kingdoms of tribe-induced sleep.

But what you've so often tried to forget or deny is what actually leads not only to all kinds of unexpected gifts to appreciate and to include along your life's journey, but also to all kinds of burdening opportunities which accompany those gifts—a paradoxical blend of everyday existence put before you not merely to delight in or to endure but to transcend.

And whether you're able or willing to acknowledge and openly receive those burdensome gifts and opportunities is yet another question altogether, isn't it?

Self-conscious awareness is a sacred gift to behold, a wondrous doorway which unlocks the imagination with paradoxical perception. It leads to the eventual emptying out of (and release from) the tribal self, if you allow it to . . . and into infinite spaciousness, into the unknowing layers of deeper and deeper holy communion with the indivisible *Self*, with the *Kingdom of God* which is always right there, even and especially within you—and within everything else.

But no evolutionary gift ever comes without a cost, does it? Even when it's freely given.

There's always a trade-off, isn't there? There's always an exchange to be made . . . if not immediately, then somewhere down the road.

And one of the more immediate, penetrating, and costly effects of receiving such a powerful gift as the one you've been given and which is your birthright . . . is the illuminating yet disturbing revelation that one day you are actually going to die. That you will not live forever. That your physical embodiment is not an eternal promise. That, as you experience each and every present moment (one moment after another), you will continue to breathe in and out as a full-fledged human being . . . until one inevitable and unpredictable point in the illusion of time when you will then shed your body like an affectionate old coat which has finally lost its reliable warmth, instantly leaving it behind to disintegrate into particles of dust for *others* to breathe in and out, before they too gradually cast off their own body of dust . . . in one inevitable and elastic future moment, for even more subsequent *others* to inhale and to inherit and to ultimately pass along with their own flesh and blood—which they will eventually shed and then bequeath to *others* as well.

One day you and everyone else will forever (physically) disappear . . . into the mystery of a dustless afterlife.

You can be sure of it.

And, shortly after your physical demise, most of the rest of the world will hardly (if at all) notice your specific disappearance . . . or that you were ever even alive and breathing in the first place.

But you will leave your legacy. And it will be relinquished to and received by the rest of the manifest universe which you've left behind, through the quality and the force of light and the presence of creative and loving energy which you've radiated during your short visit to satellite Earth.

What is a hundred years in eternity? asks the wise Mohandas Gandhi.[1]

Whatever amount of compassionate loving-kindness which you may have generated, into the life-sustaining unified field of the miraculous cosmos, will be the inheritance which you will surrender and release for all of its still-breathing inhabitants to forever absorb . . . and to benefit from.

But what of your individual or collective accumulation of power? And of your temporal achievements? And of your caches of control? Or of your fame and prestige? Or of your material, emotional, and spiritual belongings? What will become of them?

They were never the point or purpose of your entry into physical existence, don't you see? Even if so many of you still insist that they are . . . by the way you tend to attach such overweight tribal meaning to so much of it.

You can't take any of it with you, can you? As the wise and ancient human saying goes. And none of it will remain standing once you're gone.

What you insist upon accumulating and hanging on to is all destined to disintegrate, isn't it? Every bit of it. Just like your own flesh . . . along with your own blood and your own bones.

Ashes to ashes. Dust to dust.[2]

Coming to such a sudden awareness of your own mortality is one thing. But then when you add it to the percolating sense of insignificance which gnaws at so many of you, permeating your compulsive desire for security and permanence . . . well . . . then you've got some real existential angst to deal with, don't you?

To be consciously aware is to be constantly reminded of the irrefutable fact of your own mortality, isn't it? In every experiential moment, in every loss of any kind which you endure—whether it's a personal or material loss or a gradual or sudden decline of tribal means, accompanied by having less and less influence and control over more and more.

They're all instructive reminders of your own anthropological impermanence, aren't they? Reminders not only of the transience of things, titles, and works and of thoughts and of feelings and of natural and accidental events . . . but of your own physical fallibility, of your own tenuous beliefs about what matters most, and about who you think you are—which leads you to some very unsettling and unsentimental questions, doesn't it? Such as . . . who am I then, beyond this physical self? Who am I beyond the limitations of these fleeting mental objects and emotions and beyond all of these persistent self-conscious (and egomaniacal) evaluations of so much?

What will happen to this fragile empire of selfhood which I've constructed . . . with all of these material and psychological trappings? With these possessions and with these people? And with all of these events and memories? And with these concrete images of myself—which I've projected out and which I've felt and even allowed to be projected upon me from *others*?

Why did I ever enter into the body and life of a human being in the first place, especially if I'm just going to disappear . . . to eventually be eliminated from the cosmic memory bank?

Why did I show up at this particular time? And in this particular place? And in this particular vehicle?

Who is it within me that is witnessing the formation of these questions as I ask them?

Who is it that is observing my own thoughts right now?

Who is it that is *other* than yet not *other* than who I am?

How do these thoughts arise? And from where? Who is it that is watching them as they arise?

Whose thoughts are they? Are they only mine? Or are they universally shared . . . released from a deeper unifying *Source*?

What separates where they come from and what they arise into? Where is the separation?

Where is the boundary between myself and where these thoughts originate?

Is there actually a point of origination? Is there actually a point of severance? If not, then am I singular or plural? Am I infinite or finite? Or both?

Am I one and (at the same time) *not* one? Is that possible?

Can a wave separate itself from the ocean and still be a wave? Can it ever be completely independent of its source and origin of being?

When these questions are honestly faced up to then you'll only be left with *That which is incomprehensible* to the mind of the materialist, won't you? You'll be left with *That which is beyond* the containment and impermanence of perishable things, with *That which is without definable boundaries* and which is beyond the covetous traps of worldly definitions—with *That which is real and changeless* yet well beyond the grasp of complete knowing.

The immutable can only be known through a gradual process of unknowing, through the gradual shedding of all masks. Through the letting go of all of that which is *not* and of that which is momentary, leading to an uncontainable and infinite mystery—which is the only reliable guide that can ever release you from your grasping (even if unconscious) fear of death.

But most of you still cling to that fear, don't you? To the concrete belief in division and separation. To the boundaries of the familiar. To your denial of anything beyond the corporeal.

Some of you even imagine a physical and material afterlife, do you not? Resisting and denying *That which is whole* yet incomplete . . . and which is always in the elusive process of becoming. So you still try to squeeze what is often unapparent and fleeting into a parochial cage of time-hardened tribal definitions.

Most of you have not even begun to practice the art of self-surrender or even of a gentler way of holding on to what you must eventually let go of, have you?

You haven't yet begun to practice the art of dying. Of dying to yourselves. Of dying to your locked-up and locked-in self-image . . . or to the many layers of masks that you wear to secure and identify yourselves with, or to protect yourselves from what you fear most—which is the death of just about anything that you've allowed yourselves to become overly defined by.

You haven't even begun to practice dying to your own worldly enchantments, have you? To what you know will someday perish.

So then how can you possibly face the realization of your own mortality or of death itself if you still resist dying to what is essentially facile and insignificant . . . if you still struggle to let go of frivolous masks and of ancient and imaginary photographs of yourselves, if you can't release even part of whatever tribal identity you hang on to, if you can't even let go of a single piece of revered nostalgia of place, habit, or memory or of any wrong that's been done to you, or of an opinion or image that you clasp to about a friend, an enemy, or of a member of your own family, or of any fragment of a cultural, religious, or political viewpoint which has come to govern and dictate how you characterize or represent yourselves, or of any share of power which you hold over events, circumstances, or situations or over land and animals—or of any anger or resentment which you grip and aim toward *others*?

How can you courageously face death when you seldom if ever let go of anything until it's forced upon you by accident or theft or by coercion or tragedy?

You can't. Can you?

You can only keep on pretending that death does not exist despite the everyday evidence that it does. Despite the fatal proof found in every moment. Despite the fact that death can come at any time to anyone—which you've all observed and experienced at one time or another in your brief human existence.

Yet you still continue to refuse the gift, don't you?

You still refuse to die to anything without putting up a resistance, even a violent resistance, if perceived to be necessary—which has often led to the physical suffering and the painful elimination of many unfortunate beings who somehow got in your way, hasn't it?

Because if you deny the existence of death firmly enough, then the death of the *other* doesn't really feel like death, does it?

And the sufferings of *others* don't really feel like sufferings, do they?

They feel like something else instead.

And when you become *disjoined* to the agony and hardship of *others*, it can sometimes actually come to feel as though you're participating in the contradictory creation of a new form of life, in the sustaining or even in the saving of that life—which you convince yourself that you are a benevolent and even a chivalrous procreator of.

The death and misery of *otherness* can actually come to feel as though life is being preserved through its destruction, even while you continue to resist your own eventual death and dying to much of anything—which so clearly exposes the raw spiritual wounds which bleed through your hide with despair and which plead with you to cling even tighter to a deeply ingrained denial of your own mortality.

And it's continued to lead so many of you into that familiar black hole of reactionary violence, hasn't it? Filled with knee-jerk and hostile projections of blame against *others*—which you all too often justify as somehow being for their own cataclysmic good.

It became necessary to destroy the town to save it, a United States major in Vietnam was reported to have said in 1968, after the military destruction of the village of Ben Tre.[3]

Your refusal to acknowledge the power and presence of death has led to your disavowal of your own self-conscious awareness, don't you see? Which has been your most effective way of avoiding the felt experience, the costs, and the blessings of being cosmologically related to and unified with all of *Creation*—human or *other* than human.

One of the biggest challenges which you'll all be faced with tomorrow morning will be how to begin to remove the masks of *Self*-denial—which you've proudly been wearing and showing off, somehow needing to prove to yourselves that you're wrapped up safely inside the thick and secure walls of indestructible tribal skin.

But if you can't begin to peel away even the most superficial layers of that perishable shield, of that flimsy and transparent carapace of *Self*-repudiation . . . then tomorrow's going to be an extremely long day, don't you think?

You can bet heavily on it.

And when you get to the *other* side, it will become more than necessary for you to be fully aware of your own actions and to take full and unshakeable responsibility for them—which would at the very least be the adult thing to do, wouldn't it?

You must be willing to bluntly face the natural consequences which result from your very own thoughts which lead to your very own actions.

Yet if you can still deny that you're fully aware of what you think and of how you react, or that certain collective activity or personal conduct has even happened, or if you can continue to retranslate those actions into a tribal fantasy which actually validates your behavior, then consequences don't become much of an issue for you, do they? Not before, during, or even after choosing the thoughts and behaviors which you deny having chosen.

How can you absorb any enlightening consequences for something which may not have even occurred? For something which you refuse to recall or admit to taking part in yourselves, regardless of any evidence which clearly confirms that something did actually occur?

There may be horrible aftermath effects stemming from those disavowed actions . . . of which *others* often end up having to suffer. But how many internal or even external consequences are directly experienced by the actual perpetrators, by those who remain trapped and barricaded inside the safe house of tribal denial and who rely upon and often get the cult of the tribal *only-mind* to back them up?

Not a whole lot.

It's been a very common and quite effective nullifying technique, hasn't it? Used by tribes and individuals alike . . . for millennia.

It's older than the story of Cain killing Abel and then lying to God about what he did.[4]

But the unswerving *Self* cannot lie. And it cannot be lied to.

It can only be lied about.

Meanwhile, the fraudulent self can do all three at the same time . . . if it feels the urge to do so.

It can hit the trifecta of denial with the skill of a seasoned true believer whenever the impulse to run and hide or to attack shows up.

Don't you see?

CHAPTER 89

Filling the Gaps

For the grossly impudent lie always leaves traces behind it, even after it has been nailed down, a fact which is known to all expert liars in this world and to all who conspire together in the art of lying . . . But the most brilliant propagandist technique will yield no success unless one fundamental principle is borne in mind constantly and with unflagging attention. It must confine itself to a few points and repeat them over and over. Here, as so often in this world, persistence is the first and most important requirement for success . . .
—Adolf Hitler[1]

The bigger the lie, the more inclined people are to believe it.
—Anonymous

AND THE MORE the perpetrators of the *Big Lie* are inclined to believe the *Big Lie* themselves,[2] aren't they?

Much of your resistance to fully accepting your burdensome gift (of being self-consciously aware) has come from the subconscious barriers which you've constructed to block it out. But not all of it has, has it?

Whether it's been an intentional or an unwitting resistance isn't really the issue though, is it?

What the issue is and what has been revelatory is the fact that your resistance has been so constant and so committed and that you've so consistently kept yourselves cut off at such a distrustful distance from your own untapped fortune of self-reflective awareness. And while doing so, you've not only lost the knack of animal instinct which you once beheld (by naturally transcending it), but you've also lost the transcendental facility of being able to see and to experience *That which has evolved* beyond the instinctual, by sending it quick and deep into the familiar burial grounds of an arbitrary tribe which overcrowds itself with dead bodies of self-deception, with cadavers of caricature, and with the remains of its own lifeless fantasies—where the irrepressible *Self* is repeatedly entombed and then forgotten (or so you think), covered up with graveyard tribal dictates and commandments . . . and shoveled over by the uncreative imagination of the *only-mind.*

But the *Self* will not remain interred for long . . . regardless of whatever apocryphal tribal tomb it is which may again be trying to put it to sleep. It merely climbs *It-Self* out from behind your eclipsed vision. And then with ad-libbed and irreverent surprise, whenever you fall into another of the predictable naps (and traps) of the *only-mind,* the mischievous *Self* reaches over and taps you on your face once more to remind you of your fragile disconnection.

And whenever you feel that resurrected gaze and touch upon your skin . . . you react just as the tribal consciousness expects you to, don't you? By frantically shoveling even more tribal dirt onto the mountains of mass graves buried beneath the perceptual surface of the *only-mind*—where you've tried to lay any remnant of the awakening *Self* to rest.

But it just doesn't work, does it?

Because it can't work.

Most other species can't fully announce to themselves who they are yet, can they? Mostly, they just are. Which is good, beautiful, and true. Because it is just *That . . . That which is.*

Yet each and every species still moves through its own gradual awakening process, doesn't it? Through its own cross-pollinating collection of structures and lines, through its own paradoxical development, and along its own unpredictable path from which the flow of its energy is invisibly rooted, deep in a mysterious source of *Otherness* (which is not an *otherness*) in all of its inexplicable complexity, entwined with everything else in a vast cosmic relationship, tangled up with the coincidental movements of every *other* evolving species . . . with every particle and wave, miraculously comingling within an evermore spacious and infinitely expanding universe which keeps transforming and transcending itself—as it forever flourishes.

All boundaries of separation (or of solidity) are merely apparent, don't you see? Whether you want to believe that or not. They do not exist beyond their appearance or beyond what the unaware beholder can merely observe at the macroscopic (relative) level of seeing.

Whenever you break any seemingly solid object down to the quantum degree (including human beings), only waves of energy are left (waves and vibrations of exuberant energy)—along with subatomic particles. None of which can be precisely calculated or beheld.

So nothing at the larger level of material appearance is really what it seems to be. Do you understand?

When you travel into that infinitesimal microspace, you find that there are no solid objects, that nothing is absolute (besides *the Absolute* . . . *It-Self*, of course), that nothing can be grasped as certain,[3] that there are only spacious probabilities abounding in a vast and inexhaustible nanouniverse—which can never be contained or appropriated by any *disjoined* version of tribal logic.

And yet most forms of human life still tend to get stuck somewhere along the way, don't they? Or they pause for a while. Or they attach themselves to a relative vicinity (a rest stop) inside the time and space of that infinite arrangement of cosmic kinship as they move throughout the *Self*-coordinated circuitry, through the unfolding process of becoming who they are . . . until they break off again into the next adaptation or into the next level of awareness, into the next aha moment, into the next gift of spiraling grace or revelation—or even into the next surprising physical embodiment.

Evolution is always open ended, isn't it? For all of the created—without exception.

And most human beings have it in them to be able to honestly surmise from the past, don't they? And to objectively observe from the present, if they're willing . . . and if they're able to see clearly enough to do so.

Yet it's quite difficult to predict what's up ahead, isn't it? No one knows when a tragic interruption or an epiphanic moment of revelatory grace will strike, do they?

So once again, we ask you to humor us by participating in another simple experiment . . . in a simple and safe exercise in observation, which may help to begin to loosen up and expand your tightly wrapped tribal awareness. And it won't hurt a bit. We promise. It may even feel quite relaxing—even pleasurable.

Begin the exercise by trying to closely observe either a dog or a tree or maybe a rock or an ape, or perhaps a fish or a bird or a snake or even a mosquito, or a cloud or a river or maybe a flower or a turtle, or possibly a spider or an ant, or even the feel or the sound of wind—for just a short while.

Intimately watch with all of your available senses from wherever you are.

Just watch yourselves while you observe.

Who is it that is actually doing the observing?

Who is the one who is watching you observe?

Who is it again that is beholding what is beheld?

Who is the one who is aware of your present state of awareness?

Who is it that sees not only what you see . . . but who can also see through your own eyes (along with you) as you do the seeing?

Who is this ever-present and omnipresent *Other* that is (*Another* but) not an *other*?

Who is this nameless witness to everything?

These may sound like odd or incoherent questions to many of you, even though a certain minority among you (and throughout your human history) has been quite tenacious in the exploration of their meaning for some time.

But just look at the diversity in the various streams of development among sentient beings . . . and in the relationships they cultivate with and between each other. None of it is ever the be-all and end-all in itself, is it? It never is. It always continues. It forever expands. Something is always leaking out and reintegrating somewhere into an unexpected form of energy or direction.

You humans have only been here a millisecond in time, remember?

Creation. Spirit. God stuff. Energy. Or the *Life Force.* Whatever you prefer to call it. It was all here well before you were. It was speaking and expanding through its creative activity for billions of years before you even began to emerge from the quantum soup.

As a matter of fact, there is really no known beginning, is there? Even that first big bang came out of something prior to it, didn't it? In space and in time. Or in something else—which even we have no words or understanding of . . . but which always was and always is and always will be.

And it continues with or without your willfully divided consent or awareness, even without your contrived physical castes and complexions and without your isolated and *disjoined* tribal egos.

Know this: There is no *better* in any superior sense among the created.

How can there be, when there is nothing which is separate from anything else? When you are all sons and daughters who've emerged and evolved from out of the womb of the same creative and parental *Source*?

Human beings do not outrank *Brother Sun* or *Sister Moon* . . . to steal a little metaphoric wisdom (and *agape* love) from the wise Saint

Francis of Assisi, who seemed to know firsthand that he was in every other beloved part of the cosmic wholeness, didn't he? Just as they were all in him. Even before he was ever born to the physical Earth.[4]

You are not more worthy of life than any *other* thing of *Creation*, whether formless or of form and whether empty or of fullness—especially than that of any *other* human being.

How can you be?

You are of, and for, and by all of them. And they are all of, and for, and by you.

Try not to forget that when you get to the other side—if you can.

There will be no returning without it.

CHAPTER 90

The Promise of Resurrection

OUR GRATEFUL AND respectful apologies go out to the wise Abraham Lincoln for appropriating his words and for allowing us to reconnect them into a much wider context than even he was trying to stretch his listeners into hearing from, before he was caused to vanish from the Earth, largely due to the progressive dark awakenings he reluctantly received—and from the hardened tribal views he was forced to struggle against because of them.[1]

He's just one example among many *others* of what an imperfect but courageous human being can do when presented with the grace of such a tragic gift, isn't he? Yet such a gift is rarely imparted, and only to the select few who are willing to accept the offering—and only when a deeper glimpse of the indivisible *Self* begins to unfold. Then it's gradually entrusted to the receiver of that glimpse-born vision, unfurled and thrust upon him or her with much more weight than the trustee of such an inheritance ever imagined carrying—a vision which may unravel faster than anything that the *only-mind* of any single tribe is ever fully prepared to deal with.

But there were other reluctant visionaries within that same time and space—even then, as there are now, and as there always have been and always will be.

The profoundly burdened Mr. Lincoln was quite fortunate to have other receptive prophets by his side and in his midst, wasn't he? Like the wise and resolute Frederick Douglass[2] who helped to push the effect of the American presidency forward and to challenge and expand its vision even further, from within that calamitous period which fell into the enigmatic hands of uncertain mercy and fate, and of cruel and fatal circumstance . . . where greatness, fear, and bravery burned together with volcanic urgency between two men of fire conjoined to the same anguished era, propelled into the midst of enormous grief and tragedy and of spiritual struggle, of physical turmoil, and hope-filled expectations, and of harrowing and heroic transformation . . . an age of frailty and imbalance, when the sensibilities of a nation took a great and palpable leap forward, stirred up by the Harriet Beecher Stowes[3] and the John Browns,[4] by the Harriet Tubmans[5] and the William Lloyd Garrisons,[6] by the Sojourner Truths[7] and the Walt Whitmans[8]—by a prophetic choir full of aroused *bodhisattvas*, rising up from the blood of the enslaved and polarized tribal consciousness, whose collective voice would not only begin to awaken so many of the slumbering in their midst but millions more who were not yet even born—it being just one of several laborious leaps across the bewildering human terrain, which forever unfold (by grace, love, and suffering), piercing through your arduous history whenever the accumulated energy of a necessary tipping point is conjointly reached by a group of tribal renunciants—or by two or more prayerful and poetic evolutionaries (despite all of your tribal casualties of overcontainment).

Nonetheless, there's always a sizable dying that welcomes each extension of the awakening process, isn't there? You have to let go in order to reach up or to reach out, yes?

But this shouldn't really be news to anyone, should it? Especially to anyone who has ever observed a growing child or to anyone who has done even a minimal amount of studying of the history of a living organism or of the planet . . . or of the surrounding universe, or to anyone who has gone through a significant or unexpected transitional experience of any kind, or to anyone who has ever accomplished a musical skill or learned a new language or traveled out of their own culture or comfort zone, or to anyone who has ever loved and then lost their passionate link to the intimate wholeness beheld in and with another being . . . human or *other*wise.

Even so, there's always a pull back that greets each extension, isn't there? There's always a counterreaction in protest of the anguish which accompanies the death or dying of any individual (or tribal) habit, attachment, or certitude.

It's to be expected.

Maturation always has its price, doesn't it?

There's always a death (or some type of loss) which accompanies each emerging differentiation. Yet when the loss is fought off too vigorously, the emergent begins to deform and to dissociate . . . to disunite instead of integrate, to fragment instead of harmonize—which is where so many of you are so often being pulled, aren't you? If you're not already there.

You've developed a strong strain of resistance, haven't you? Against being unified with any unfamiliar slice of *Creation* and even against any genuine unification with the familiar . . . or even into a relevant and merciful fusion within yourselves.

Each step in the awakening process is so often chaperoned by an equal force of tribal impedance or obstruction, isn't it?

It's that old, well-known fear of death . . . routinely shadowed by an unacknowledged fear of life.

But you no longer believe that you can fall off the edge of the planet, do you?

Grab on to that example and add it to your list of present-day beliefs or to your limited knowledge base . . . even to your restricted tribal memories and experiences, to your current scientific discoveries or to your cultural integrations, to your occasional spiritual eye-openers and to your technological advances, to your evolving social customs, to all of what you know, do, and comprehend—which has replaced so much of so many of the ancestral ways when it comes to how things were once perceived and thus understood, the ways that were informed by such a limited ground of knowledge and experience, and with such thin apprehension when compared to what informs you now.

Many of the old ways which have been transcended were once considered to be at the top of the tribal truth heap, weren't they?

Weren't they clung to at one time as if they were eternal? As if they were unshakable absolutes? And yet, now they're seen by a slow growing number of you as mere baby steps in the expanding human (and spiritual) journey, aren't they? In the ongoing evolution of the Homo sapien consciousness.

But try not to forget this: They were also quite necessary, weren't they? Those beginning baby steps?

Because if the baby doesn't get up and if it doesn't start to walk, then the adolescent (or even the adult) is stuck with laying down those same stumbling footprints years later, even decades or centuries later—which is what has happened to so many of you, and even to entire tribes, hasn't it? Particularly during the more immature stages of your spiritual development, where so many among you still cling (psychologically and emotionally) to frozen and fundamentalist beliefs and rituals which merely imitate and reinforce long-lost tribal superstitions and which lead so many of you to violently defend those apocalyptic desires.

What so often then culminates is the contraction of wisdom and of the spaciousness once generated from within the metaphoric myths from which they were originally derived, the very wisdom and spaciousness passed down to you (with an open hand) by the frequently forgotten prophets of the past . . . whose intentions were for you to keep opening yourselves up to however truth, goodness, and beauty may evolve.

And the more forgotten those prophets have become the more they've been fictionalized into becoming mere caricatures of themselves, through the recasting logic of the amnesiac *only-mind*, don't you see? Only to fit even tighter into the confinement of the tribal container, kidnapped . . . even to this day, fantasized to be holding and waving a hypnotic wand above your head . . . made from the same fabric of that same *disjoined* superstition, a superstition which was once fervidly devoted to by a much less consciously evolved and a much less intellectually enlightened group of ancestors—and which is now being used to hijack so many of your overpoliticized myths and religions, pushing its way to the forefront of your divisive and violent attacks against those all-too-familiar *others* . . . especially against those who refuse to comply with or devote themselves to such intolerant and infantile beliefs and practices.

Many of you not only reject but condemn the credibility and integrity of anyone who might take a minimal or even an exploratory step onto any unconventional or impartial spiritual path, especially once you've found a comfortable and secure spot for yourselves inside the isolated confinement of the tribal container . . . from which to dig into and defend, as if it were the very end of the human road, where any travel outside of that isolated cul-de-sac is prohibited by the authorities of contingent power and by the false truths which are spread and clung to by those who worship at the altar of the Tribe-Almighty—and upon its unforgiving judgments of *others*.

Each footstep forward takes death and rebirth, don't you see? It takes struggle then release in every way real or even imaginable. Yet each and every step along the way toward honest transcendence (toward genuine resurrection) always faces inner and outer opposition, doesn't it?

Just ask anyone who has ever lived and died for anything that matters. They'll tell you. Resurrection cannot be realized without death. Transcendence is unattainable without surrendering up the image of who you've forced yourselves to think you are—especially without being liberated from whom the tribe says you are.

Awakening is out of the question without removing the masks of convention.

Emergence into any newly integrated life is stifled and denied whenever you refuse to let go of the ancestral baton. It's actually impossible. Although so many of you like to think and act otherwise, don't you? Even while remaining trapped in a circular game of tribal charades.

Remember this: Without the death of stars (and dinosaurs) there would be no human beings.

Convergence, death, and resurrection. That is what tomorrow morning is all about. We're just trying to fast-track things a bit . . . with some heads-up preparatory work.

We're not attempting to convince you to chase after anything. It's being present to where you are that's most important, where the beginning of each next footprint in the evolutionary awakening process arises and leans forward from deep inside of each vast and expanding present moment.

You all have access to the whole radical realm you've been born into (or that you've grown into). Yet there are always other more expansive realities beyond and within the ones you're familiar with.

Aren't there?

And they're all accessible to you right from where you are. You don't have to go anywhere. You don't have to steal from anyone or destroy any part of the whole. You don't have to accumulate anything to prove that you exist. You don't have to go back in time or travel to the *other* side of the world. You don't have to wait for another change in your physical evolution. You don't have to grow or transform another body part or develop a larger brain. You don't have to wait for the perfect moment.

You just have to die.

And so you will, as you'll all be getting that brand new face of which we've been promising you—tomorrow morning, no matter what.

You will all be dying. We guarantee it.

And we're certain that it will drive home the point in a way that these late words may never do.

This is just the preparation. It's meant to assist you, to help lead you to your resurrection. Remember?

We hope it does you some good and maybe some justice as well.

CHAPTER 91

The Importance of Readiness

MANY OF YOU act quite surprised whenever you actually observe some previously hidden or unique quality revealed or demonstrated by one of your *other* than human Earthly cohorts, don't you? At least when you keep your eyes wide open and uncovered long enough in order to see what's right there and in front of you.

You've directly witnessed that at least some of your *other*-than-human kinfolk seem to be living right in the present moment, haven't you? Right there in the presence of *That which is always becoming.* You've seen it. You've seen a dog or a cat in full acceptance of who they are, in full concentrated action or attention.

Some of you have even entered into similar states of higher alertness yourselves, and for longer than a brief chemically induced few hours of window shopping, haven't you?

Some of you have practiced your way there, moving beyond temporary states of illusion or excitement and into direct contact with the larger *Life Force*—which includes all other co-inhabitants of the miraculous universe, of which you all share.

It can be done by each and every one of you—as a way. As a *Way of Being.*

You humans are the most singular of all species. You're not even obliged to leave your present physical structures in order to continue to evolve—or to even widen your limited perception.

Maybe that's what's been so confusing to so many of you. And maybe that's what's frozen so many of you into your destructive holding patterns of rigid beliefs and loyalties. Maybe you just can't accept your own unconfined actuality and its lack of restrictions.

A new face with new eyes may help. It may lead you away from holding on to self-defeating beliefs, or out of the constricting grasp of tribe-determined beliefs (and thoughts) period, and into the essential reality of direct life-and-death experience—not instead of thoughts and beliefs, but engaged with yet moving beyond them.

And if it does do that?

Then here's the way it works:

When you begin to explore the unrepressed and infinite depths of even one *wave* of development . . . you will then gradually begin to have access into the next one.

That's how it's done.

That's the way things have been moving ever since you broke through and arrived here as an incarnated and partially realized human being—following the second *big* (awakening) *bang*. And it all began even before you completely came into being who you think you are right now.

The infinite has no literal or imaginary boundary lines (or dividing walls) which separate itself from *Its-Self*. It's never an either/or (or this or that) chopped up or compartmentalized process of linear evolution. The *Great All* is forever *One*. It can't be anything else. Don't you see?

Or perhaps a better way of describing it is . . . as the *Great All in One*.

A true awakening *state* can open you up anywhere along the way, no matter where you are on any of the developmental paths which are entwined within the paradoxical human journey.

And it doesn't matter which path it is.

Each path is important. That's true. And moving yourselves up and through the expanding ladder of each significant artery and groove is essential. But it's not the same thing as waking up.

Yet the awakening *state* and the expanding *path* can work quite well together, can't they? As long as you don't confuse one for the other.

That's the great thing about this whole adventurous excursion. The more of the unifying *Self* that you become acquainted (and integrated) with, the more you tend to grow along the various spiritual channels and pathways. While at the same time you become even more susceptible to coming across aha moments of pure awareness by pure happenstance—through the unclouded and open avenues of an elastic synchronicity.

The chance of this type of coincidence of grace increases as your awareness of each moment deepens and expands, even though any one moment of grace or enlightened awareness has nothing much to do with anything you've actually done.

The paradox is quite stunning, isn't it? Even while there really are no self-sustaining coincidences. Because everything is interconnected and interdependent, remember?

Nonetheless, it's still vital that you persist in the practice of paying attention, while continuing to exercise creative self-discipline in multiple spheres of your life—in order for you to remain open (with a steady aim) toward moving up that dizzying staircase of self-conscious awareness.

As each sphere develops and strengthens it also tends to heighten, deepen, and expand other fields of creativity (and of parallel awareness).

It's not a certainty. But it helps.

If you practice living in the present moment, your concentration may improve. And if you practice daily concentrated meditation and regular physical exercise, it may help you to polish your skills with a musical instrument or to learn to stand up and speak out for the disadvantaged and the oppressed. Or it may help you to pay better attention to your personal finances or to what kind and amount of food you put into your mouth—or to how you treat *others*. It might even begin to clear your head of all those tired, compulsive, and repetitive ego-defending thoughts and arguments which dominate and control so much of your interior life.

Your compassion and loving-kindness for *others* and your overall sense of justice and fairness may begin to increase—even when considering your so-called enemies.

Your addictive behaviors may actually begin to diminish and dissipate.

You may smile more and sleep better.

You may begin to pray spontaneously without ever saying a word. Your body may simply and suddenly exude prayer out into the cosmic energy field. And then the prayers might pass themselves right back through you—even more powerfully then when they spilled themselves out.

But there's always the danger of ignoring or denying that you have a blind spot, isn't there? One which may have crawled into a crucial hidden corner of your life . . . one that somehow got under your imperfect radar, one that stubbornly refuses resurrection, refusing to allow itself to die—hiding itself in the tribal shadows of self-containment.

So you've got to stay vigilant. Do you understand?

Just look around at all the influential or charismatic gurus and priests and at the thought-to-be intelligent and ambitious political and business leaders, and at all the *other* so-called respectable and highly esteemed figures whom you've relinquished so much authority to. How many of them have violated their office of authority or neglected their own virtuous and exalted ethical codes? How many have ended up abusing followers (even children) while exploiting and deceiving so many *others* who've mindlessly yielded so much trust and allegiance to them, or who were overly infatuated by their charisma or by their elevated positions of power and prestige?

The shadow of death can be denied for only so long before it takes on a life of its own. And the greater the light it exudes, the more daring the shadow tends to be that projects itself on to the available or vulnerable *otherness*—which is another paradox, isn't it?

Try to remember that. Okay? Especially whenever you begin to actually believe your own self—(or tribe-) adulating fan mail.

A good activity to begin to practice at the beginning of each day (when you get to the *other* side) is to make sure that you catch a glimpse of your actual physical shadow each morning, even if it's only by waving your hand in front of a lightbulb to make dancing shadow-play figures on a basement wall.

It's a healthy and harmless reminder. Yet it may help to prevent you from blinding yourselves by exaggerating your own light or from trying to convince yourselves that light is all that you consist of (big, bright, and shadowless light), and that it will last forever—that it will never die out.

There's nothing the *disjoined* ego would like better, is there?

Yet having said all that, none of what you can do in the way of practice has any direct cause-and-effect connection to waking up.

You will wake up when you're ready to wake up. And that's that.

That which is the *Self* is always there and always awake. So wakefulness is always present. It's always available. It's never *not* here. And neither are you. So waking up just might be a matter of realizing that you're already awake.

Wouldn't that be interesting?

The distinctions reveal themselves through whichever dominant level of self-reflective awareness you're inhabiting at the time of a realized moment of awakening—however long that moment lasts.

If you awaken while mostly residing at a lower level of self-reflective awareness, then you'll be confined to the limitations of that lower level . . . to the range and field of its depth of perception, to the internalized parameters and mythologies of whatever dominant cultural influence you've absorbed and accepted, to what it represents—to what is most comfortably comprehensible to you.

So if you happen to wake up while you're still heavily attached to your tribal belief systems, then your enlightened state will only be lit by the available candlelight from within that level of spiritual intelligence and awareness (or lack thereof).

A barely awakened mind may be able to easily rationalize as normal (and without question) that certain *others* may be owned as property—as slaves, as disposable objects to be treated however you wish, for one's own pleasure and profit.

A bit higher but still a low level of awakening may tell you that slavery is sometimes justifiable . . . but only as an economically necessary evil or (as strange as this may sound to many of you) as part of God's will and design, as it actually had been irrationally justified (and not all that long ago) by many of your tribal ancestors, by your most dominant ancestral religious configurations, and by many of the most acclaimed so-called moral philosophers of the given time period.

A midlevel of awakening may lead you to condemn the expansion of slavery and to protest the mistreatment of current slaves, but not to question the actual institutions which profit from their bondage . . . and hence not to question the actual institution and system of slavery itself or the current status of current slaves as still being slaves—and never to question the most powerful and rich slave owners themselves, whose calculating ambition in the trade and subjugation of human beings routinely generates financial opportunities for many of the less savvy but thoroughly conditioned loyalists of the tribe . . . blood-drenched opportunities, hoisted upon the bruised and scarred backs of the enslaved who've become the principal material resource which propels the tribal economy forward.

A higher level of awakening may tell you to privately (and to sometimes publicly) protest all institutions and systems which have anything to do with enabling slavery at all—as being morally wrong.

And an even higher level of awakening may break you wide open to the eternal and ethical truth of the matter. It may drive you to do whatever you can (even to risk your own physical life) to free all slaves, to destroy all institutions and systems of slavery, to acknowledge that if anyone is held as a slave (or if anyone is even held in a lower view among the created) then everyone is held as a slave, that *All are in the Oneness* together, that all are equal in the eyes and heart of God—and that there are no exceptions to that truth.

A lower level of awakening may lead you to have an overly contained understanding of what God actually is, as something concrete (even material) . . . with only one allowable, given, and specific tribal name, who is somehow completely separate from who you are and who has the power and the need to interfere . . . to save or destroy, and whom you must fear and seek approval from in order to be rescued from eternal destruction.

A higher level of awakening may lead you to *That which is your true unifying Self* . . . where nothing and no one is separate and where everyone (human and *other* than human) is neither saved nor doomed to be destroyed, but instead are always eternally embraced and forever loved by the indivisible God that lives and breathes in the *Ground of All Being*.

So pounding a nail can become a moment of pure bliss. Don't you see? Washing dishes can be an entrance through the gates of heaven. Making love can melt you into the boundless ocean of the *Divine*. A lucid dream can transport you into a miraculous universe of untold awareness which you can visit and move about in at will.

Watching yourself breathe can so open up your heart that you can love without needing any specific object to love. Breathing (itself) becomes loving.

But you don't have to take our word for any of this. And we know that most of you won't. So beginning tomorrow morning the new faces will take their shot at it.

Remember: You are latecomers to all of this.

And you're only able to be here, wearing those clothes, because you were given the gift of birth (through death and resurrection) by all of *That which is becoming* . . . which always was and always will be, by the eternal, unifying, and compassionate *Self* which includes the entire infinite cosmos, together with every cosmic particle and every speck of paradoxical dust—excluding no one and nothing, neither human nor *other* than human.

Repetitio mater studiorum est (Repetition is the mother of all learning) . . . wrote the wise Thomas Aquinas.[1]
Repetitio mater studiorum est.

Repetitio mater studiorum est.

Repetitio mater studiorum est.

CHAPTER 92

Almost There

MANY OF YOU still insist on inhabiting only what you consider to be your preassigned tribal slot, don't you? Seldom (if ever) allowing yourselves to enjoy even a partial pull into *other* realities or perspectives.

While many among the *others* who usually dwell on the fringe of most tribal norms can (and often do) consciously access and appreciate an awareness which extends well beyond the restrictions of most tribal logic.

Even so, some of you (among the invited) have on exceptional occasion accidentally slipped and fell into a beginning glimpse of nontribal reality yourselves, haven't you? It's been rare. But it's happened. Although usually you've been quick to discount, reject, or sever yourselves from the occurrence—often quicker than it took the sudden uncharacteristic slipup to surprise you itself.

In the meantime, most of your *other*-than-human family members have made no entry at all into the tribal ways of the so-called human being—unless they've been forced into it (by humans, of course).

A dog doesn't ridicule an *other*. A tree doesn't torture an *other*. A river doesn't go to war with an *other*. A bullfrog doesn't starve an *other*. An eagle doesn't gossip about or impose its views on an *other*. A horse doesn't reject or dismiss an *other's* understanding of God. A dolphin doesn't exterminate an *other*. A wolf doesn't hunt an *other* for the mere sport of it. A mountain doesn't rape an *other*. The soil doesn't intentionally pollute an *other*. A rock doesn't lie to or about any *others*. A cloud doesn't target or drop vindictive bombs on an *other*. An ocean doesn't hoard from an *other*. A flower doesn't kidnap and traffic in *others*. A field of wheat doesn't envy or steal from *others*. A thorn doesn't demonstrate any pride-filled pleasure in the downfall or suffering of *others*. A chicken doesn't put *others* in cages. Even a weed doesn't exploit or condescend to *others*.

Meanwhile, most of you among the invited keep yourselves purposely wedged in at a safe tribal distance from any nearby gate which could open and then lead you into the next wave of your own evolutionary impulse, don't you?

Many of those who occupy that seeing fringe (whom you may not even recognize) have grown into and become accustomed to inhabiting a much more relaxed altitude than you find yourselves breathing at. They sustain and revitalize themselves through an impartial candor and openness, having passed through many gates which you seem to be unwilling to allow yourselves to fathom, let alone pass through and experience.

And for most of them . . . there's no turning back.

Yet they (like you) can still backslide . . . as we've already documented. Even so, they can't return to clinging to what they've already allowed themselves to let go of. They can only proceed on the path of further unknowing. Although they can rest at any time or even stop for a while. But they just can't go back to relying upon any knowledge or experience which they've already transcended. And neither can you—no matter how hard you try or how much you imagine that you already have. That part of the path has disappeared from *That which is always becoming.*

And it's actually less confusing than it seems.

Think of a dog's nose (not to mention its loyalty); the radar of a dolphin or the spider's spinning of a web; the migratory flight of birds . . . or of Monarch butterflies; how about the depth of emotion of elephants or the reproduction of an apple tree; the miracle of a salmon run or the stride of a galloping horse; the strength of a mountain or the spring and beauty of a deer on the run; the cleansing rush and energy of a waterfall or the enigmatic power of thunder and lightning; the hibernation of a bear or the mystery of a sunset; the ghostliness of an early-morning fog or icicle covered trees in a frozen forest; a sudden cloudburst of rain, hail, or snow; a tornado or a hurricane; a rainbow; a billion newly discovered galaxies; or the light still shining down to Earth from a star that died a thousand years ago; the self-reflective awareness of a single human being or the collective unconscious awareness hidden in all of humanity, in all of *Creation.* (There should be no surprises here . . . even though it may feel surprising).

But it's still . . . only and always partial, isn't it?

A dog can smell mightily. But it doesn't *think* about it. No dog is self-aware of its own nose power. It just uses it. It's instinctual. That's the partial piece that you humans have transcended but have also lost.

You're aware that you're listening to these words right now, aren't you? And it's a conscious awareness. It's not an instinct. But you have to pay attention to be consciously aware, don't you? Or if not, then you're not even able to skillfully eavesdrop. You'll drift off into monkey mind instead. And so many of you still revert into allowing yourselves to become just such creatures of unconscious conditioned habit, don't you? Instead of creatures of awakened mindfulness—which is your unique gift waiting to be received, moment to moment.

Breathing in, I calm body and mind. Breathing out, I smile. Dwelling in the present moment I know this is the only moment, repeats the wise Thich Nhat Hanh.

You're uplifted in your wholeness through a simple transaction—by that of breathing; by a gentle gust of air which nourishes and sustains life through an unspoken understanding; through an interweaving of complexities; by way of atoms, cells, and molecules; by a cosmic interconnection between all that *is*; through an exchange of divine and mysterious gifts; between the inner and the outer; between the human and the *other* than human; between the animate and the inanimate; between all that exists—between *others* that are not and never have been *others*.

And it all waits for you on the *other* side . . . seen from within the quick peeks which you are allowed, into the *something more* of who you are—through the invitations to become. And it's always there, reflected back to you from the *otherness* which is not an *otherness*—from the *other* side which is not an *other* side.

An interactive field of universal love and intelligence bursts with activity—each face disappearing into the faceless sea of the *Infinite*.

And it's all so immeasurable, isn't it? Yet so liberating when it flows into *That which is the oceanic Self*.

But so many of you still remain blamelessly ignorant or in firm denial of your own immense spaciousness . . . of your own original face as it awaits patiently for you to release yourself, and then to enter into that eternal space of *now*—once and for all.

Instead, you've spent much of your time on the planet trying to cut up and nail down your own overly contained version of what is good, of what is true, and even of what is beautiful.

You deny the vastness and depth of your shared reality by trying to bottle it up and by trying to force it into the overcrowded container of one single tribal perception—which is understandable. Isn't it?

But it's also heart blind and fear driven. And it's led you to all of that endless fighting (and physical and spiritual dying) over whose bottle is the most pure or the most holy one to drink from.

We suppose, however, that you could have chosen to resist your own evolutionary pull. But you didn't. Did you?

And that was a long time ago.

So it's a little too late now to reject your own self-reflective abilities at this aging stage in the cosmic scheme of things, yes?

Once you've become self-consciously aware you're always self-consciously aware . . . barring a serious head injury, of course, or a serious denial of your own cognizance—which is what has led so many of you to your own current state of *disjoined* tribal stuckness, hasn't it?

But those among you who have lost their self-reflective powers due to physical injury or disease are exempt from the new rule.

And they can thank God (by whatever name) for that.

And you're almost there now.

We hope you're ready.

CHAPTER 93

What Will It Be?

S O HERE WE are.

You now have this new opportunity facing you by way of the new rule—of the new and fast-approaching universal face exchange.

And just what are you going to do with it?

The time to choose has just about run out of itself.

So what will it be?

It's your choice.

Just like it's always been.

CHAPTER 94

A Stumbling Response

YOU ALREADY KNOW that suffering exists, don't you? Everybody does.

Every human being who has ever been born into the light of self-conscious awareness has intimately experienced and has come to know that suffering is an ever-present reality in every aspect of their lives—ever since that very first explosive emergence into human consciousness.

There have been no exceptions.

You came forth from the prehuman world of unconscious instincts and of unsuspecting innocence . . . to enter into a miraculous new universe, into a strangely sophisticated and even frightening existence where you suddenly became aware of yourselves for the very first time—in all of your imperfect and vulnerable perfection.

And not only could you still feel the agony of physical suffering whenever it cut through to your fleshly senses, but you suddenly found yourselves trying to anticipate its advent, didn't you? You came to expect it . . . to reluctantly predict it, and even to wildly imagine it. You came to fear and to thus exaggerate its coming arrival based on enough experiences of being caught off guard by the likes of a tragic accident, the onset of a serious illness, a major disappointment, a surprise attack by a stranger or an acquaintance—or by the sudden death of a loved one.

You came to sense that suffering was somehow ever present, that its haunting yet strangely valuable whereabouts was always just a second or an inch or merely a deceptive smile away from you. It was just a matter of when or how often you would bump into it by fate, habit, or innocence.

You could feel yourself becoming more hypervigilant to things that you once gave no thought to at all. You came to sense that you had less and less influence over more and more of the events, situations, and circumstances that came to restrict or define your life. It seemed that the more self-reflective you became, the more you sensed that you were losing control of things, didn't it?

Suffering on the physical plane was bad enough when it was the only kind you had ever experienced. But now it had entered into the psychological, emotional, and spiritual realm. Suffering had suddenly been humanized. And regrettably, more and more of you over time turned to the *only-mind* of the tribe to try to numb you out of your fears. And many of you seem to think that it's just what the doctor ordered, don't you?

You were abruptly thrown from the protection and innocence of the metaphoric Garden of Eden.[1] You were expelled, banished, and sent out to be reborn into a self-conscious and unsettling world which was suddenly inhabited by a newly awakened and wandering exile (meaning you)—into a vast yet volatile complexity of awareness. Into a second big cosmic bang . . . preceded along the evolutionary spiral by millions of smaller awakening explosions, stretching or slam banging themselves out into the realm of overflowing self-reflection, emerging just as powerfully and just as full of intensifying uncertainties as the first big cosmic bang.[2]

And just like the surrounding physical universe which continues to spread out from the force of that first *Great Radiance*, as the wise Philemon Sturges renamed it,[3] the awakening of awareness has no defined limits. It has no boundaries to restrict its ever-reaching cosmic arms.

But somewhere along that elaborate and spiraling energy wave, evolving out of that second *Radiant Awakening Bang*, the wise Buddha made a simple yet profound observation, didn't he?

He observed that the existence of suffering is a Noble Truth—which seems quite curious to most of you who try to hide or run away from it, doesn't it?

But then he also pointed to a simple way to get beyond it. And we are (now) simply building upon that promise.

So this is your chance to enter and move into that paradoxical place beyond yet into suffering—beyond the numbing effects of the *only-mind*. It's your chance to invest in the noble activity of letting go . . . and to begin to practice the *bodhisattva* craft, to enter the narrow field of self-detachment and of self-giving where the very few among you (who we've so often mentioned) continue to evolve in that difficult and deep tradition and discipline.

MICHAEL J. GAJDA

But first you must admit and realize your tribal fixations and repulsions, in order to even begin to unmask them.

Remember this: Repulsion is often the deceptive twin of attachment, isn't it?

But how can you let go of something if you deny that you ever picked it up?

You can't, can you?

And you've already walked that path of denial long (and often) enough, haven't you?

Although you've also strode along another path—the one of actually *not* picking up what is yours to behold.

Now you'll have an opportunity to traverse a much nobler way, one which has rarely been taken seriously by anyone in your either/or tribal universe and which straddles both of those worn out, confusing, and conventional paths while preventing you from falling back into either of them—which has been the opportunity you've had all along.

Hopefully this practice in the shedding of masks and in the wearing of an *other's* face (or of many *other* faces) will help you to get to the place along the cosmic track which you've ignored for so long in your existent facial life (which is the place of no-face)—being forever empty and forever full (forever refilling *It-Self* with its ever-expanding and ever-fulfilling emptiness), revealing the paradoxical face of the *Self* which is beyond all relative knowledge and understanding.

Have we mentioned that enough yet?

So much paradox. And so many tribal clichés to ponder. Yet so little time, eh?

But not really. You see, you've got all the time in the world. And for many of you . . . well . . . you've actually got all the time contained in multiple worlds . . . or in a multiplicity of faces.

But by the way, do you really think that something is less true because it's become a cliché?

Think again. But try not to think in too many catchy tribal sayings—if you can.

The actual process of becoming a hackneyed phrase is quite on purpose in the human psyche. Although it doesn't completely understand that yet. Which means most of you don't completely understand that yet.

If something becomes so true that it hurts, then reducing it into a buzzword appears to disempower it, doesn't it?

But that's just another illusion. Don't you see?

It merely moves it to remanifest itself into yet another form somewhere else while trying to dodge the bullets of addiction (to either power and control, to approval and esteem, to security and certainty, or even to mere physical survival)—which so many of you believe will eventually solve all of your problems. But they don't. And they won't. And neither will your clichés . . . or your lack of them.

So anytime you see or hear a tribal catchword from now on . . . just try to remember that it's simply a stumbling response to too much truth. It's neither good nor evil nor profound, nor unimportant nor shallow nor deep—nor memorable nor forgettable.

It's just trying to listen to the truth in a lighter weight form because it came out too heavy for the handling—too weighty for the listening audience.

Unfortunately, sometimes it misses the mark . . . or its original responsive meaning gets lost in the impermanence of time.

But that's a whole other subject, isn't it?

Maybe not.

But let's move on anyway.

Shall we?

CHAPTER 95

The Noble Way

THE GOOD THING is that you still get to apply the previous rule, if you so choose . . . the Golden one which we've already referred to, the one that the wise Jeshua made famous. You get another crack at it. It hasn't disappeared. It will still be waiting for you on the other side of this announcement.

Now that is *good news*, isn't it?

And if you felt like his version of the Golden Rule was tough enough or too radical and impractical to handle in the so-called *real* world (of the *disjoined* tribal *only-mind*), then just take a contemplative look at the words of quixotic wisdom which he famously preached on that mythological hillside all those centuries ago—which many of his most professed followers even today seldom (if ever) quote from directly or even indirectly refer to, let alone encourage the serious practice of.

Those words still seem to expect too much for too little in return for most of them—and for most of you among the invited, don't they? In order to inspire you enough to intentionally pattern your lives after them with much honest effort or intent.

They don't quite fit into the theological models which praise and encourage the achievement of material success, do they? Or of achieving religious or personal prestige or tribal superiority—or of following narrow rules of tribal belonging. There isn't anything in those words to inspire anyone to attain power over *others* or about trying to convince or force *others* to accept a certain belief system or of justifying violence of any kind—or of trying to be a resolute and steadfast believer now so you can enter a magical kingdom later on.

It's quite the opposite of all of that, isn't it?

His words point to the practice of living and dying inside the present moment, where the kingdom of *That which is always becoming* is always available in the *Eternal* (and expanding) *Now*. They don't aim you toward a collection of rules to follow or to attaching yourselves to a system of mental belief in order to prepare for a later reward. They don't even pretend to tease anyone to go in that direction. He never tried to bribe or browbeat anyone to do anything, did he? As a matter of fact, he often strongly criticized those who mouthed formulaic tribal beliefs or who tried to walk and talk perfectly by using proper (tribal) rituals and words—especially when they blatantly failed to attempt to live out of the higher principles of unconditional and uncontainable love, faith, compassion, and humility.

Although a certain amount of belief is sometimes necessary, isn't it? In order to advance any worthwhile practice. And if you claim to be one of his followers, then it seems to us that you would be making that quite evident by following the way of seeing and doing things that he regularly demonstrated—which was how the first group of followers of the wise Nazarene were described by others, and by themselves.

As followers of the *Way*.

But just go ahead and try to follow that particular *Way* for a while . . . and see what happens.

Just try practicing being poor in spirit for a while . . . or being intentionally poor at all. Or try being gentle with everyone (human or *other* than human) while hungering and struggling for justice. Or try showing mercy to *others* (human or *other* than human) while keeping your hearts clean. Or try striving to work for peace . . . without the use of violence. Or try responding with loving words and actions toward those of whom you feel no love for at all, and who don't love you . . . including your so-called enemies. Or try refusing to swear an oath of loyalty to anyone especially to any national, corporate, or tribal entity . . . including religious entities. Or try never staying angry with *others* and never vilifying them or never objectifying anyone no matter what . . . while praying for those who hurt you or for those who are different from you, while refusing to ever let anyone see you pray or even to know that you do or do not pray. Or try refusing to let anyone see you do any act of charity or of fasting or even to know that you have . . . while forgiving everyone (no matter what) and never retaliating for any wrong done against you, while living intentionally and simply, storing up nothing that you can't let go of at a moment's notice and never worrying about where you'll live or how you'll pay the bills or where you'll get your next meal or even where you'll get your clothes. And try never worrying or acting anxious about anything for that matter . . . not even about your own physical survival or death . . . while never judging anyone's personhood, but being honest and critical about actions, including your

MICHAEL J. GAJDA

own—while being self-forgiving, and always demonstrating faith and trust in *That which is beyond all understanding* (no matter what), while seeking guidance from that faith, always treating others how you would want them to treat you—even as if they are you. Or try being able to detach yourselves from any circumstance, situation, or outcome . . . whether pleasurable or painful. And try never surrendering to any addiction (or to any idolization) of tribal ways or to tribal symbols or to any individual from any tribe, no matter what their tribal ranking is and no matter what the consequences.

Try any of that for a good while and see what kind of response you get from your fellow human beings . . . especially from those who consider you as part of their tribe, and especially from many of those who claim to worship the man who preached and lived that *Way* of doing and of being, and who instructed his followers to do the same, and who told them that they would do *even greater things* than he did, who never put himself on any pedestal above anyone else . . . who did just the opposite, who came down from the mountain and lived and breathed by example at ground level, in the mud of everyday life alongside everyone else, getting his hands and his feet dirty—demonstrating what he meant by how he lived.

Watch this, he would say. *Now . . . you do the same. Only improve upon it. You have in you exactly what I have in me. We are one. All of us. We all come from the same Parental Source. From the same Father of joy and protection. From the same Mother of guidance and peace.*

Trying to hoist him up onto a tribal throne (which he regularly shunned), while separating and elevating him above the rest of you, has perhaps been the most disrespectful and falsifying disservice that's been done to his central message, hasn't it? To the message that he emphasized by the way he lived and died—and for what he was eventually murdered for.

But can you even start to see why so many of you would rather make the much easier choice, of stressing the elevation and the worship of the man, instead of trying to better follow in his footsteps, instead of walking beside him—instead of practicing the *Way?*

He's left behind some pretty big and difficult shoes to fill, hasn't he?

And that does seem to be what he's calling *others* to do, doesn't it? To do the walk . . . not so much the talk. To try to walk like he walked . . . but even to journey well beyond how far he was able to take things. To do what he did and expand upon it instead of spending so much of your time trying to clean up the man's sandals . . . to make them sparkle and shine and to praise them as footwear which only he is able to slide his feet into, as if his most important accomplishment while on Earth was that of being an awe-inspiring and otherworldly magician . . . a miracle man who did tricks in order to mesmerize and to show off his power and then to have a religion named after him which worshipers could then claim to be the one-and-only true religion for which they could frequently judge, proudly condemn, and even piously imprison or execute *others*, or even to make murderous war against them in defense of its superior status and name. None of which can be found in any part of the message of the *Way*—and which this Son of *That which is in and of everything*, and this Brother of *All*, never encouraged or taught anyone to do. Did he?

You can bet that the rest of *Creation* might be quite appreciative if and when you start to take even a few small steps in his actual direction, along that most difficult of paths, as you slip your own clumsy feet into that spacious footwear and start to actually imitate the *Way* he walked.

But somehow, despite all of your other great advancements, this is the practice field where you humans so often seem to break down or to function at an almost unevolved level of participation, isn't it? It's on this field where every other sphere of your momentary (and relative) existence and all of your interactions with *others* is most affected, yes?

It's on the field of your everyday lives.

And while you're at it . . . if you feel like really testing yourselves, when you get to the *other* side, while you're out there exploring more care-filled and profound ways to walk, you might want to try experimenting with the Buddha's *Noble Eightfold Path* too,[1] in the same way you might try to explore the *Beatitudinal Path* of Jesus.[2] The difficult but doable way of travel, which both of these sages insist upon, may differ somewhat from each other. But they also intersect and fit quite well together.

But (similar to the *Way* of the Nazarene) just watch what kind of reaction you get when you begin to practice the *Way* of Siddartha, of understanding the nature of things just as they are (for instance) without delusion or distortion of any kind, or of keeping your thoughts in harmony with the rest of creation and with the way things actually are (not how you wish them to be, nor how your tribe wants you to see things); or of only speaking truthfully . . . yet without harm toward anyone (human or *other* than human); of acting ethically, honorably, and responsibly at all times with no excuse at all for doing otherwise; of earning your living only through life-affirming ways without deceit or dishonesty . . . and without exception; of demonstrating continuous effort to strengthen your mind and heart and to restrain negative feelings, thoughts . . . and other unwholesome states of mind from arising; or of being fully mindful and aware of all of your bodily actions, sensations, and feelings and of the activity of your thoughts at all times; and of keeping your mind one pointed in its concentration in whatever you do; and of being exactly where you are—not where you desire to be or where you imagine you should be.

Practicing these two demanding-yet-noble and beautiful paths of discipline may speed up the process of returning. It may even help in the transformation of your face. It may expand your consciousness. And it may increase your compassion for others. It may even wake you up enough and infuse you with enough clarity to be able to overcome obstacles which you thought were impossible to surmount. Who really knows?

But it won't make the transformation or the waking up any easier. Real transformation is never easy. And waking up is by invitational readiness only, from the welcoming and persuasive inner voice (and grace) of God, who namelessly abides in the infinite and inexhaustible *Self*—which includes everyone and everything, human and *other* than human.

That's the truism that so many of you have tried to escape (and cover up) for so long. And it's what the great prophets, sages, scientists, and saints have pointed to even longer through the way they lived, the way they died, and the way they walked a path for you to follow . . . a path for you to practice living and to practice dying to—not just to talk about it, but to walk it, with no predetermined expectations of your own.

If you die before you die then when you die you will not die, affirms the wise Buddhist proverb.

But so many of you want your transformation the fast-food way, don't you? You want wake up on a stick, with rewards for tribe-approved good behavior and only for yourselves . . . or maybe for your self-selected, so-called chosen group of true believers, applied with all of the easy excesses and with all of the obese benefits—but with none of the difficult sweat or stretch which the sharing of courageous humility requires.

You'd rather sit inside of a loud tribal echo chamber, lined with cushy seats and with a list of inhibitory rules and beliefs to dress up in, for *others* to see . . . but not with any of the dull and hard facts or the necessary daily practice and discipline which leads to more freedom, not less—and for all, not just for yourselves.

But when you pray, go to your private room and, when you shut the door, (then) *pray,* said the wise Jesus.[3]

Did you ever wonder what *private room* he was talking about, since most of the houses (of those who were listening to him at the time) had no private rooms?

Could it be the private room of the inmost and spacious *Self?* The private room of the universal and embracing heart?

CHAPTER 96

The Unchosen

HAVE YOU EVER considered how many different tribes there are that announce themselves to be uniquely *chosen*, and set apart (or something comparably unique and separate) from *other* tribes?

It seems to be a pretty fashionable thing for you humans to do, doesn't it? Especially if it helps you to justify some stealing, invading, demonizing, or destruction of some kind.

And there always seems to be plenty of those unchosen (and disposable) *others* around, doesn't there? To teach another violent lesson to and to protect and defend yourselves against—even if your defense is usually offensive in nature.

But here's some historical news for you to chew on.

There really isn't any such communal creature as a uniquely chosen (or unchosen) tribe of human beings to turn into or against. If you're a human being (if you're a member of the human family), then you're automatically chosen just by being one, no matter how you might want to explain that it happened—and no matter what tribe you currently overidentify with.

You already exist—all of you. So you've *all* been chosen. Haven't you? And if you've all been chosen . . . then (paradoxically) none of you have been chosen.

And it's quite possible that many of you may not really want genuine transformation after all. Isn't it? Because it always includes the goal of bringing back as many of the *others* along with you that you can, and never by force or indoctrination, but by the transmission of loving-kindness and with compassion—by loving them as if they're actually you.

But if you don't work for a change of face, if you don't practice being ready, then you probably shouldn't expect much in the way of waking up, should you? Even if you really are human. Even if you really are who you think and say you are. Even if you are among the (unchosen) chosen ones.

CHAPTER 97

The Theory of the One-and-Only Rule

B UT ONE THING at a time.
The new rule does not trump the old rule. It's just an additional way to approach this thing.

You all get to try again (to reexplore) . . . but just from a different perspective. From a new expression . . . or from many different perspectives and expressions. Through the lives and faces of *others*. And for some of you . . . through many *others*. But now with two rules—instead of just the one.

As a matter of fact, you're not even limited to the two rules which we've discussed.

How good is that?

You might even become so brazen, from the pure shock of newly formed facial recognitions, as to try to bring a whole slew of *others* back with you (through your example and effort) as you make your way back. Not just a few. But a whole slew!

Imagine that.

It's quite doable, you know. But only if and when you begin to take advantage of the forest of underused rules which are hidden in plain view all around you and which aren't actually rules at all—as you've previously perceived them to be. Yet they're still available if you choose to see them and if you choose to benefit from their availability and usefulness.

The door leading into the unmasking arena just seems to keep opening up wider for you, doesn't it?

Options ahoy are crawling out of the woodwork from everywhere— like starving tribal ants.

But just try to recall how so many of you have limited yourselves to only one rule to follow for so long, the rule which you so often claim to be the one-and-only true rule of the tribe, so often and only followed and adhered to through your *disjoined* thoughts and words—and by your knee-jerk rejection of *otherness*.

It's the antirule. The rule of *against*. And you're all quite familiar with its characteristics. Aren't you?

So many of your predictable tribal rules flesh themselves out that way, don't they? No matter how they're handed down—whether in spoken language or in written words.

And they're most easily identified not by how they demonstrate a striving *for* something, but by demonstrating a clear, rigid, and automatic *againstness* (which we've earlier discussed and emphasized), while still remaining the one-and-only, true-blue rule of your select tribal following—which, as you know, so many of you remain willing to kill and die for, as we've plainly laid out for you with our list of undeniable examples (in order to debunk your irrational tribal logic), and of which you've been more than willing to have your less fortunate stand-ins kill and die for you in your place, over and over again, haven't you? In your dogged defense of tribal logic.

Of course most of your one-and-only rules have many subsections and subtexts . . . and laws, rituals, and rule variations, don't they? To reinforce the actual following of the one-and-only rule of the tribe—to make sure that it's being deliberately and properly followed.

But then there's always those of you who've tried to falsely distinguish yourselves from the rest of the pack, isn't there? By cradling yourselves in the no-rules-at-all shtick—which has been *your* cellophane way of trying to masquerade yourselves, to try to hide the fact that you actually do follow your own one-and-only formula of *againstness* (which you too have been willing to kill and die for).

It's the same old *disjoined* tribal logic but which clumsily pretends to be different and distinct.

Hopefully, when you take a good look at it all, you'll begin to see what a waste of time and aliveness much of this playacting has been.

But if you don't get it now . . . well . . . then maybe soon enough on the other side.

But let's move on, shall we? It's getting late.

And we do want to complete our introduction before the lights grow too dim and then eventually go out.

You'll all be needing a good night's sleep in order to come out of those starting gates tomorrow morning with your eyes wide open and with your wings spread and rested—and ready to fly.

Wouldn't you agree?

CHAPTER 98

Name Your Pleasure

S O.
    Our announcement is gradually coming to a close.

You will all be losing your face tomorrow morning—the one you've been trying so hard to save for so long.

We hope that simple fact has settled in by now . . . whether you like it or not. Because, as you already know, acceptance is always the first, the most essential, and often the most difficult step to take along any path which can lead you to any lasting, actual, or transcendent return to who you really are, isn't it?

We admitted we were powerless over alcohol—that our lives had become unmanageable, states the first step of acceptance in the spiritually wise Twelve-Step Program of Alcoholics Anonymous.[1]

Most of you could substitute your own containing word for *alcohol*, couldn't you? And then you would feel a similar kind of anxious or compulsive desire rising up to the surface of your own skin.

The reality within can never be completely hidden from the heart and soul of the spacious *Self*, can it? Not unless you're wearing the mask of a totally dissociated psychopath.

But then if you are . . . well . . . then you'll be doing some extra heavy lifting tomorrow morning in order to turn your particular boat around, won't you? Once you splash yourselves headfirst into those uncharted waters of facial exploration.

The heart and soul (the spirit-body-mind) of everyone will eventually come to know that *That which is always becoming* excludes no one and nothing. That's indisputable.

How that knowledge will come to light will just depend upon your specifically denied addiction. Don't you see? And how deeply you've buried it.

Just try plugging in any one of the following words (which represent what many of you feel powerless over) into that first step, and see what lights up with discomforting desire or with obsessed attachment in your *disjoined* tribal veins and arteries.

Work, religion, food, belief, greed, intimacy, *fear* of intimacy, owning, power, hoarding, busyness, sex, entertainment, status, television, tradition, computer use, hurry, cynicism, rebellion, socializing, obedience, conformity, aggression, submission, phone use, texting, isolation, violence, fame, shopping, noise, guilt, routine, being right, cleanliness, order, risk taking, excitement, the past, the future, cigarettes, lying, jealousy, possessiveness, attention seeking, staying physically young, hatred, worry, nonstop talking, gossip, clothes, shoes, property, narcotics, pornography, travel, *fear* of socializing, security, apathy, activism, recognition, distraction, disorder, vindictiveness, appeasement, tribal overidentification . . . etc., etc., etc.

Or just pick a word of your own choice—one that's not already on the list. You've all got at least one or more that could easily fit for you personally. You all know that. But that first step of acceptance is always so difficult to take, isn't it?

You can just feel the resistance tightening around your bones, can't you? Which partially explains why so many of you try to cope with so much of it from inside and behind the secret lives which you hide yourselves—even while aching to unlock and let go of the camouflaged addictions that have come to have so much power over you.

But you'll soon have your chance (to begin) to let it all go, in just a few more hours from right now and as soon as you open up your eyes tomorrow morning—even while the same opportunity has been there all along, hasn't it?

And there will be no bargains made in advance of (or during) this unusual facial transaction. Are we all clear on that? It's the only way to save whatever face you've got left to unmask. But you already know that too. Which (again) is just the opposite way most of you among the invited have been viewing it (and playing it) up to now, isn't it?

You've all worked very hard at saving the *tribal* face. Haven't you? And in the process you've been slowly losing track of your *original* face (which is faceless) . . . behind the masks covering your *individual* face.

But tomorrow morning, you'll be losing all of that window dressing in order to begin to save what's behind that spacious window, to begin the return trip back to that original face—which (we repeat) is forever faceless.

As you already know.

CHAPTER 99

The Field of *You*

THERE'S ONE HUGE (and invisible) playground of awareness which surrounds and embraces all of you. Don't you see? An unfolding cosmic playing field quietly hidden within an expanding universe, a centralizing force which somehow links and holds all of your various facial inclinations together in one infinite rhythmic pattern of interweaving energy, reinforcing memory and behavior, while reinvesting in itself through the unifying discretion of a morphic resonance—a resonance which flows out and beyond yet includes all of you (to loosely borrow from the theory and observations of the wise Rupert Sheldrake).[1]

It's been utterly eye popping to observe how so many of you tend to replicate certain specific patterns of behavior once they've first been displayed by maybe only one small handful of human beings from way over on the *other* side of the planet—or even from right next door, but unbeknown to you.

Once a new behavior is practiced and expanded upon (anywhere in the boundless cosmos), a spreading wave of replication is soon set into motion.

Somehow it weaves its way throughout the vibrational field which envelops and absorbs your entire little planet, allowing *others* to unconsciously plug right into it, enabling them to reproduce similar patterns of thoughts, feelings, and behaviors themselves—with one constant proviso. In accordance with the universal law of impartiality, the patterns of reproduction take hold irrespective of the quality of goodness, truth, or beauty which any particular vibration oozes out.

Yet that's exactly where the hope lies in tomorrow morning's experiment. Don't you see?

Whatever genuine effort you put into practicing compassionate interactions, the more likely those same enhanced patterns will more likely emerge into the skill set and the interplay of everyone else who is trying to turn the cosmic ship around. That's where the sacred mystery lays hidden—in the all-inclusive realm of *That which is always becoming*.

Practicing the Golden Rule and all of the aligned disciplines we've talked about will help. So don't stop practicing. You'll just be getting a taste.

Yet there's so much more to wake up to. Isn't there?

So once again, let us remind you of something: *That which is always becoming* is beyond your current understanding of time and space. It's an endless field in an undiscovered paradise—a silent and serene celestial antidote for your tribal separation sickness.

And even when you and every object that's familiar to you eventually ceases to be subject or object, the interpenetrating bliss of the inexhaustible *Self* will still be there to back you up. Because there is nowhere that its interwoven presence is not.

That which is changeless remains the same at its essential core. But it can always become more obvious and more inviting. It can always expand and deepen in your consciousness. It can always change shape. It can manifest *It-Self* in infinite ways. Can it not?

And it does.

Because it is always becoming. Remember? Holding everything together in one big evolutionary *Body of Christ* . . . or by whatever other name you try to grasp its unconditional presence with.

Another paradox? Perhaps.

But the unifying *Self* isn't too concerned about which moniker you reach for or by what tribal cloth you attempt to wrap it up in when trying to capture its essence, even while most of you still anxiously cling to your tribal labeling and to its *disjoined* logic—confining yourselves to the inherited language of the tribe which you've submitted to.

Yet what would you do if all of your spoken and written words were suddenly taken away from you? What if they no longer existed? Would all of your religious traditions instantly lose their significance? Would their meaning and value disappear? What about all of your theories and theologies and philosophies? Would your ability to discern simply disintegrate into thin air, without the might of your tribal words there to speak and decide things for you—to hold the tribal mother tongue together? Or what about your heated arguments over whose belief system is superior? And what of your tribal memories? Would they be forgotten without the recall of words? How would you be able to prejudge or project your tribal hatred onto *others* anymore without the harsh insistence of words? Is it possible that the true heart of compassion is only allowed to grow in accordance with the loss of divisive tribal diction? Is that the only way for the heart to be unhindered enough to pump compassionate loving-kindness out of itself? Is the constant threat of reprisal which seeps in from the *only-mind* that which mainly corrupts the heart? And what about your tribal face and its unsmiling and habitual convictions? Would it suddenly suffer from the loss of self-identification? What about what you call yourselves? Or how you describe and define who you are? Would you no longer exist without your tribal language? And what of all of that tribal clothing, and the visual baggage which you stuff it into and wrap around it? And all of what you claim to exclusively own (with words)? Would it all vanish? What would you have left to hold on to or to fight over? What would you have left to possess it with, without the *disjoining* grip of your tribal words?

You would have what you've always had.

You would have the ever-present paradoxical reality of being *One* . . . but not one.

You would have the complimentary coexistence of the dual with the nondual.

You would have *That which is changeless* . . . and yet is always becoming.

You would have love in all of its nakedness. And naked love is a powerful force to reckon with, isn't it? The less it's clad in the conventional costumes of the tribe, the less there is to water it down or to cover it up with or to try to reshape or redefine it—or to try to shame it into hiding itself.

So when it comes right down to it, it's the pure nakedness of love that scares so many of you away from the *Self*. Don't you see? And yet that's exactly what you'll be entering into for the first time in your lives tomorrow morning. Scary stuff indeed.

Each one of you is a unique manifestation of the underlying and all-inclusive *Self* . . . which is always beyond complete knowing, and whose nondual nature can only be revealed through each arising concrete expression of itself in the cocreative world of duality—which includes all of you. Every single one of you. Human or *other* than human.

That which is always becoming is one big inexhaustible paradox, isn't it? One big cosmic joke with one huge inexhaustible punch line—which transcends but includes you.

So we heartily suggest, as you prepare yourselves to enter into the unmasking amphitheater, that you begin the practice of learning how to crack a smile on whatever face you inhabit . . . and upon whatever circumstance you face. Even if it's only an interior smile. For it's the cracking that matters most. Because it's the cracking that precedes the smile. And it's the smile that leads to love. And it's love that leads to peace.

Smiling can only help to speed up and smooth out the process that leads to an inner awakening. (Well . . . it can't hurt anyway, can it?) And it's the inner awakening that will lead to your return.

Smiling is very important. If we are not able to smile, then the world will not have peace. It is not by going out for a demonstration against nuclear missiles that we can bring about peace. It is with our capacity of smiling, breathing, and being peace that we can make peace, wrote the wise Thich Nhat Hanh.[2]

To borrow again from the wise Paul Tillich and others . . . it is the *Eternal Now* which forever interpenetrates and transcends yet embraces you (and everything else).[3]

So stay alert as you lean forward.

And remember: There is no separation between you and *You.*

God is closer to me than I am to myself, wrote the wise philosopher Augustine of Hippo.[4]

I pray God to rid me of God, wrote the wise Christian mystic Meister Eckart.[5]

God finds himself by creating . . . wrote the wise Hindu poet Rabindranath Tagore.[6]

CHAPTER 100

When Do You Want to Leave?

NOW . . . LET US digress just a bit more. Shall we? Before we get into some of the more detailed and meaty examples of what you might expect to encounter on the *other* side of this thing. There's a few lingering loose ends that can use some cleaning up, which include some (predictable) resistant thought patterns that we're picking up on, which are hard to miss . . . from more than just some of you. They need at the very least to be exposed if not directly addressed, before we wrap things up.

And by the way, we know that you're all still listening intently enough, even if some of you pretend to go about your business as if it were business as usual while still confined to those small tethered-off containment areas which we've temporarily assigned you to.

We've included all of the necessary preparations to ensure that this event is kicked off without a hitch . . . just as we promised. We've considered and planned for any and all likely countermaneuvers on your part.

We've been closely monitoring for any stray or delinquent thought patterns which might try to throw a monkey wrench into the mechanisms of this undertaking—an undertaking which is only meant to help you return to who you really are (even if many of you still doubt our words, or even if you continue to pretend that you don't understand them).

But our open surveillance will only be in operation until takeoff . . . until sunrise tomorrow morning. After that you'll be on your own. We will have unplugged the active monitoring system by then, when you'll then be launched firmly into the refacing dimension. And that dimension will only be able to take you where you direct it to go . . . through your actions, through your thoughts, and through your feelings—but more so through your total being.

We will still be available if and when you request or require our assistance. We won't be abandoning you. But we'll be staying out of your way. We can't bring you back. Only you can do that. We can only help to guide you.

It's a self-correcting process which you'll be in complete charge of. However smooth or rocky things go will be entirely up to you at that point. That's the way the whole operation is programmed. That's when your self-conscious choices will kick in and really matter. Not that they haven't always mattered. After all, it's been your own actions and your own thoughts, your own feelings and your very own way of being which has ultimately delivered you into this unique quandary, hasn't it? Which you already know, of course.

But here's the thing.

We can see that some of you may be thinking of taking the easy way out of this peculiar predicament—through self-annihilation maybe?

Others of you seem to be considering the possibility of going out in a blaze of tribal glory, by getting stupefyingly violent before tomorrow morning even has a chance to wake you up, to blow off your steam of fear and frustration while taking out a lot of *others* in the process, along with yourselves—similar to the way you've addressed so many of your overdramatized tribal dilemmas during your short and confused sojourn upon your fledgling planet.

So we might as well make things clear about this right now.

It won't happen.

None of it.

Anybody who goes a little too far past the pondering point of ending it all or of doing even more damage than they've already done (either physically, emotionally, psychologically, or spiritually) . . . well . . . if you go over that edge even from within your own small and limited portion and capacity of the tribal *only-mind*, you'll be shipped right over and into your own buffet of ready and waiting faces, to be reembodied—instantly.

You'll be shot to the other side in the blink of an eye . . . denied even a preparatory nap, let alone a good night's sleep.

Most of you who may be plotting things out in those reactionary ways have a lot of facial reconversions to work yourselves through. And you know it. And you're feeling a tad overwhelmed, aren't you?

And you haven't even dipped your big toe into the transformational pond yet.

But you might at least consider taking advantage of the time that you still have left . . . to prepare yourselves, don't you think? To at least say your proper good-byes, yes?

Just let us repeat it one last time: There's no way to escape from this thing. Okay? It's simply down to a matter of *when.* There will be no ifs, ands, or buts to try to cling to. Whatever you choose to do (or whatever you choose *not* to do) won't affect the inevitable. You will still be leaving on a singular face ship (with full group participation) tomorrow morning—or in a premature New York minute if you insist upon forcing us to send you off the quick and easy way.

But whichever way it goes—you'll still be departing from the tribal premises. Do you understand?

And don't forget this part of it either. You'll not only be leaving your face behind, but you'll be leaving everything and everyone else behind too. Until the return. And we'll get to that part of the process in a little bit. So for the time being . . . just hold your herd of horses on that issue. Got it?

Right now we just want to encourage you to begin using your time wisely. Starting . . . well . . . immediately. You don't need to waste any more of it than you already have. And you don't have much left to waste anyway.

It may be an opportune moment to finally get real with the people you care about, or even with some of those whom you've convinced yourselves that you can't even sympathize with, or for whom you can't even allow yourselves to feel much of anything for.

This life that you've been simulating is coming to an end tomorrow morning, like it or not—and at the very most, in only a few hours from this very moment.

You're all approaching a place of death and a place of rebirth . . . at the same time. Which is always the same place and time, isn't it?

But now you've got the added enticement of being able to completely reconstruct things all over again, from a new point of entry . . . into a new flow of departure, with a clean and fresh slate, right along with all the *others*.

So all for one then, eh? And one for all. Just as it's always been.

Can you feel a rising of hopefulness? Does it spring eternal for you after all? Have we asked that question yet?

We've been telling you all along to look at this thing as a unique opportunity, as difficult as that is to comprehend or to realize and as painful as it may be for some of you to endure.

But this is yet another area where you'll have the choice. And it's really all you've got. It's your reality. You can use it or just keep losing it. Because you won't have this chance to be so real again for a very long time. At least it'll feel that way in the refacing process.

But when you do eventually return, it'll simply feel like you just went to sleep for the night and then woke up after a few bizarre dreams which you can't quite understand or explain to yourself, and of which you'll lose all meaningful threads of connection to within minutes (or maybe even within seconds) of pouring that first cup of dark-brown coffee into that flea-market ceramic cup or after that first simmering sip of it while still staring into nothing in particular and for no apparent reason other than it feels good to do so, as it gives you a sense of safety while you peacefully ponder what it is that you're staring out into or looking for, as you try to absorb what it is that you're experiencing which feels so unfamiliar yet so tranquilizing.

Or maybe you'll do the same within minutes or seconds of massaging your naked back with the hot water spraying down upon you from the shiny steel showerhead which you'll stare back up at and into, as the contorted steel reflection of your face wonders back to you . . . *who or what is it that is disappearing into my thoughts and what was it that was dangling about in my dreams?*

That's what it will feel like. And then it will all go away as if it never happened.

And when you all safely return (and here's another thing we neglected to make clear, although we've hinted at it)—nobody returns alone.

This is an all-for-one deal.

You'll all return safely together or not at all. You can toss all that rugged-individualism gear out the door. This is a community endeavor. You'll all be riding the same horse back to the corral. Or if things go really well, you and the horse will be walking back into an open pasture of spaciousness . . . side by side, right along with the lion and the lamb and along with all the *others* who will have lost their projected-upon and *disjoined otherness* by then. Because the *only-mind* will have disappeared into the *One*-and-only mind of the all-embracing *Self.*

Your returning wake up should have you nestled back into your homes with an altogether realigned and reinvigorated dharma—and with a much more spacious capacity to behold the world after all that, don't you think?

So when do you want to leave? And how do you want to leave?

It's all up to you. Instant transportation is available right now. And it will be used if necessary. Or you can take the next few hours or the next several hours, depending on which time zone you're getting this announcement from, and allow the transformational process to wisely and to gradually begin—once and for all.

You will soon inhabit a brand new face. No matter what. There's no bargaining on that poker chip.

Is that abundantly clear by now?

We hope so.

Okay then.

Enough of that.

On to another subject.

CHAPTER 101

Something Else to Consider

B UT HERE'S SOMETHING else to consider.
There are many (far too many) human beings out there in
your present-day world who are clothed in hopeless and even terribly
agonized facial expressions. We've mentioned many of them already.
They're right there among you. They can't wait to jump at a second,
third, or however many chances it takes to reface themselves. Many of
them will actually be volunteering to leave tomorrow morning (which
is permissible within our guidelines). Even though they weren't on the
initial list of the invited.

And many of them are easy to identify.

They fill up your prisons.

They're being physically or emotionally tortured as we speak.

They live in fearful anticipation of the cruelty under which the
tyrannical conventions of the overly contained tribe is forced upon them.

They're coerced into running away from any actual or awakening
present moment by the dogmatic protocols of faithless fundamentalist
religion, by unscrupulous politics, by corrupt corporate power, by
out-of-control militarism—and by violent and senseless ideologies.

Many remain trapped and buried beneath the rubble of escape by
physical and emotional addictions.

Think of the people in Haiti or Tibet; Iran, Iraq, or Afghanistan; of
Sudan, the Central African Republic, or parts of Mexico; or of North
Korea, Gaza, or Somalia; or of Syria or Burma. To name just a few.

Or think of the many poverty stricken, depressed, and insecure city
dwellers in the so-called *developed* world . . . usually confined there by way
of their darker skin, by trauma-filled childhoods, by blocked opportunities,
by economic violence, or by brutal neighborhoods. Or those stranded in
abandoned or deprived rural outposts or on neglected and apartheid-like
reservations where the First People have been huddled and thrown together
in the United States and Canada, or on the streets and under the bridges
of Europe where the looked-down-upon so-called gypsies (the Romani

people) wander along the fragile underbelly of those rejecting nations—or where *others* are simply locked into hypnotic, religious, or political cults which keep them emotionally trapped and psychologically arrested.[1]

Or maybe they're the millions of children who so often are abandoned and forgotten or taught the spineless virtues of violence by their vagrant or merely biological fathers, by their cowardly uncles and cousins—while being battered and scarred in your next-door neighbor's house. Or maybe in your own house.

They're the powerless of the world. The homeless and the hungry. The thirsty. The physically and mentally weak. And the more easily addicted. They live in despair. They live under the thumb of exclusion and intimidation, under any of the prevalent tribalisms that dominate so much of your world's isolated and overly contained pockets of incestuous thinking and under its elite pyramid schemes—where expediency snuffs out the common good. They try to breathe under the weight of conventional ignorance, where the ease and gutlessness of habitual blame outguns the compassionate and truthful witness; where joblessness is blamed on the jobless; where homophobia is blamed on the homosexual; where hunger is blamed on the hungry; where violent misogyny is blamed on women; where the abuse and neglect of children is blamed on the abused and neglected child; where blame is routinely dumped onto the blameless; where excessive cravings for utility and so-called progress trump any truth, justice, or mercy that may slow down or disrupt the compulsive pleasures idolized by the tribal machine; where the comforts and accumulation of the few outweigh the betterment of the many; where the disease of consumerism is hailed as an honorable addiction to pursue; where religious bigotry and habits of ethnic or racial hatred or of cultural and economic injustice smother out the undreamt dreams of those on the vulnerable fringe.

Many of them have lost their homes or their families, their livelihoods, their very sense of who they are . . . due to war and terror, or to hurricanes and tornadoes or earthquakes, to drugs, to tsunamis and floods or to fires, to pollutions and poisonings or to sickness, or due to fear and ignorance, to an imbalance of power, to savage money systems, to fraudulent banks, to parents who should have never been parents—or to their own habits of despair and surrender.

Many of them have lost limbs or have succumbed to terrible diseases or they may embody congenital physical disfigurements—or they may be locked in the broken arms of other mental or physical impairments.

Millions of them wake up every day without access to clean drinkable water or to enough food or to affordable or decent (or even available) health care.

Many of them live in deep depression, in deep sadness and guilt, or in shame . . . wanting badly to make amends, wanting to face their own demons, to be free of your demons—to be free of the collective, corporate, and tribal demons who dominate and oppress so much of their world (which is so much of your world).

They're ready for this opportunity to replace and transcend their current face. They can't imagine it being any worse for them in any *other* face. They're especially ready for most of you to transcend your face and the tragic consequences that you as a species have pushed upon so many *others* and even upon yourselves.

And (for many of you among the invited) much of your own pain has been self-inflicted, related to your own habits and behaviors . . . many of which we've already summarized, haven't we? They include your own crimes or corrupting ways which you've inherited, adapted to, and passed on; your own violent soldiering; your emotional cowardice; your lust for power or status; your ingrained tribal hatreds; your fragile and frightened self-righteousness; your inner poisons of distraction; your undeniable intolerance of so many *others*; your self-indulgent *disjoined* desires; your following of the fear-and-doubt mongers; your compulsive hoarding; your addiction to the cultish tribal belief that you are an actual separated self—disconnected from *That which unifies*.

Yet unlike so many of you, these volunteers seem to know that this is an actual (not merely a potential) opportunity, which they've been waiting for most of their lives—an opportunity which they haven't yet had the courage to face up to or to take up on their own. They didn't take up their own cross when they had the chance.

So we will help them. And you will help them. And they will help you.

Because when you get to the *other* side of this holy mountain of death and resurrection, the return ticket will have everybody's name on it. There's only one ticket home, remember? It's a whole-group, round-trip ticket through all the tunnels and across all the tightly mapped-out over—and underpasses. It's all for one and one for all. Because there is no separation. There is no *other*.

You are the *otherness*. And the *otherness* is you.

So when it gets to the tipping point of which we spoke of earlier, when there's enough accumulated empathic energy for *others*, and enough freed-up sorrow and self-forgiveness, when there's enough growing kindness in spirit, in thoughts, and in actions . . . when there's enough wide-open compassion for those who you've hurt or for those who are just plain hurting and even for yourselves, when there's enough of you realizing and entering into that loving space of *That which is actually You*—then the ship will begin to turn around and come home.

But only then.

Amazing Grace, how sweet the sound, wrote the wise reformed slave trader John Henry Newton.[2]

CHAPTER 102

A Feast of *Good-Enoughness*

WE'VE SAID IT before. And we'll say it again.

We're not looking for perfection.

It's the movement toward goodness that we're after. In all of you. Because there actually is such a desirable state (and/or level) of being—which is *good enough*.

As a matter of fact, without it, without being able to get to that opening or to that evolving nonplace of being, without even being able to imagine such a space of freer movement, without being able to stretch your reach and your imagination at least that far, many of you will just continue to convince yourselves to seek out the fantasies of false perfection instead, to seek out some kind of final state and stage of completion—which doesn't exist in your impermanent world.

It never has existed. And it never will.

You've been sold a bill of nonexistent goods, a dreamt-up tribal exactness which you've mentally clung to. And so you almost always come up short and eventually empty-handed—while reaching for that final all-or-nothing attainment of utopian flawlessness.

You've even tried to force fit *others* into your artificially perfected reality, with your intrusive methods of persuasion and control.

But you never get there, do you? Because *there* does not exist, even though you keep hammering away at it to try to pound it into existence.

And you've done plenty of damage along the way with all of that pounding, haven't you? As you've tried so desperately to get everybody else squeezed into your ark of perfection or to be condemned to drowning for refusing to climb aboard your overcrowded tribal slave ship.

But tomorrow morning, when you get to the *other* side, your job will not be to perfect yourselves. It will simply be to strive to do your part. That's all. That's the whole crux of it. And when all of the individual parts are interconnected, when it gets to be *good enough*—you'll then begin to feel the turn around. But only then.

So do your part. For yourselves. And for the *others* who are also *You.* And then when you do make your way back, you'll know that the rest of the world which stayed behind will be throwing you one hell of a nontribal bash out of the sheer joy of feeling unified again, out of feeling that you'll be watching their back, just as they'll watch yours—and that there really won't be much left to watch for anyway.

There will be one giant sigh of relief heard throughout the universe once you accomplish your return and come back together as *One.*

The great separation will be over.

The prodigal sons and daughters will be welcomed home with open arms.

A feast of *good-enoughness* will be thrown for all.

CHAPTER 103

The Hard Part

OKAY. NOW FOR your introduction into the hard part, for the actual facing-up to what you might expect to run into on the other side.

We won't waste any valuable time here. And we won't beat around the bush with any lightweight illustrations either.

You might as well get a cogent glimpse into the sharp and disfigured divide which you'll be crossing over and entering into tomorrow morning.

But it won't be too unfamiliar to many of you.

It's just that when you do get there you'll be fully awake to *That which is*. There will be no more illusions. It'll be the beginning of the rebirthing process. Some of it won't be pretty or easy to experience. But if you start right now with a giant push, giving it all you've got, with courage and commitment, maybe even retrieving the bravery that you've stored away behind so much shame, fear, guilt, and regret for so long . . . that it just might get you off to a well-grounded start, sturdy enough when the floodgates open up to enable you to cut the tribal umbilical cord—once and for all.

Either way, there's simply no painless way of getting there or of getting back. But there is a *good-enough* way. There always has been. And there always will be. But most of you have always known that, haven't you?

So let's get right into the hard lesson then, shall we? With our emblematic yet quite disturbing example.

But you should know that we've been preparing you for this particular part of the presentation from the beginning.

And this first approach is probably the more daunting of the two you'll be offered. At least it may feel that way . . . initially. There will be a secondary option which may seem to be the easier way to go. But in reality, it might actually be the more vexing of the two. You'll have to decide that for yourselves. And as always the choice will be yours. We'll describe option number 2 after giving you a strong dose of the first alternative.

So here we go . . . with selection number 1.

Take a deep breath.

We're about to discuss and describe an extreme case in point for your consideration. But perhaps it's not so obvious or extreme. We'll leave that judgment up to you.

So let's begin with it, shall we?

Try to imagine that you're one of the many thousands of active and armed combatants who've been roaming your world for centuries or maybe that you're (what's become more and more common these days) one of the many violent mercenaries (aggressors of fortune) fighting in one of the many ongoing wars or smaller but no-less-violent conflicts which you've frequently participated in as a tribal species (some tribes more than others), with most of the warring instigated by the rich and powerful who employ the poor and the powerless along with the greedy and the gullible (as well as the eagerly submissive) to fight their battles for them.

But you already know that part of the story, *yes?*

Well, if you don't, then you might just end up wearing the face of at least one failed history student (or of one self-deluded tribal loyalist) along the way.

But let's take a serious look at just one of you, one of you who not only took on the role of the hired gun but was also a violent participant in the rape, torture, and murdering of mostly women, girls, and boys . . . or of any *other* weak or defenseless human being who may have tragically crossed your rampageous path of aggression . . . a path mixed with fear and violent lust, with obedience to power, injected with avarice—all of which have so easily and so often been aroused by hellish acts of organized or even chaotic tribal violence, haven't they?

And it doesn't really matter whether the violence is premeditated or simply executed out of convenience, does it?

No government, no religious institution, no military branch, no street gang, and no corporation that collaborates in any willful or reactionary act of terror at any level or from any distance can honestly deny its own culpability in causing or contributing to the pain and suffering of *others*, can it? And all acts of violence are acts of terror, are they not? Whether a contributing cause is direct or indirect in its nature makes no real difference to those who feel the suffering impact of terrorism. A cause is still a cause.

Yet so many of the contributors tend to either boast or minimize, justify and defend, or even outright lie about their own acts of flagrant cruelty, don't they? Unless (of course) they happen to be boorishly gloating about their shameful acts to each other, to drown out their own internal disgrace—for some of them only months or maybe even years before they slowly drink themselves to death or suddenly blow their own brains out after too many nightmares full of the wailing, agonized, and extinguished victims of their tribal (and cowardly) carnage.

So what do you think one or more of your faces will look and feel like if you were to wake up into that homicidal participant's nightmarish morning?

And by the way, there will be multidimensional refacings going on throughout the process. We'll explain that in more detail in a little while.

But back to the mercenary example.

Let's discuss some possibilities.

Let's start with just one young child who you've raped and tormented.

You may rise up right away into tomorrow's wake up wearing the face of that child (from the moment you open your eyes)—right in the middle of your own act of brutalization.

You will be able to enter into that experience through that child . . . right into the very act itself. That may be where you land. You will feel the pain and the fear of forced penetration, of being stripped and slapped and held down and mocked and insulted—while a sweating man's body part is violently pushing itself into you.

You will feel your own genital weapon forcing itself into you as your own breath and sweat and arms cover you with your own laughter and anger and mockery and dirt.

Do you think some essential changes in your consciousness might get stirred up by going through that horrific experience? By wearing the complete suffering face of that innocent child of God for a while?

Are you beginning to perceive the potent possibilities for waking up that this option can evoke? Of what prospects there are for developing a deep and compassionate opening in the heart? Of the opportunities that can be seized for allowing yourselves to actually feel empathy and remorse? For realizing their transformational powers?

And if you think this feels real ugly right now by simply listening to this description, then just begin to think about how it actually felt to the actual child . . . and how it will feel to you tomorrow morning.

Let's stick with this example. But let's take it a few steps further . . . to expand the optional frontier a bit.

Is everybody paying close attention here?

There's nowhere to run and hide anymore, is there?

So why keep trying?

It's time to face up. You can start right now or tomorrow morning. But as we've stressed all along, there will be no escape hatch to climb out of. So get used to it already. Although it's still your choice, isn't it? In the end, it is still always your choice.

So . . . what if the young child's mother and father were forced to watch this act of terror while it's being perpetrated. How would they feel? What would they be experiencing?

You may enter into their face as well, watching their own son or daughter being brutally tortured right before their very own eyes.

But those will be your eyes behind that face.

And it will be your daughter or your son or your wife or your mother whom you will be watching this happen to, behind whose face it is which you must experience. Because you will experience the whole thing as if this was really happening to you, until you make enough inner changes to move on to the next face and eventually to the last face until you can look forward to returning to your own original face—the one you wore before you were born, the one everyone shares, the face of the inmost (and outmost) *Self*, the face that you and the young child and their parents and their brothers and sisters and your parents and your brothers and sisters all share. The face of God.

But this won't be anything like an "as if" experience. It will be actual . . . in real Earth time.

There will be nothing left to your imagination. You won't have to imagine any of it. You will *be* it.

You will be her or him. You will feel your heart break. You will feel like a helpless, frightened coward . . . even though there was really nothing you could do to stop any of it.

You will feel like a failure unable to protect your own son or daughter. You will feel the shame. You will feel those tortuous seconds and minutes that seem instead to last for hours and days.

And then you will live the rest of your life with that. You will dream it.

You will see it in your son's or daughter's eyes—if they survive.

You will never again be at complete peace with anything or anyone. You will die a sad and broken man or woman.

And you will live way longer than you wish to live.

Your body will outlive your sense of spirit and your sense of soul.

Years of lessons. Right there.

But let's spread it out even a little more. Let's say that the young child survives . . . and then lives for several more decades with that experience.

So will you.

You will live out their shaming from their culture and from their family and from their friends.

You will live out their fears and their repeated memories and with their physical pain and damage—and with the psychological and spiritual hurt done to them. You will feel all of their raging self-blame.

And you will die with them when they die, to look back at your life as they would . . . wondering why this happened to you.

You will ask yourselves—how could my life have been different? You will curse life, replaying all of the self-rejection and the rejection by *others* because of what happened to you, feeling all of the rage and the fear (and even more) that their parents felt—that your parents will feel. Sadness, fear, and rage will dominate your thoughts and feelings—or even worse, you will stuff them all away into a tightly wrapped ball of torture and denial that will one day suddenly explode into another rage of violence upon even more unsuspecting and undeserving *others*, unexpectedly triggered by a seemingly harmless annoyance—extending the depth of its pain and suffering even further into the cosmic wound.

Are you all still listening? What do you think and feel so far?

This face exchanging is pretty powerful stuff . . . eh?

Look at all the depths and levels of meaning and awareness you will be brought into. You will surely be different when you return from all this, won't you? But if this doesn't do it, then it will just continue until it does. Because each included face must be transcended.

Once again: There is no escape.

You will return more compassionate and more loving and more forgiving and more caring—or you won't return at all.

But let's take it in another direction, shall we? Suppose the young girl becomes pregnant.

Then you will become pregnant.

You will carry the child all the way to birth, whether she decided to on her own . . . or if she was forced to by circumstances or by *others*.

And you will feel all the pain and emotional stress and anguish through the skin of the mother into the child as it grows within her—as it grows within you. You will feel the hate and the unloving and confused fear generated through the blood and the skin of your mother as you approach delivery into the world—as you wear the face of the unborn and unwanted child.

And then you will live out the life of that unwelcome child of your rape when it's born. And you will live out all the strain and pain, anger and abuse, and the hatred which will come your way from your birth mother and from all who know how you were conceived.

You will feel the judgment and the ridicule and the repudiation that the world offers children and mothers like you.

You will feel the suicidal feelings as your mother and as your child, even as your parent, or maybe even as your sister or your brother or your husband, or your lover—whose faces you will also be wearing to full fruition, or until you make the necessary changes in consciousness (and in your heart) to move on.

You may even take your own life as he or she eventually may have—as many victims (and perpetrators) of traumatic torture, terror, and abuse have done.

Or you may kill or violently hurt others out of your own building rage.

And then you will wear the faces of the those victims too, and all of the faces of all of the victims who were created along the way by that one tortuous degradation of that one child—which you perpetrated to begin this long line of unspeakable pain and consequences for so many.

And by the way, this is not merely an opportunity for your own transformation. Don't you see? But it's a chance for you to break (once and for all) the chain of suffering and terror which includes so many who are tragically affected by terrible acts of unloving unkindness.

This is a repulsive and violent example. We know that. But unfortunately, it's not so uncommon as to be rare either. Is it?

We wanted to make the point as sharp as a knife, and crystal clear, in order to cut through any layers of denial that have hardened themselves like steel so deeply into so many of you that they've come to feel like a natural response—or even like an ingrained tribal part of your being.

But all unloving and unkind acts of violence have their own painfully long line of unsuspecting victims of consequence, don't they? Resulting from any and all levels of withdrawn love—from any and all levels of violent unkindness.

And all unkindness (no matter how small the dose) as well as all withdrawn love feeds and participates in cowardly violence, doesn't it?

None of it is justifiable, valid, or even sane—except in the *disjoined* thought world of the tribal *only-mind*.

If you were to watch the damage done by one insensitive, unloving, and unkind spoken word, (which so often and so easily comes out of so many of your mouths) from the moment it is spoken, as it leaves the mouth of the one person who speaks it, until the chain of insensitive, unloving, and unkind effects it generates multiplies and expands and is finally (if ever) broken, you would be shocked and amazed at all the heartbreak which is incurred by so many precious beings along the way—from the power of one small (and so often xenophobic) but hurtful word.

But maybe some of you wouldn't be so surprised, would you?

Every cause has its multiple effects.

How far does a word travel? Can a word change into other forms of violence along the way?

And how far does a rape travel? Or a murder? Or even one moment of neglect? Or a public shaming? How far does enforced ignorance travel? Or untreated illness? Or suppressed freedom of speech? Or political or media exploitation? Or restrictions on movement? Or repressed self-expression? Or abuse of one's position of authority? How far does poverty or destitution travel? Or fear? Or lack of nutrition? Or an act of fraud or theft? How far does a hateful thought travel? Or a car full of explosives? Or a bomb dropped from a jet plane? Or the poisoning of the atmosphere? Or an act of bullying? Or a life of apathy? Or a handful of lies? Or any blind act of loyalty which gives its support to any brutal act of tribal violence?

What is the sound of one hand clapping? asks the wise Zen koan.[1]

The rapist wasn't born into your world as a rapist. And he wasn't a rapist prior to entering into his human birth. And he won't be a rapist when he leaves. He will return to the *Self.*

But meanwhile the interconnections of his actions on earth are endless, aren't they? As too are all the opportunities for enlightened awareness and compassionate loving-kindness and even for forgiveness— especially self-forgiveness, which is too often disowned and abandoned as the abused inner descendant, forced to hide itself beneath the rubble of violence which overcrowds and corrupts so much within so many of you.

Yet just as one act of violence takes its toll, so too does each and every act of nonviolent loving-kindness.

A long list of good, true, and beautiful consequences evolve from each and every act of goodness, from each and every act of truth, from each and every act of beauty—just as a much uglier list of consequences evolve from each and every act of hatred and brutality that comes from the *disjoined* one.

Are you even beginning to see how vital, deep, and wide each and every speck of action really is? That just as no human being stands alone so too no human thought, word, or action stands alone? That everything really does interconnect? That there is no such thing as a noneffectuating response? That everything counts? That nothing created is without consequence? That not even a simple almost invisible drip of unintentional or routine thought goes unnoticed or without impact? That it really does all matter?

We're trying to wake you up to a *good enough* or better set of actions and aftermaths while eliminating (as much as is possible) the other kind—the kind of tribal illogic which seeks to violently fill up, perfect, and contain your world.

But we're trying to get you to do the leg work. After all, it is your awareness of being which we're working with and talking about, isn't it?

And all of you must be able to forgive yourselves in order to return.

There's no healing without self-forgiveness.

And without healing, there's no conversion of faces. The chain will not be broken. Which means that the possibility of just returning to and refitting yourselves with the same old face which led you into tomorrow morning's facial event is just a waste of time—a head fake that fools no one anymore, not even you.

But here's another possibility in our example, to try to drive it all home to you even deeper.

Suppose the young girl decides to abort you . . . or she is forced to by circumstances or by *others*.

You will know it ahead of time. You will be wearing the face of the unborn child or fetus—whichever word you prefer to name it with. And what you choose to call it is not the issue right now. This is not the time to reflexively march to your side of the politically, philosophically, or religiously correct street of tribal belief with all of its predictable and projected hostilities aimed at those on the *other* side of the street, with none of it really proposed (if it ever was) for the sake of the unborn child or for the mother, but which is so often intended instead for the sake of the *disjoined* ego who must always be right—no matter how violent its righteousness is.

What is important is the act of entering into the experience of living as it actually is and of dying as it actually is and of suffering as it actually is, in its original and true being and in its true form (or its true formlessness) and in its true face with all of which that entails—which you will need to experience in order to transcend yourselves.

And you will find out what that entails and includes.

You will live that short time in the womb of a body that desperately wants to reject you, or that is so confused and hurt that it doesn't know what you mean to it—or what you mean to the young girl or woman whose body it is.

You will live in the womb of a body which may even hate you—which hates what you represent. Which wants to kill you. Which fears you because of what you will always remind it of. Which doesn't want to see you come into this world alive.

You will feel it (all of it), all the way up to the moment of your death and destruction.

You will feel whatever physical pain is involved. And you will suffer an anonymous and lonely death while dying at whatever speed is allowed—raped into conception, hated and rejected, and then destroyed just because you exist—and for no fault of your own.

Imagine the power in that experience—combined with all the others.

If you can see clearly at all at this point you should be able to realize the impact that one person's actions can have on so many and how there are no either/or, all or nothing, or any other (easy-healing) simplistic solutions which are isolated or cut off from *That which is always becoming* or which are separated from the unifying *Self.*

It's an all too common yet painfully tragic story to tell, isn't it? The more damage you've done to *others* translates into more rocks being thrown into the tribal pond—which keep the rings of pain moving out.

And how many rocks have you thrown into that pond up to now?

That will be what all of you have to look forward to—and what all of you will have to reface.

A revitalizing and sacramental body of water will pour over you, which is ancient and eternal. You'll be immersed into that baptismal liquid to retrieve every last rock you've thrown and to wear every last face—or until the transformational turnaround begins to take hold.

So as you can see, and as we've been warning you, you'll need to be very strong and very committed to this, or else you'll be going through a whole lot more suffering and sorrow before your facial realization (and ultimate deliverance) can come about, before honest compassion and loving-kindness for *others* will begin to develop, to take hold, and to stick.

But maybe that's what you need. It won't be wasted in any case. The turnaround will happen—no matter how long it takes. You can count on it.

What has been wasted has been what you did to get here, to all those *others*, to those who had to experience every last pound of pain you put upon them at whatever level or excuse you used—and what you put yourselves through as well.

And maybe you haven't even allowed yourselves to realize the extent of the waste until now, whether you're one of those in the hideous extreme . . . as in the brutalizing mercenary or if you're simply a common thief or a habitual liar to those whom you claim to love; or if you manipulated and cheated people in your business or if you commanded violent subordinates; or if you willingly sold weapons to murderers or sold drugs to children; or if you looked the other way when someone needed your help or if you deceived *others* to get your own way . . . to get more possessions or to accumulate more power or prestige; or if you took part in the willing destruction and disruption of any part of nature's beautifully balanced forests, seas, mountains, and air . . . or of any other mixture of *Creation*; or if you simply remained as neutral and apathetic as you could so as not to offend anyone . . . to avoid taking the risk of being rejected by your tribe for adding even a speck of doubt or criticism into the mix of the *disjoined* tribal idolatry or to avoid adding even an ounce of extra effort toward making it a *good enough* or better world.

You can name your own wasted poison.

You know who you are and what you've squandered up to now. Don't you? And you know who you're not.

You still have a chance to minimize your trauma by how you respond from your first refacing onward. It will all be up to you. It will always be up to you. Just as it always has been and always will be—as we've so often repeated.

Some of you will probably have to reexperience every last bit of the pain you caused or contributed to or of every bit of *good-enoughness* you withdrew from your world by giving up or turning inward. That's how stuck you are.

But you'll all get every last chance that's possible.

No one who needs it will be denied the opportunity.

We've just given you one brief (however disturbing) description and overview of a possible combination of faces that you'll be wearing in order for you to return.

In most cases, that would seem to be more than enough to enhance and mobilize the sought after transformation.

If not, there will be more. Not to worry.

We do not give up.

We never give up.

CHAPTER 104

Coconspirators, Past and Present

B UT BEFORE WE leave this sampling of option number 1 (which will be our only and final sample) and before we begin to describe option number 2, and before you begin to prepare yourselves for your last night of sleep with the face that you're still wearing, let's consider any other conspirators in the case of the mercenary abuse of the young children we've been describing, who, for all practical purposes, is really you that we're talking about since it will be their face which you will be entering into in our case study (but merely as an example of course).

They (the coconspirators) will be going through the same refacing experience as you. All of them will be included, reaching all the way back to the persons providing the funds or giving the orders that got the ball rolling in the tribal system of events with all of its subservient participants, which led you to your crime—and even way beyond and before that, no matter how far back it goes.

That's the beauty of selecting option number 1.

The line of interrelated faces which must be entered into to be re-worn will actually go all the way back to your first self-consciously aware human ancestor. Because each line of consequence reaches far beyond what even your spirit-body-mind can remember. And it involves every kind of interaction as well as the corresponding effects upon everyone in that same line, and even outside that line . . . reaching into related lines, into infinity if necessary—which now brings us to our multidimensional level within the refacing process.

Since everything and everyone is interconnected, we will be bringing everybody back who, if they were actually still living and breathing in your world today, would be invited to join you on the *other* side tomorrow morning.

So as you can see there will be countless *others* who must and will be allowed to rework and retrace their lives. Through the face of millions.

What an interesting and revealing prospect, eh?

You'll actually be able to work alongside your long-gone earthly ancestors, to expand and deepen the collective return even more. Even your most infamous brothers and sisters will be unforgotten, brought back, and entered into tomorrow morning's events.

So if you happen to see the face of Jack the Ripper or Genghis Khan, or of Jim Jones or Al Capone, or of Vlad the Impaler or Marcus Brutus Junius, or of Marie Antoinette or Pol Pot . . . don't be too surprised.[1]

They're all coming back.

They'll all be waking up from their long slumber tomorrow morning—just like the rest of you. They might even look a little wide eyed when and if you run into them. But they'll know what the game plan is. They'll know it's time for another chance to retrace and reface their lives. Because just like you, they're listening to us . . . right this very second.

We've covered all of our bases. And like we've already said so many times before—now it's all up to you.

Every one of you.

You can generalize this specific example to any of the facial conversions which you will be a part of. It will all work the same.

The more culpable a face has been, the more depth and expanse of faces it will be rewearing. All the dots and lines will be connected.

Anyone's culpability in your specific face adaptation is a contributing cause to what you will have to reface. They will have to retrieve your rock from the pond and reface themselves with it—and vice versa of course, if the culpability moves in the other direction.

The more damage done or the more *others* you've influenced into doing damage, then the more faces you will wear and the more trauma you will experience—and the wider your net will be cast in order to make your way back. But the more depth and expanse of discovery that you will experience too, and the deeper and wider your wake up into *That which is always becoming* will be.

How each of you perform in your sequence of facial adaptations will also partially determine how many faces and how deep into the refacing operation everyone else will have to travel too—in the returning transformational process.

Everything and everyone is interdependent and affected by everything and everyone else. It's always been that way ever since that first *big bang*—maybe even before. And after you wake up tomorrow morning, you will never have any doubts about that again.

It will all become real to you.
Beyond your wildest dreams.
And beyond your wildest fears.
And beyond your wildest imagination.

MICHAEL J. GAJDA

CHAPTER 105

The Closing Argument

OKAY. NOW FOR option number 2.
It's pretty simple and straightforward.

Option number 2 consists of this: You will live your own whole life all over again, rewearing only *your* own face all the way to your eventual return.

How you wear and reface yourself will have the same effect upon all the others. How well you do will still matter in the bigger picture of things, including the fact that everyone returns together or not at all. Everything still connects. Everything remains interconnected. That will never change.

But (with this option) you'll have to reface every bit of your own self-reflective adult life all over again—which means that the events will change as you slowly reface yourself, as you slowly recover into who you actually are.

If you're moving in the direction of the *good enough* and the *true enough* and the *beautiful enough*, then your life and face will automatically move in an all new and challenging direction. Once you make your first new turn, the whole path of your life will then transform. Which means that you will have new and different friends and lovers and even children.

So even though you won't be required to wear the face of anyone else, you will be losing much of who you think you are and who you're used to being with and what you're so used to imagining that you care about—even at the deepest levels.

You'll still be taking off all of your masks. You'll just be working through the same superficial face all over again.

The trade-off is huge, isn't it?

If you go it alone (which is what option number 2 will demand of you) you will lose every bit of your previously faced adult life . . . with all of its ups and downs and with all of its likes and dislikes. You'll even lose (forever) most of the considerable luggage, trappings, and human beings which and whom you feel so attached to.

A big sacrifice waits for you in this option. But can you see how this selection so cleverly disempowers the influence of the *disjoined* tribal *only-mind* which you've been so used to filtering yourselves through.

And as you let go of all those previous attachments and addictions, so too are you letting go of the corrupting power of tribal (and hence self-absorbed) overidentification.

Are you willing to let go of your friends? Your wife or husband? Your children? Your longtime next-door neighbors?

How about your occupation or vocation? Your travels and experiences? Your fond recollections? Your dog or cat? How about your accomplishments? The things you've created, learned, or discovered? Your entire early adulthood and beyond? They'll all be wiped clean from your memory banks.

Maybe some of you are willing, even anxious, to let go of so much. We shall make no judgment—either way you choose.

But there's always that dependable trade-off isn't there. And the outcome of letting go of so much cannot be nailed down with any of your overprotective tribal certitudes anymore either, can it?

Do you see what we meant when we said that this option may seem to be the easier one at first glance—but may actually be the more traumatic one to reface yourselves with?

But there you have it anyway.

Those are your choices.

So now it's still (but finally) up to you, isn't it? Like it always has been. Which you must be thoroughly (and paradoxically) aware of by now. But if, for some reason, you still can't accept that fact . . . you soon will. Which is something you will not have a choice in deciding.

Refusing this particular gift of choice and responsibility is not an option. You must choose one of the two travel alternatives. And you must take full responsibility for the consequences of the choice you make. Just like it's always been. Which you've forever tried to avoid and deny.

There really is nobody left to blame anymore, is there? No matter which option you choose. There never has been.

That which is real is not a choice—even though you can still deny its reality.

But it is getting late, isn't it? And we've prepared you as much as we can up to this point.

You'll now have some time to reflect upon how you want to leave, who you might want to say good-bye to before you go, and what option to choose.

We respectfully pass you the ball.

Try not to drop it.

CHAPTER 106

One Last Thing

B UT BEFORE WE let you go—there is one last thing.
We've decided that we will answer one of your remaining questions after all—even though we previously stated that we wouldn't have time to do that.

But this won't take long.

There's been this lingering curiosity that we've detected among you in your collective attention which we think may be worth addressing and which we don't expect to be too much of a distraction from the work at hand.

And most of you already know what the curious question is.

Don't you?

But here it is anyway—just in case some of you are still trying to deny your own natural tendency to speculate or inquire.

Who are we?

That's the question that so many of you are wondering about, isn't it? Which is quite understandable.

You want to know who we are.

Meaning—us. Right?

Who is it that's behind the voice which you've been listening to for these past several hours?

That's your question.

We can't blame you for wondering. We really can't.

So here's your answer. It may or may not satisfy your curiosity.

Ready?

We are the Seventh Generation ahead of you, the ones whom your Iroquois brothers and sisters take in such serious regard and consideration when making collective decisions about how to care for and treat each other and how to care for and treat the rest of the planet (as well as the surrounding universe).

We've seen you coming for centuries. And we've gradually come to the conclusion that if we didn't intercede in some fundamental way that you may not even get here, that you may not survive the oppressive buildup coming from all of that tribal blockage long enough to make it this far (and from the subsequent *Self*-denial which has kept you from realizing *That which is always becoming*)—which obviously would mean that we would not even be allowed the chance to do our part, that we would not be able to join our ancestors or contribute to the health and welfare of future generations. And that thought alone was just too much for us to ignore.

So here we are.

And so now you know not only who we are but that our very lives and the lives of all future generations are in your hands, that our lives depend on how well you unmask your tribal ways and begin to wear your own original face. That our face is in your face. That our face is your face. That our face is also faceless. And that our face is held together in the same grace of *That which is always becoming* (in the grace of the inexhaustible *Self*), which excludes nothing and no one, neither human nor *other* than human—or not yet human.

So when you finally make it back to this side of things, you will not only be bringing back everyone else from that side with you, but you will be bringing forward anyone else who will ever have a chance to breathe or to laugh or to love.

Huge task ahead . . . eh?

Astronomical.

But the rewards are almost impossible to imagine, aren't they? Let alone to count or appreciate.

We'll be watching it all with our cosmic fingers crossed—closely. Very closely. And we'll be praying constantly—for you, and for all of us.

But it's getting quite late, isn't it? Very late. As it has been getting for some time now.

So try to get a good night's sleep, if you can. We plan to.

You'll all need it. We'll all need it.
Tomorrow promises to be a very long day, yes?
And very interesting indeed.

Evolve or die, many among the wise have said.

Sitting quietly, doing nothing, Spring comes, and the grass grows, by itself, wrote the wise Basho.[1]

NOTES

Opening Quotes:

(1) Taken from a talk given by Eknath Easwaran. Blue Mountain Center for Meditation & Nilgiri Press. Talks of Eknath Easwaran, 1 Kabir: Stages of Desire http://www.easwaran.org

(2) Quote attributed to Meister Eckart. For more information on Eckart see The Eckart Society. Accessed January 15, 2014. http://www.eckhartsociety.org/

(3) Emily Dickinson, The Complete Poems of Emily Dickinson. (Boston: Little, Brown and Company, 1960)

(4) Remarks at the 11th Annual Presidential Prayer breakfast, Washington, D.C., Feb. 7, 1963. "This morning we pray together; this evening apart. But each morning and each evening, let us remember the advice of my fellow Bostonian, the Reverend Phillips Brooks: "Do not pray for easy lives. Pray to be stronger men! Do not pray for tasks equal to your powers. Pray for powers equal to your tasks.""

(5) Richard Rohr, "Things Hidden, Scripture as Spirituality", Saint Anthony Messenger Press and Franciscan Communications (2007).

Chapter 1:

(1) Helen Schucman, A Course in Miracles (ACIM). (New York: Viking, 1996)

Chapter 3:

(1) William Johnston, editor, The Cloud of Unknowing. (New York: Image Books/Doubleday, 1973)

Chapter 4:

(1) Eknath
Easwaran, adapted for meditation from the version in his *Dialogue with Death: The Spiritual Psychology of the Katha Upanishad* (Petaluma: Nilgiri Press, 1981). This line is taken from the translation of the Katha Upanishad, Part 1, Canto 3.

Chapter 5:

(1) Ibid
(2) Widely attributed to Saint Francis of Assisi.
The line has also been translated or quoted in various places as "What *we* are looking for is who is looking," or "What *you* are looking for is what is looking."

Chapter 6:

(1) a) Thich Nhat Hanh. Being Peace. (Berkeley, California: Parallax Press, 1996)
b) Plum Village http://www.plumvillage.org

Chapter 7:

(1) Opie and P. Opie, *The Oxford Dictionary of Nursery Rhymes* (Oxford: University Press, 1951, 2nd ed., 1997), p. 418.

Chapter 8:

(1) Niels Bohr, Comment to observers when an experiment took an unexpected turn. In Bill Becker, "Pioneer of the Atom," *New York Times Sunday Magazine* (20 Oct 1957).
(2) a) Quote that is widely attributed to Shana Alexander.
b) Shana Alexander. Wikipedia, the Free. Accessed March 3, 2013. http://en.wikipedia.org/wiki/Shana_Alexander
http://www.brainyquote.com/quotes/authors/s/shana_ alexander.html Accessed June 15, 2013
(3) Consciousness of Reality.

Accessed June 15, 2013. http://www.peterrussell.com/Reality/RHTML/R2.php

Chapter 10:

(1) a) Right Mindfulness: Samma Sati—Buddhist Meditation
Accessed June 16, 2013. http://www.vipassana.com/resources/8fp6.php
b) Right Mindfulness: Samma Sati—Access to Insight
Accessed June 16, 2013. http://www.accesstoinsight.org/ptf/dhamma/sacca/sacca4/samma-sati/index.html

(2) Ira Progoff. At a Journal Workshop: Writing to Access the Power of the Unconscious and Evoke Creative Ability. (New York: Jeremy P. Tarcher, 1992)

(3) Eric Butterworth. Discover the Power Within You: A Guide to the Unexplored Depths Within. (San Francisco: Harper & Row, 1989)

(4) New Testament. Luke 17:21. King James Version.

(5) Quote attributed to Thomas Merton.
For information on Merton go to ITMS Information—The Merton Center site at http://www.merton.org/ITMS

(6) George Bernard Shaw Accessed January 10, 2014. http://www.whale.to/v/shaw1.html
http://www.newworldencyclopedia.org/entry/George_Bernard_Shaw

(7) a) Tao Te Ching by Lao Tsu, Chapter 7, Sentence 2. Unknown translation/translator.
b) Tao Te Ching—Index of Chapters
Accessed January 10, 2014. http://www.wayist.org/ttc%20compared/indexchp.htm

Chapter 11:

(1) Abraham Maslow. The Psychology of Science, (New York: Harper & Row. 1966) *Maslow's hammer,* popularly phrased as "If all you have is a hammer, everything looks like a nail," and variants thereof. Maslow's actual written words were, "I suppose it is tempting, if the only tool you have is a hammer, to treat everything as if it were a nail."

(2)   Picasso. Conversations and Memories. With 17 Portraits and Drawings. German title and text. Translated by Oswalt of Nostitz. Sabartés, Jaime (Zurich, Ark. Germany: 1956)

(3)   Quote widely attributed to Picasso.

Chapter 12:

(1)   The Lord's Prayer—Comparison from Bible Translations. Accessed May 2, 2013.
      http://www.csdirectory.com/biblestudy/lords-prayer.pdf

(2)   Eknath Easwaran, Blue Mountain Center of Meditation. From the Metta Sutta, part of the Sutta Nipata, a collection of dialogues with the Buddha said to be among the oldest parts of the Pali Buddhist canon. Accessed August 12, 2013. http://www.easwaran. org/sutta-nipata-discourse-on-good-will.html

(3)   Pierre Teilhard de Chardin. The Future of Man. (San Francisco: Harper & Row, 1964)

Chapter 15:

(1)   Radical Humanist. Small is Beautiful. E. F. Schumacher. 1973. Quotymologist: Investigating the True Origins of Famous Quotations. Accessed May 12, 2013.
      http://www.quotymologist.com/einstein-anyintelligent.html

(2)   Alice Calaprice, Freeman Dyson, Albert Einstein. The New Quotable Einstein. (Princeton: Princeton, University Press, 2005. Page 173)

(3)   Joseph Conrad. Lord Jim. (New York: Doubleday & McClure, 1900)

(4)   Peace Pilgrim: Her Life and Work in Her Own Words. Peace Pilgrim. (Ocean Tree Books, 1983)

(5)   a) Quote attributed to Soren Kierkegaard. b) Soren Kierkegaard (Stanford Encyclopedia of Philosophy)
      http://plato.stanford.edu/entries/kierkegaard

Chapter 18:

(1)   First Law of Thermodynamics—Wikipedia, the Free Encyclopedia. Accessed January 12, 2014. http://en.wikipedia.org/wiki/ First_law_of_thermodynamics

(2) a) The Paschal Mystery in Every Day Life—Loyola Press. Accessed May 1, 2013.
http://www.loyolapress.com/the-paschal-mystery-in-everyday-life.htm
b) Focusing—A Way of Living the Paschal Mystery. Accessed May 1, 2013.
http://daneoservices.weebly.com/focusing—a-way-of-living-the-paschal-mystery-pat-duffy-cp.html

(3) a) Editor's Choice, Silence is God's First Language. Accessed January 10, 2014.
http://www.adishakti.org/_/silence_is_gods_first_language.htm
b) Catholic Encyclopedia: St. John of the Cross
http://www.newadvent.org/cathen/08480a.htm

(4) Kahlil Gibran. The Prophet. (New York: Alfred A. Knopf, 1991)

(5) Thomas Merton. The Wisdom of the Desert. (New York: A New Directions Book, 1970)

Chapter 19:

(1) a) "To Be Or Not To Be," Hamlet's Soliloquy by Shakespeare
http://www.nosweatshakespeare.com/quotes/hamlet-to-be-or-not-to-be
b) William Shakespeare. Hamlet. (New York: W. W. Norton,, 1996)

Chapter 20:

(1) a) Parables, Young Men's Buddhist Association of America. Accessed January 9, 2014.
http://www.ymba.org/books/thus-have-i-heard-buddhist-parables-and-stories/parables. Parable 0117: Raft of Dharma.
b) Thich Nhat Hanh, Daniel Berrigan. The Raft is Not the Shore: Conversations Toward a Buddhist/Christian Awareness. (New York: Orbis Books. Maryknoll, 2000)

(2) Zen Story.
The nun Wu Jincang asked the sixth patriarch, Huineng, "I have studied the Mahaparinirvana sutra for many years, yet there are many areas I do not quite understand. Please enlighten me."

The patriarch responded, "I am illiterate. Please read out the characters to me and perhaps I will be able to explain the meaning." Said the nun, "You cannot even recognize the characters. How are you able then to understand the meaning?"

"Truth has nothing to do with words. Truth can be likened to the bright moon in the sky. Words, in this case, can be likened to a finger. The finger can point to the moon's location. However, the finger is not the moon. To look at the moon, it is necessary to gaze beyond the finger, right?"

(3)   Snow White and the Seven Dwarfs, Freely Translated and Illustrated by Wanda Gag. (New York: Coward-McCann, 1938), pp. 9-43.

(4)   Nirvana—Wikipedia, the Free Encyclopedia
http://en.wikipedia.org/wiki/Nirvana

(5)   a) Lost Horizon: The Haunting Novel of Love in Shangri-la. James Hilton. (New York: Pocket Books, 1939)
b) Underworld—Wikipedia, the Free Encyclopedia
http://en.wikipedia.org/wiki/Nether_realm

(6)   New Testament. Matthew 6:21. (Garden City, New York: The Jerusalem Bible. Doubleday & Company, 1968)

Chapter 21:

(1)   a) Book of Leviticus—Wikipedia, the Free Encyclopedia
http://en.wikipedia.org/wiki/Book_of_Leviticus
b) Book of Leviticus—New World Encyclopedia
http://www.newworldencyclopedia.org/entry/Leviticus
c) Book of Leviticus 1-27: New International Version
http://www.biblegateway.com/passage/?search=Leviticus+1-27 &version=NIV

Chapter 22:

(1)   In the Vision of God. By Swami Ramdas. (Bombay: Bharatiya Vidya Bhavan. 1974)

(2)   The quote is attributed to Sinclair Lewis responding to an interviewer's question about his Popular Front novel, It Can't Happen Here. Sun Dial Press, Garden City, NY. 1935.

Chapter 23:

(1) Texts on the Universality of Sufism—The Sufi Way. Accessed April 13, 2013.
http://www.sufiway.org/history/texts/origins_and_nature.php
"To be 'in the world, but not of it,' free from ambition, greed, intellectual pride, blind obedience to custom, or awe of persons higher in rank; that is the Sufi ideal."

Chapter 24:

(1) Every Particle of the World is a Mirror. Mahmud Shabestari, *The Essential Mystics,* edited by Andrew Harvey, (San Francisco: HarperSanFrancisco, 1996)
(2) Mein Kampf. Adolf Hitler. (New York: Stackpole, 1939)
(3) Letter From Birmingham City Jail. Martin Luther King, Jr. (Philadelphi, PA: American Friends Service Committee, 1963)
(4) Satyagraha & Ahimsa: Stories of Nonviolence in Action (blog). Accessed May 10, 2013)
http://satyagrahaandahimsa.blogspot.com/2006/04/satyagraha-and-ahimsa.html
(5) The Inclusive New Testament. (Brentwood, Maryland: Priests for Equality, 1996) Matthew 5:46.

Chapter 25:

(1) Compiled by TV-Free America, 1322 18th Street, NW, Washington, D.C. 2003. Statistics were taken from the website, The Sourcebook for Teaching Science. Copyright, 2007. Accessed September 21, 2012.
http://www.csun.edu/science/health/docs/tv&health.html
(2) a) An Introduction to Skillful Means—Mountain Source San
http://www.mtsource.org/articles/skillful.htm
b) Skilful Means: A Concept in Mahayana Buddhism. Michael Pye. Ge Duckworth & Company. London. 1978.
(3) Theodore Roszak. Quoted in *Thinking Green! Essays on Environmentalism Feminism, and Nonviolence* by Petra K. Kelly, Parallax Press, Berkeley, California, 1994.

Chapter 26:

(1) In the Vision of God. By Swami Ramdas. (Bombay: Bharatiya Vidya Bhavan, 1974)

(2) a) Bodhisattva. New World Encyclopedia. Accessed May 15, 2013.
http://www.newworldencyclopedia.org/entry/Bodhisattva
b) Wikipedia, the Free Encyclopedia. Accessed May 15, 2013.
http://en.wikipedia.org/wiki/Bodhisattva

(3) New Testament. Matthew 25:35-40. The Message. The Bible in Contemporary Language. Eugene H. Peterson. (Colorado Springs, Colorado: NavPress, 2002)

> "I was hungry and you fed me,
> I was thirsty and you gave me a drink,
> I was homeless and you gave me a room,
> I was shivering and you gave me clothes,
> I was sick and you stopped to visit,
> I was in prison and you came to me . . . Whenever you did one of these things to someone overlooked or ignored, that was me—you did it to me."

(4) World Military Spending. Accessed November 23, 2012.
http://www.globalissues.org/article/75/world-military-spending

(5) World Hunger and Poverty. Accessed November 24, 2012.
http://millionsofmouths.com/blog/nfblog/2006/11/13/global-expenditure-on-defense-over-1000-billion

(6) a) War and Civilian Deaths. Accessed November 24, 2012.
http://agencyandresponsibility.typepad.com/ethics/2011/09/war-and-civilian-deaths.html
b) Civilian Casualty Ratio. Accessed November 22, 2012.
http://en.wikipedia.org/wiki/Civilian_casualty_ratio

(7) New Testament. 1 Corinthians 12. Contemporary English Version.

Chapter 27:

(1) The Big Bang—NASA Science. Accessed November 21, 2013.
http://science.nasa.gov/astrophysics/focus-areas/what-powered-the-big-bang

(2) The Dragons of Eden: Speculations on the Evolution of Human Intelligence. By Carl Sagan. (New York: Random House, 1977)

(3)   New Testament. Luke 11:9, The Jerusalem Bible, Reader's Edition.

(4)   Theory of Relativity—Wikipedia, the Free Encyclopedia. Accessed December 12, 2012.
       http://en.wikipedia.org/wiki/Theory_of_relativity

(5)   Spherical Earth—Wikipedia, the Free Encyclopedia. Accessed December 24, 2012.
       http://en.wikipedia.org/wiki/Spherical_Earth

(6)   The Great Work: Our Way into the Future. Thomas Berry. (New York: Bell Tower, 1999)
       "We need merely understand that the evolutionary process is neither random nor determined but creative. It follows the general pattern of all creativity. While there is no way of fully understanding the origin moment of the universe we can appreciate the direction of evolution in its larger arc of development as moving from lesser to great complexity in structure and from lesser to greater modes of consciousness. We can also understand the governing principles of evolution in terms of its three movements toward differentiation, inner spontaneity, and comprehensive bonding" (p. 169).

(7)   The Inclusive Hebrew Scriptures, Volume I: The Torah. (Brentwood, Maryland, Priests for Equality, 2000) Genesis 1:26

(8)   The Inclusive New Testament. (Brentwood, Maryland: Priests for Equality, 1996) The Gospel of John. 1:1-1:5

(9)   The Holy Qur'an. 49:13. This is a routinely used/quoted translation of this verse. Unfortunately, the author could not pin down its source.

(10)   Black Elk Speaks: being the life story of a holy man of the Ogalala Sioux (1961), as told to John Neihardt. (Lincoln: University of Nebraska Press, 1961)

Chapter 28:

(1)   The Perennial Philosophy. Aldous Huxley. (New York: Harper & Brothers Publishers, 1945)

(2)   a) Shamanism: Foundation for Shamanic Studies. Accessed February 21, 2013.
       http://www.shamanism.org
       b) Shamanism: Wikipedia, the Free Encyclopedia. Accessed February 21, 2013
       http://en.wikipedia.org/wiki/Shamanism

(3)   a) Vision Quest of the Native American: Native Americans Online. Accessed February 22, 2013.
http://www.native-americans-online.com/native-american-vision-quest.html
b) A Native American Vision Quest: Webpanda.com. Accessed February 23, 2013.
http://www.webpanda.com/There/uot_vision_quest.htm

(4)   a) Dreamtime: Wikipedia, the Free Encyclopedia. Accessed February 26, 2013.
http://en.wikipedia.org/wiki/Dreamtime
b) Australia. Aboriginal Dreamtime. Jane Resture's Oceania Page. Accessed February 26, 2013.
http://www.janesoceania.com/australia_aboriginal_dreamtime/index1.htm

(5)   a) Khan Abdul Ghaffar Khan. Wikipedia, the Free Encyclopedia. Accessed March 1, 2013.
http://en.wikipedia.org/wiki/Badshah_Khan
b) A Man to Match His Mountains: Badshah Khan, Nonviolent Soldier of Islam. Eknath Easwaran. Blue Mountain Center for Meditation. (Berkeley, CA: Nilgiri Press, 1984)

(6)   Osama Bin Laden. Wikipedia, the Free Encyclopedia. Accessed March 2, 2013.
http://en.wikipedia.org/wiki/Osama_bin_Laden

(7)   Albert Schweitzer. A Biography by James Brabazon. (New York: G. P. Putnam's Son, 1975)

(8)   Timothy McVeigh—Wikipedia, the Free Encyclopedia. Accessed March 6, 2013.
http://en.wikipedia.org/wiki/Timothy_McVeigh

(9)   Hildegard of Bingen, 1098-1179, A Visionary Life. S. Flanagan. (New York: Routledge, 1990)

(10)   Radio Priest: Charles Coughlin, The Father of Hate Radio. (New York: Free Press, 1996)

(11)   Abraham Joshua Heschel: Prophetic Witness. Edward K. Kaplan, Samuel H. Dresner. (New Haven: Yale University Press, 1998)

(12)   Ku Klux Klan. Wikipedia, the Free Encyclopedia. Accessed March 14, 2013.
http://en.wikipedia.org/wiki/Ku_Klux_Klan

(13)   Wangari Maathai—NobelPrize.org. Accessed March 21, 2013.

http://www.nobelprize.org/nobel_prizes/peace/laureates/2004/maathai-bio.html

(14) Joseph Kony. Wikipedia, the Free Encyclopedia. Accessed March 14, 2013.
http://en.wikipedia.org/wiki/Joseph_Kony

(15) a) Why the Dalai Lama Matters. Robert Thurman. (New York: Atria, 2008)
b) A Simple Monk: Writings on His Holiness, The Dalai Lama. (Novata, CA: New World Library, 2001)

(16) The Rise of the Taliban in Afghanistan: Mass Mobilization, Civil War, and the Future of the Region. Neamatollah Nojumi. (New York: Palgrave/Macmillan, 2002)

(17) Autobiography of a Yogi. ParamahansaYogananda. (Los Angeles, CA: Self-Realization Fellowship, 1994)

(18) Mao: A Biography. Ross Terril. (Old Tappan, New Jersey: Touchstone Books, 1993)

(19) Becoming Human. Jean Vanier. (New York: Paulist Press,1999)

(20) a) Wall Street's Economic Crimes Against Humanity—Business Week. Accessed March 1, 2013.
http://www.businessweek.com/managing/content/mar2009/ca20090319_591214.htm
b) Griftopia: A Story of Bankers, Politicians, and the Most Audacious Power Grab in American History. Matt Taibbi. (New York: Random House, 2011)
c)   Christian America and the Kingdom of God. Richard T. Hughes. (Champaign-Urbana: University of Illinois Press, 2009)

(21) Zen Mind, Beginner's Mind. Shunryu Suzuki. (Boston: Shambhala, 2001)

(22) Newtonian Mechanics: The M.I.T. Introductory Physics Series. A.P. French. (United Kingdom: W. W. Norton, 2011)

Chapter 29:

(1) Chabad.org—The Complete Jewish Bible. Accessed April 23, 2013.
http://www.chabad.org/library/bible_cdo/aid/16183

(2) This translation is by Eknath Easwaran, adapted for meditation from the version in his *Dialogue with Death: The Spiritual Psychology of the Katha Upanishad* (Petaluma: Nilgiri Press, 1981)

(3) BibleEncyclopedia—Solomon. http://bibleencyclopedia.com/solomon. htm

(4) New Testament. Matthew 23:26. English Standard Version.

Chapter 30:

(1) Theodor Adorno, "Education after Auschwitz," in *Critical Models: Interventions and Catchwords*, (New York: *Columbia University* Press, 1998)

Chapter 31:

(1) a) Perfect is the Enemy of the Good. Wikipedia, the Free Encyclopedia. Accessed August 12, 2013.
http://en.wikipedia.org/wiki/Perfect_is_the_enemy_of_good
b) Voltaire Quote-The Perfect is the Enemy of the Good. Accessed August 12, 2013.
http://www.famous-quotes.net/Quote.aspx?The_perfect_is_the_enemy_of_the_good

Chapter 32:

(1) My Religion. Mahatma Gandhi. (India: Navajivan Publishing House, 2007)

Chapter 33:

(1) William James. Wikipedia, the Free Encyclopedia. Accessed August 12, 2013.
http://en.wikipedia.org/wiki/William_james

Chapter 34:

(1) Reference.com—A Free On-line Encyclopedia. Accessed October 13, 2013.
http://www.reference.com
Metanoia (from the Greek μετάνοια, "changing one's mind," "repentance") is a word which has a few different meanings in different contexts.

Metanoia in the context of theological discussion, where it is used often, is usually interpreted to mean repentance. However, some people argue that the word should be interpreted more literally to denote changing one's mind, in the sense of embracing thoughts beyond its present limitations or thought patterns (an interpretation which is compatible with the denotative meaning of repentance but replaces its negative connotation with a positive one, focusing on the superior state being approached rather than the inferior prior state being departed from).

In the context of rhetoric, metanoia is a rhetorical device used to retract a statement just made, and then state it in a better way. As such, metanoia is similar to *correctio*.

In the psychological theory of Carl Jung, metanoia denotes a process of reforming the psyche as a form of self-healing, a proposed explanation for the phenomenon of psychotic breakdown. Here, metanoia is viewed as a potentially productive process, and therefore patients' psychotic episodes are not necessarily always to be thwarted, which may restabilize the patients but without resolving the underlying issues causing their psychopathology.

Theological Meaning

Biblical references

From the Greek μετάνοια—compounded from the preposition μετά (after, with) and the verb νοέω (to perceive, to think, the result of perceiving or observing)—metanoia means "a change of mind." In Christianity, the term refers to spiritual conversion. The word appears often in the Gospels. It is usually translated into English as "repent":

> And saying, The time is fulfilled, and the kingdom of God is at hand: **repent ye**, and believe the gospel.

καὶ λέγων ὅτι πεπλήρωται ὁ καιρὸς καὶ ἤγγικεν ἡ βασιλεία τοῦ θεοῦ: **μετανοεῖτε** καὶ πιστεύετε ἐν τῷ εὐαγγελίῳ.
(Mark 1:15)

Theology

In theology, metanoia is used to refer to the change of mind which is brought about in repentance. Repentance is necessary and valuable because it brings about change of mind or metanoia. This change of mind will result in the changed person hating sin and loving God. The two terms (repentance and metanoia) are often used interchangeably.

However, the prefix "meta-" carries with it other variants that are consistent with the Eastern Greek philosophical mind-set, and perhaps is at odds with Western views. "Meta-" is additionally used to imply "beyond" and "outside of," e.g., metamorphosis as "beyond change" and metaphysics as "outside the limits of physics." "Meta" also means "next to" or "after" as in metaphysics, where the books we call metaphysics were placed *next* to or after the books on physics.

The Greek term for repentance, *metanoia*, denotes a change of mind, a reorientation, a fundamental transformation of outlook, of man's vision of the world and of himself, and a new way of loving others and God. In the words of a second-century text, the Shepherd of Hermas, it implies "great understanding," discernment. It involves, that is, not mere regret of past evil but a recognition by man of a darkened vision of his own condition, in which sin, by separating him from God, has reduced him to a divided, autonomous existence, depriving him of both his natural glory and freedom. "Repentance," says Basil the Great, "is salvation, but lack of understanding is the death of repentance." Repentance thereby acquires a different dimension to mere dwelling on human sinfulness and becomes the realization of human insufficiency and limitation. Repentance then should not be accompanied by a paroxysm of guilt but by an awareness of one's estrangement from God and one's neighbor.

Rhetorical Meaning as Correction
Metanoia is used in recalling a statement in two ways—to weaken the prior declaration or to strengthen it.

Weakening
The use of metanoia to weaken a statement is effective because the original statement still stands, along with the qualifying statement. For instance, when one says, "I will murder you. You shall be punished," the force of the original statement ("I will murder you") remains, while a more realistic alternative has been put forward ("you shall be punished").

Strengthening

When it is used to strengthen a statement, metanoia works to ease the reader from a moderate statement to a more radical one, as in this quote from Marcus Aurelius's *Meditations*

> I still fall short of it through my own fault, and through not observing the admonitions of the gods, and, I may almost say, their direct instructions (Book One);

Here Aurelius utilizes metanoia to move from a mild idea ("not observing the admonitions of the gods") to a more intense one ("not observing . . . their direct instructions"). He uses the clause "I may almost say" to introduce the metanoia.

Psychological Meaning

In Carl Jung's psychology, metanoia indicates a spontaneous attempt of the psyche to heal itself of unbearable conflict by melting down and then being reborn in a more adaptive form. Jung believed that psychotic episodes in particular could be understood as existential crises which were sometimes attempts at self-reparation. Jung's concept of metanoia influenced R. D. Laing and the therapeutic community movement which aimed, ideally, to support people while they broke down and went through spontaneous healing, rather than thwarting such efforts at self-repair by strengthening their existing character defenses and thereby maintaining the underlying conflict.

Source:

Cuddon, J. A., ed. *The Penguin Dictionary of Literary Terms and Literary Theory*. 3rd ed. Penguin Books: New York, 1991.

Chapter 35:

(1) a) The Power of Myth. Joseph Campbell. (New York: Doubleday, 1988)
b) The Power of Myth. Wikipedia, the Free Encyclopedia
http://en.wikipedia.org/wiki/The_Power_of_Myth
(2) Rip Van Winkle. Wikipedia, the Free Encyclopedia
http://en.wikipedia.org/wiki/Rip_Van_Winkle

(3)   Homer. Wikipedia, the Free Encyclopedia http://en.wikipedia.org/wiki/Homer

(4)   The Odyssey. Homer. Robert Fagels (translator). (New York: Viking Press, 1996)

Chapter 36:

(1)   Intentions. The Decay of Lying. Pen, Pencil and Poison. The Critic as Artist. The Truth of Masks. Oscar Wilde. (New York: Dodd, Mead & Company, 1891)

(2)   The Wisdom of Holy Fools in Postmodernity. Peter C. Phan. Accessed September 9, 2013) http://www.ts.mu.edu/content/62/62.4/62.4.3.pdf

(3)   Tricksters. Myth Encyclopedia. Accessed September 9, 2013. http://www.mythencyclopedia.com/Tr-Wa/Tricksters.html

Chapter 37:

(1)   a) The Eye of the Spirit. Ken Wilber. (Boston and London:Shambhala, 1997). p. 74
      b) Transcend and Include Accessed October 1, 2013. http://www.enlightennext.org/magazine/j27/gurupandit.asp

(2)   New Testament. Matthew 15:10-11. The Message. (Colorado Springs, CO: Navpress, 2002)

(3)   Free Thesaurus—Synonyms for Fundamentalism. Accessed October 12, 2013.
      http://freethesaurus.net/s.php?q=fundamentalism

(4)   a) Sex, Ecoloy, Spirituality: The Spirit of Evolution. Ken Wilber. (Boston/London: Shambhala, 1995)
      b) Boomeritis: A Novel That Will Set You Free. Ken Wilber. (Boston/London: Shambhala,, 2002)

Chapter 40:

(1)   a) Basic Quantum Mechanics for Dummies. http://www.buzzle.com/articles/basics-of-quantum-mechanics-for-dummies.html
      b) Introduction to Quantum Mechanics. Wikipedia, the Free Encyclopedia.

http://en.wikipedia.org/wiki/Introduction_to_quantum_mechanics
c) Quantum Physics for Dummies. Steven Holzner. (United Kingdom: John Wiley & Sons, 2009)

Chapter 42:

(1) Facts about Induced Abortion—Guttmacher Institute. Accessed October 23, 2013.
http://www.guttmacher.org/pubs/fb_IAW.html
(2) Henry Ward Beecher. Wikipedia, the Free Encyclopedia.
http://en.wikipedia.org/wiki/Henry_Ward_Beecher
(3) Mother Mary Jones. Wikipedia, the Free Encyclopedia.
http://en.wikipedia.org/wiki/Mary_Harris_Jones

Chapter 45:

(1) "Sympathy for the Devil," Jagger/Richards; Beggars Banquet Album. The Rolling Stones. (London: ABKCO, Decca, 1968)
(2) a) Hubblesite. Accessed October 19, 2013. http://hubblesite.org
b) NASA—Hubble Space Telescope. Accessed October 19, 2013.
http://www.nasa.gov/mission_pages/hubble/main/index.html
c) Kepler: Home Page. Accessed October 19, 2013. http://kepler.nasa.gov
(3) Species Extinction and Human Population. Accessed October 21, 2013.
http://www.whole-systems.org/extinctions.html
(4) a) Nondualism—Wikipedia, the Free Encyclopedia. Accessed October 25, 2013.
http://en.wikipedia.org/wiki/Nondual
b) Center for Nondual Awareness. Accessed October 25, 2013.
http://nondualcenter.org

Chapter 46:

(1) The Ghost in the Machine, Arthur Koestler. (New York: Macmillan, 1968)

Chapter 47:

(1)   New Testament. Mark 6:4. Jerusalem Bible. Reader's Edition. (Garden City, New York: Doubleday & Company, 1968)

(2)   a) The Suicide of Socrates—Eyewitness to History. Accessed November 21, 2013. http://www.eyewitnesstohistory.com/socrates.htm
b) *The Trial and Execution of Socrates: Sources and Controversies.* Thomas C. Brickhouse; Nicholas D. Smith. (New York: Oxford University, 2002)

(3)   The Death of Al-Hallaj: A Dramatic Narrative. Herbert Mason. (South Bend: University of Notre Dame Press, 1991)

(4)   Akiba: Scholar, Saint, and Martyr. Louis Finklestein. (Northvale, New Jersey: Jason Aronson, 1990)

(5)   John of the Cross—Wikipedia, the Free Encyclopedia. Accessed November 12, 2013.
http://en.wikipedia.org/wiki/John_of_the_Cross

(6)   Teresa of Avila—Wikipedia, the Free Encyclopedia. Accessed November 12, 2013.
http://en.wikipedia.org/wiki/Teresa_of_%C3%81vila

(7)   Crucifixion of Jesus—Wikipedia, the Free Encyclopedia. Accessed January 12, 2013.
http://en.wikipedia.org/wiki/Death_of_Jesus

(8)   Francis of Assisi: A New Biography. Augustine Thompson. (Ithaca, New York:Cornell University Press, 2012)

(9)   a) A Testament to Freedom. Dietrich Bonhoeffer. (New York: Harper Collins, 1995)
b) The Life and Death of Dietrich Bonhoeffer. Mary Bosanquet. (New York: Harper & Row, 1968)

(10) IACHR Condemns the Murder of Keila Esther Berrio in Columbia. Accessed November 1, 2013)
http://notiwayuu.blogspot.com/2011/08/iachr-condemns-murder-of-keila-esther.html

(11) The Life and Death of Mahatma Gandhi. Robert Payne. (New York: Smithmark, 2005)

(12) a) The Death and Life of Malcolm X (Blacks in the New World). Peter Goldman.

(Champaign-Urbana: University of Illinois Press, 1979) b) Malcolm X. The Movie. Written, Produced, Directed by Spike Lee. (Brooklyn, New York: 40 Acres & a Mule Filmworks, 1992)

(13) a) Franz Jagerstatter: A Man of Conscience. Documentary Film. Directed by Jason A. Schmidt. (December 2nd Productions, 2010)

b) Film: The Refusal—Story of Franz Jagerstatter, a Martyr for Justice.

(14) a) A Testament of Hope: The Essential Writings of Martin Luther King, Jr., Edited by James Washington. (New York: Harper & Row, 1986)

b) An Act of State: The Execution of Martin Luther King, Jr. William F. Pepper. (London/New York: Verso, 2003)

(15) The Pope and the Heretic: The True Story of Giordano Bruno, the Man who Dared to Defy the Roman Inquisition. Michael White. (New York: William Morrow, 2002)

(16) Long Walk to Freedom: The Autobiography of Nelson Mandela. (Boston: Little Brown & Company, 1994)

(17) A Man to Match His Mountains: Badshah Khan, Nonviolent Soldier of Islam. Eknath Easwaran. (Petaluma, California, Nilgiri Press, 1984)

(18) a) Dance the Guns Away: 100 Poems for Ken Saro-Wiwa. (Flipped Eye Publishing Limited, 2005)

b) Ken Saro-Wiwa and Mosop: The Story and Revelation. Ben Wuloo Akari. (Bloomington, Indiana: Xlibris, 2007)

(19) a) Word Remains: A Life of Oscar Romero. James Brockman. (Maryknoll, New York: Orbis Books, 1982)

b) A Martyr's Message of Hope: Six Homilies by Archbishop Oscar Romero. (Celebration Books, 1981)

(20) a) Ghosts of Mississippi: The Murder of Medgar Evers, the Trials of Byron de la Beckwith, and the Haunt. (Boston: Little Brown & Company, 1995)

b) The Autobiography of Medgar Evers: A Hero's Life and Legacy Revealed Through his Life, Letters. Myrlie-Evers Williams. (New York: Basic Civitas Books, 2005)

(21) Martyr of the Amazon: The Life of Sister Dorothy Stang. Roseanne Murphy. (Maryknoll, New York: Orbis Books, 2007)

(22) Assassination of Benigno Aquino—Wikipedia, the Free Encyclopedia. Accessed August 3, 2013.
http://en.wikipedia.org/wiki/Assassination_of_Ninoy_Aquino

(23) a) Crazy Horse: A Lakota Life. Kingsley M. Bray. (Tulsa: University of Oklahoma Press, 2008)

b) The Killing of Chief Crazy Horse. Robert A. Clark. (Lincoln, Nebraska: Bison Books, 1988)

(24) a) The Self-Immolation of Thich Quang Duc. Accessed September 1, 2013.
http://www.buddhismtoday.com/english/vietnam/figure/003-htQuangduc.htm

b) Thich Quang Duc. Jesse Russell & Ronald Cohn. (United Kingdom: Books on Demand, 2012)

(25) Betrayed: The Assassination of Digna Ochoa. Linda Diebel. (New York: Carroll & Graf,2006)

(26) Setting the Gospel Free: Experiential Faith and Contemplative Practice by Brian C. Taylor. (United Kingdom: SCM Press, 1997)

(27) Agape. The New World Encyclopedia. Accessed July 13, 2013.
http://www.newworldencyclopedia.org/entry/Agape

(28) a) Moses—Wikipedia, the Free Encyclopedia
http://en.wikipedia.org/wiki/Moses

b) Jeremiah—Wikipedia, the Free Encyclopedia
http://en.wikipedia.org/wiki/Jeremiah

c) Muhammad—Wikipedia, the Free Encyclopedia
http://en.wikipedia.org/wiki/Muhammad

(29) New Testament. Matthew 25:42.

(30) a) Quote attributed to Mahatma Gandhi.

b) Welcome to Mahatma Gandhi http://mkgandhi.org

(31) a) Quote attributed to Fyodor Dostoevsky.

b) Fyodor Dostoevsky—Wikipedia, the Free Encyclopedia
http://en.wikipedia.org/wiki/Fyodor_Dostoyevsky

(32) a) Quote attributed to Jean Cocteau.

b) jeanCocteau.com http://www.jeancocteau.com

(33) a) Quote attributed to Oscar Wilde.

b) Oscar Wilde: Biography and Works
http://www.online-literature.com/wilde

Chapter 49:

(1) a) The Impact of Illiteracy. Accessed May 3, 2013.
http://washingtoncountyliteracycouncil.org

b) Mental Health and Crime. Jill Peay. (United Kingdom: Taylor Francis, 2012)

c) Crime and Poverty Essay. Accessed June 12, 2013.
http://www.pubdef.ocgov.com/poverty.htm

d) Poverty and Crime: Breaking the Vicious Cycle. Accessed June 12, 2013.
http://www.poverties.org/poverty-and-crime.html

e) Drug Addiction in Relation to Crime. Accessed June 13, 2013.
http://www.druglibrary.org/schaffer/Library/studies/dacd/appendixa_9.htm

(2) The Headless Way. Accessed November 13, 2013.
http://www.headless.org

(3) a) *"For I was hungry and you gave me food, I was thirsty and you gave me drink, I was a stranger and you welcomed me, I was naked and you clothed me, I was sick and you visited me, I was in prison and you came to me . . .*

Truly, I say to you, as you did it to one of the least of these my brethren, you did it to me" (Matthew 25:35-36, 40).

b) The Corporal Works of Mercy

To feed the hungry.

To give drink to the thirsty.

To clothe the naked.

To shelter the homeless.

To visit the imprisoned.

To visit the sick

To bury the dead.

Chapter 50:

(1) Machiavellian-Merriam-Webster Online
http://www.merriam-webster.com/dictionary/Machiavellian

(2) a) Soviet Empire—Wikipedia, the Free Encyclopedia
http://en.wikipedia.org/wiki/Soviet_Empire
b) Islamofascism—Wikipedia, the Free Encyclopedia
http://en.wikipedia.org/wiki/Islamofascism

(3) a) World Communism—Wikipedia, the Free Encyclopedia
http://en.wikipedia.org/wiki/World_communism
b) International Terrorism—Definition / WordIQ.com
http://www.wordiq.com/definition/International_terrorism

c) Pirates and Emperors, Old and New: International Terrorism in the Real World. Noam Chomsky. (Cambridge, MA:South End Press, 2003)

(4)   a) Ho Chi Minh: A Life. William J. Duiker. (New York: Hyperion, 2000)

b) Vietnam: A History. The First Complete Account of Vietnam at War. Stanley Karnov. (New York: Viking Press, 1984)

c) Crisis in Allende's Chile: New Perspectives. E. Kaufman. (New York: Praeger, 1988) d) Salvador Allende—Wikipedia, the Free Encyclopedia. Accessed December 12, 2013.
http://en.wikipedia.org/wiki/Salvador_Allende

(5)   Angolan Civil War—Wikipedia, the Free Encyclopedia. Accessed June 11, 2013.
http://en.wikipedia.org/wiki/Angolan_Civil_War

(6)   a) Iran-United States Relations—Wikipedia, the Free Encyclopedia. Accessed June 1, 2013.
http://en.wikipedia.org/wiki/United_States-Iran_relations

b) 1953 Iranian coup de'tat—Wikipedia, the Free Encyclopedia. Accessed June 1, 2013.
http://en.wikipedia.org/wiki/Iran_Coup_d'%c3%a9tat

(7)   a) Timeline: Nicaragua—Stanford University. Accessed July 8, 2013.
http://www.stanford.edu/group/arts/nicaragua/discovery_eng/timeline

b) United States Occupation of Nicaragua—Wikipedia, the Free Encyclopedia. Accessed August 4, 2013.
http://en.wikipedia.org/wiki/United_States_occupation_of_Nicaragua

(8)   Invasion of Grenada—Wikipedia, the Free Encyclopedia. Accessed August 4, 2013.
http://en.wikipedia.org/wiki/Invasion_of_Grenada_(1983)

(9)   United States Invasion of Panama—Wikipedia, the Free Encyclopedia. Accessed August 5, 2013.
http://en.wikipedia.org/wiki/United_States_invasion_of_Panama

(10) Korean War—Wikipedia, the Free Encyclopedia. Accessed August 5, 2013.
http://en.wikipedia.org/wiki/Korean_War

(11) a) 2003 Invasion of Iraq—Wikipedia, the Free Encyclopedia. Accessed August 5, 2013.
http://en.wikipedia.org/wiki/2003_invasion_of_Iraq

b) Gulf War 1991 Invasion of Iraq—Wikipedia, the Free Encyclopedia. Accessed August 5, 2013, http://en.wikipedia.org/wiki/Gulf_War

(12) al Qaeda—Wikipedia, the Free Encyclopedia. Accessed August 6, 2013.

http://en.wikipedia.org/wiki/Al-Qaeda

(13) United States Invasion of Afghanistan—Wikipedia, the FreeEncyclopedia. Accessed August 6, 2013.

http://en.wikipedia.org/wiki/United_States_invasion_of_Afghanistan

(14) Somalia—Wikipedia, the Free Encyclopedia. Accessed August 6, 2013.

http://en.wikipedia.org/wiki/Somalia

(15) War On Yugoslavia: Ten Years Later. Accessed August 7, 2013.

http://www.fpif.org/articles/the_war_on_yugoslavia_10_years_later

(16) a) War on Drugs—Wikipedia, the Free Encyclopedia, Accessed August 7, 2013.

http://en.wikipedia.org/wiki/War_on_Drugs

b) Mexican Drug War—Wikipedia, the Free Encyclopedia. Accessed August 8, 2013.

http://en.wikipedia.org/wiki/Mexican_Drug_War

(17) a) Bolivarian Alliance for the Americas—Wikipedia, the Free Encyclopedia. Accessed August 9, 2013. http://en.wikipedia.org/wiki/Bolivarian_Alliance_for_the_Americas

b) United States-Venezuela Relations—Wikipedia, the Free Encyclopedia. Accessed August 1, 2013.

http://en.wikipedia.org/wiki/United_States_%E2%80%93_Venezuela_relations

c) Bolivia-United States Relations—Wikipedia, the Free Encyclopedia. Accessed August 1, 2013.

http://en.wikipedia.org/wiki/Bolivia%E2%80%93_United_States_relations

d) Ecuador-United States Relations—Wikipedia, the Free Encyclopedia. Accessed August 2, 2013.

http://en.wikipedia.org/wiki/Ecuador_%E2%80%93_United_States_relations

(18) a) Syria-United States Relations—Wikipedia, the Free Encyclopedia. Accessed January 3, 2012.

http://en.wikipedia.org/wiki/Syria_%e2%80%93_United_States_relations

b) 1986 United States Bombing of Libya—Wikipedia, the Free. Accessed August 4, 2013.

Encyclopedia http://en.wikipedia.org/wiki/1986_United_States_bombing_of_Libya

c) Libya-United States Relaions—Wikipedia, the Free Encyclopedia. Accessed January 3, 2012. http://en.wikipedia.org/wiki/Libya_%E2%80%93_United_States_relations

(19) a) Hamas—Wikipedia, the Free Encyclopedia. Accessed January 3, 2013.
http://en.wikipedia.org/wiki/Hamas
b) Hezbollah—Wikipedia, the Free Encyclopedia. Accessed January 3, 2013.
https://en.wikipedia.org/wiki/Hezbollah

(20) Cuba-United States Relations—Wikipedia, the Free Encyclopedia. Accessed November 12, 2012.
http://en.wikipedia.org/wiki/Cuba_%E2%80%93_United_States_relations

(21) a) Guerrilla Prince: The Untold Story of Fidel Castro. Georgia Anne Geyer. (Riverside New Jersey:Andrews McMeel Publishers, 1992)
b) Fidel Castro: Cuban Revolutionary. Brendon January. (New York: Franklin Watts, 2003)
c) The Man Who Invented Fidel: Castro, Cuba, and Herbert L. Matthews of the New York Times. (New York: Public Affairs, 2006)
d) Fidel Castro—Wikipedia, the Free Encyclopedia. Accessed June 12, 2012.
http://en.wikipedia.org/wiki/Fidel_Castro

(22) a) Saddam Hussein—Wikipedia, the Free Encyclopedia. Accessed June 12, 2012.
http://en.wikipedia.org/wiki/Saddam_Hussein
b) Muammar Gaddafi—Wikipedia, the Free Encyclopedia. Accessed June 12, 2012.
http://en.wikipedia.org/wiki/Muammar_al-Gaddafi

(23) a) Supreme Leader of Iran—Wikipedia, the Free Encyclopedia. Accessed June 12, 2012.
http://en.wikipedia.org/wiki/Supreme_Leader_of_Iran
b) Daniel Ortega—New World Encyclopedia. Accessed June 12, 2012.
http://www.newworldencyclopedia.org/entry/Daniel_Ortega

c) Mohammed Omar—Wikipedia, the Free Encyclopedia. Accessed June 12, 2012.
http://en.wikipedia.org/wiki/Mohammed_Omar

d) Kim Jong il—Wikipedia, the Free Encyclopedia. Accessed June 13, 2012.
http://en.wikipedia.org/wiki/Kim_Jong-il

e) Kim Jong un—Wikipedia, the Free Encyclopedia. Accessed June 13, 2012.
http://en.wikipedia.org/wiki/Kim_Jong-un

f) Hugo Chavez—Wikipedia, the Free Encyclopedia. Accessed January 2, 2012.
http://en.wikipedia.org/wiki/Hugo_Ch%C3%A1vez

g) Mahmoud Ahmadinejad—Wikipedia, the Free Encyclopedia. Accessed January 2, 2012.
http://en.wikipedia.org/wiki/Mahmoud_Ahmadinejad

h) Evo Morales—Wikipedia, the Free Encyclopdia. Accessed January 3, 2012.
http://en.wikipedia.org/wiki/Evo_Morales

i) Bashar al-Assad—Wikipedia, the Free Encyclopedia. Accessed January 3, 2012.
http://en.wikipedia.org/wiki/Bashar_al-Assad

j) Khaled Mashaal—Wikipedia, the Free Encyclopedia. Accessed January 4, 2012.
http://en.wikipedia.org/wiki/Khaled_Mashal

k) Hassan Nasrallah—Wikipedia, the Free Encyclopedia. Accessed January 4, 2012.
http://en.wikipedia.org/wiki/Hasan_Nasrallah

l) Rafael Correa—Wikipedia, the Free Encyclopedia. Accessed January 5, 2012.
http://en.wikipedia.org/wiki/Rafael_Correa

(24) a) Julian Assange—Wikipedia, the Free Encyclopedia. Accessed June 3, 2012.
http://en.wikipedia.org/wiki/Julian_Assange

b) Bradley Manning Support Network. Accessed June 3, 2012.
http://www.bradleymanning.org

c) Wikileaks. Accessed June 3, 2012. http://wikileaks.org

d) Edward Snowden—Wikipedia, the free encyclopedia. Accessed November 23, 2013.
http://en.wikipedia.org/wiki/Edward_Snowden

(25) Manuel Noriega—Wikipedia, the Free Encyclopedia. Accessed June 3, 2012.
http://en.wikipedia.org/wiki/Pineapple_face

(26) Merchants of Doubt: How a Handful of Scientists Obscured the Truth on Issues from Tobacco Smoke to Global Warming. Naomi Oreskes, Erik M. Conway. (New York: Bloomsbury, 2010)

(27) a) Habeas Corpus in the United States—Wikipedia, the Free Encyclopedia. Accessed November 29, 2012.
http://en.wikipedia.org/wiki/Habeas_corpus_in_the_United_States
b) Habeas Corpus—Wikipedia, the Free Encyclopedia. Accessed November 29, 2012.
http://en.wikipedia.org/wiki/Habeas_corpus

(28) Einstein & Infield. The Evolution of Physics. (New York: Simon & Shuster, 1938)

(29) Quote is widely attributed to Helen Keller.

(30) The Complete Poems of Emily Dickinson. (Boston: Little, Brown & Company, 1924)

(31) Quote is widely attributed to Muhammad Ali.

Chapter 51:

(1) a) Human Rights in Burma (Myanmarr)—Wikipedia, the Free Encyclopedia. Accessed January 12, 2012.
http://en.wikipedia.org/wiki/Human_rights_in_Burma
Myanmarr Human Rights—Amnesty International. Accessed January 12, 2012.
http://www.amnestyusa.org/our-work/countries/asia-and-the-pacific/myanmar

(2) a) List of Largest Empires—Wikipedia, the Free Encyclopedia. Accessed January 23, 2012.
http://en.wikipedia.org/wiki/List_of_largest_empires
b) Blowback: The Costs and Consequences of American Empire. Chalmers Johnson. (New York: Owl Books, 2001)
c) The Sorrows of Empire: Militarism, Secrecy, and the End of the Republic (American Empire Series). Chalmers Johnson. (New York: Metropolitan Books, 2003)
d) Dismantling the Empire: America's Last Best Hope. Chalmers Johnson. (New York: Metropolitan Books, 2010)

e) House of War: The Pentagon and the Disastrous Rise of American Power. James Carroll. (Boston/New York: Houghton Mifflin, 2006)

(3) a) The Age of Anxiety: McCarthyism to Terrorism. Haynes Johnson.
(Orlando: Harcourt Brace, 2005)
b) Let History Judge: The Origins and Consequences of Stalinism. (New York:Columbia University Press, 1989)
c) Stalinism: Essays in Historical Interpretation. Various authors. (New York: W. W. Norton & Company, 1978)

Chapter 52:

(1) a) Israel and Palestine: A Brief History. Accessed September 18, 2013.
http://www.mideastweb.org/briefhistory.htm
b) Paradoxes of Peace: German Peace Movements Since 1945. Alice Holmes Cooper.
(Ann Arbor: University of Michigan Press, 1996)
c) Memorialization in Germany Since 1945. Bill Niven, Chloe Paver (editors). (London: Palgrave Macmillan, 2010)

(2) a) The Galileo Project. Accessed June 13, 2013.
http://galileo.rice.edu/sci/theories/ptolemaic_system.html
b) Copernicus, Kepler, and Galileo. Accessed June 13, 2013.
http://www.fsmitha.com/h3/copernicus.htm

(3) a) Relativity: The Special and General Theory. Albert Einstein. (New York: Three Rivers Press, 1997)
b) Evolution Resources from the National Academies. Accessed August 24, 2013.
http://www.nationalacademies.org/evolution
c) Overwhelming Scientific Confidence in Evolution. Accessed August 24, 2013.
http://www.scienceeducationreview.com/open_access/wiles-evolution.pdf
d) AAA Statement on Evolution and Creationism. Accessed August 24, 2013.
http://www.aaanet.org/stmts/evolution.htm

e) Evolution's Purpose: An Integral Interpretation of the Scientific Story of Our Origins. Steve McIntosh. (New York: Select Books, 2012)

(4) Home Page of the Pontifical Academy of Sciences. Accessed August 29, 2013.
http://www.casinapioiv.va/content/accademia/en.html

(5) Islamic World Academy of Sciences. Accessed August 29, 2013.
http://iasworld.org

(6) Long Walk to Freedom: The Autobiography of Nelson Mandela. (Boston: Little, Brown and Company, 1994)

(7) a) The Jim Crow Encyclopedia: Milestones in African American History. Nikki L. M.
Brown & Barry M. Stentiford. (Westport: Greenwood Press, 2008)
b) Transformations in Slavery: A History of Slavery in Africa. (African Studies) Paul E. Lovejoy. (West Nyack, New York: Cambridge University Press, 1983)
c) Civil Rights Act of 1964—Wikipedia, the Free Encyclopedia. Accessed October 12, 2012.
http://en.wikipedia.org/wiki/Civil_Rights_Act_of_1964
d) Voting Rights Act—National Archives and Records Administration. Accessed October 12, 2012.
http://www.archives.gov/historical-docs/document.html?doc=18&title.raw=Voting%20Rights%20Act
e) African American Candidates for President of the United States. Accessed October 12, 2012.
http://en.wikipedia.org/wiki/African_American_candidates_for_President_of_the_United_States

(8) a) Inquisition—Wikipedia, the Free Encyclopedia. Accessed February 5, 2013.
http://en.wikipedia.org/wiki/Inquisition
b) Separation of Church and State—Wikipedia, the Free Encyclopedia. Accessed February 12, 2013.
http://en.wikipedia.org/wiki/Separation_of_church_and_state

(9) Council for Secular Humanism. Accessed February 12, 2013.
http://secularhumanism.org

(10) a) Catholicism: New Study Edition. Richard P. McBrien. Revised and Updated Edition.
(San Francisco: HarperSanFrancisco, 1994)

b) The Documents of Vatican II: In a New and Definitive Translation, with Commentary and Notes by Catholic, Protestant and Orthodox Authorities. William M. Abbot, S.J., General Editor. Introduction by Lawrence Cardinal Shehan. Translation Directed by Joseph Gallagher. Published by (London: Geoffrey Chapman, 1966)

(11) Interfaith Dialog—Wikipedia, the Free Encyclopedia. Accessed June 25, 2013.
http://en.wikipedia.org/wiki/Interfaith_dialogue

(12) Topia.net: Interspirituality Homepage. Accessed June 21, 2013.
http://www.topia.net/interspirituality.html

(13) Understanding Interbeing: Bodhi Leaf. Accessed June 21, 2013. http://bodhileaf.wordpress.com/2009/05/25/understanding-interbeing/

(14) a) The Role of International Law in the Elimination of Child Labor. Holly Cullen. (Martinus Nijhoff, 2007)
b) Child Labor in the United States—The Child Labor Education Project. Accessed July 22, 2013.
http://www.continuetolearn.uiowa.edu/laborctr/child_labor/about/us_history.html

(15) a) Women Prime Ministers and Presidents: 20th Century. Accessed July 28, 2013.
http://womenshistory.about.com/od/rulers20th/a/women_heads.htm
b) Women Presidents and Prime Ministers. Accessed July 28, 2013.
http://www.squidoo.com/women-presidents-women-prime-ministers
c) Wilma Mankiller: Chief of the Cherokee Nation (Signature Lives: Modern America Series). Pamela Dell. (Minneapolis: Compass Point Books, 2006).

(16) a) Patriarchal Religion, Sexuality, and Gender: A Critique of New Natural Law. Nicholas Bamforth & David A.J. Richards. (United Kingdom: Cambridge University Press, 2007)
b) Women's Leadership in Marginal Religions: Explorations Outside the Mainstream. Catherine Wessinger. (Urbana: University of Illinois Press, 1993)
c) Religious Institutions and Women's Leadership: New Roles Inside the Mainstream (Studies in Comparative Religion). Catherine Wessinger (editor). (Columbia, SC: University of South Carolina Press, 1996)

d) Women's Oppression, Suppression and Repression in Islam—A Total Blocade of their Leadership Quest. Ikechukwu Aloysius Orjinta. (Germany: Grin Verlag, Publisher, 2012)

e) Gender Equity in Islam: Basic Principles [Is Female Circumcision Required?; Foundation of Spiritual & Human Equality; Right to Possess Personal Property; Financial Security & Inheritance Laws; Women in Leadership Positions; Islamic Reformation . . . Jamal A. Badawi. (Plainfield, Indiana: American Trust Publications, 1999)

f) Gender Equity in Islam. Accessed May 14, 2013.
http://www.islam101.com/women/equity.html

g) Gender Roles in Christianity. Accessed May 14, 2013.
http://en.wikipedia.org/wiki/Gender_roles_in_Christianity

(17) a) Muslim, Christian, and Jew: Finding a Path to Peace our Faiths Can Share. David Liepert. (United States:Faith of Life Publishing, 2011)

b) The Gift of Responsibility: The Promise of Dialogue Among Christians, Jews, and Muslims. Lewis S. Mudge. (United Kingdom: Continuum International Publishing Group, 2008)

c) People of the First Crusade: The Truth about the Christian-Muslim War Revealed. Michael Foss. (New York: Arcade, 2011)

d) Holy Warriors: A Modern History of the Crusades. Jonathan Phillips. (New York: Random House, 2010)

(18) A Hidden Wholeness: The Visual World of Thomas Merton. Thomas Merton and John Howard Griffin. (Boston: Houghton Mifflin, 1970)

Chapter 53:

(1) New Testament. Matthew 7:3. English Standard Version.

(2) Quote widely attributed to the Buddha.

(3) The Sayings of Muhammad. (New York: Citadel Pres, 2000)

(4) The Bhagavad Gita for Daily Living: The End of Sorrow, Volume 1. Eknath Easwaran. (Petaluma, California: Nilgiri Press, 1983)

(5) New Testament. Matthew 8:22. Darby Bible Translation.

(6) Pied Piper of Hamelin—Wikipedia, the Free Encyclopedia. Accessed March 12, 2013.
http://en.wikipedia.org/wiki/Pied_Piper_of_Hamelin

(7)   Eyes Wide Shut, A Film directed by Stanley Kubrick. (Warner Bros., 1999)

Chapter 54:

(1)   Oscar Romero's Opposition. Accessed May 16, 2013. http://dwkcommentaries.wordpress.com/2011/10/06/oscar-romeros-opposition

(2)   a) Army School of the Americas. Accessed May 17, 2013. http://pangaea.org/street_children/latin/soa.htm
b)   School of Americas Watch. Accessed May 17, 2013. http://www.soaw.org

(3)   a) United Fruit Company—SourceWatch. Accessed May 17, 2013. http://www.sourcewatch.org/index.php?title=United_Fruit_Company
b)   United Fruit Company Chronology. Accessed May 17. 2013. http://www.unitedfruit.org/chron.htm
c)   Cry of the People: United States Involvement in the Rise of Fascism, Torture, and Murder and the Persecution of the Catholic Church in Latin America. Penny Lernoux. (Garden City, New York: Doubleday and Company,1980)

(4)   a) Monsanto versus Farmers—The Institute of Science in Society. Accessed November 3, 2013.
http://www.i-sis.org.uk/MonsantovsFarmers.php
b)   Monsanto—Wikipedia, the Free Encyclopedia. Accessed November 3, 2013.
http://en.wikipedia.org/wiki/Monsanto
(c)   Monsanto Uses Patent Law to Control Most U.S. Corn, Soy Seed Market
http://www.cleveland.com/nation/index.ssf/2009/12/monsanto_uses_patent_law_to_co.html

(5)   Pioneering Study Shows Richest 2 Percent Own Half World Wealth. Accessed March 4, 2013.
http://www.eurekalert.org/pub_releases/2006-12/unu-pss120106.php

(6)   a) The New Resource Wars: Native and Environmental Struggles Against Multinational Corporations. Al Gedicks. (Boston:South End Press, 1993)
b)   Rome: The Rise and Fall of the First Multinational Corporation (Enterprise). Stanley Bing. (New York: W.W. Norton, 2006)

c) Global Inc.: An Atlas of the Multinational Corporation. Gabel Medard, Henry Bruner. (New York:The New Press, 2003)

d) The Politics of Resource Extraction: Indigenous Peoples, Multinational Corporations, and the State. (United Kingdom: Palgrave/Macmillan, 2012)

e) Corporations—Global Issues. Accessed November 3, 2013. http://www.globalissues.org/issue/50/corporations

f) Key Facts—Share the World's Resources. Accessed November 4, 2013.
http://www.stwr.org/multinational-corporations/key-facts.html

7) a) Post-SovietConflicts—Wikipedia, the Free Encyclopdia. Accessed December 1, 2013.
http://en.wikipedia.org/wiki/Frozen_conflict

b) Yugoslav Wars—Wikipedia, the Free Encyclopdia. Accessed December 1, 2013.
http://en.wikipedia.org/wiki/Yugoslav_Wars

8) a) Cultural Revolution—Wikipedia, the Free Encyclopdia. Accessed December 2, 2013.
http://en.wikipedia.org/wiki/Cultural_Revolution

b) Why the Dalai Lama Matters: His Act of Truth as the Solution for China, Tibet, and the World. Robert Thurman. (New York:Atria Books, 2008)

c) Tiananmen Square Protests of 1989—Wikipedia, the Free Encyclopdia. Accessed December 3, 2013.
http://en.wikipedia.org/wiki/Tiananmen_Square_protests_of_1989

9) The World According to Monsanto: Pollution, Corruption, and Control of the World's Food Supply. Marie-Monique Robin. (New York: The New Press, 2010,)

10) a) Farmlandgrab.org Accessed January 2, 2014. http://farmlandgrab.org

b) The Global Farms Race: Land Grabs, Agricultural Investment, and the Scramble for Food Security. Michael Kugelman, Susan L. Levenstein. (Washington: Island Press, 2012)

11) Richest Two Percent Own Half the World's Wealth. Accessed June 19, 2013.
http://www.commondreams.org/headlines06/1222-04.htm

12) Social Darwinism—Encyclopedia Britannica. Accessed February 12, 2013.

http://www.britannica.com/EBchecked/topic/551058/social-Darwinism

Chapter 57:

(1) a) Acid Rain: Deposition to Recovery. Peter Brimblecombe, Hiroshi Ha Daniel Houl Martin Novak. (New York: Springer Verlag, 2007)
b) Acid Rain (Pollution): History—Brittanica Online Encyclopdia. Accessed February 13, 2013.
http://www.britannica.com/EBchecked/topic/3761/acid-rain/299480/History

(2) a) The Media and Rwanda Genocide. Allan Thompson (editor). (London: Pluto Press, 2006)
b) The Role of the Media in the Yugoslav Wars—Wikipedia, the Free Encyclopdia. Accessed March 6, 2013.
http://en.wikipedia.org/wiki/Propaganda_in_the_Yugoslav_Wars

(3) Warspeak: Linguistic Collateral Damage. Accessed March 10, 2013.
http://www.alphadictionary.com/articles/drgw008.html

(4) a) The Truth about Rainforest Destruction. Russel G. Coffee. (Better Planet Press, 1996)
b) The Causes of Rainforest Destruction. Accessed March 11, 2013.
http://www.rainforestinfo.org.au/background/causes.htm
c) Coal Country: Risinig up Against Mountaintop Removal Mining. (San Francisco:Sierra Club/Counterpoint, 2009)
d) Bringing Down the Mountains: The Impact of Mountaintop Removal Surface Coal Mining on Southern West Virgini Communities, 1970-2004. Shirley Stewar Burns. (Morgantown, West Virginia:West Virginia University Press, 2007)
e) A Review of Oil Exploration and Spillage. Kadafa Adati Ayuba. (Lap Lambert Academic Press, Print on Demand, 2012)
f) The Largest Oil Spills in History: 1901 to the Present. Accessed January 15, 2014.
http://chartsbin.com/view/mgz
g) UNHCR (UN Refugee Agency) Annual Report Shows 42 Million People Uprooted Worldwide. Accessed July 9, 2013.
http://www.unhcr.org/4a2fd52412d.html

(5) Free the Slaves—About Slavery. Accessed July 9, 2013.
http://www.freetheslaves.net/Page.aspx?pid=348

Chapter 58:

(1) The Hidden Gospel: Decoding the Spiritual Message of the Aramaic Jesus, Neil Douglas-Klotz. (Wheaton, IL: Quest Books, 1999) Matthew 6:24. Page 146.

Chapter 61:

(1) a) Ishi. Wikipedia, the Free Encyclopedia. Accessed May 6, 2013. http://en.wikipedia.org/wiki/Ishi
b) Ishi, Last of his Tribe. Theodora Kroeber. (Berkely: Parnassus Press, 1964)

(2) Amish Society. John A. Hostetler. (Baltimore/London: The John Hopkins University Press, 1993)

(3) Corporate Farming: Behind the Veil. Food Inc. Accessed May 10, 2013.
http://www.takepart.com/foodinc/film

Chapter 62:

(1) a) Charles Darwin—Wikipedia, the Free Encyclopedia. Accessed September 2, 2013.
http://en.wikipedia.org/wiki/Charles_Darwin
b) Aleksandr Solzhenitzyn—Wikipedia, the Free Encyclopedia. Accessed September 2, 2013.
http://en.wikipedia.org/wiki/Aleksandr_Solzhenitsyn
c) Catholic Worker Movement—Dorothy Day. Accessed September 2, 2013.
http://www.catholicworker.org/dorothyday/ddbiographytext.cfm?Number=72
d) The Hollywood Ten—The Library, University of California. Accessed August 3, 2013.
http://lib.berkeley.edu/MRC/blacklist.html
Hollywood Blacklist—Wikipedia, the Free Encyclopedia. Accessed August 3, 2013.
http://en.wikipedia.org/wiki/Hollywood_blacklist

(2) Christianity: The Official Religion of the Roman Empire. Accessed June 4, 2013.
http://www.unrv.com/culture/christianity.php

Religion: The Roman Empire. Accessed June 4, 2013.
http://www.roman-empire.net/religion/religion.html
The Hierarchy of the Roman Empire now called the "Holy Roman
See" . . . Accessed June 4, 2013.
http://philjayhan.wordpress.com/2007/02/12/the-heirarchy-of-
the-roman-empire-now-called-the-holy-roman-see-the-roman-
catholic-church-or-the-vatican

(3)　Old Saint Peter's Basilica—Wikipedia, the Free Encyclopedia.
Accessed June 5, 2013.
http://en.wikipedia.org/wiki/Old_St._Peter%27s_Basilica

Chapter 65:

(1)　a) Job Outsourcing Statistics: Statistic Brain. Accessed July 7,
2013.
http://statisticbrain.com/outsourcing-statistics-by-country
b) Outsourcing America: What's Behind Our National Crisis
and How We Can Reclaim American Jobs. Ron Hira, Anil Hira.
(AMACOM, Kindle Edition, 2005)
c) 21st Century Globalized Workforce: Job Outsourcing, The
Necessary Evil. Godson Obiagwu. (Lambert Academic Publishing,
2012)
d) Outsourcing Jobs to Foreign Countries (Essay). James Tallant.
(New York: Grin Verlag, 2012)
e) Outsourcing U.S. Jobs. Jacqueline Ching. (United States:
Rosen Publishing Group, 2009)
f) SweatFree Communities: Home Page http://www.sweatfree.
org
g) Making Sweatshops: The Globalization of the U.S. Apparel
Industry. Ellen I. Rosen. (Berkeley: University of California Press,
2002)
h) Can We Put an End to Sweatshops: A New Democracy Forum
on Raising Global Labor Standards. (Boston: Beacon Press, 2001)
I) Beyond Sweatshops: Foreign Direct Investment and
Globalization in Developing Countries. Theodore H. Moran.
(Washington D.C: Brookings Institute Press, 2002)

(2)　Nineteen Eighty-Four, George Orwell. (London: Secker and
Warburg, 1949)

Chapter 69:

(1) Taken from a talk given by Richard Rohr. For more information on Richard Rohr go to the Center for Action and Contemplation website (home of the Rohr Institute) https://cac.org/

(2) New Testament. Matthew 6:22-23. The Inclusive New Testament. (Brentwood Maryland: Priests for Equality, 1996)

(3) Carny—Wikipedia, the Free Encyclopedia. Accessed August 6, 2013. http://en.wikipedia.org/wiki/Glossary_of_%27carny%27_slang

(4) Vegan: The New Ethics of Eating. Erik Marcus. (Ithaca, New York: McBooks Press, 2001) Revised.

(5) a) Facts on Induced Abortion Worldwide: Guttmacher Institute. Accessed January 15, 2014.
http://www.guttmacher.org/pubs/fb_IAW.html
b) Abortion Statistics and Other Data: Johnston's Archives. Accessed July 4, 2013.
http://www.johnstonsarchive.net/policy/abortion/index.html
c) Consistent Life—Home Page. Accessed July 4, 2013. http://www.consistent-life.org
d) UN Report Uncovers Global Child Abuse. Accessed July 23, 2013. http://www.independent.co.uk/news/world/politics/un-report-uncovers-global-child-abuse-419700.html
e) Childe Abuse: Statistics, Research, and Resources for Recovery, Accessed July 23, 2013.
http://www.jimhopper.com/abstats
f) Criminal Abuse of Women and Children: An International Perspective. (CRC Press, 2009)

Chapter 70:

(1) a) Iroquois Constitution. Accessed June, 15, 2013. http://www.indigenouspeople.net/iroqcon.htm
b) Seven Generation Sustainability. Wikipedia, the Free Encyclopedia. Accessed June 15, 2013
http://en.wikipedia.org/wiki/Seven_generation_sustainability

(2) Mark Twain, "Consistency," paper read at the Hartford Monday EveningClub on 5 December 1887. Inscription beneath his bust in the Hall of Fame. U.S. humorist, novelist, short story author, & wit (1835-1910)

(3) Essays: First Series. Ralph Waldo Emerson. (Boston: Houghton Mifflin and Company, 1900) The Quote is from the essay, "Self Reliance."

(4) Interior Castle (Classics of Western Spirituality). Teresa of Avila. (Mahwah, New Jersey: Paulist Press, 1979)

Chapter 71:

(1) Meister Eckhart's Sermons. Sermon IV. Translated into English by Claud Field. No publication date. Quote taken from a text taken from a public domain source first published about 1909. Sermons: Meister Eckhart. Wikisource—the Free Online Library. Accessed February 12, 2013.
http://en.wikisource.org/wiki/Sermons_(Meister_Eckhart)

(2) Einstein, "What I Believe," originally written in 1930 and recorded for the German League for Human Rights. It was published as "The World as I See It" in Forum and Century, 1930; in Living Philosophies (NewYork: Simon and Schuster, 1931); in The World As I See It, 1-5; in Ideas and Opinions, 8-11. The versions are all translated somewhat differently and have slight revisions. Talk: Albert Einstein—Wikiquote. Accessed March 8, 2013.
http://en.wikiquote.org/wiki/Talk:Albert_Einstein

Chapter 73:

(1) Hebrew Scriptures (Old Testament). Exodus 3:1-4:17.

Chapter 75:

(1) Strange Case of Dr. Jekyll and Mr. Hyde. Robert Louis Stevenson. (London: Longmann, Green and Company. 1886)

(2) a) The Zensite: The Textual History of Linji lu. Accessed May 16, 2013.
http://www.thezensite.com/ZenEssays/HistoricalZen/welter_Linji.html
b) Linji Yixuan—Wikipedia, the Free Encyclopedia. Accessed May 16, 2013.
http://en.wikipedia.org/wiki/If_you_meet_the_Buddha_on_your_path%2C_kill_him

(3) a) Spiritual Emergency: When Personal Transformation Becomes a Crisis. Stanislav Grof. (Los Angeles: Jeremy P. Tarcher, 1989)
b) Stormy Search for the Self: Understanding and Living with Spiritual Emergency (Classics of Personal Development). Christina Grof, Stanislav Grof. (Los Angeles: Jeremy P. Tarcher, 1995)
c) Spiritual Emergency Resource Center. Accessed June 14, 2013. http://www.spiritualcompetency.com/se/resources/senciis.html
(4) M-theory, the theory formerly known as Strings. Accessed December 22, 2013.
http://www.damtp.cam.ac.uk/research/gr/public/qg_ss.html

Chapter 78:

(1) Biography of Augusto Pinochet—Latin American History. Accessed April 10, 2013.
http://latinamericanhistory.about.com/od/20thcenturylatinamerica/p/pinochetbio.htm
(2) Biography of Idi Amin—African History. Accessed April 10, 2013. http://africanhistory.about.com/od/biography/a/bio_amin.htm

Chapter 79:

(1) An Autobiography: The Story of My Experiments with Truth. Mohandas K. Gandhi.
(Boston: Beacon Press, 1957)
(2) New Testament. New International Version. 1984. Matthew 18:21-22.

Chapter 81:

(1) New Testament, John 17: 20-22. The Message.
(2) "I Am the Walrus," Lennon/McCartney, Magical Mystery Tour film and album, 1967. The Beatles. Parlophone, United Kingdom; Capital Records, USA.

Chapter 84:

(1) New Testament. Luke 6:31. New International Version.

(2)   Golden Rule—Wikipedia, the Free Encyclopedia. Accessed March 3, 2013.
http://en.wikipedia.org/wiki/The_Golden_Rule

Chapter 85:

(1)   The Secret History of Nursery Rhymes. Linda Alchin. (Surrey, England: Babyseen Ltd., 2010)
Humpty Dumpty Story and Picture. Accessed April 6, 2013.
http://www.rhymes.org.uk/humpty_dumpty.htm

Chapter 86:

(1)   The Razor's Edge, page 80. God Makes the River to Flow, An Anthology of the World's Sacred Poetry & Prose, Eknath Easwaran, (Tomales, California: Nilgiri Press, 2009)

(2)   Man's Search for Meaning: An Introduction to Logotherapy, Victor Frankl. (New York: Washington Square Press, 1963)

Chapter 87:

(1)   The Way of Life, Tao Teh Ching. A New Translation by Gary N. Arnold, Ph.D. (Metairie, Louisiana: Windhorse Corporation, 1996)

Chapter 88:

(1)   Self Surrender, page 248. God Makes the River to Flow, An Anthology of the World's Sacred Poetry & Prose, Eknath Easwaran, (Tomales, California: Nilgiri Press, 2009)

(2)   Ashes to Ashes—Wikipedia, the Free Encyclopedia. Accessed October 2, 2013.
http://en.wikipedia.org/wiki/Ashes_to_Ashes

(3)   a) This Day in Quotes. Accessed October 2, 2013.
http://www.thisdayinquotes.com/2010/02/it-became-necessary-to-destroy-town-to.html
b) Ben Tre. Wikipedia, the Free Encyclopedia. Accessed October 22, 2013.
http://en.wikipedia.org/wiki/Ben_Tre

(4)   Hebrew Scriptures. Genesis 4:1-16

Chapter 89:

(1)   Mein Kampf. Adolf Hitler. (New York: Stackpole, 1939)
(2)   Big Lie—Source Watch. Accessed May 6, 2013.
       http://www.sourcewatch.org/index.php?title=Big_lie
(3)   The Uncertainty Principle (Stanford Encyclopedia of Philosophy).
       Accessed June 24, 2013.
       http://plato.stanford.edu/entries/qt-uncertainty
(4)   The Canticle of the Sun. Saint Francis of Assisi. Accessed January
       15, 2013.
       http://www2.webster.edu/~barrettb/canticle.htm
       Most high, all powerful, all good Lord! All praise is yours, all glory,
       all honor, and all blessing. To you, alone, Most High, do they
       belong. No mortal lips are worthy to pronounce your name.
       Be praised, my Lord, through all your creatures, especially through
       my lord Brother Sun, who brings the day; and you give light
       through him. And he is beautiful and radiant in all his splendor!
       Of you, Most High, he bears the likeness.
       Be praised, my Lord, through Sister Moon and the stars; in the
       heavens you have made them, precious and beautiful.
       Be praised, my Lord, through Brothers Wind and Air, and clouds
       and storms, and all the weather, through which you give your
       creatures sustenance.
       Be praised, My Lord, through Sister Water; she is very useful, and
       humble, and precious, and pure.
       Be praised, my Lord, through Brother Fire, through whom you
       brighten the night. He is beautiful and cheerful, and powerful and
       strong.
       Be praised, my Lord, through our sister Mother Earth, who feeds
       us and rules us, and produces various fruits with colored flowers
       and herbs.
       Be praised, my Lord, through those who forgive for love of you;
       through those who endure sickness and trial. Happy those who
       endure in peace, for by you, Most High, they will be crowned.
       Be praised, my Lord, through our Sister Bodily Death, from whose
       embrace no living person can escape. Woe to those who die in

mortal sin! Happy those she finds doing your most holy will. The second death can do no harm to them.

Praise and bless my Lord, and give thanks, and serve him with great humility.

(translated by Bill Barrett from the Umbrian text of the *Assisi codex*.)

Chapter 90:

(1) The Gettysburg Address—Abraham Lincoln. Accessed July 9, 2013. http://showcase.netins.net/web/creative/lincoln/speeches/gettysburg.htm

(2) Frederick Douglass—History.com. Accessed July 9, 2013. http://www.history.com/topics/frederick-douglass

(3) Harriet Beecher Stowe—History.com. Accessed July 9, 2013. http://www.history.com/topics/harriet-beecher-stowe

(4) John Brown—History.com. Accessed July 9, 2013. http://www.history.com/topics/john-brown

(5) Harriet Tubman—History.com. Accessed July 9, 2013. http://www.history.com/topics/harriet-tubman

(6) William Lloyd Garrison—New World Encyclopedia. Accessed July 9, 2013. http://www.newworldencyclopedia.org/entry/William_Lloyd_Garrison

(7) Sojourner Truth—History.com. Accessed July 9, 2013. http://www.history.com/topics/sojourner-truth

(8) The Walt Whitman Archive. Accessed July 9, 2013. http://whitmanarchive.org

Chapter 91:

(1) Thomas Acquinas—Wikipedia, the Free Encyclopedia. Accessed September 12, 2012. http://en.wikipedia.org/wiki/Thomas_Aquinas

Chapter 94:

(1) a) History or Metaphor—The Lookstein Center for Jewish Education. Accessed February 13, 2013. http://www.lookstein.org/articles/history_or_metaphor.htm

b) Creation Stories—Myth Encyclopedia. Accessed February 16, 2013.

http://www.mythencyclopedia.com/Ca-Cr/Creation-Stories.html
c) Creation Stories from Around the World. Accessed February 16, 2013.
http://www.gly.uga.edu/railsback/CS/CSIndex.html

(2)	The Big Bang—NASA Science. Accessed August 3, 2013.
http://science.nasa.gov/astrophysics/focus-areas/what-powered-the-big-bang

(3)	Philemon E. Sturges—Wikipedia, the Free Encyclopedia. Accessed September 18, 2012.
http://en.wikipedia.org/wiki/Philemon_E._Sturges

Chapter 95:

(1)	a) The Noble Eightfold Path: The Way to the End of Suffering. Accessed June 6, 2013.
http://www.accesstoinsight.org/lib/authors/bodhi/waytoend.html
b) The Noble Eightfold Path. Accessed June 6, 2013.
http://www.thebigview.com/buddhism/eightfoldpath.html

(2)	a) Prayers of the Cosmos: Meditations on the Aramaic Words of Jesus, Translated and with Commentary, Neil Douglas-Klotz. (New York: Harper & Row, Publishers, 1991)
b) The Eight Beatitudes—Catholic Encyclopedia. Accessed June 8, 2013.
http://www.catholic.org/encyclopedia/view.php?id=1615

(3)	New Testament. Matthew 6:6, Jerusalem Bible, Reader's Edition. (Garden City, New York: Doubleday & Company, 1968)

Chapter 98:

Alcoholics Anonymous: The Story of How Many Thousands of Men and Women have recovered from Alcoholism. (New York: Alcoholics Anonymous World Services, 1976)

Chapter 99:

(1)	The Presence of the Past: Morphic Resonance and the Memory of Nature, Rupert Sheldrake. (United States: Inner Traditions, Bear and Company, 4th Revised and Expanded Edition, 2012)

(2) Being Peace. Thich Nhat Hanh. (Berkeley, California: Parallax Press, 1987)

(3) The Eternal Now, Paul Tillich. (New York: Charles Scribner's Sons, 1963)

(4) Saint Augustine (Stanford Encyclopedia of Philosophy). Accessed March 10, 2013.
http://plato.stanford.edu/entries/augustine

(5) The Eckart Society. Accessed March 12, 2013. http://www.eckhartsociety.org

(6) a) Rabindranath Tagore—Biography. Accessed March 13, 2013.
http://www.nobelprize.org/nobel_prizes/literature/laureates/1913/tagore-bio.html
b) The Writings of Rabindranath Tagore—Internet Sacred Text Archive. Accessed March 13, 2013.
http://www.sacred-texts.com/hin/tagore/index.htm

Chapter 101:

(1) John Newton—Wikipedia, the Free Encyclopedia. Accessed March 27, 2013.
http://en.wikipedia.org/wiki/John_Newton

Chapter 103:

(1) a) thezensite: koan studies. Accessed November 12, 2012.
http://www.thezensite.com/MainPages/koan_studies.html
b) The Sound of One Hand: 281 Zen Koans with Answers. Yoel Hoffman. (New York: Basic Books, 1975)

Chapter 106:

(1) Matsuo Basho—Poems and Biography by Poetry Connection. Accessed January 14, 2013.
http://www.poetryconnection.net/poets/Matsuo_Basho

ABOUT THE AUTHOR

Michael J. Gajda is a writer who lives in the middle of nowhere, somewhere in the southern part of a midwest state which has at least two peninsulas . . . with his two dogs Bud and Woodrow, surrounded by woods and rumors of paved roads. He's recently retired from working thirty years with troubled kids, among other things. And he's currently putting the final touches on an old new work of fiction (so he says).

CPSIA information can be obtained at www.ICGtesting.com
Printed in the USA
BVOW02s1202100415

395648BV00001B/3/P